House of Midnight Fantasies
KRISTI GOLD

A Single Demand
MARGARET ALLISON

MILLS & BOON®

*MILLS & BOON and MILLS & BOON with the Rose Device
are registered trademarks of the publisher.*

*First published in Great Britain 2007
Harlequin Mills & Boon Limited,
Eton House, 18-24 Paradise Road, Richmond, Surrey TW9 1SR*

The publisher acknowledges the copyright holders of the
individual works as follows:

House of Midnight Fantasies © Kristi Goldberg 2006
A Single Demand © Cheryl Guttridge Klam 2005

ISBN: 978 0 263 85015 4

51-0407

*Printed and bound in Spain
by Litografia Rosés S.A., Barcelona*

House of Midnight Fantasies
by Kristi Gold

ᗡ ⅍ ᗡ

*He was a very persuasive man…
Many a woman could attest to
that…*

The kiss had been a part of a carefully crafted
plan of seduction, and she'd walked right into
his trap without a moment's hesitation.

"We'll forget what just happened."

He backed up a few steps. "Go ahead and try
to forget it."

"We need to maintain a professional
relationship."

"Selene, I didn't hire you. Ella did. As far
as I'm concerned, you work for her, not me.
Which means we don't have a professional
relationship."

Without responding, Selene turned, and
sprinted down the narrow steps to the safety
of her bedroom. No doubt about it, Adrien
Morrell had cast his spell over Selene. Now
it was up to her to break free, before she,
too, found herself caught in the clutches of
obsession and allowed him to do anything
he pleased.

A Single Demand
by Margaret Allison

ᗝᔍᕷᕼᙅ

"This is not personal, Cassie."

Hunter took another step towards her. To prevent himself from touching her, he kept his hands clenched at his sides. "Whether you like it or not, I'm your boss. And you're costing me money."

"So fire me," she said.

"If I thought it would solve anything, I would. But I'm not about to give up the one degree of control I have."

This time it was Cassie's turn to step towards Hunter. She looked up at him with anger smouldering in her eyes. "I don't care who you are. I'm not afraid of you. You can't control me."

It was a dare, plain and simple. But as he stared into Cassie's cool green eyes, his anger once again gave way to passion. Hunter remembered their night together, how he'd made her sigh with pleasure and burn with desire. How could he forget her?

No, she was wrong. He may not be able to control her mind, but he damn well could control her body.

Available in April 2007 from Mills & Boon Desire

The Convenient Marriage
by Peggy Moreland
&
Reunion of Revenge
by Kathie DeNosky
(The Illegitimate Heirs)

ᗡ ⌇ ᘉ

Totally Texan
by Mary Lynn Baxter
&
Only Skin Deep
by Cathleen Galitz

ᗡ ⌇ ᘉ

House of Midnight Fantasies
by Kristi Gold
(Rich & Reclusive)
&
A Single Demand
by Margaret Allison

HOUSE OF MIDNIGHT FANTASIES

by
Kristi Gold

KRISTI GOLD

admits to having a fondness for major league baseball, double cheese enchiladas and creating dark and somewhat dangerous – albeit honourable – heroes. She considers indulging in all three in the same day as the next best thing to a beach holiday!

Kristi resides in central Texas with her retired physician husband and the occasional guest in the form of one of her three grown children. She loves to hear from readers and can be contacted through her website at http://kristigold.com or through snail mail at 6902 Woodway Drive, #166, Waco, TX 76712, USA. (Please include SAE with return postage for a response.)

To my good friend and fellow author
Karen Rose Smith. A heartfelt thanks for your
gentle guidance and unwavering support.

One

Maison de Minuit. The House of Midnight.

The name alone seemed ominous, but the forbidding Louisiana plantation symbolized Selene Albright Winston's first serious step toward freedom.

Gathering her courage, Selene left her sedan, apprehension shadowing every step while she walked the flagstone path that led to the lengthy porch. Not even the whisper of a wind ruffled the leaves and only the occasional sound of a cicada disturbed the eerie silence. Ancient gnarled-finger oaks, dripping with Spanish moss, covered the lawns like sinister sentries warding off intruders. The tall grass held a cast of brown and a spattering of milkweeds, and no flowers adorned the overgrown beds lined with withering hedges.

She stopped a few feet from the porch to study the house that seemed as if it had been abandoned, too. In many ways it had, at least superficially. The Greek

Revival mansion's pale yellow facade showed definite signs of aging, and so did the shutters, trim and the six massive columns supporting the structure—all oddly painted as black as the entry sign. She hoped the interior had fared better than the exterior, otherwise not even the most curious person would dare step foot in this place. In fact, turning around and heading for safety was Selene's initial instinct. Not this time. Safety also came with a price.

When she ascended the first wooden stair leading to the entry, it groaned as if it might buckle. Yet the abrupt assault on her psyche proved to be much more disturbing.

Eyes. Ice blue eyes. Intense eyes.

Selene closed her mind as well as her own eyes against the image until it disappeared. But when she scaled the second step, the vision came back, stealing her breath and her confidence. She refused to let this happen. Refused to invite this into her world, not when she had tried so hard for years to keep it reined in.

She drew in a deep breath and raised the invisible mental shield she'd developed for self-protection, relieved to discover it didn't fail her when she took the third and final step onto the porch.

After only a slight hesitation, she rapped on the peeling black door then smoothed a hand down her tailored sleeveless red dress. Though the fabric was lightweight, she felt as if she were wearing a winter parka. She'd pulled her hair back into a band low at her nape, yet that, too, provided little relief from the relentless June heat. Of course, a solid case of nerves contributed to her discomfort, and so did the fact that no one answered her summons.

She knocked one more time, both relieved and anxious when she heard the sound of approaching footsteps. She had no idea who might be on the other side of the door. No idea if she would find friend or foe—or maybe even the owner of the disturbing eyes.

The door finally opened to a woman with keen dark eyes who appeared to be in her sixties, her black-and-silver hair styled in a short, severe cut. She wore a loose-fitting pale green shift and a guarded expression, but she didn't appear to be at all threatening. "May I help you?" she asked in a soft voice that contrasted with her sharp features.

"Are you Ms. Lanoux?" Selene asked.

"Yes, and you are?"

At least Selene was in the right place, even if the woman didn't seem to have a clue as to why she was there. "Selene Winston. I'm here about the restoration."

The woman's hand fluttered to her hair. "I wasn't expecting you until tomorrow."

When they'd spoken last Friday, Selene could have sworn they'd agreed she would interview for the job on Monday. Maybe she should return to the local inn where she'd been residing for the past ten days since her spontaneous escape from Georgia. Maybe she should consider this misunderstanding as a Do Not Enter sign. "If it's not a good time, I can come back tomorrow."

"I wouldn't hear of it," she said as she stepped aside and gestured Selene forward. "Welcome to *Maison de Minuit*… It's Mrs. Winston, isn't it?"

"Winston's my married name, but I'm divorced." Selene internally flinched over the bitterness that resonated in her tone. "Actually, I'd rather you call me Selene."

The woman thankfully maintained a pleasant demeanor. "And you may call me Ella. Now let's get you out of the heat."

When Selene stepped inside the wide foyer, she immediately noticed two things—the house wasn't much cooler than the porch outside, and the light was all but filtered out by heavy shutters covering the windows. A gloomy atmosphere encompassed the area, along with the scent of aged wood and musty air.

She followed Ella down the vestibule where they paused at a small parlor that proved to be as dark as the entrance, any natural light blocked by thick blue drapes. The Federal-style antiques set about the room were most likely original furnishings, and worth a fortune, Selene decided. Nothing she hadn't seen—or owned—in her former life. A life she had gladly left behind. Still, she'd always had an affinity for all things historical, and the pieces were definitely worth investigating.

"This is only one of the common areas," Ella said. "And like the rest of the house, it needs refurbishing." She fanned her face in a rapid succession of waves. "Inside and out. You would have to obtain estimates on a new cooling system and most likely a new roof, which means you'll have to find a suitable contractor."

"Wait a minute," Selene said as soon as the woman's words registered. "I had no idea the job would be quite this extensive."

"My dear, you can hire anyone you'd like," Ella said. "Unless you have a problem supervising workers."

In reality, no, Selene didn't. She'd managed a household staff for years. Besides, she had nowhere else to be. No place to go aside from her former home, and that wasn't an option. "I can handle it, as long as I have a substantial budget to follow."

"Money is no object."

Obviously Ella Lanoux had sufficient wealth even though she wasn't at all like the well-heeled matrons Selene had known most of her life, including her own mother. Although Selene wasn't exactly comfortable with the magnitude of the restoration, she had to remember why she'd come here—to seek employment. To be her own person, make her own money. To start over.

Ella brushed her damp bangs from her forehead, then motioned Selene forward. "Follow me and we'll continue the tour." She strode down the foyer, stopped at a set of double doors and faced Selene again. "This is by far the most impressive part of the house."

With dramatic flair, Ella threw open the doors to reveal a massive circular room covered in what appeared to be original wood-plank floors. In the center of that room, a freestanding, wide red-carpeted staircase spiraled to the second floor. Selene's gaze tracked to the ceiling that show-cased gold-winged cherubs flitting about a large expanse of cloud-bedecked blue sky, a chandelier dripping with crystals serving as the focal point. She'd seen this type of room before, but only in photographs that couldn't compare to witnessing the real thing with her own eyes. "This is absolutely breathtaking."

Ella smiled proudly. "It had that effect on me the first time I saw it." She pointed across the way. "The kitchen and dining room are through there. We can see those later. I'll show you the second floor now."

As she followed Ella up the stairway, her hand firmly gripping the white iron railing, Selene felt as if she were climbing toward heaven. A tranquil piece of paradise among the darkness.

When they reached the landing, Ella stopped and nodded to her left. "That corridor leads to the front of the house where you'll find two rooms. One was formerly a nursery, the other's been converted into a private office."

Heavy emphasis on *private,* Selene noted. She motioned to her right. "And down that way?"

"The rest of the second-floor bedrooms, including where you'll be staying if we come to an agreement."

"I would be expected to live on-site?"

"Room and board would be included while you're here."

Selene supposed it would make things more convenient. She wouldn't have to drive the ten miles or so into town, or find a suitable place to live. *If* she decided to accept the job. A decision not to be taken lightly, Selene thought as she trailed behind Ella, who made an immediate right into a narrow paneled hallway illuminated by the occasional dimly lit lamp mounted to the wall.

They'd only walked a few feet when Selene's attention landed straight ahead on a bronze life-size statue looming at the end of the corridor. A demonic creature complete with horns, pointy teeth and claws with a terrified, scantily clad woman in its grasp. The menacing figure definitely contrasted with the angels keeping watch over the rotunda downstairs. A classic illustration of good versus evil. Heaven opposed to hell.

Selene suddenly found herself in the grip of another vision. Unlike her first images on the entry steps, this came to her as if she were watching somewhere on the sidelines, as it always had in the past. The image of a hand sliding down her bare arm. A very large, very male hand that continued down her back, formed to her waist, drifted to her bottom, before she blinked and forced the image away. She had no idea where the vision had originated since there seemed to be no one around. And she found that more than a little troublesome.

She hadn't realized she'd come to a complete stop until Ella turned and favored her with another smile. "It's rather grotesque, isn't it? I call him Giles, after the former owner. The crazy man loved that thing, but then he was always known for being eccentric."

Eccentric wouldn't be the term Selene used to describe the former owner. *Scary* would be more like it. She couldn't imagine wanting the "thing" around every morning, or at bedtime. "I'm surprised he didn't take it with him." She was sorry he hadn't.

Ella laughed. "Unfortunately, it was too big to fit in his coffin."

Selene internally cringed. Was that the source of her vision—the mental musings of a ghost? That had never happened to her before. Normally she channeled the thoughts of living, breathing humans, at her own peril at certain points in her life. "I'm sorry to hear he passed away."

"Don't be," Ella said. "He was almost ninety and quite frankly, I thought he was too cantankerous to die. In fact, he had a mistress forty years his junior. She's the one who did him in."

"She killed him?" Selene couldn't disguise her distress.

Ella shook her head and laughed again. "Not intentionally. Let's just say the Morrell men have virility down to a fine art. Unfortunately, Giles didn't know his limitations."

"Well, at least he left this world a happy man." Now for the question foremost on Selene's mind. "Did he pass away in this house?"

"No. He died in France." Selene's frame relaxed from relief until Ella added, "But unfortunately, this place has a reputation for tragedy."

Great. Just what Selene wanted to hear—the mansion could be home to restless spirits intent on haunting her brain. But only if she let that happen, which she wouldn't, if she could prevent it.

They continued on for a few steps until Ella stopped at a closed door. "Your quarters would be in here." She pointed toward the end of the hallway where the demon held court. "That guest room over there is closed for the time being. The current owner keeps it locked and prefers it not be disturbed."

Selene gaped for a few moments. "I thought you were the owner."

Ella frowned. "Oh, dear, I'm sorry if I gave you that impression. Adrien Morrell, Giles's grandson, inherited the plantation. I'm his assistant." Her frown melted into a cynical smile. "And his maid and cook. I also advise him from time to time, whether he asks for my advice or not."

Selene was beginning to suspect she had a lot to learn, and worried some of it might not be pleasant at all. "Does Mr. Morrell live here?" she asked.

"That's his room." Ella indicated a closed door nearby. "It's the master suite and adjacent to your room, but I promise he won't bother you."

"Where is your room?" Selene asked.

"Off the kitchen. I spend much of my time there. And this would be your room." Ella opened the door to the prospective living quarters and waved Selene inside.

As it was with the rest of the house, the bedroom was adorned with more antiques, including a huge cherry-wood Victorian double bed covered in a white lace spread. Several colorful braided rugs covered the hard-wood floors that had lost their sheen. Straight ahead, the white curtains were pulled back to reveal double French doors opening to a veranda that apparently faced the back of the heavily wooded property. Several fans were set about the room, including two overhead, but they did little to alleviate the heat.

"I'm afraid it doesn't have a private bath," Ella said. "You would have to use the one across the hall that serves this wing."

Now that was just wonderful, sharing a bathroom with a total stranger. And a man, no less. Of course, she'd shared a bath with a virtual stranger before—her husband. And toward the end of the marriage, Richard had slept in another bedroom altogether. Lived in his own private world. A world that hadn't included his wife. "Then I assume that means Mr. Morrell uses it, too."

"Actually, his suite has its own bath. The younger Mr.

Morrell had it installed before he moved in. Unfortunately, that's the only improvement he managed."

At least he wouldn't be in her way. "I could live with those arrangements."

Ella wrung her hands several times before saying, "Then the job is yours if you want it."

Selene decided this was almost too easy. "Wouldn't you like to see my portfolio first? Or at the very least, let me prepare some kind of estimate for my services?"

"That's not necessary. I promise, you'll be paid much more than you would normally receive for this type of work. I'll have all the details outlined in a simple contract that Mr. Morrell drew up himself."

"What about consulting with him first?"

"He's left the hiring up to me. He trusts my judgment, and my judgment tells me you'll do a fine job."

Could she really afford to decide something so important on the spot? A better question—could she afford *not* to accept since she was armed with an interior design degree that she'd never really utilized and a very limited résumé? If she turned down the offer, she might have to search long and hard for another opportunity, especially one that would allow her the freedom to take a project with so much potential and see it to fruition. "Pending the contract is in order, I'll take the job."

Ella looked very pleased. "Wonderful. When can you move in?"

"Right now if I need to. I'm staying at the local inn. I will have to go back there and get my things." Very few things. Most of what Selene had owned she'd left behind, except for the harsh memories of a doomed marriage.

"Today would be wonderful." Ella started toward the door. "I'll show you the contract first, and while you're in town, I'll see if I can arrange a time for you to meet him."

Him, as in Mr. Morrell, Selene decided. "I'm looking forward to it." If for no other reason aside from curiosity.

"One thing you need to know about Adrien," Ella said once they reentered the hallway. "He's a hard case. I've known him for many years, and the best way to handle him is to stand your ground."

Considering Ella's cautions, Selene wondered if she'd already made a colossal error in judgment. "I'll remember that."

On the drive back to the inn, Selene entertained more than a few second thoughts even though she'd found the agreement satisfactory and the pay much more than generous. She should have questioned the woman more thoroughly, particularly about the mysterious owner. Yet the opportunity had practically fallen into her lap at a time when she'd been uncertain over her future. Sheer serendipity.

Besides, the man was probably a middle-aged codger, as peculiar as his grandfather, set in his ways and, she suspected, cranky. She could handle cranky. She could handle anything as long as she could be her own person, make her own decisions, at least when it came to her private life.

Yes, she would deal with Adrien Morrell, through whatever means necessary, be it killing him with kindness or hanging tough. Better still, she would ignore him altogether.

"Who the hell is she, Ella?"

Adrien immediately noted the surprise in his longtime companion's near black eyes, followed by a flicker of guilt before she said, "You've seen her?"

Yes, he'd seen her. He'd watched her from the window as she'd left her car. Saw her brief hesitation. Witnessed her wariness. He'd noticed the way her golden blond hair, bound at her neck, spiraled down her back in soft curls. Noticed her slender throat, her flawless pale skin, the length of her legs and the curve of her hips. From the shadows near the stairs, he'd also observed her walking the corridor, and imagined more than only watching her. A reaction he didn't welcome but hadn't been able to stop.

Adrien leaned forward and rolled a pen back and forth over the desk's surface. "What does she want?"

"A job."

He tossed the pen aside. "I assume you told her she was in the wrong place."

"No, I did not." Ella stepped forward from the door and displayed her usual toughness. "Her name is Selene Winston, and I've hired her to oversee the restoration."

A sharp prick of seething anger threatened Adrien's tenuous self-control. "I didn't give you permission to hire anyone."

Ella planted her palms on the desk and leaned into them. "Someone needs to go forward with the plans before this house falls down around our heads."

Damn her interference. "That's my decision, not yours."

"That's the problem, *shâ*. You're making no decisions. That's why we need someone to get this place into shape so you can put it on the market and leave."

Right now he didn't care to leave. The house had become his haven, his own private hell. "How did you find her?"

"I put an ad in the St. Edwards newspaper and she answered it. She's the *only* one who answered it. And you're the one who told me you wanted someone who would give the house personal attention. Otherwise, I could have hired a firm from Baton Rouge months ago."

Adrien didn't like the way Ella's gaze suddenly faltered. "Where is she from?"

"Georgia. She's a divorcée. From the looks of her car and clothes, I suspect she has money, or did at one time. But for some reason she's decided to settle in St. Edwards. As long as she's a hard worker, I don't really care how she got here."

Adrien cared. He had no use for a woman who'd probably never had her diamond-bedecked hands dirty in her whole damn life. "How much experience does she have?"

She shrugged. "Why don't you ask her since you're the all-knowing, all-seeing entrepreneur?"

If Ella were anyone else, he'd fire her. "I really don't give a damn because I have no intention of letting her stay."

"You don't give a damn about anything, Adrien." She straightened and sighed. "It's been well over a year now. You have to go on with your life."

A life filled with remorse. A life that had become static, by his own hand. And he liked it that way. "Tell her she's not needed here." Or wanted.

Ella scowled. "Oh, she's needed here, all right. And she's staying, or I'll go with her."

More empty threats, Adrien decided. Nothing he hadn't witnessed before from his surrogate mother. Ella wasn't going anywhere because she had no desire to leave him alone. In order to keep the peace, at least externally if not internally, he'd humor her for now. "Fine. Do what you will. Just make sure she stays out of my way."

"Maybe you should tell her yourself. She's agreed to live here until the house is finished. I put her in the room next to yours." With that, Ella spun around without giving him a glance and headed out the door.

Adrien streaked both hands down his face and leaned back in his chair. He didn't need any of this. Didn't need this Winston woman anywhere near him. Even if she was beautiful. Even if he'd been numb for months now and when he'd seen her, he'd begun to come alive, at least in a carnal sense.

He'd be damned if he'd bed some Georgia debutante,

and he had every intention of persuading her to leave. He wasn't exactly sure how he would manage it, but he would. He definitely would.

Selene had been granted a delay in the official meeting, at least for the time being. According to Ella, the plantation's owner hadn't requested an audience, nor had he joined them for dinner. She hadn't run into him on her way to retire for the night, but earlier she had heard him passing through the corridor outside the bedroom, followed by a closing door. The sound of creaking floorboards, as if he'd been pacing, continued for a time before ceasing a few moments ago. Now if only she could get some sleep.

But sleep seemed as elusive as her employer. The fans only served to stir the warm air, and the open windows provided little relief. She'd tossed and turned so much that her thin white gown was practically wrapped around her neck. And although she'd taken a bath before turning in, at this rate she would probably need another. She couldn't imagine how people survived before the advent of air-conditioning. But then they couldn't miss what they'd never had.

What Selene really needed at the moment was some fresh air to provide some temporary comfort. On that thought, she pushed out of the bed, opened the French doors and stepped barefoot onto the veranda, hoping she didn't encounter any splinters jutting up from the wooden decking as she moved to the edge of the balcony. With her hands braced on the black railing, she turned her gaze to the three-quarter moon hanging overhead and the host of stars scattered across the midnight sky.

The temperature had mercifully dropped to a more tolerable level, the gentle wind she'd been seeking flowing over her damp body and ruffling her unruly hair. The bayou's summer sounds surrounded her—chirping locusts and bellowing bullfrogs. She inclined her head and listened for the rush of the Mississippi that knit through the terrain not far away. She only heard the rustle of brush from below. No doubt, the swamps were full of nasty creatures. Probably a few bobcats and alligators with large, treacherous teeth waiting to snap up unsuspecting wildlife. Definitely snakes slithering about, coiled and ready to strike. Maybe even a wolf foraging the forest, searching for prey.

A brief image flashed in her mind—another mental photo shoot of someone watching her—followed by a low, rugged male voice saying, "Too hot to sleep?"

Two

Selene spun to her right to find a dark figure seated in a wicker settee at the end of the veranda a few feet away. She released a ragged breath, one hand resting on her chest above the gown's scooped neck, the other gripping the rail tighter for support. "You startled me."

"Obviously." His tone dripped with sarcasm.

Wonderful. A midnight encounter with a jerk. She was so looking forward to this. "I take it you're Mr. Morrell."

"Correct."

That relieved Selene somewhat, even if his attitude needed adjusting. At least he was a real man, not some ghostly apparition.

What now? She could bid him good-night and return to her room. Or she could get the official introduction out of the way then go back to bed. With that in mind, she shored up her courage and moved closer, the moonlight providing enough illumination for her to make out a few details.

Details such as he couldn't be much beyond his mid-thirties and not the curmudgeon she'd envisioned.

His slightly wavy dark hair fell below his chin and his lips formed a line as hard and unyielding as his jaw that was covered in evening whiskers. Then her gaze came to rest on his eyes. She suspected the same eyes that had flashed in her mind upon her arrival. Unearthly blue, predatory eyes.

She could also see he wasn't wearing a shirt, while she was wearing a cotton gown that provided little cover. Not necessarily the proper attire for her first encounter with her boss, but she might as well get it over with.

Selene finally gathered enough wherewithal to step forward and offer her hand along with a forced smile. "I'm your new employee, Selene Winston."

"I know who you are." His gaze tracked down her body slowly in a blatant size-up before he centered it on her extended hand. After a slight hesitation, he took her palm into his grasp and curled his fingers around hers. Selene reeled from the bolt of sensation, the abject pain emanating from him. A deep, wounding pain.

She quickly dropped her hand and took a step back, as if she'd suffered an electrical shock. In reality, she had. She'd lived with the "gift" for as long as she could remember, keeping it concealed from the world. Well-bred Southern girls didn't read minds; they read the society page. But in all her years, never before had she been empathetic. She'd been able to discern others thoughts through imagery and occasionally words, but she'd never been able to channel feelings. Until him.

"It's nice to meet you," she murmured once she again had control over her voice.

He didn't return the greeting, yet he did continue to stare at her, making her want to twitch where she stood.

Making her want to run from him even though she felt oddly drawn to him. Drawn to his aura. His pain.

She struggled for something casual to say despite the uncomfortable situation. "I'd appreciate your input on how you want the restorations handled. Not right now, of course, since I need something to write with. Maybe tomorrow. Or the next day, if you prefer." Heaven help her, she was rambling like an idiot.

He failed to respond for a few moments until he finally said, "Only one thing you need to know. I expect perfection."

Selene knew all about perfection. She'd lived the perfect life with the perfect family. Had gone to perfect schools and had married the perfect man. The perfect lying bastard, she corrected. "I'll do my best to please you."

He laced his hands atop his bare belly. "That remains to be seen. I'm not easy to please."

That certainly didn't surprise Selene considering Ella's assessment that Adrien Morrell was a "hard case." She would have to concur. And after her reaction to him when they'd touched, she sensed that perhaps he had his reasons. "Do you have any particular preferences?"

He inclined his head and surveyed her face from forehead to chin, settling his gaze on her mouth. "In reference to what?"

Another image filtered into her mind, regardless of her attempts to stop it. She only caught a glimpse of his thoughts, but enough to realize those thoughts involved questionable considerations involving naked bodies. *Her* naked body.

Selene couldn't fathom why her well-honed ability to block this kind of thing failed her now. Couldn't understand why he would be fantasizing about her, a woman she'd just met. More disturbing, she couldn't comprehend why that excited her.

"I'm referring to how you would like the restoration handled," she said once the images dissolved.

He shifted slightly in the chair. "I prefer not to be involved at all. Unless you have no idea what you're doing."

That made her bristle, her defenses on high alert. "Any reason why you believe I wouldn't know what I'm doing?"

"You've given me no evidence to believe that you do."

How was she going to answer? Easy. By telling only a partial truth. "I have an interior-design degree. I've also supervised staffs and redecorated my own house in the past. I've even refinished furniture with my own two hands."

"Was that before or after your tennis game with the ladies down at the club?"

She resented his condescending tone. Resented even more that he was right about her former life. "Actually, I believe that was the day I had tea with the Daughters of the Confederacy," she said in her sweetest drawl. "Right before I went to my lessons on how to be genteel and polite even when confronted by ill-mannered jackasses. Those lessons seem to be escaping me now."

He looked as if he might actually smile, but it didn't quite form. "Are you calling me a jackass, Ms. Winston?"

If the moniker fits. She laid a dramatic hand above her breast. "Why, no, Mr. Morrell. That would be totally improper."

Again he raked his gaze down her body and back up again. Slowly. "Nothing wrong with impropriety now and then, Selene."

And no doubt he had that impropriety market cornered. He'd been brazen enough to call her by her given name. Bold enough to fantasize about her. And he hadn't even bothered to stand…until that moment.

He came to his feet slowly and, as she'd guessed, he was

an inch or two over six feet. His chest was lean, well defined and dusted with a layer of dark hair, his flat abdomen sporting a sequence of ridges above the waistband of his black slacks. His proximity alone jumbled her mind, hindered her breathing, as did his scent. A subtle clean scent that seemed perfectly in sync with the summer night, as if he were an integral part of the atmosphere. Mystifying, intoxicating, forbidden.

If he'd meant to intimidate her, it was working. But Selene wasn't going to let that happen. Not anymore. Not by any man. Especially not a man like him, even if he was absolutely awe-inspiring—in a threatening kind of way.

But instead of backing up, she turned her attention to a pair of dark vines circling his solid bicep, a grouping of letters centered in the middle that spelled out the word *Imperium.* "Interesting tattoo. My Latin's a little rusty. What does it mean?"

She lifted her eyes to find his gaze boring into her. "Absolute power."

Both his declaration and his overwhelming presence paralyzed her, even though she knew what he was about to do. The way he studied her mouth again gave her the first indication. His musings that broke through her mental haze served as confirmation. If she didn't leave now, he was going to kiss her. And she might actually let him.

Forcing herself back into reality, Selene folded her arms tightly around herself, as if that might offer some protection, and stepped back to regain her resolve. "I don't believe power is absolute, Mr. Morrell."

With the last of her shredding strength, Selene turned away from him and headed back to the safety of the bedroom. But she'd only managed a few steps before he said, "Some power is absolute, Selene. And you know it."

She didn't dare face him again, or respond at all. Doing

so would only prove to him that he did possess a certain power—over her.

She returned to the room, closing the doors behind her. Closing him out. But she couldn't drive him from her thoughts, nor could she rid herself of the persistent heat that had little to do with the elements.

She climbed into bed and tried to clear her mind. Tried to sleep. Tried to think about anything but him. But as she drifted off, Adrien Morrell was the last thing she thought about. The last thing she saw.

The minute Selene stepped from the bathroom into the hallway the following morning, she knew he had been nearby. She'd immediately caught the scent of his cologne, but more importantly, she sensed his presence. An intangible feeling that totally consumed her. She wondered if he'd been standing at the door or if he'd simply just passed through the corridor. Whatever the case might be, he wasn't anywhere in sight now. That should please her, but in a way, she was disappointed—only because she wanted to get a look at him in the daylight. A good, long look.

Glancing to her right, she intended to check to see if his bedroom door was open. Instead, she made contact with the devilish statue, its vicious features causing her to physically jump. Demon Giles would definitely have to go somewhere else. Anywhere else. If she thought she could actually haul him up and carry him out, she would deposit him in the nearby swamp.

Selene returned to her bedroom, slipped out of her robe and into a pair of white linen slacks and a coral knit sleeveless top. At least her summer apparel provided a respite from the heat that had already begun to creep into the house.

Selene headed down the spiral staircase at a fast clip, relieved to be out of the dark corridor and into the light, surrounded by cherubs. As she made her way across the rotunda toward the kitchen, she paused at a painting hanging on the wall of a young woman with bright green eyes and raven-black hair swept up from her slender, pale neck, her hands folded primly in her lap. Considering the lady's clothing—a soft white, long lace dress with a full skirt—Selene would guess that she'd probably resided at the plantation many years before. But when she studied the inscription on the brass plate anchored to the bottom of the frame, a series of chills raced up her spine as well as a sense of foreboding.

Grace— She sleeps with the angels.

Maybe this was a key to one of the tragedies Ella had spoken about the previous day. Maybe this beautiful young woman had died before her youth was spent, and perhaps even in this house. As disconcerting as that thought was, Selene wanted to know more about the plantation's past, if for no other reason than to satisfy her own curiosity. Who better to ask than the owner's right-hand woman?

As she entered the kitchen, Selene found Ella at the ancient white stove scrambling eggs and humming a cheerful song.

"Good morning," Selene said as she pulled back a chair and took a seat at the weathered pine table.

Ella regarded her over one shoulder while she continued to cook. "Good morning to you, too. Did you sleep well?"

"Fairly well. It's going to take me a while to get used to the surroundings." To get used to the idea that Adrien Morrell resided right next door. She'd intermittently heard the sounds of his footsteps throughout the night, as if he'd been restless. But then so had she. She still was.

Ella turned from the stove, balancing a full plate in one hand and a cup of coffee in the other. She crossed the small space and slid the fare in front of Selene. "Enjoy."

Selene resisted wrinkling her nose. She didn't care for

eggs or bacon. Toast she could do, and coffee. Definitely coffee. "It looks good, but I'm never very hungry in the morning. I also want to get an early start today."

Ella returned to the table with her own cup of coffee and took the chair across from Selene. "If you stay around for a while, you might be able to meet Mr. Morrell when he comes down for breakfast."

"I've already met him." Selene waited for Ella's apparent surprise to subside before she added, "Last night, on the veranda outside our rooms."

Ella slid a fingertip around the rim of her own cup. "How did that go?"

It had gone places Selene had never expected. "Not too badly. He wanted to know about my work experience, and I got the impression he doesn't want to be bothered with the details of the restoration."

Ella sighed. "He wants to be left alone."

Selene had sensed that about him last night, even in light of his fantasies about her. "What exactly does he do for a living?"

"He's an entrepreneur. He turned his inheritance into a small fortune through various ventures, mainly buying faltering businesses, restoring them and selling them for a large profit. He's very good at what he does, or he was until…" Ella's gaze drifted away with her words.

"Until what?" Selene asked.

"Until he decided to take a break from it all."

Again, Selene wanted to know more about Adrien, to ask more questions. But she sensed Ella wasn't up to answering, which called for a subject change. "If you can point me to a phone, I'll contact a few prospective contractors and set up appointments."

Ella took a quick sip of her coffee. "You'll have to find someone from Baton Rouge since you won't find anyone locally, at least not anyone who's willing to come out here. The townspeople are a superstitious lot. They believe the place is cursed."

Ella had unknowingly provided Selene with a good opening. "That portrait near the staircase. Is that woman somehow involved in the tragedies?"

"I'm not really sure," Ella said. "I assume she probably is, but I don't know any details about her."

Selene had always embraced the past, and she truly believed the woman named Grace had an interesting one at that.

She took another quick drink of coffee, pushed back from the table and stood. "I'm going to go into town and pay a personal visit to a few of the business owners. Maybe someone can suggest a local contractor who isn't superstitious."

"Good luck." Ella nodded toward Selene's untouched food. "You should eat something first, put on a few pounds so you don't make me look quite so portly."

"You're fine just the way you are. And I'm in a hurry to get this restoration underway." In a hurry to get away because she sensed Adrien's imminent arrival as surely as if she'd heard his approaching footsteps, which she hadn't. Any minute now, he could walk into the kitchen and throw her off balance. Better to head into town before that happened. Before she had to look at him again, this time in the daylight where all her fascination and preoccupation with her boss would be bared like a flashing billboard. Because she was fascinated by him, completely intrigued. He had his share of secrets, that much she knew, and most she would probably never know.

Yet she also knew those secrets had brought on his pain, and she had always been a sucker for lost souls. She'd manned a couple of hotlines on a volunteer basis, had championed several causes. She'd also learned that some lost people didn't care to be found. She suspected that Adrien Morrell had no desire to be saved from his solitude. For that reason alone, she vowed to pay no heed to him, as long as he stayed out of her head.

Alone in his office, Adrien stood at the window and watched Selene Winston drive away. Curiosity sent him immediately to her room, to see if she had left for good. In his experience, everyone eventually left. Not so in this case, at least not yet.

The white gown she'd been wearing on the veranda last night was draped over the bed's footboard. The sheer fabric had revealed only a few details, but enough details to set him on edge and keep him there. Striding across the room, he passed his palm over the gown that was as soft as her skin. He knew that much, even though he hadn't touched her. Yet. But he would.

Last night, he'd warred with what was wise and what he wanted. Many considered him predatory, territorial in both business and in pleasure. Until recently, he'd lived for the thrill of the chase, the rewards of capture. Selene Winston had resurrected that desire. Though he'd made a solid effort to ignore his baser urges, he was still a man. A man on a mission.

He planned to draw her into his world with a slow and carefully crafted seduction, guiding her into the darkness he'd created. She might be reluctant at first, but eventually she would come without reservation. Willingly. Openly.

She would provide a respite from his remorse, a means to temporarily forget what he hadn't done. More importantly, what he *had* done…to Chloe.

Fifteen minutes later, Selene drove into St. Edwards and pulled her sedan in front of Abby's Antiques, a place she had visited several times. The shop was situated along a row of small businesses that lined the single downtown street, an ancient red brick church serving as the town's cornerstone. After only a moment's hesitation, she left the car and entered the glass door, the subtle chime announcing her arrival.

The proprietor, Abby Reynolds, a fortysomething tiny woman with bobbed auburn hair and kind hazel eyes, looked up from behind the counter positioned at the back of the store and greeted Selene with a smile. "Hello, Ms. Winston. I thought you'd left town."

"As it turns out, I'm going to be here awhile." Selene skirted the helter-skelter antiques as she traveled down the narrow aisle, basking in the blessedly cool air flowing over her. If only she could bottle some to take back to the plantation.

When Selene reached the counter, Abby pushed her black glasses up onto her head and set aside the book she'd been reading. "You've decided to stay?"

"Yes, thanks to you. Remember that ad you showed me? As it turns out, it's a plantation west of town, and I've been hired to oversee a complete restoration."

"Maison de Minuit." Selene immediately noticed the wariness in Abby's tone and the stiffness of her small frame. "That should be challenging."

"Yes it will be, and that's why I'm here." Selene set her purse on the counter and folded her hands next to it. "Do you happen to know a local contractor who'd be willing to take it on?"

The woman shook her head. "You won't find anyone here who'll go out there."

Exactly what Ella had told Selene earlier. "What is it about the place that has everyone avoiding it like the plague?"

"Well, there's the matter of the lovers who supposedly

died there, and the voodoo woman who lived there after that. And the somewhat insane Giles Morrell who fortunately wasn't there very long. Take your pick."

Selene wondered if Grace happened to be one of those lovers. "Do you know any details? Names, that sort of thing? I'd like to know a little bit about the plantation's history."

Abby shrugged. "I've only been in town a couple of years. When I have heard people speak about the place, it's been brief, as if they're afraid to talk about it. And there's also the woman who mysteriously disappeared about a year ago."

"What woman?" Selene couldn't mask her surprise or uneasiness.

"Supposedly Adrien Morrell was holed up with her for over a year," Abby said. "Ralph Allen works for a delivery service and used to make runs out there every week or so to deliver packages. He says he saw her looking out an upstairs window a couple of times."

Surely Adrien didn't have an unidentified woman locked up in the mysterious bedroom. A totally ludicrous thought, Selene decided. Still… "But as far as anyone knows, she left?"

"The deliveries stopped suddenly, and no one's seen her since. Except Ralph swears he passed a coroner's car coming from that direction one morning."

Selene swallowed hard. "She died?"

Abby showed her discomfort by shifting her weight from one hip to the other. "There isn't any real proof of that. No death notice or anything. But Mr. Morrell has enough money to pay for silence, so I guess anything's possible. If he wanted her dead, he could arrange for it, even if he didn't do it himself."

Selene wasn't sure she wanted to explore those possibilities, though she didn't really view Adrien as a murderer. But what did she really know about him? Not much, other than he was a physically attractive, powerful man. "Maybe she just left on her own accord."

"Maybe she was a ghost." Abby attempted a reassuring smile. "You know how it is with gossip, Selene. People are like coon hounds with a rawhide bone. They chew on it for a while, then bury it for a time, but they always bring it out, along with more dirt."

Selene wanted to believe that that's all it was—idle gossip from the depths of idle minds. Rumor or not, she was still uneasy. "Do you know anyone who knows about the plantation's previous owners? Maybe a historian of some kind?"

"Unfortunately, the town doesn't have a library, otherwise I'd point you in that direction. You could try the courthouse, but I don't know how far back their records go. They don't even have a computerized system yet. And they lost quite a bit during a flood in the 1920s."

That sounded like a surefire dead end to Selene. "I suppose it wouldn't hurt to try that."

"Good luck," Abby said. "In the meantime, I can ask around and let you know if I find someone who knows the history."

"That would be wonderful." Selene rummaged through her purse, withdrew a pen and paper, jotted down her number, then handed it to Abby. "This is my cell phone. You can call me anytime."

Abby reached beneath the counter, took out a notepad and began to write. "I'm going to give you the address of a friend of mine, Linda Adams. She's in Baton Rouge and she specializes in antique restoration." She tore off the page and slid it in front of Selene. "She can help you with fabric selection and anything you need done with the furnishings. Her husband's a contractor and he's worked on several historical homes in the area, so he might be willing to help you out."

Selene took the paper and tucked it into the side pocket of her bag. "Thanks so much. I'll pay her a visit today."

After giving her thanks and a goodbye to Abby, Selene slid into her car for the trip to Baton Rouge. But before she could pull out into the street, a name jumped into her mind, as clear as the sound of the church's bell now tolling in the town square. The name meant nothing to her at all, but the voice that spoke it did.

Adrien Morrell's voice.

"Who's Chloe?" Following the query, Selene watched her dinner companion's expression herald first shock, then caution.

"Where did you hear that name?" Ella asked.

"In town." She didn't dare tell her exactly where the name had originated—in her mind.

Ella sent her a suspicious glance before pushing the pile of peas around on her plate. "That's not possible. No one in town knows about her."

"They believe a woman named Chloe was here for a while with Mr. Morrell, and then she was gone. Rumor has it she died."

Ella dropped her fork, pushed her plate aside and folded her hands tightly before her on the table. "First, you can't always believe what you hear, Selene. Second, I don't know who told you about her, but if I were you, I'd drop it. Now."

Selene couldn't ignore Ella's adamant tone, or the hint of anger. She worried that if she pushed too hard, Ella might push back. Or worse, dismiss her immediately regardless of the contract. "I drove into Baton Rouge today and found a woman who's going to help me restore the furniture. Her husband has agreed to come by and give us an estimate on repairs. But he's busy until next week."

Ella thankfully smiled. "You definitely accomplished quite a bit today."

"I also went by the courthouse," Selene added. "The woman told me it would take several days for her to locate any plans, and that's if they actually have any. Do you think I might find some here?"

Ella shrugged. "I'm sure Adrien probably has a set, but you'll have to ask him."

Not something Selene wanted to do, at least not tonight. "Is there some kind of attic where I might find old documents, maybe original abstracts?"

Ella picked up both hers and Selene's plates, then stood. "Yes, there's an attic. You'll find the door at the end of the hallway past Adrien's office. Feel free to explore it." The look Ella sent her said, "If you dare."

"Think I'll check it out in the next few days." In the daylight, Selene decided, because she definitely didn't want to traipse around in a dusty attic in the dark, in case she should come across the stuff scary legends were made of, including an idiot. That thought almost made her laugh. Almost.

Selene pushed back from the table and stood. "Let me do the dishes."

Ella waved a hand in dismissal. "I'll do them, dear."

"I insist," Selene said as she began to gather the serving bowls. "I could use something to do while I think."

"In case you haven't noticed, we don't have a dishwasher."

Selene had noticed, and that would be the first appliance on the purchase list. "I have no problem using my own two hands."

Ella sent her a cynical smile. "Have you ever washed dishes before, dear?"

"As a matter of fact, I have." Much to her mother's horror.

"Then I'll gratefully take you up on your offer. I need to speak with Adrien before I retire, anyway."

Most likely reporting to him about the new employee, Selene decided. But that didn't really matter. So far, she had done nothing wrong other than bring up the name Chloe. And although she'd decided to steer clear of that topic for now, she suspected Ella knew much more than she was willing to reveal. A mystery that might never be solved, unless Selene made a conscious—or subconscious—effort to solve it.

No. She wouldn't invade someone's mind to gain information. She'd done that before, only to suffer for it. If she discovered anything at all, it would have to come from someone verbally volunteering the information, not by her intruding into an unsuspecting mind. She highly doubted Adrien Morrell would serve as that volunteer, even though she instinctively knew he held the key. But then again, she might not want to know.

Adrien didn't bother to look up from the newspaper, even when Ella slid the covered plate and utensils in front of him. "If it's cold, don't blame me. You should come to dinner like a normal person."

He sent a disinterested glance at the food before finally bringing his attention to Ella. "I'm sure it's fine."

Ella remained in the same spot, obviously in the mood for a little chat. "Don't you want to know what our new houseguest has been doing?"

He knew exactly what she'd been doing—keeping him in sexual high gear, and she didn't even realize it. Yet. He went back to the paper, hoping Ella might take the hint and leave. "I've told you, I'm not interested in her plans." But he was definitely interested in her.

"She's been asking about the house's history," Ella continued despite his comment. "I thought you might like to help her out with that."

Adrien only wanted to help her out with one thing, and it had nothing to do with the past. He was much more interested in the immediate future. After folding the paper in precise creases, he set it aside. "What do you suggest?"

"First, she needs a set of blueprints," she said.

He opened a drawer, withdrew a cardboard tube and offered it to her. "Here."

Ella waved his offer of the plans. "You give them to her. It wouldn't kill you to be nice to her."

If Ella only knew how badly he wanted to be *nice* to Selene, she'd probably rescind the suggestion. "I'll think about it. But right now, I have some work to do. Anything else that needs my attention?"

"Yes, *shâ.* Your manners."

She spun around and headed out the door before Adrien could even offer a parting good-night. He wasn't expecting to have a good night. He'd rarely had one for almost two years now. Sleep had been as elusive as peace over the past months, and last night had been no exception. It hadn't helped that he'd encountered a woman who had shattered all his expectations. A woman who'd started a slow burn that had begun to heat up at a rapid pace.

Maybe Selene would like to spend a little time with him tonight. If she wanted to explore some history, he could accommodate her. He would willingly take her on a different kind of exploration, if she gave him some kind of sign she welcomed his attention. He had no cause to think she might, at least not now.

But he wouldn't let that deter him. He would have never gotten anywhere in business if he'd avoided challenges. Now he had to convince Selene Winston she had nothing to fear from him, as long as she never learned the truth.

Three

When Selene crossed through the "angel arena" on the way to her room, an eerie feeling slowed her steps on her ascent up the spiral staircase. As she turned the corner into the dark corridor, her heart immediately jumped into her throat. A few feet away, Adrien stood in the hallway, dressed in a steel-gray shirt and black slacks, one shoulder leaned against the wall, hands firmly planted in his pockets. He was as stone-still as the statue behind him, although he had much more physical appeal.

Selene planned to send him a polite greeting and good-night before she retired to her room. But before she could even utter a word, he said, "Going to bed already?"

His voice was low and provocative, but then so was he. A sullen stranger set in shadows. The light was muted, but at least now she could fully appreciate the details of a face that could have been sculpted by the angels keeping vigil nearby. No horrid disfigurement.

No mask of death. No real innocence, either, especially when it came to his eyes. Those deadly cut-glass blue eyes that he kept trained on her while she simply stood there as if in a trance.

Again Selene hugged her arms to her middle and finally snapped out of her stupor. "I've had a busy day," she said. "I'm tired."

He pushed off the wall but kept a safe distance. "Too tired for a little adventure?"

The question shook Selene's waning calm so strongly she couldn't speak for a few moments. "What kind of adventure?"

He took a slow step toward her. "Ella told me you're interested in the history of this house. I have something that might satisfy you."

His emphasis on *satisfy* shook her up even more. "What exactly would that be?"

"I could tell you, but I'd prefer to show you."

Selene checked her watch, more out of nervousness than true concern with the time. Although it was barely past nine, she said, "It is getting late."

"I'll make it worth your while."

He'd lowered his voice a notch and Selene responded with a slight shiver. A pleasant one that was both unexpected and inadvisable. "Where exactly would we be going for this adventure?"

He nodded toward the opposite end of the corridor. "To my office."

An office seemed relatively safe, but could she really be safe around him? She had two options—to trust him or use her gift to sift through his thoughts. She opened her mind briefly, but came up with nothing. No visions of him holding her hostage or doing her bodily harm. At least not yet.

"Lead the way." The words spilled out of her mouth

without any further consideration. If she really intended to work for him, she had to give him some of her trust, unless he proved he didn't deserve it. And hopefully not after it was too late for her to turn back.

She followed him down the hall, past the stairway and into the wing Ella had described to her during the initial tour, a place she had yet to explore. They passed by the closed door leading to the nursery, Selene presumed. When they reached another door adjacent to that, Adrien opened it and stepped aside for her to enter.

The large office was thoroughly modern, from the solid oak desk lit by a lone lamp to the computer sitting on a counter in the corner. Several binders were stacked neatly in an in-box and a silver canister housed various pens. Everything in its place and not at all what Selene had expected. But at least the room was sufficiently cool. In fact, it was cooler than most of the house, thanks to that modern convenience known as a window unit. Might have been nice if someone had bothered to install them everywhere.

When she heard the door close behind her, Selene fought the urge to spin around and display some serious panic. For all intents and purposes, she was trapped. He could do with her what he wanted and she doubted Ella would hear a single cry of distress.

Still, she wasn't getting any strange vibes or sense of looming disaster. When she faced him, she did get the full effect of Adrien's slight smile. The first she'd witnessed so far. "What do you want to show me?"

He slid his hands into his pockets again and looked much more relaxed than she felt. "A journal."

Selene had learned nothing was of more value in recreating the past than personal writings. "Where is it?" she asked, her tone revealing her enthusiasm over the discovery.

Adrien crossed the room to his right, opened a door and flipped on a light. "Up here."

Selene moved closer to see a dimly lit, narrow staircase and made a mental note to have someone replace all the low-wattage bulbs in the house as soon as possible. She took a mental step back when she realized she would have to accompany her employer into a remote area. "It looks like you might find a bat or two up there." She'd said it with humor to mask her wariness.

He hinted at another smile. "No bats, but maybe a few spiders."

"Lovely."

He studied her for a moment. "Are you afraid of spiders, Selene?"

Insects had never been her best friends, but she wasn't exactly arachnophobic. "No. As long as they keep their distance."

"Are you afraid of me?"

A very good question, one that Selene needed to seriously ponder. "Any reason why I should be?"

"Not at all."

He sounded convincing to Selene, but could she really believe him? She could usually rely on her instincts, though, and they were telling her he had no plans to injure her. As far as any other plans went—questionable plans— she supposed she would have to take her chances and keep a firm grip on self-control.

She made a sweeping gesture toward the staircase. "After you."

He took the first step and when she hung back, he shifted slightly and offered his hand. "I'll make sure you don't fall."

Selene wasn't all that concerned with falling. Years of ballet lessons had cured her of any serious clumsiness. But she was concerned about touching him again. Concerned that she might experience another blow to her senses. Yet instead of insisting on managing without his help, she reached out and accepted his offered hand. This time, the contact sent a rush of heat coursing through her body, as if she were being warmed from the inside out. The sensation was overwhelming and as they started to ascend the stairs, it only grew more intense. He glanced back at her now and then with eyes as blue as the ceiling in the rotunda. By the time they reached the top, Selene was both winded and very, very warm, even when he released his grasp on her.

The landing opened into another room, this one smaller with a narrow shelf housing volumes of aged books. In the corner sat a mahogany pedestal desk, and a lone straight-backed chair covered in red satin. The area was dusty, the ceiling draped with a few cobwebs, but other than that, it didn't look at all menacing. At least where bats and bugs were concerned.

"At one time this was the *garçonnière*," Adrien said as he remained at her side. "The original bachelor's quarters, probably used by a previous owner."

But obviously not used by Adrien, Selene thought. "Your grandfather?"

He forked a hand through his hair. "No. Giles wasn't one to stay in the same place for very long. He had a solid case of wanderlust. I inherited that from him."

She sent him a smile. "You're inclined to travel, I take it."

"Not in a while." He strolled to the bookshelves then faced her again. "I've been all over the world. Europe. Africa. Central America. Mostly off the beaten path. Spain is one of my favorite spots."

She walked to the desk and leaned against it. "Don't tell me. You've run with the bulls in Pamplona."

"Actually, no. I would be more inclined to root for the bulls since I believe that animals sometimes have more merit than humans."

A point in his favor, Selene decided. "So you're a thrill seeker as long as it doesn't involve cruelty to animals."

"At one time, yes."

He looked and sounded regretful, and that only served to spur Selene's interest. "I've been to Europe several times," she said to break the brief span of uncomfortable silence. "Mostly London. The usual tourist spots."

He rested one elbow on the edge of the shelf. "Ever done any cliff diving in Mexico?"

She laughed. "I'm not fond of heights."

"Ever stood on a deserted beach, naked, and watched the sun come up?"

Only in her wildest dreams. "I'm afraid not."

"You should experience it at some point in time."

Little did he know, he'd taken her there through his recollections, images that were too strong to bar from her mind. She experienced the salty breeze blowing over her bare skin and the sun on her face, smelled the scents of the sea, felt his palms forming to her waist, curving over her abdomen and lower....

Forcing herself out of his fantasy, she turned her attention to the shelves to avoid his steady gaze. "I've often wondered what it would have been like to live years ago, when times were less complex and modern conveniences were nonexistent."

"I've been in places where you had to rely solely on nature," he said. "It's a rush."

Selene decided his deep, steady voice was a rush. "I'm too old and set in my ways to rough it too much."

He inclined his head and narrowed his eyes to assess her. "You're what, maybe late twenties?"

"Thirty-two. And you?"

"Thirty-five. How old were you when you married?"

Obviously he knew much more about her than she knew about him. "Twenty-four. I've been divorced for a year."

He paced the room's perimeter, glancing at her now and then, as if he were some wild, agitated creature of the night assessing his quarry. "Seven years, just in time for that proverbial itch."

"You could definitely say that."

He stopped and leaned back against the shelves a few feet away from her. "Did that itch include both of you?"

As much as she wanted to know Adrien better, she was growing increasingly uncomfortable with the conversation. Drudging up her past with Richard always made her ill at ease. "Maybe you could show me the journal now."

"If that's what you want."

He headed straight for her with slow, stalking steps and Selene's gaze immediately tracked to his mouth, the softness of his lips that contrasted with the rigid set of his jaw, the slight cleft in his chin. All too late she realized he'd noticed her interest when he showed some semblance of another smile. Knowing. Sensual.

When he reached the desk, Selene stifled a catch of breath even though he passed by her. She regarded him over her shoulder to see him opening a drawer and withdrawing a small black journal that had seen better days. Olden days, she would guess.

Adrien rounded the desk and offered it to her. "I've marked the place that might interest you."

She took the diary, opened it where a pale pink satin ribbon indicated the spot and noted the date at the top of the page—July 1875. But before she could scan the faded script, Adrien said, "Read it out loud."

She turned her attention from the page to him. "You haven't read it?"

"Yes, I have. But I want to hear your voice."

His voice was so indisputably sensuous, so compelling that Selene couldn't think of one argument. She turned and laid the journal open on the desk while he began pacing the room once more. After clearing her throat, she began to read.

"'This afternoon, I again met Z. at the abandoned sharecropper's cabin near the swamp at his plantation. Should my father discover I am keeping company with his enemy, he would be furious. If he knew what I have done, he would surely kill him.'"

Selene paused and glanced back at Adrien to find him no more than a foot away. "Who wrote this?"

"I don't know. I came across it one day a few months ago."

"I'm wondering if maybe the woman named Grace in the portrait downstairs is the author."

"That's possible," he said. "Keep going."

Selene went back to the journal, driven by her need to know more about the unidentified author's rendezvous. "'I have given freely of my affections to Z., accepted his stolen kisses. He spoke to me about the ways between a man and a woman, and told me things that any proper lady would never consider. Yet I listened, and then I begged him to show me.'"

Again she glanced back at Adrien only to discover he'd moved closer. "I'm feeling a bit like a voyeur."

"I think it's an interesting commentary on the mores of the past," he said. "But if it makes you uncomfortable, hand it to me and I'll read it."

She noted the challenge in his tone, and she intended to answer it. After all, they were both adults, and she highly doubted anything written in this journal would compare to what was featured in modern literature in terms of sexuality. "I'll do it."

After drawing in a deep breath, she turned her attention back to the journal entry. "'In Z.'s arms, I am a wanton. I barely recognize myself. I allowed him to lower my chemise, allowed him to touch my breasts. Never before have I experienced such pleasure. Never before have I been so open or so free. I wanted more. I wanted all that he could give me.'"

Selene's words faltered when a hand came to rest on her shoulder. *Adrien's hand.* As his fingertips idled over her bare arm, she tried to ignore the rhythmic, enticing motion. Tried to disregard the frisson of pleasure brought about by his touch. "Continue," he whispered. "It only gets better."

Good judgment failed Selene and so did her resolve to avoid this very thing. "'He lifted my skirt and slid his hand beneath my drawers. He touched my most secret place, touched me in ways I had never imagined. My body was no longer mine. It belonged to him....'"

Adrien chose that moment to slide his hand down Selene's hip, brushing her pelvis briefly before settling his palm on her lower abdomen. She studied his golden skin against her white slacks, the width of his hand, his blunt fingers. He moved completely against her, his solid chest meeting her back.

She only had enough strength to close the journal and mutter, "That's enough for now." But she didn't push his hand away. Didn't scold him. Didn't move.

"It's not enough."

As if he'd bound her with invisible twine and gave it a tug, she slowly turned to face him. She knew exactly what he planned to do when the image flashed in her mind a split second before he lowered his head.

The minute Adrien's mouth met hers, Selene stepped

into a sensory minefield, bombarded by his subtle, clean scent, the taste of scotch on his lips, the suggestive foray of his tongue against hers. And suddenly it seemed she'd melted into his body, into his soul, experiencing his pleasure as well as her own. Because of this psychic communion, she also knew he needed more from her, wanted more from her.

Still, she had no desire to escape him, no will left to fight. No cause to loosen the grasp she now had on his shoulders even though she'd lost all grip on reality. But the mental as well as the physical connection ended when he stepped back and scrubbed a hand over his jaw.

"My apologies," he said. "I forgot myself for a few minutes."

As far as Selene was concerned, he hadn't forgotten a thing. The kiss had been part of a carefully crafted plan of seduction, and she'd walked right into his trap without a moment's hesitation.

She reached back, picked up the journal from the desk and tapped it against her open palm. "I'm going to read the rest of this later, and we'll forget what just happened."

He backed up a few steps and hid his hands in pockets again. "Go ahead and try to forget it."

I won't....

His thought came to Selene as sharp as a dagger, traveled along the mental passage connecting her mind with his. "We need to maintain a professional relationship."

He brandished his grin like a pirate wielding a sword, cutting her determination to shreds. "A little late for that."

All heaven and hell might break loose if she didn't escape that instant. Self-preservation sent her to the door, clutching the journal to her chest. "I'm going to my room now."

"One more thing, Selene."

The soft sound of her name sliding from his lips acted on her like a potent magnet, drawing her around to face him, where she found him holding out a cardboard tube. "What's that?"

"The plans for the house."

She moved only close enough to take the tube from his grasp. "Thank you."

"And let me set you straight on something. I didn't hire you. Ella did. As far as I'm concerned, you work for her, not me. Which means we don't have a professional relationship. In fact, if I'd had my way, you would already be gone."

Selene was so incredulous she almost couldn't speak. "Is that what this whole thing is all about? You're trying to drive me away?"

"In the beginning, yes. But not now. Not any longer. I've decided I like having you here."

Without responding, Selene turned, sprinted down the narrow steps and kept a fast pace until she reached the safety of her bedroom. But she feared she might never be safe as long as she lived under the same roof with him.

As she readied for bed, her thoughts kept turning to the absolute bliss she'd experienced in his arms. Too many years had passed since a man had touched her that way, or kissed her with such command.

Looking for a distraction, Selene climbed into bed and opened the diary to the place where she'd left off earlier.

We met again today at the cabin although I realized the risk in that. Yet I could not stay away from Z. He kissed me again and again, and I trembled with pleasure. I craved his touch. He then took my hand and placed it against his trousers where I felt his hardness. He said that when he was certain I was ready, he would join his body to mine. I insisted I was ready, I pleaded with him to show me. At first he denied me, but when I opened my arms to him, it was as if I had unleashed something wild in him, my sweet, gentle Z. He tore away his clothes and removed mine before laying me back on the cot to fill my body. I experienced some pain, as he told me I would, but the pain did not compare to the pleasure.

I knew in those moments I was forever his. I knew that no matter what the future held, he would always be mine. But I fear our time might end in terrible ways after today, for as I left the cabin, I saw one of my father's field hands lurking in the swamp, and knew I had been caught. I have no idea what fate awaits me and my lover when my father returns from Savannah tomorrow. I only know that whatever happens, every moment I have spent in Z.'s arms will have been worth it. He is my all. My one true love.

Disappointed to find the journal ended with that passage, Selene closed the diary, turned down the light and tried to sleep. She thought about the mysterious lovers and questioned how a man could have so much power over a woman that she would risk it all to be with him. Perhaps even risk her own life.

No doubt about it, Adrien Morrell had cast his spell over Selene. Now it was up to her to break free, before she, too, found herself caught in the clutches of obsession and allowed him to do anything he pleased.

She was quickly becoming his obsession.

Adrien knew all about obsession. Possession. Once he set a plan in motion, be it business or pleasure, he dove in with dogged determination until he got what he wanted. And he wanted her.

Tonight had been a first step toward his goal. A good step. He'd expected her to resist him a little more, but instead she had responded to his kiss with surprising enthusiasm. Unfortunately, even that minimal contact had set him on fire.

After stripping out of all his clothes, he downed the last bit of scotch, set the glass aside and walked to the double doors leading outside. He parted the curtains to see if Selene had ventured onto the veranda, as she had the other night. He found only an empty balcony to match the emptiness in his soul.

He shut off the lights, stretched out on his back across the bed and ran a slow hand down his abdomen. Knowing Selene was only a few steps away made him harder than he'd been in some time. Had him gritting his teeth and firming his resolve not to go to her. He wouldn't do that until he had an invitation. And he expected to have one, signed, sealed and delivered, very soon.

Right now, he would do whatever he had to do to keep his need for her in check—until the time was right.

He sat motionless at the end of the veranda in the same wicker sofa he'd occupied when Selene had first met him. The full moon cast his imposing frame in bluish light, yet it failed to soften his features, particularly his eyes. Those spellbinding eyes that he kept aimed on her. He looked every bit the stoic king holding court. A dark king.

Totally entranced, Selene maintained her distance a few feet away, watching, waiting. Waiting for him to speak, to move. To say her name.

Like a practiced hypnotist, he called to her simply with his gaze and a slight nod of his head. She effortlessly walked toward him, her mind caught in a fog, her lungs all but absent of air. She noticed immediately the lack of noise—

no rustling breeze, no sounds from the swamp below. Not even the chirp of a cricket. Although she found that odd, she kept moving forward until she stood before him. She also realized he was completely nude—and aroused.

Though he didn't utter a word, she recognized exactly what he wanted. As if bankrupt of free will, she clasped the hem of her gown, pulled it over her head and dropped it onto the ground beside her. Without the least bit of hesitation, she reached out and took his extended hand, allowed him to position her thighs on either side of his thighs. She released a soundless sigh when he lifted her up, then guided himself inside her. The sensations were potent, indescribable. She wanted more, needed more. Needed him to alleviate the dull ache, erase all the years of disappointment. Yet when he failed to move, she knew what he was asking of her. Knew that he waited for her to move first. She began a steady cadence and, in that moment, she became a woman she didn't recognize. An uninhibited woman who strived to please him, as well as herself, as he joined her in reckless abandon.

Still, there was no noise, no sounds of broken breaths, no quiet moans of satisfaction. Only absolute silence. Selene could feel the beat of her heart, the flutter of her pulse, the pressure beginning to build as she hurled toward a climax. Then Adrien stopped moving altogether and buried his face in the cleft of her breasts.

She wanted to ask why he had stopped, but she couldn't speak. She could only lift his head and force him to look at her. Again she saw his utter pain immediately before his face began to blur and fade completely, followed by a flash of white light that blinded her.

Selene forced her eyes open and bolted upright. She wasn't on the veranda, or outside at all. She was in bed.

Frantically she searched the darkened room, only to

discover she was completely alone. She patted her body to find her gown was still intact. Obviously she'd been dreaming. A very detailed dream that had seemed so very, very real.

Then awareness dawned. No, not a dream at all. A fantasy. *His fantasy.*

Selene collapsed back onto the mattress and rolled to her side, taking the spare pillow and slipping it between her knees. Adrien had unwittingly invaded her mind, bringing with him erotic images that she wouldn't soon forget. She couldn't comprehend why she was so open to his thoughts, or why those thoughts were so strong that they would disrupt her sleep. She also found it amazing that he would imagine her to be so unrestrained. If he knew that wasn't her normal self, would he still want her? She also recognized what he had been doing, because she had experienced all the sensations that he had through this wondrous, disturbing connection they now shared. Yet something had caused him to pull back, to stop before reaching the release he'd obviously been seeking.

Another bright flare of light drew Selene's attention toward the curtained doors, and so did the shadowy figure moving across the veranda. A storm was brewing on the horizon, and someone was outside her room. She suspected she knew the identity of that *someone*. Still, she had to know, had to confirm that before she could rest.

On wobbly legs, she left the bed, tiptoed to the doors and opened the curtains ever so slightly. She discovered him standing at the railing only a few feet away staring off into the distance, his arms crossed on the ledge, his leg bent at the knee, his foot propped on the bottom rail. The occasional flash of lightning revealed the finer points of his form turned slightly profile to her—beautifully naked and a wonder to behold. A steady rain began to fall and still he didn't move, seemingly unconcerned with the light show playing out above him. Rivulets of water gathered on his skin and slid down his body—over the coil of muscle on his bicep, down the path of his spine and the curve of his buttocks. He turned his face up, slicked both hands through his hair and let the rain wash over him, as if engaged in some kind of cleansing ritual.

Selene continued to be transfixed by the image he created against the turbulent skies…until he looked back at her. As if he'd ordained it, another bolt of lightning illuminated his face.

In that moment, she noted the flash of remorse in his beautiful face. She also saw the hunger in his eyes. The desire. And Selene feared she saw something else she might not welcome. Her destiny.

Four

For the past two mornings, Selene had waited until she'd heard Adrien leave his room before she got out of bed. Waited until she was certain she wouldn't have to face him before she took her morning bath and headed downstairs. She hadn't seen him at all since their encounter in his office, or since he'd occupied her mind, and she thought that was probably best for the time being.

Today Ella had left a note stating she had gone into town and would be out until that evening, allowing Selene some privacy to make a call she'd needed to make for a while now. After closing herself in the small office off the kitchen, she withdrew her cell phone from the pocket of her jeans and keyed in the number.

When her sister answered with a cheerful, "Hello," Selene released the breath she'd been holding.

"It's me, Hannah," she said.

"It's about time you called. I've been worried sick about you."

"I'm sorry. I've been busy." Busy trying to keep her brain above water and out of the clutches of the master of the house. "Are you feeling okay?"

"Other than I've got an extra ten pounds sitting on my bladder, I have another couple of weeks before I deliver this kid and Mother is still upset that I'm having the baby at home, I'm fine. Now it's my turn. Where the hell are you, Selene?"

Her little sister was nothing if not direct. She'd been that way for as long as Selene could remember. "I'm in Louisiana. I have a job—get this—at a plantation."

"Doing what? Sending out invitations to parties?"

Selene might have resented Hannah had she not said it in such a teasing tone. "Very funny. I'm overseeing the house's restoration from top to bottom."

After a long silence, Selene asked, "Are you still there, Hannah?"

"Yes, I'm still here. I'm just trying to picture you gainfully employed. Didn't the jackass leave you enough money to survive?"

"He left me plenty of money. A nice check every month. And I need the job because I need to be my own person. I thought you'd understand that."

"I do understand that, Selene. Mother, on the other hand, doesn't. You need to give her a call and explain so she'll quit bugging me."

Their mother understood little beyond untimely disruptions of her social calendar, and that was one phone call Selene would put off for as long as she could. "I will eventually. In the meantime, tell her I'm fine and I'll be in touch. I just wanted to let you know I'm still alive and kicking. And to make sure you're okay."

"I'm wonderful. Doug's been great. He treats me like a queen. I have no real complaints."

Selene had secretly envied Hannah's relationship with Doug. The man had been a saint during his and Hannah's five-year marriage, even though their mother and father hadn't approved of Hannah's choice—a man whose blood was lacking a certain shade of blue, but not his collar. A car mechanic, no less. Dear, rebellious Hannah, who'd always gone after what she wanted, and who'd had the temerity to ignore their parents' ideas on what constituted a good match for their daughters. If only Selene had been so strong. If only she hadn't kowtowed to their insistence that she and Richard take the next step, before Selene had been ready. Come to think of it, she had never really been ready.

"I'll definitely be home for the baby's birth, Hannah. Just give me time to get there if you can."

"Great, and Selene, just one more question. Are you happy?"

Selene rarely asked herself that question these days, or over the past few years, if the truth were known. "Yes, right now I'm happy. For the first time in a while, I feel free."

"I'm glad." Hannah sounded as if she truly was. "But I hope you finally decide to take a few chances, make a few friends. Maybe even meet a man."

Selene released an abrupt laugh. "It's only been a year since I got rid of one man. Why would I want another one so soon?"

"You don't have to marry him," Hannah said. "It's just nice to have a guy around for other things."

Those other things had weighed heavily on Selene's mind over the past few days, thanks to Adrien Morrell. "Actually, I've met someone."

"Wow! Who?"

"The plantation's owner," Selene said. "He's very nice looking although he's somewhat mysterious."

"Nice looking is good. Mysterious is really good. Have you two done it yet?"

"We haven't done anything yet." With the exception of the kiss and the shared fantasy. "I'm only saying that I find him interesting. Nothing may come of it at all." And that was likely considering Adrien's continued absence.

"You should make something come of it," Hannah said. "You've been lonely for too long, Selene."

How well Selene knew that. Yet she had the feeling that even if she did take a few chances with Adrien, she might still be lonely. Worse, she might even be in danger of many things, the least of which was getting her heart crushed. "Look, Hannah, I've already made one mistake with Richard. I don't want to make another. So don't get your hopes up."

Hannah released a long sigh. "Don't be so cautious, Selene."

"What's wrong with being cautious?"

The door creaked open right before the very deep, very clear male voice said, "Because playing it safe isn't very rewarding."

Selene's grip tightened on the cell phone, her mind unable to register what her sister was saying. When she didn't respond, Hannah asked, "Are you still there?"

"Yes, but I have to go now. I'll call you next week."

After saying goodbye and hanging up, Selene swiveled the chair around to find Adrien filling the doorway, wearing a tailored white shirt, plain black slacks and a half smile.

"I was beginning to believe you were permanently living in your office," she said in a slightly unsteady voice.

"I only come out when I have something important to do."

"And what would that be?"

"Another adventure. With you."

Selene wasn't certain she could handle any more of his kind of adventure, especially after the one she'd experienced two nights ago, both in his study and in his mind. "Give me the details and I'll decide if I'm interested."

He leaned his shoulder against the doorjamb. "Did you finish reading the diary?"

"Yes, but there wasn't very much left."

"I know. I've read it. But that doesn't mean other journals don't exist."

"You have more?"

"No, but I know where the cabin is. We might find one there."

"Where is it?" Selene's eagerness came out in her tone, despite the fact she didn't want to seem too excited, even if she was.

He favored her with a slow smile. "It's at the back of the property, next to the swamp. I can take you there."

Selene definitely wanted to see it, but she wasn't sure that was wise. At least not with him tagging along, bringing with him a surplus of sensuality. "If you'll just point me in the right direction, I'm sure I can find it myself."

"I want to show you the way."

She had no doubt he did, and no doubt that he could show her many things. Make her feel things she'd never felt before, if she gave him any indication she wanted that from him. But did she?

Don't be so cautious, Selene….

Maybe Hannah had been right. Maybe she was too cautious. Perhaps that caution had prevented her from knowing the best things in life. And no maybes about it, she was tired of playing it safe. As long as she kept a cool head, remained in control, she could avoid any emotional entanglement.

After pushing back from the desk, she came to her feet.

"I'd love to go with you, but I still have a few things I'd like to do today."

"So do it." He pushed away from the door. "I'll meet you at the back door at five this afternoon."

"Fine. I'll be there."

He turned and walked away, leaving Selene to ponder her decision, and definitely to question her sanity.

Standing at the kitchen door, Adrien Morrell looked like every teenage girl's fondest dream—and every over-protective father's worst nightmare. He wore a black T-shirt cut off at the sleeves that revealed his "power" tattoo, his thumbs hooked into the pockets of a pair of jeans that were faded in several notable places. His air of confidence was palpable, his raw sensuality undeniable. Selene wanted to run—straight into his strong arms. She cautioned herself to remain tough, although that seemed incredibly difficult when he smiled.

As Selene approached him, he gave her a long once-over and a disapproving stare. "That's not a good idea," he said.

Selene frowned. "What's not a good idea?"

"Your choice in clothes."

She looked down at her beige thin-strapped tank top, denim shorts and sneakers before glancing at him again. "It's hot outside. And my feet are sufficiently protected."

"It's rough terrain. Plenty of briars and poison ivy along the way to attack your bare legs."

Obviously she wasn't cut out for this outdoor stuff. "I'll go change into something more appropriate."

"We don't have much daylight left." He opened the door and held back the screen. "You'll have to manage. I'll help you."

Selene brushed past Adrien and he remained behind her as they descended the three steps. Once they reached the overgrown yard, he moved to her side as they walked the well-marked path leading to the swamp. The clearing soon gave way to thick underbrush and twisted trees that hovered overhead, filtering out some of the sun, but not the heat. Because of the recent intermittent rain, the atmosphere was almost unbearable, at least for Selene. Adrien didn't seem to be at all affected by the high humidity and the stifling steam that rose from the soggy ground. He remained silent, staring straight ahead as if deep in thought.

Selene watched her feet, careful not to come too close to anything that looked poisonous or pointy. When the scrub grew thicker, that proved to be a challenge, and that challenge led to a few scratches around her ankles while she fended off several mosquitoes attacking her limbs. But she refused to complain about the bugs and the briars. Refused to come off sounding like some kind of spoiled ninny who didn't have the fortitude to take on the elements. She could deal with a few bites and scrapes for the sake of seeing a part of the past. She couldn't avoid the thornbush that seemed to reach out and grab her leg, leaving a nice long welt down her calf, prompting her to hiss out a breath between her gritted teeth.

Without warning, Adrien swept Selene up in his arms before she realized he'd moved. A sharp gasp left her parted lips and she clung to his neck, immediately noticing the breadth of his shoulders and the dampness beneath the soft curls at his nape.

"This really isn't necessary," she said. "I was managing okay by myself."

"You were getting cut to shreds. Now shut up and enjoy the ride."

Shut up? He'd actually told her to shut up? If he didn't look like a veritable god, she might have slugged him.

A glint of gold where her forearm met his neck caught

her attention. Taking a chance, she kept one arm draped around his neck and used her free hand to pull the chain out from beneath his shirt to study the medallion. "What's this?"

He kept his gaze centered on the trail. "It's a Chinese talisman. The symbol of the snake."

She couldn't resist rolling her eyes. "No doubt, it has some sort of phallic significance."

He sent her a brief glance. "Actually, it symbolizes intuition and perception. And strengthens willpower."

Selene decided she could use a bit of willpower now, especially when he leveled his gaze on her. Only then did she notice his eyes seemed to darken in the daylight, taking on a more cobalt hue. When he turned his profile to her, she also noticed the near perfection of his face, the golden cast of his skin and the temptation of his mouth. She had the strongest urge to reach out and touch his lips, to see if they were as soft as she remembered. Only she didn't care to use her fingertips. She wanted to use her own lips.

"We're here," he announced before she gave into temptation.

Selene tore her gaze away from Adrien's face to see the small log cabin set out in the clearing before them. When they reached the front door, he deposited her back on her feet and released his hold on her—just when she was beginning to enjoy the ride.

He opened the door to a small one-room hut that was dingy and dark even though it was still afternoon. After breezing past her, he opened the heavy shutters on one window, allowing the daylight to stream in. Selene followed his lead, going for another window on the opposite side of the room. As poor luck would have it, the stubborn shutter took a moment to cooperate, and in the process, gifted her with a nice long splinter in her thumb.

"Damn." The oath spewed out of her mouth before she

had the foresight to stop it. She turned to see Adrien smiling at her—a very amused smile. "What?" she asked as she examined her throbbing thumb.

"I didn't know Southern belles knew those kind of words."

"Actually, I have a book of cuss words. I like to practice now and then."

His grin expanded, taking the sting out of her wound. "Good to know I don't have to watch my language around you. Now let me see that."

She shook her hand as if that might dislodge the splinter. "It's not that bad. I'll get it out when we go back to the house."

"I'll take care of it." He crossed the room and caught her hand, turning her palm up to inspect her thumb. He then reached into his back pocket, pulled out a knife and flipped it open with a twist of his wrist.

It took all Selene's power not to jump out of her cross trainers. "I'd really like to keep my thumb, Adrien."

His gaze shot from her hand to her. "What did you say?"

"I said my thumb comes in handy, so I'd like to keep it."

"Not that. You said my name."

Funny, she hadn't even thought about it. The word had flowed as naturally from her mouth as the curse a few moments before. And considering what they'd been through together two nights ago, they should probably be on a first-name basis. "Isn't that amazing?"

He shook his head slightly before returning to tending to her injury. With little effort, he dislodged the splinter and slid the knife into his back pocket. "You'll live," he said, keeping his eyes leveled on her face and her hand still firmly in his grasp.

"I'm sure I will." Even if her respiration wanted to fail her at the moment. "Can I have my hand back now?"

"Sure."

When he released his grip, Selene distracted herself by

studying the area. A lone wooden cot in the corner near the fireplace and a rickety chair by the far window were the only two pieces of furniture to be found. The floors, like the walls, were made of wood and looked as though they hadn't seen foot traffic in decades.

"Not much here," Selene said as she wandered around the room, surveying the cobweb-covered ceiling. "Do you really think this is the place where our unidentified lovers rendezvoused?"

"What do you think?"

"I suppose it's possible. It's a sharecropper's cabin by a swamp." She strolled to the bed and lifted the flattened feather mattress, hoping to find another journal, but no such luck. "Nothing here."

"No discarded chemise or drawers?"

Selene looked up to find him smiling again. She definitely liked his smile. She liked everything about him at the moment. "No. And no journal either. The mystery continues." She straightened and sighed. "I'll just have to search harder. Maybe go into town and see if anyone knows the story."

He leaned his back against the far wall. "You do that, but you might be disappointed with what you learn."

"True. Maybe it's best I don't know. Then I can go on believing they had this grand, passionate affair. Sometimes the fantasy is better than the reality anyway."

"Not always. When two people have enough heat between them, the reality is always better."

Selene was definitely heating up, both from the musty, unventilated cabin and that unmistakable take-me look in Adrien's eyes. "I wouldn't know about that."

Needing some air, she strode to one window and stared out over the marshy terrain. Changing the subject seemed wise. As it was, she'd already said too much. "I think I see some kind of pond in the distance. You know, if this acreage was cleared out, and this cabin restored, it could provide a nice secluded guesthouse for a couple wanting to escape. Before the passion goes away completely." Her cynicism was definitely showing.

She heard the sound of Adrien's footsteps and sensed he was close. He confirmed that when he asked, "You didn't have any passion in your marriage?" from immediately behind her.

She opted not to turn around even though she decided to be honest. "Not exactly."

"Then he didn't do it for you?"

"I didn't do it for him." Too much honesty, she decided. Too much laid bare for him to take the bait.

And he did when he said, "He told you that's why he cheated on you."

Now who was reading whose mind? "Yes, he mentioned that." Right after she'd tapped into Richard's thoughts only to see another woman residing there. A woman who "did it" for him.

Adrien's hands coming to rest on her shoulders sent a pleasurable succession of shock waves along her nerve endings despite the disturbing conversation. "Did he ever encourage you?"

No, but she had tried to encourage him—from intimate meals to sexy lingerie. Eventually, she'd given up. "Define *encourage*."

He breezed his fingertips up and down her bare arms. "Did he ever make love to you in a dark alley after midnight?"

Had it not been for Adrien's close proximity and heady strokes on her flesh, she might have laughed. "Heavens, no."

"He never made love to you in a car in your driveway because he couldn't wait to get into the house before he had you?" He moved flush against her back, wrapped one arm around her middle and breezed his fingertips along the side of her exposed neck. "He never arranged for a private dining room in an exclusive restaurant, then touched you beneath the table until you wanted it right then, right there?"

Selene was certain Adrien had done all those things with a lover, maybe several, even though she couldn't channel his thoughts at the moment. But she could imagine doing all those things with him, and more. "Richard's not that resourceful."

"Richard's a damn fool."

He wouldn't get any argument from Selene on that point, but he did manage to extract a slight shudder when he stroked his knuckles above the rise of her breasts, back and forth in a sultry rhythm. She closed her eyes and absorbed the sensations, leaving her mind open for his thoughts, his fantasies. Yet she saw nothing other than white light, heard nothing but the lyrical cadence of his voice as he continued to speak to her in a steady, stimulating tone.

"We all have the capacity to reach incredible heights during sex." He slid one strap off her shoulder and brushed his warm lips down the bend of her neck before bringing his mouth back to her ear. "You only have to be open to the possibilities."

He lowered his palm to her breast and softly, slowly circled his fingertip around her nipple through the thin knit. Only then did she choose to open her eyes, to watch what he was doing, and she wasn't at all sorry. "This is only one erogenous zone, Selene," he said. "There are a lot more all over your body. Even so, just this little bit of fondling has you hot, doesn't it?"

Selene could do no more than nod her affirmation. Speaking seemed completely out of the question, especially when Adrien slid his palm down to the waistband on her shorts. "Right here, right now, you want me to touch you everywhere." He toyed with the button on her fly, twisting it slightly, torturing her with anticipation. "You want me to take these off you and find out how hot you really are."

Yes, she wanted it. Wanted it more than anything she'd wanted in a long time, even her hard-won freedom. So much so she thought she might actually beg him to do it. But instead of answering her silent plea, Adrien turned her around and readjusted her straps. When she gave him a look of confusion, he simply said, "Not here. At least not now. Tonight."

Selene hugged her arms close to her middle to fend off the unexpected chill. "I'm not sure that's what I want."

He inclined his head and surveyed her face. "You want it as badly as I do, and you know it." He reached over and tucked a random strand of hair behind her ear. "But I'll give you time to think about it between now and then. Think about what it's going to be like with us."

He did no more than draw another line with his fingertip down her throat to her cleavage and back up again along her jaw. But it was enough to make Selene lose all sense of reason. Enough to cause her to wrap one hand around his nape and bring his mouth to hers. He let her take the lead, let her explore, cajole, taste and tempt him. He kept his hands loosely about her waist for a time but as the kiss grew deeper, he moved closer until their bodies meshed together. Until every curve and crevice fitted perfectly against the other, practically interlocked like a human puzzle.

When he pressed one hand on her bottom, bringing her in maximum contact with his erection, and ground his hips against her, she ran her hands up his back beneath his shirt just so she could feel his bare flesh. And she did feel it, every amazing inch of corded muscle, his smooth skin hot and damp beneath her palms. She wanted his shirt gone. She wanted all his clothes gone, and hers, too. She wanted him to lay her down on that ancient cot and thrust inside her, as he had in his fantasy. As the mysterious Z. had taken his lover all those years before. She wanted to know if the reality would be as remarkable, even though she instinctively knew it would.

Without any warning, Adrien broke the kiss and wrested out of her arms. He ran both hands through his hair and then laced his fingers behind his neck. "We need to go now. Before I change my mind and take you right where you stand."

Selene tugged at the hem of her top. "That's probably a good idea."

He sent her a half smile. "Taking you where you stand?"

Oh, yes. Definitely. "Going back to the house before we both do something we regret."

"I promise you, Selene, you won't have any regrets after I'm done with you."

With that, he headed toward the door and Selene followed him outside, her mind whirling with all the possibilities. This time he didn't carry her, but in a welcome display of chivalry, he did take her hand as he navigated the path, kicking aside any rogue limbs and thorns that might reach out and grab her.

Once they made it to the back door, he tugged her back against him, formed one hand to her jaw, and kissed her again, but only briefly. "I want an hour of your time, Selene. Tonight. After it's over, you'll know your own body like you've never known it before. You'll also know the lack of passion in your marriage wasn't your fault."

Then he disappeared into the house, leaving Selene alone to ponder exactly what she was falling into, aside from Adrien's sensual snare. Vigilance came calling, along with a voice that implored her not to be too hasty. Not to listen to her carnal needs. Not to throw out all her caution.

But her sister's voice telling her not to be so cautious drowned out all the warnings. Tonight, she would give Adrien an hour and hope that she came away with all that he'd promised, and more. Why wouldn't she? After all, he was a master of seduction.

"You summoned me, oh master of the household?"

Adrien spun his chair around from his computer to find Ella standing before the desk. "Yeah. I just spoke with your brother. He's expecting you tonight."

Confusion showed in her expression and resonated in her tone when she asked, "Since when?"

"Since I told him you were coming to visit for a few days. I've arranged for a driver to take you to the airport and the plane will be waiting. You can leave immediately after dinner."

"But—"

"No buts, Ella. You haven't seen him in almost two years."

Ella narrowed her eyes. "What are you up to, Adrien?"

He leaned back in his chair and stacked his hands behind his head. "I'm not up to anything. I'm giving you some time off to be with your family. I know you wouldn't go before now because you had this crazy idea I shouldn't be alone. Now you can go without having to worry about me."

She tapped a finger against her chin. "I see. Since Selene's here, you won't be alone."

"That's correct."

The suspicion didn't subside from her face. "Then I take it you two are getting along well."

Damn well, and he planned to get to know her better later this evening. "I'm getting used to her being here."

She propped both hands on her hips and took on her

motherly stance. "I know what you're up to. I see it in your face. You're going to use that charm of yours to seduce her."

If he lied, she would know. Glossing over his intentions seemed the best alternative. "What I do is my business. You don't have to concern yourself."

"I am concerned, Adrien. She's a nice woman. You need to be careful, otherwise she'll be just another one of your casualties."

Adrien could see that she regretted the comment the moment it left her mouth. "I'm not going to force her to do anything she doesn't want to do," he said.

"You don't have to force her. All you have to do is look at her a certain way and she'll follow you anywhere you want her to go. She's vulnerable."

"She's tougher than you think." Tougher than Adrien had first assumed, and he liked that about her. "Now go pack a bag."

"Anything else?" she asked in an overly sweet voice. "Perhaps draw you a bubble bath, light a few candles after I prepare your dinner?"

"That's not necessary. We're only having dinner together." And that's all Ella needed to know right now. He did have a few more plans, but he didn't require candles or warm baths to execute those. He only needed Selene's trust, and he planned to have it tonight.

Ella released a long-suffering sigh. "Okay. I admit it, I'm looking forward to seeing my brother and my nephews." She pointed a finger at him. "But I'm only going to stay the weekend."

"Stay a week, Ella. Or two. You deserve it."

"But—"

"That's an order."

She held up her hands in surrender. "Fine." She left out the door, letting loose a string of Cajun oaths directed at him.

Now that the plan was in motion, Adrien only had to set the stage, beginning with dinner. And after dinner, he intended to keep Selene occupied for at least an hour, if not longer.

Five

Selene was surprised to find the evening meal set out in the formal dining room, not at the small dinette in the kitchen. But she was even more shocked to see Adrien seated at one end of the rectangular table, wearing a crisp white shirt that matched the tablecloth, his dark hair framing his shadowed jaw in soft waves. His very first appearance at dinner.

When she noticed only one other place setting aside from his, she asked, "Is Ella not joining us?"

"She's already had her dinner." He picked up a knife and ran his fingertips along the blunt end of the silver blade. "She's about to leave."

Another surprise among several, and one Selene wasn't certain she welcomed. "Where is she going?"

"Why don't you ask her?"

"I will."

Once in the kitchen, Selene found Ella sliding two

plastic containers inside the refrigerator, a lone paisley bag set out on the floor not far way. "Going somewhere?"

Ella straightened, closed the door and faced Selene with a smile. "To visit my brother and nephews in Shreveport. I'm about to leave as soon as I finish up here. A car's waiting to take me to the airport."

"When did you decide to do this?" Selene heard uneasiness in her voice and tried to temper it when she added, "I don't remember you mentioning a trip."

Ella grabbed a dish towel, wiped her hands and then tossed it aside. "That's because I only decided to go this afternoon."

"Not a family emergency, I hope."

"No, dear, just a visit that's long past coming. I'll only be gone a week, maybe two."

A week or two? Selene resisted wringing her hands from a nervousness she couldn't control. In a matter of moments, she would be in the house with Adrien, completely alone. That created some more cause for concern, although admittedly the thought excited her. "When you return, we need to discuss some of the particulars on the restoration. I have a few ideas I would like to run past you."

"I look forward to it." She picked up the bag and gestured toward the refrigerator. "I've prepared several meals for you to heat up. Just make sure he eats on occasion. He's lost too much weight as it is. He's too thin."

Granted, Adrien was lean, but Selene wouldn't exactly describe him as *thin*. Not in the least. "I'll try, but I don't know if I'll make much headway."

"All I ask is that you try. The rest is up to him." Ella patted Selene's cheek. "Now see me to the door, then you can eat before it gets cold."

Silently they walked past the dining room where Adrien

was still seated, then through the angel rotunda and into the vestibule. At the front door, Ella turned to Selene, concern calling out from her eyes. "Remember what I've told you. Stand your ground with Adrien. Don't let him talk you into anything."

Selene clasped the hem of her blouse and held it tightly. "You don't have to worry. I'm not one to do anything I don't want to do." Not in this lifetime. Not any longer.

"And you don't have to worry about Adrien doing you any harm."

"That's good to know." When Ella's gaze drifted away, Selene's worry increased. "What is it you're not telling me, Ella?"

"He is a very persuasive man, *shâ*. Many a woman could attest to that. But no one knows the real man behind that steel exterior. Take care to protect your heart."

Selene released a humorless laugh. "Believe me, Ella, falling in love is the last thing on my mind. Let's just say I'm rather jaded when it comes to that sort of thing."

"Falling in love isn't always a terrible thing." Ella studied Selene a moment longer, looking thoughtful. "But now that I think about it, you could be the one."

"The one?"

"The one who saves him from his isolation. Saves him from himself, in a manner of speaking. It will take a strong woman, but you could be that woman."

After a brief hug, Ella walked out the door, leaving Selene to analyze her assertions. She'd never seen herself as being all that tough, at least not in recent years. Yet it had taken a good deal of strength to walk away from the only home she'd known and set out on her own. But was she strong enough to prevent her emotions from overtaking good sense if she did become further involved with Adrien?

He is a very persuasive man…. Many a woman could attest to that….

All along, Selene had acknowledged she would be only another conquest. Another woman among heaven only knew how many more. But then, if she viewed it logically, he could be her conquest, too. Her ticket to the adventure of a lifetime. For that reason, she intended to explore all the possibilities with him, beginning tonight. She could play it safe and always wonder what she might be missing, or she could gain firsthand knowledge of his skill as a lover. She wanted that firsthand knowledge. She wanted to know what it would be like to have a man pay complete attention to her needs, as she knew he would.

Driven by anticipation and adrenaline, Selene made her way back through the house at a fast clip. She only paused to take a brief look at Grace's portrait, questioning again if the young woman had been, in fact, the journal's author. If so, Selene could definitely relate to how Grace had felt when she'd met her mysterious lover—excited, winded and somewhat wicked. Which would make Selene a "wanton," she supposed. Well, not yet anyway, but possibly before the night was over, if all went as planned.

When she reached the dining room, Selene discovered Adrien had waited to begin eating. She took her designated place at the opposite end of the table and draped the napkin in her lap.

"Looks great," she said as she inspected the food—blackened fish, a vegetable medley and rice. Unfortunately, she wasn't at all hungry, even though she probably should be.

"Did you and Ella have a nice chat?"

Selene looked up from the plate to find Adrien staring at her. "We didn't really have a chat. I told her to have a nice time and she told me to make you eat." She picked up her fork and gestured toward his plate. "So eat, otherwise

I might be out of a job if she comes back and finds you've totally wasted away."

"I won't be wasting away. In fact, I've had an increase in my *appetites* in the past few days."

Selene concentrated on eating while considering he'd said "appetites," meaning those not only having to do with sustenance. Needless to say, hers had improved as well, but not when it came to this particular meal. The fish was a bit too spicy for her taste and, although the vegetables were good, the rice seemed to stick in her parched throat. For the most part, she pushed the food around on her plate while the silence continued.

"I'm finished," Adrien said after a time, drawing her attention to find his plate absent of any food.

Selene nudged her plate away and dabbed at her mouth with the napkin before setting it aside. "I'm finished, too."

He leaned forward and studied her half-full dish. "You didn't eat much at all."

"It's the hot weather," she said. "I'm never that hungry in the summer."

Without saying a word, he pushed back from the table, stood and strolled toward her, his gaze fastened firmly on hers.

Selene braced for what he might do next until he picked up her plate and said, "I'll be back in a minute. Don't go anywhere."

She wasn't sure she could move even if she'd wanted to.

Adrien grabbed his own plate, headed for the kitchen, then returned a few moments later with an open bottle of red wine. He came back to her, filled the glasses he'd brought with him and set one before her.

She waved it away. "No thanks."

He nudged the wine closer. "Take it. You look like you could use a drink."

Selene decided not to argue since a little libation might not be such a bad idea. Maybe it might even untangle the nervous knots in her belly. "Okay, I guess I could have a glass." Or two or three should she decide she needed to find courage in a bottle. Ridiculous. She didn't have to get drunk to enjoy Adrien's attention. He was already intoxicating enough, particularly the way he filled out his slacks, something she couldn't help but notice when he turned away to reclaim his place at the opposite end of the table.

After he settled back into his seat, he took a long drink of the port before he asked, "What were you like as a child?"

She wasn't expecting that at all. "Serious, I guess you could say. An above-average student. I was fairly reserved." And different, something she'd recognized at a very young age, thanks to the "gift."

He rubbed a hand along his jaw. "Interesting. I had you pegged as a social butterfly."

She'd never quite left her cocoon, the one she'd weaved for self-protection. "Not really. Now my baby sister, on the other hand, was quite the hellion. Someone had to keep her in line."

That seemed to pique his interest. "Are you and your sister still close?"

"Yes. Very close. She's back in Georgia and about to have her first baby. Do you have any siblings?"

He drank the last of his wine and set the glass down hard. "No."

Selene sensed that was somewhat of a sorry subject from the somber look on his face. "What were you like growing up?"

He flashed a wry grin. "Trouble."

She couldn't help but return his smile. "Why does this not surprise me?"

He rimmed a slow finger along the edge of his glass,

drawing her attention. "Unlike you, I wasn't a great student. You could label me the classic underachiever, at least during high school. I did manage to obtain an MBA from Notre Dame."

Selene didn't consider that an underachievement at all. "I went to the University of Georgia for my undergraduate studies. No master's although I did consider going back at one time. But then I made that fatal mistake of getting married instead."

"To Richard the fool."

Selene wrapped both her hands around her glass and stared into the burgundy liquid. "Yes, to Richard the fool."

She heard the scrape of his chair but failed to look up, her pulse accelerating with the sound of his approaching footsteps. She finally did give him her attention when he pulled her chair from the table, turned it to one side, then positioned another chair to face her and dropped down into it.

He rested his hands on her thighs. "I like what you're wearing tonight," he said in his chill-inducing voice.

"Thank you." She'd actually chosen the sleeveless red silk blouse and black mid-thigh skirt for him, as absurd as that seemed.

He inched his hands higher, just beneath the hem. "Have you thought about what I proposed earlier?"

She sighed. "That's all I've been thinking about."

"And?"

"I need to think a little more." As if she could really think at all with his hands on her. "I'll do that while I'm washing the dishes."

"The dishes can wait."

"I need something to do while I think."

He hinted at a smile, as if he might have a suggestion on what she could do. "Leave your veranda doors open in your bedroom. I'll come to you." He leaned over and brushed a soft kiss on her lips, then stood.

"I guess I'll see you in a while, then." She'd agreed without hesitation, but then she'd known all along she would. Known that buying more time would only delay the inevitable, and he knew it, too.

He turned away briefly before facing her again. "Don't get undressed. Wear what you're wearing now."

"Anything else?" she asked.

"That's it. For now."

Then he was gone, leaving behind his sandalwood scent and leaving Selene with a heightened sense of excitement and impatience.

Whatever he had in store for her, Selene doubted she would easily forget it—and she hoped she didn't regret it.

Twenty minutes later, Selene walked into the darkened bedroom, fumbled for the lamp on the dresser and switched it on. After slipping off her sandals, she crossed the room, the floorboards creaking beneath her bare feet, her knees practically knocking from nervousness. She knew what she was about to do would be deemed risky, the reason why she hesitated when she clasped the brass handles. As soon as she opened the doors, she would be opening herself up to several possibilities that could be very good, or very bad, at least in the long term. The long term didn't matter. Being with Adrien tonight did. A risk she planned to take.

Selene opened the doors wide, letting in a draft of warm, humid air. The moon had returned, fuller this time, washing the veranda in a blue glow. She backed away, uncertain what to do next or where to go. Should she lie back on the bed? Or would that make her seem too eager? After deliberating a few moments, she turned off the light, took the wing-back chair across the room and waited. And waited…

Just when she decided Adrien had changed his mind, he appeared at the open doors, causing Selene to startle even though she'd been staring at the spot for several minutes. He moved into the room like some ethereal being. A dark, imposing presence.

Surprisingly, he strode to the dresser and clicked on the same lamp Selene had turned off. Obviously he didn't prefer darkness in every instance. He still had on his slacks, but he'd removed his shirt, and his wavy hair looked as untamed as his eyes. He touched the gold medallion hanging against his bronzed chest then ran a slow palm down from his sternum to his belly. For a minute she thought he might remove his pants but instead, he stalked toward her.

With great effort, Selene maintained a relaxed posture despite the rapid beat of her heart. "I thought you weren't coming."

Adrien braced both hands on the arms of the chair and leaned toward her. "I had every intention of coming, and soon you will, too."

He topped off the suggestive comment with the hint of a smile that did little to ease Selene's urge to twitch in the chair. She clasped his offered hands and allowed him to pull her up into his arms, against his solid body that radiated heat. When she pressed her palms against his chest, intending to explore, he caught her wrists and held her arms at her sides.

"I'll do all the touching," he told her, his voice impossibly deep.

"Does this mean you expect me to be submissive?"

"Yes."

Nothing new there. She'd played the submissive to Richard, but then she hadn't really cared enough to actively participate. Their married life had involved little more than occasional, perfunctory sex. Although she'd avoided too much analysis during their time together, she realized now that any true passion had been lacking from the beginning. During lovemaking—if she could really call it that—she'd always been detached. At times, even uncomfortable. Yet she sensed that with Adrien, detachment or discomfort wouldn't be an issue.

He glanced behind him toward the bed before bringing his gaze back to hers. "Normally I prefer the unconventional, but I might have to make a few concessions tonight."

She was more than curious and a tiny bit nervous over the possibilities. "What do you consider unconventional?"

He brushed her hair away from her shoulders. "Anywhere other than a bed. But after I get started, you might be too weak to stand."

Weak? She was already feeling weak only imagining the potential in his promise. And in order to see this through, Selene would have to give him her trust. She honestly believed he didn't intend to hold her down and torture her, or at least not any way that would put her in serious jeopardy.

Adrien kept his eyes leveled on Selene while he turned her palms up and kissed each wrist. "You don't have to worry," he said, as if he sensed her concerns. "It's up to you to tell me when to stop or to go." He lifted one of her hands and rubbed her knuckles along his jaw. "Although you'll be saying *go* more than *stop*. *Yes* more than *no*."

Selene appreciated his confidence. In fact, she appreciated everything about him at the moment—the length of his dark lashes, the definition of his incredible mouth, the breadth of his shoulders and the clear-cut control he emitted.

Absolute power.

"First, you need to relax," he said as he took her hand and led her to the open doors, then stood behind her. A chorus of locusts seemed to keep time with Selene's thrumming heart as Adrien circled his arms around her waist and pulled her back against him.

"The swamp is a powerhouse of biorhythms at night." He moved his palm to her neck and rubbed his thumb up and down the column of her throat. "Unlike humans, animals don't fight the force of nature."

"They don't overanalyze, you mean." Selene was proud she could assimilate any thoughts at all with Adrien so close.

"Exactly." He tipped her face back with his fingertips and pressed a kiss on her cheek. "They only consider their natural urges."

Selene decided taking a lesson from nature seemed like a fine idea. Right now she would give up all reason for his attention. The pleasure of his touch. He kissed her lightly, chastely, before pulling away until she sought his mouth again. Twice more he retreated, and each time Selene went back for more. Finally he deepened the kiss, suckling her lips, nipping lightly, exploring meticulously with the soft thrust of his tongue.

So wrapped up in that kiss, it took a moment for Selene to register the waft of warm air on her chest. She hadn't even noticed that Adrien had managed to unbutton her blouse, leaving her red lace bra exposed.

He halted the kiss to rest his lips against her ear. "Are you relaxed yet?"

Relaxed, not exactly. Heating up with every passing moment, definitely. "I'm getting there."

"Good."

When he circled her nipple through the thin lace with his fingertip, Selene's whole body felt as if it might liquefy. She could only imagine how she would react when he finally touched her without any barriers at all.

He slid his hand down her bare midriff and around the skirt's waistband, as he had in the cabin earlier that day.

"Stop or go?" In the instant that she hesitated, he told her, "Don't think too much, Selene. Listen to your body, not your mind."

"Go." The word rode out on a shaky breath that halted altogether as Adrien reached down and worked her skirt up her thighs. When he formed one palm between her legs outside her panties and applied only a slight pressure, her knees practically buckled.

He released a rough, sensuous laugh. "We definitely need the bed."

Again he took the lead, and she followed him back into the room without any real qualms. He seated her on the edge of the mattress and left her to open the screened windows flanking the closed doors, then walked to the middle of the room and pulled the chain that set the overhead fan on high.

He came back to the bed and stood over her. "Take off your blouse and your bra." His voice was a firm command. His steadfast gaze demanded she answer.

As if she had no choice but to do his bidding, Selene slid the gaping top off her shoulders with ease and draped it on the footboard. But when she attempted to tackle the bra's front closure, her hands trembled. Adrien knelt in front of her and gently moved her hands away before effortlessly flicking the bra open, proving he'd done this before. Probably many times, Selene decided. When he leaned forward and touched the tip of his tongue to her nipple, Selene experienced a pleasurable shock to her system and drenching dampness between her legs.

He stood, pulled her to her feet and, after he'd proficiently discarded her skirt, he tossed back the bedspread and sheets. "Stretch out on your back, Selene."

Selene was naked except for her panties, and he was still wearing his slacks. That seemed somewhat unfair. "What about you?" she asked.

"What about me?"

"Aren't you going to get undressed?"

"This is all about you right now."

Well, that was definitely a first in Selene's experience, so she chose not to argue even though she was somewhat disappointed. She doubted that her disappointment would last very long. After climbing into the bed, she laid her head back on the pillow, waiting and wondering what Adrien planned to do next.

Following a long look down her body, he sat, leaned over and braced his palms on either side of her. "I want you to watch what I'm doing."

"I want to close my eyes so I can concentrate." The truth, but only in part. She wanted to remain somewhat disconnected. She wanted to treat this exclusively as a visceral experience, leaving all emotions out of it. She didn't want to become too attached to a man who lived only for the moment.

"If that makes you more comfortable, fine," he said. "At least for now."

Selene closed her eyes when he kissed her again with a highly evocative play of his tongue against hers, driving all reservations from her mind. When he broke the kiss and drew her nipple into his mouth, she absorbed the sensations, savoring every pass of his tongue, every pull of his lips. Then something happened that was both unexpected and enthralling—she could see as well as feel what Adrien was doing through the mystical workings of her mind now joined with his. She could see him skim his hands down her sides at the same time she experienced the slight abrasion of his callused palms. Could see as well as feel him draw a line with his fingertips from her pelvis to her hips before drifting down to bend her knees.

For endless moments he caressed her with delicate

strokes all along her body, from her arms to her feet, leaving nothing untouched. After another stimulating kiss, he used his mouth and tongue to follow the path he'd taken with his hands. He tenderly manipulated places that at one time had seemed inconsequential to Selene when it came to lovemaking. Yet with Adrien, every spot he explored became overly sensitive, as if he had found undiscovered erogenous zones. Undiscovered to her, at least.

And all the while, she watched from his perspective from behind closed lids, taking an erotic journey into his mind, sensing his building excitement as well as her own. By the time he sucked a small patch of skin between her thighs, she was bordering on coming totally undone. And when he clasped the elastic band below her belly, she experienced an undeniable ache and another rush of damp heat between her thighs.

But instead of sliding her panties down, Adrien paused and said, "I want you to hold out as long as you can before you climax."

Selene opened her eyes and met his intense gaze. "I'm not sure I can."

He gave her the most patently sexy look she'd ever witnessed from a man. "Then I guess I'll be forced to give you another orgasm."

This had to be a dream. Never before had Selene encountered a man so determined to give her complete pleasure with no thought of his own needs.

Without wavering, Adrien worked the lace down her legs and tossed her panties aside. Again Selene closed her eyes and saw what he saw as he parted her legs. Now she was completely exposed to him and more vulnerable than she'd ever been before. Yet any concerns she might have entertained gave way to an unqualified rush when he divided her flesh, tested her with a fingertip, then two as he fondled her inside and out. He knew how to tease. He knew how to tempt. He knew exactly where to concentrate his attention until she lifted her hips in response.

Holding back wasn't going to be possible, that much Selene knew as the first contraction hit her, causing her to clasp fistfuls of the sheet. She gritted her teeth, tried to cling to her control, but that control clashed with the need for release. The climax surged through her, shaking her entire body. She tipped her head back and a steady moan threatened to leave her mouth, saved only by Adrien's own mouth closing over hers to absorb the sound.

When he broke the kiss, Selene opened her eyes to find him studying her. She draped an arm over her damp forehead and sighed. "I'm relaxed now."

He released another low, grainy laugh. "You're almost too hot to handle. But I'm going to do it to you again."

"Adrien, I…"

Can't handle any more. She had no choice but to try as Adrien began touching her as ardently as he had before.

"I want to use my mouth on you," he said as he slid a finger inside her. "But I'll save that for later, when I know you're ready."

If he did use his mouth, Selene had no doubt she would dissolve into the mattress beneath her back. And she wasn't concerned with later. She was focused only on the here and now as Adrien worked his spell, speaking to her in a low steady voice, telling her how sweet she was and describing what he was doing to her in very detailed terms. In a matter of moments, he had her back on the brink, ready to plummet again. When he whispered, "I'm going to make you scream," that was all it took.

Selene didn't exactly scream when the orgasm hit, but she did groan. A long, almost mournful groan that she couldn't believe actually came from her. She had no idea what he had done, only that she was practically panting by the time the sensations subsided. Then suddenly Adrien was next to her, enfolding her in his arms, soothing her with gentle kisses on her lips and cheeks.

"Where did you learn to do that?" she finally managed to say.

He brushed her hair from her forehead and kissed her there. "I studied tantric sex. Since then, I've done some modification and experimenting. And I've practiced."

"With several partners, I take it." Something that didn't set well with Selene.

"No. Only a chosen few."

That relieved her somewhat. "Should I be flattered?"

"Yes, you should. I'm very selective. And I always begin with the singular purpose of pleasing a woman. I've only scratched the surface with you."

He'd scratched a few itches she hadn't realized she'd had until now. "I'm not sure I can take much more of that."

He rose up on one elbow, using his fist to support his jaw while keeping his free hand idling on her breast. "You can. But right now, you need to sleep."

Selene could only gape when Adrien left the bed and started toward the door. "Wait a minute. That's it?"

He faced her again. "That wasn't enough?"

"Actually, I thought we were going to…" She wasn't quite sure how to say it.

He leaned back against the door. "Anyone can climb on and have it over in a matter of minutes, Selene. But not everyone takes the time to get to know their partner's body. I want to know yours before I'm inside you. And I'm only getting started."

Then he left the room, the sounds of his footsteps and the opening and closing door echoing in Selene's ears.

Adrien Morrell was a sexual savant bent on demonstrating his genius on her. And she would continue to be a willing study, as long as he eventually gave in and gave her his all.

Six

Selene awoke the next morning, still restless even though she'd slept remarkably well, thanks to Adrien's undivided attention. She couldn't recall the last time she'd been so relaxed, even if she hadn't gotten everything from him that she'd wanted. Hopefully that would be included in the next phase. In the meantime, she had work to do.

She went through every room on the first floor, taking inventory of the furnishings as well as jotting down ideas and making a few preliminary sketches. She wanted to retain as much of the original atmosphere as possible, which meant eventually scouring antique stores to fill in wherever necessary, unless she found more items in the attic. She made a note to explore there in the next few days.

By the time afternoon rolled around, her head began to spin when she considered how much she needed to do with a house this size, including refurbishing the flooring and updating the kitchen. Right now, she needed to get out of the house, if only for a while. She also needed to see Adrien, the reason why she set out for his office before she drove into town.

When she knocked, he called, "Come in," in a gruff voice.

She opened the door to find him standing with his back to her, one hand holding back the curtain as he stared out the window. His white shirt was rolled up at the sleeves and it appeared he might be wearing the same pair of slacks he'd worn last night. Had he slept in his clothes? Had he slept at all?

She cleared her throat to garner his attention. "I'm about to go into town for a while, if that's okay with you."

He let the curtain drop and slowly turned to face her. His rumpled unbuttoned shirt hung open, revealing his incredible chest. "You don't need my permission to leave the house."

She centered her gaze on his coveted medallion resting flush against his chest. "I thought you might have something you need me to do first."

When she forced her gaze back to his face, along came the suggestive look he flaunted so well. "I do, but we'll save that for later." He rounded the desk and leaned back against it. "Unless you're reconsidering after last night."

Selene fumbled in her purse for the car keys, unsuccessful in her first two attempts to find them. "I'm leaving all options open. In the meantime, is there anything you need me to pick up from the store?"

"Do we need condoms?"

She gripped the keys tightly in her palm as a hot blush raided her cheeks. "As far as birth control is concerned, no, I'm on the Pill. But we do have other things to consider."

"I've made more than a few mistakes in my time, Selene, but carelessness during sex isn't one of them. Trust me, you don't have to worry that I have some sort of disease. I wouldn't do that to you."

"The same holds true for me." She had spent several months after she'd tossed Richard out making certain her ex-husband hadn't left her with any reminders of his infidelity, other than bitter memories.

"Good," he said. "When I make love to you completely, I don't want anything between us at all."

"It's nice to know you still plan to make love to me, hopefully before I'm too old to care." Where on earth had that come from? Apparently from that recently discovered area of her brain known as "sex central."

He gave her a smile as he pushed off the desk. "You are an impatient little minx, aren't you?"

She was now. "I should go so I'll be home before dark."

He moved in front of her and drew a line down her jaw with his fingertip. "You want to get home to have more of what you had last night."

Very true, Selene decided. But she wouldn't give him the satisfaction of knowing that. "I was thinking about dinner."

He snagged the belt loop on her jeans and tugged her against him. "To hell you were. You're thinking about sex. About me touching you again. If I said the word, you'd let me take you right here on my desk."

Selene received a very detailed vision of that, thanks to Adrien. She glanced behind him and frowned. "I believe I'll wait."

"Fine, because I have no intention of taking you on a desk the first time."

So long as he took her, Selene didn't care where it happened. She formed her palm to his stubbly jaw. "Do me a favor and shave before tonight."

He moved her hand to his lips and streaked his tongue over her palm before placing it against his chest. "I'll definitely do that. I wouldn't want you to suffer from whisker burn."

"I do have a very sensitive mouth."

His smile was oh so wicked. "I wasn't referring to your mouth."

She backed out of his hold and tugged at the hem of her T-shirt. "I see."

"Not yet, but you will."

"I'm leaving now."

He crooked a finger at her. "Not until you come here."

Selene knew exactly what he wanted and she wanted it, too. A quick kiss goodbye. A prelude to what he had in store for her that evening. She easily moved back into his arms and tilted her face up in a blatant offering of her mouth. Instead of kissing her, he brought his lips to her ear. "If you think you want it badly now, wait until tonight. I'm going to take you places you've never been before."

Only then did he meld his lips to hers, driving her wild with the sweep of his tongue before he released her.

Selene wanted him to take her to those places, wanted him to take her beyond the limit. And that want had her counting the minutes until she again entered Adrien's dark, seductive world.

He didn't show up for dinner. In fact, Selene hadn't seen him since she'd come back to the house from her errand run. After she did a load of laundry and cleaned up the kitchen, she went to her bedroom in hopes of finding him waiting for her, only to find the place deserted.

She opted to take a quick bath and ready for bed before she decided what to do next. Dressed in a mid-thigh pink satin robe, her wet hair bound in a towel, she stepped into the hallway and encountered her least favorite demon. Even after a few days of enduring Giles, her heart leaped into her throat every time she laid eyes on his murderous guise. Tonight she was jumpy enough without having to deal with him. On that thought, she pulled the towel from her hair and tossed it at him, making a perfect three-point landing on his horns and effectively covering his snarl. Unfortunately, the poor terrified woman was still exposed and, unless Selene retrieved a blanket to use as a drape, she would have to ignore her.

She returned to her still-empty bedroom and ran a brush through her hair. On afterthought, she dabbed on a little lip gloss and applied a touch of mascara, just in case she might actually get lucky with Adrien. Now the time had come to execute plan A—make the short trip to his office in hopes she might find him there. She padded down the corridor on bare feet, trying desperately to ignore the rasps and groans of the floor, the darkness down below and the dim light in the hallway.

She stood outside his office for a time, and when a knock received no response, she listened carefully and heard nothing. She tested the handle only to find it locked. Disappointed over her lack of success, she headed back down the corridor and paused at the staircase's landing to look down into the dark depths of the rotunda. She wondered if Adrien was prowling around like some restive creature of the night. Even if that was the case, she had no intention of going outside to find him.

When she reached her room, Selene sent a quick glance at the demon only to find the towel was gone. Either he'd managed to remove it himself—a thought she preferred not to entertain—or Adrien had been around at some point in time.

Maybe it was time for plan B—checking out Adrien's inner sanctum. She stopped outside his bedroom and, after finding the door partially ajar, called his name. When she received no answer, she stepped inside. The room was much bigger than hers, much cooler thanks to an operable window air-conditioning unit, and definitely more opulent.

That didn't exactly surprise her. After all, he was the lord of the manor. A gilded bed, the headboard and footboard upholstered in heavy blue brocade with a matching spread, sat angled in the corner across the room near the doors leading out to the veranda. To the left of those doors, a long Victorian walnut chaise covered in gold damask and two blue-and-gold striped armchairs formed a sitting area lit by a lone brass floor lamp.

Selene noted a door not far from the right of the bed and presumed that was the master bath. It didn't seem wise to try and find out if he might be in there. Of course, she didn't actually have to go in. She could stand by a few minutes and listen to see if he was taking a shower. She crossed the room to investigate and discovered no light filtering through the door, no sound coming from inside, indicating he was somewhere else in the house. But where? She supposed he could have taken a drive, but she didn't recall seeing any car other than Ella's hatchback.

She started to leave but instead turned back to survey the room. She had two more options—wait for him here in hopes he'd eventually come to her, or wait in her own bedroom with the veranda doors opened wide in invitation as she had last night. Or she could explore a bit more, beginning with the locked chamber across the hall. But did she dare? If he happened to be in there and she knocked, he would either allow her in or tell her to go away. He might also be angry over the intrusion. If so, he would simply have to get over it.

Filled with determination, Selene took one last glance at the room then spun around—only to run into a solid wall of prime male.

With one hand against her pounding heart, Selene stepped back to find Adrien dressed in a T-shirt and jeans,

his jaw clean shaven, his hair shower damp, his feet bare...
and a towel dangling from one hand. Her discarded towel.
"Did you lose something?" he asked.

She suddenly felt very silly. "I was wondering where
that went."

He slid a slow glance down her body. "I was hoping you
were leaving a trail so I could find you."

"Actually, I got tired of that monster leering at me. I took
the towel from my hair and covered him up."

"Too bad the towel wasn't around your body."

Selene felt as if she were totally naked now under his
perusal as he took a step toward her. "Did you need something from me?" he asked.

He knew exactly what she needed, but Selene wasn't
about to bite. "I needed to tell you that the contractor will
be here first thing Monday morning to assess the repairs."

"It's only Friday."

"I was afraid I might forget to mention it."

"You were afraid I might not pay you a visit tonight."

She shrugged. "Since it's late, maybe some other time."

When she started past him, he grabbed her arm and pulled
her around. "It's not too late to give you what you need."

"I don't *need* anything from you." Another tiny lie.

"Okay, what you *want*." He slid his hands inside the
collar of her robe and rubbed her neck with his thumbs.
"It's already started, the addiction. Don't bother to deny it."

She wasn't a card-carrying Adrien addict yet, but she
could be. Which is what made this situation so hazardous.
"Look, whether you want to continue this or not is imma-
terial to me."

"It's everything to you." He clasped her waist and
hauled her against him. "Now that you know what you've
been missing, it's difficult to do without it."

"I can do without it, thank you very much."

"Are you sure about that?"

She was only sure of one thing—he could do things to her that no man had ever done with only a look.

Without the least bit of warning, he pulled up the back of her robe and ran his hands over her bare bottom. "For someone who doesn't want it, you're certainly prepared to get it."

She shivered slightly despite her efforts to stop it. "I didn't have the opportunity to get dressed after my bath."

"You didn't have any intention of getting dressed after your bath." He took his hands from her bottom and brought them to the robe's sash, releasing it with only a minimal tug. After parting the fabric, he took a step back and a visual excursion down her body that was already flushed. "Now to decide exactly what I'm going to do to you, and where I'm going to do it."

She closed her robe and redid the sash for the sheer pleasure of having him open it again. "I don't remember giving you permission to do anything to me."

He gestured to the door. "Go, then. I'm not going to force you into anything."

Damn him. And damn herself for her inability to resist him. "Well, I suppose since I don't have anything better to do, we could spend some time together."

His smile was smug and tremendously sexy. "That's what I thought."

Clasping her hand, he led her to the chaise and sat her down. Then he took the chair across from her, tugged his T-shirt over his head and tossed it behind him. Selene held her breath when he toyed with his fly before lifting his hand and settling it on his thigh without lowering his zipper.

He was taunting her. And she wasn't going to let him get away with it. "You can take off your pants, Adrien. It's nothing I haven't seen before."

He stretched his long legs out before him and laced his hands atop his belly. "Don't be so sure about that."

A tiny shiver ran up and down her spine. "A bit egotistical, are we?"

"This isn't about ego. It's about your experience." He leaned forward and nailed her with his deadly gaze, the medallion dangling from his neck serving as a reminder of his strength of will. "Have you ever really looked at a man before, Selene? Studied all the details of his body?"

She'd lost her virginity in the dark after a fraternity fling and had married a man who was a lights-out kind of guy. "I guess I would have to say no, not really."

"Then you still have a lot to learn."

"Let's get to it then." Obviously she was suffering from an overdose of enthusiasm.

"Not yet." He slowly rose from the chair and stood before her. "We're going to take this slowly."

"I don't want slowly."

He pulled the sash, parted her robe again and slid it off her shoulders. "You're going to get slowly whether you want it or not. Now recline on the chaise."

Selene scooted up against the angled tufted back and stretched her crossed legs before her, propped her elbow on the rolled arm and draped her other arm across her middle. In a way, she felt like a queen waiting to be tended by a dark, dangerous knight. She found it odd that she didn't feel uncomfortable over being totally nude in his presence, until he continued to stand there, sizing her up like a sculptor preparing to mold his next masterpiece.

In a fit of self-consciousness, she started to fold her arms across her breasts until Adrien said, "Don't you dare cover yourself."

"Okay." Her voice sounded pathetically weak, which complemented the way she felt at the moment.

"You have no idea how beautiful you are, do you?" he asked.

"I've never thought much about it." Other than she'd always believed her nose was too sharp, her hair too thin, her brown eyes too wide set and nondescript. All those little worries that women often obsessed about when things could be so much worse.

He moved a little closer. "Did he ever tell you that you're beautiful?"

She sighed. "I don't understand your preoccupation with my ex."

"Because he's the reason you're unable to let go."

Maybe so, but what were Adrien's reasons? She wanted to ask but she didn't want to anger him and, in turn, send him away. "I was under the impression I let go quite well last night."

"Not completely. And that's what I want from you tonight. I don't want another man in your mind aside from me."

He had no idea how deeply ingrained he'd been in her mind since they'd met. "I can manage that."

"Good. But as tempting as you look right now, there's not enough room for both of us on that damn lounger."

Selene pointed to her left. "There's always the bed."

"And there are other alternatives, too."

Obviously Adrien had an aversion to beds, Selene decided. And to lights, her next thought when he snapped off the floor lamp, sending the room into darkness. When she heard the rasp of his zipper and the rustle of denim, she stopped thinking altogether, her mind caught in the grip of anticipation even though she couldn't see much more than the outline of his body.

"Stand up," he said.

When Selene left the chaise, he clasped both her hands

and held them against his chest. "I'm giving you the chance to learn all the details."

"How can I when I can't see you?"

He took her palm and pressed it against his face. "After last night, you should know the answer to that."

She did know the answer—by using her hands. While Adrien stood there, his arms at his sides, she began by streaming her fingertips along his jaw before tracing a line along his full lips, pausing to briefly touch her lips there. She traveled down the column of his throat, past his Adam's apple, and used her splayed palms to explore his collarbone before roaming down to the solid plane of his chest covered in a slight dusting of hair. When she grazed his nipples, she detected a slight shudder that led her to linger for a while longer before breezing her hands down his sides and over his rib cage.

Deciding to save the best for last, Selene moved behind him and felt her way over his broad shoulders, joining her hands in the middle of his back to follow the path of his strong spine. His skin grew damp beneath her palms and the cadence of his breathing quickened as she discovered the dip below his waist. She fashioned her palms to his buttocks, kneading slightly before following the crevice with her fingertips and curling them between his legs. He opened his stance slightly, allowing her more room to delve as far as she dared, which she did for a time before she touched the backs of his hair-roughened thighs.

She returned to stand before him, taking up where she'd left off, beginning with his rigid abdomen that grew tauter when she touched him. She circled her fingertip around his navel and his breath hitched slightly. Yet he kept his arms dangling at his sides, even when she moved her palms lower to stroke his pelvis, finding the ribbon of hair that created a path leading to all that made Adrien premium male.

But now that the moment she'd been anxiously awaiting had arrived, Selene hesitated, and that was absurd. She'd touched a man intimately before. Why was touching Adrien so different?

"Do it, Selene."

Buoyed by Adrien's demand, in a voice grainy with need, Selene didn't have to journey far before discovering he was definitely aroused. She explored the length of his erection with a slow glide of her fingertip before taking him completely into her hands. She didn't have to ask what he liked, what spots were particularly sensitive to her touch. She only had to open her mind and tap into his thoughts to learn his reaction as she began to caress him with long, fluid strokes. She soon sensed his emergent need, his battle with control. She knew he was nearing the edge and that he would prevent her from continuing a moment before he clasped her wrist and lifted her hand to his pounding heart.

"Stop." Selene heard the effort in that one word, felt his slight tremor.

After Adrien tugged her down to the floor and positioned her on the plush Oriental rug, he left her for a moment to turn on the lamp, the beam illuminating her body like a movie premiere searchlight, and giving her a great view of the places she had touched only moments before. And what a glorious view it was.

He joined her on the rug, propped a throw pillow beneath her neck and lifted her arms above her head. In only a few moments, he had her body weeping for him, trembling for more, and he knew it, apparent by the perception in his dark gaze. When he came to his knees between her parted legs, Selene wasn't sure she could stand the anticipation.

After spending a few moments finessing her breasts with his mouth, he drew a line with his tongue down her torso. And when he went as far as he could go before reaching his ultimate destination, Adrien lifted his head and commanded, "Watch, and don't think."

Selene could do nothing more than watch when he dipped his head between her legs and went on an all-out assault on her body, the kind that would definitely lead to an explosion. She laid her palms on his dark, damp hair as he explored, using his mouth to gain supreme advantage. As good as Adrien had made her feel last night, nothing could match this incomparable intimacy. Nothing. Her gratification only intensified when she opened her mind to him and saw the scene from his perspective, knowing that as he gave her that pleasure, he in turn received pleasure.

Selene could only remain mute and motionless…until he used gentle suckling as his weapon of choice. Her hips bucked when the climax crashed down on her, wresting another long groan from deep within her throat. But Adrien wasn't through yet. With his gaze firmly locked into hers, he paused to blow his warm breath over her sensitized flesh before swooping back in with his clever mouth. He remained relentless with his goal through gentle yet single-minded manipulation. She wanted to beg him to stop. She also wanted more. After the second orgasm consumed her, bringing with it a series of shudders, she clawed at his shoulders and the word "Please," left her mouth in a desperate, pleading tone.

Adrien worked his way up her body and kissed her deeply while she raked her fingernails down his back. He rubbed his chest over her breasts in a deliberate, rhythmic motion while she shifted her hips in encouragement. She sensed his sudden struggle, felt his faltering control and the nudge of his erection between her legs, until his mind went totally blank as if he'd raised a mental fortress to block her out completely.

Without any explanation, he rolled away from her and

stood. Keeping his back to her while he shrugged on his jeans, he said, "That's enough for now. We'll continue this tomorrow."

Selene recognized there was more to his reticence than taking it slowly. Much more. "Then you're saying if I want you to make love to me now, you won't do it?"

He turned, snatched her robe from the floor and tossed it at her. "Not tonight."

She sent a direct look at his fly as she clutched the robe to her breasts. "Are you into masochism or are you trying to prove your strength?"

"I'm patient. I can wait. I also have some work to do."

Selene pulled the robe on and thought back to the night when he'd first invaded her mind. When he'd denied himself then, as well. As he started to leave, she said, "What are you afraid of, Adrien?"

He turned and frowned. "I'm not afraid of anything."

She rose and joined him at the door. "You're afraid you're going to feel something, aren't you? That it won't be only meaningless sex between us." She lined the ridge beneath his slacks with a fingertip. "That has to be it since there's not a thing physically wrong with you."

She saw it then, another slide show coming from his mind—him backing her against the wall, shoving his pants to his thighs, thrusting inside her. But he forced the image away at the same time he took her hand and held it at her side. "I'm not afraid, Selene. But I say when and where we make love. You don't have to understand why I want to wait. You only have to respect it."

She understood all too well. A woman in his immediate past kept him guarded. Most likely, the woman named Chloe who was still influencing him, even if Adrien couldn't admit it to Selene or himself. But Selene didn't dare mention that woman's name, otherwise she would have to explain how she'd come by the information. Right now she would keep her own secrets, and let him have his.

Resigned to letting him have his way, she stepped back and cinched the robe tightly. "Fine. You go ahead and leave now. But remember what I've said before, no power is absolute. I could very well be the one who says when and where."

She knew he still battled with coming back to her, but when he touched the medallion dangling from his neck before turning away again, it became apparent his will-power had won out. At least for now.

After Selene returned to her bedroom, she forged her own plan. She vowed to help Adrien get past his fears and if that meant taking the lead, so be it. She might only be a temporary fix for his problems, a means to help him over the life-altering hurdle that had caused him to retreat. But as long as he didn't turn her away, she believed anything was possible.

Adrien locked himself in the room across the hall to keep from going to Selene to finish what he'd started. He also needed to remember why he couldn't become too deeply involved with her. What better place to do that but in this dark, desolate tomb? The room didn't serve as a shrine; no real reminders of Chloe remained. At least not those that revealed what she had been, and not what she had become.

He walked to the window where she had once stood looking out over the grounds while dreaming of those things that had been outside her reach because of him. He collapsed into a chair by that window and, in the cover of darkness, plagued by the physical pain of needing and not having, he analyzed Selene's conjecture.

He did have fears, all justified. He feared she could be the one woman who would force him to face his downfall, tear open his wounds and make him bleed again. He also recognized she was a woman who under normal circumstances wouldn't interest him at all. But nothing about their liaison was normal. From the beginning, he'd realized she was special, unique in ways he didn't quite understand. He only knew that something about her had drawn him from the moment he'd seen her.

He also recognized the risk in that. A risk he couldn't afford. He'd set a dangerous course the moment he'd touched her, and he needed to halt it soon. Before he did something that they would both regret.

Seven

The following morning, Selene needed something to do other than worry over Adrien. For that reason, she opted to explore the third-floor attic, afforded only a brief glance at Adrien's closed office door and kept right on walking until she located the attic's entry. After last night, she decided she'd been too accessible. Too compliant. The time had come for her to take control.

When she opened the attic door, she encountered another steep staircase and flipped on the switch that turned on a lone bulb hanging high overhead. With each step she took, an ominous feeling assaulted her. She scolded herself for overreacting and continued on, not certain of what she would find. Hopefully not a passel of rodents and spiders. Or wandering spirits.

She opened a second door and entered the area that spanned the length of the house. Although rays of light filtered in from the three dormer windows, the place still retained a gloomy atmosphere, from the weathered wood floors to the cobwebs draped in the corners. A pile of helter-skelter planks and fabric near one window immediately caught her attention, and upon further investigation, she discovered several splintered chairs and tables, as if someone had taken a sledgehammer or hacksaw to them. Someone who obviously didn't like the furniture, or had chosen to expend their anger on the antiques.

A sense of foreboding sent chills up her spine like menacing fingers, and she gladly left the furniture remnants behind to examine the two boxes across the room. She came upon a gold mine—several pieces of fine china and glassware, all carefully wrapped in white cloth, a definite contrast to the destruction. But she found no missing journals, no other pieces of the past. And she wasn't up to searching for more clues at the moment.

After organizing the boxes, Selene left the attic and made her way to the room that Ella had claimed was once the nursery—a happier place, she hoped. She again paused outside Adrien's office door and considered knocking, until she heard the sound of muffled conversation. Apparently he was on the phone discussing business, so she decided not to disturb him. At least not yet.

Selene opened the door to another lengthy room painted a bright yellow, sunshine spilling from the uncovered windows casting golden light on the walls, dust motes floating about like miniature snowflakes. And in the corner rested a tiny spindled cradle and a lone wooden rocking chair that looked as if they'd had limited use. When she crossed the room and nudged the cradle, a strong sense of sadness overcame her. Perhaps this room, too, had been the site of some tragedy, and she hated to think that tragedy involved a child.

A series of shrill rings jerked Selene back into the

present. She pulled her cell phone from her pocket and answered with a melancholy, "Hello."

"Hi, Selene. It's Abby. Are you busy?"

"Not at all. As a matter of fact, I was about to call you. I've found a few pieces of china I'd like you to take a look at when you have time."

"I'll be out of town until the end of next week, but feel free to bring them by then. And I'm calling you because I think I found someone who might be able to help you with the house's history."

The timely twist of fate definitely elevated Selene's optimism. "Who?"

"His name his Jeb Gutherie and he lives in an assisted-living community in Baton Rouge called Briar Oaks. I don't have an exact location, but it shouldn't be too hard to find."

Not much to go on, but Selene was willing to take her chances. If she left now, she could arrive before lunch. And if lucky, she might have at least one mystery solved today. "Thanks, Abby. You've come to my rescue again."

"You're welcome. How's the job going?"

The job was going fine. Her relationship with Adrien was going places it probably shouldn't. "I'm making slow progress, but it's still progress."

"Seen any ghosts yet?"

Only in her dreams, particularly last night. She'd seen Grace's face that had turned into another unidentified face—a woman with light brown hair and vibrant blue eyes. She'd woken up twice, practically paralyzed, before drifting off to sleep only to have more fitful dreams of falling. "No, no spirits. Only the occasional creepy house sound."

"Let me know if anything changes, and good luck."

Following the phone call, excitement over the prospect of unraveling the plantation's past sent Selene out of the house and to her car without telling Adrien goodbye. After all, he'd said she didn't need his permission to leave, and she didn't intend to request it. Having him wonder where she might be going could prove to be a good thing.

He stood at the window and again watched her leave, wondering where she might be going this time. Maybe back to Georgia, although she had no suitcases in her possession. He'd heard her footsteps and had opened his door to see her entering the attic and knew what she'd seen—the result of his fury. Yet she had no way of knowing he'd been responsible for the destruction. No way of knowing why he'd taken out his anger on several priceless antiques, and he didn't plan to tell her.

He had no plans to return to her tonight, either. He needed time to assess his next move. To decide how much farther he would go before he put an end to their liaison. Creating some distance between them would be wise. But his wisdom warred with his desire, and only time would tell if he could stay away from her. Correction, how *long* he would stay away from her.

Little by little, she was wearing him down. Tearing away at his resistance and, if not careful, he'd end up traveling down a road he didn't dare take.

An hour later, Selene pulled into the parking lot at a high-rise retirement community north of Baton Rouge. She entered the foyer and was immediately greeted by a young woman seated behind a reception desk. "Welcome to Briar Oaks. May I help you?"

"I hope so. I'm looking for Jeb Gutherie."

She eyed Selene suspiciously. "Is he expecting you?"

"Actually, no. But I believe he has some information I need." Selene glanced at the woman's name tag. "Tisha,

could you tell him I'm inquiring about the history of a plantation in St. Edwards?"

Following a sigh, the young woman slid a clipboard in
front of Selene. "If you'll sign in and wait here, I'll see if
I can find him."

Selene jotted down her name and waited a few moments
until the receptionist returned. "He'll see you," Tisha said.
"But I have to warn you, he tires easily and might nod off
now and then. And he'll need to be in the dining room in
about twenty minutes for lunch."

As long as she could garner some information, Selene
could live with that. "I won't keep him too long."

Selene followed Tisha through the vestibule that opened
into a large atrium with an open-air dining room to the right
and offices on the left. Just beyond that, Tisha stopped at
a smaller room and faced Selene. "This is the game room.
If you need to speak with him privately, you can use the
conference area next door."

Selene peeked inside to find a group of four elderly gentlemen playing cards at a round table. "Which one is he?"

Tisha pointed discreetly. "On the far end facing us."

Selene homed in on the man seated in a wheelchair, his
shock of gray hair contrasting with his mocha-colored
skin. He wore a neat brown suit and a number of years on
his thin face. "The one in the bow tie?"

"That's him. And good luck."

"Thanks."

After Tisha departed, Selene stepped into the room and
cleared her throat. "Mr. Gutherie?"

He glanced up from his cards, mischief calling out from
his light brown eyes. "Well looky here, boys. I have a
guest. And a mighty pretty one at that."

All eyes turned to Selene and, after the rest of the card
players muttered polite greetings, Mr. Gutherie said,

"Could you give us some privacy, gentlemen? We'll take up where we left off after lunch." He spoke with Southern sophistication, his voice as clear as the summer skies.

The men pushed back from the table, stood and passed by with greetings and cautions not to believe a word Gutherie said. After they'd filed out, Selene approached the table. "Thank you for seeing me, Mr. Gutherie."

"Call me Jeb," he said as he gave her offered hand a gentle shake. "And forgive me for not standing. My legs don't work well, but my mind's still as sharp as a steel trap."

Selene took the vacated chair next to him and set her purse on the floor beside her. "I'm here about the House of Midnight."

His expression turned somber. "The House of Sunshine, you mean. Or at least that's what it was called a long time ago."

A piece of the puzzle had already fallen into place, and that pleased Selene greatly. "I didn't realize that about the name. In fact, I know very little about the plantation's history, and that's why I'm here." She briefly explained her role in the restoration, and then asked the first question that came to mind. "Someone told me you might know something about the previous owners, specifically a woman named Grace. Her portrait hangs in the rotunda."

"Ah, Miss Grace." He tented his fingers beneath his chin and tapped them together. "She lived in the house a long time ago and died before I was born. But my grandmother spoke fondly of her. They grew up together and remained good friends, even after the war."

"Which war would that be?"

He chuckled. "The Civil War, although it wasn't too civil."

Selene tried to hide her shock but doubted she succeeded. "If you don't mind me asking, how old are you?"

"I've seen one hundred years as of this past May," he said proudly. "Miss Grace was my aunt."

Another surprise among many. "Your grandmother and Grace were sisters?"

"No. Miss Grace and my father were half siblings by Stanton Gutherie, a heartless bastard. He owned the plantation next to Sunshine House and thought he owned everything and everyone, including his workers. My grandmother, Effie, was one of his slaves, orphaned at a young age when her parents died after the war. She had no place to go, so she stayed on at the Gutherie plantation. And when she was only fifteen, Stanton got her with child. That child was my father."

Selene had never expected such a disturbing history. "How did Grace come to live at the plantation?"

His face lit up with remembrance. "Ah, Miss Grace was as pure as her father was evil, according to my grandmother. She fell in love with Zeke Cormier, the owner of Sunshine House and a man Stanton hated. But she defied her father and married Zeke against his wishes."

Now Selene knew the identity of Z. in the journal— Grace's journal. "And your grandmother continued to live with Stanton?"

"Luckily, no. Grace took Effie and my father to live with her after she married."

Jeb went on to explain how Grace had become pregnant two years into the marriage, how Effie had described the pure joy in the house, until Grace passed away from black fever a few weeks before the baby was born, a little boy who perished as well.

Jeb sat back and shook his head. "Mr. Zeke went crazy after that. He painted the house black. He refused to let my grandmother clear out the nursery."

Selene recalled the sad little cradle in the corner. "How awful."

"It only got worse," Jeb said. "Mr. Zeke took to the bottle. He eventually drank himself to death. My grandmother tried to help him, but he wouldn't let her. He did leave her the house when he died." Again his expression softened. "I spent summers at the plantation when I was growing up. Many of my fondest memories are tied up in that place. In the grove at the west of the property, my father built a tree house." He rubbed his chin and looked thoughtful. "I wonder if it's still there."

Selene didn't know, but she would find out. "And your grandmother—"

"Died in a rest home back in the sixties. I owned the house until Giles Morrell bought it in a public auction because I couldn't pay the back taxes. I haven't been back since."

"You probably wouldn't want to see it now," Selene said. "It's in a sad state, but I hope to change that soon."

"I wish you luck."

She took Jeb's hand into hers. "Thank you so much. I don't know how to repay you."

He patted her arm. "Treat the house with kindness, Miss Selene. Bring back the joy and the sunshine."

If only she could promise him that, but unfortunately more sadness resided there, resonating from Adrien, although she still didn't know any of those facts yet. But she hoped eventually to come by that information.

Selene had one last question she needed to ask, although she felt a little foolish. "Did your grandmother ever claim to have seen any ghosts?"

Jeb chuckled again. "She swore she talked to Zeke after he passed until she told him to go to the light and find Miss Grace and their boy child. He supposedly left after that and she didn't see him again. Might seem crazy to some folks, but I believed her."

Zeke accepting the call to glory was definitely good news. Selene had one wounded man to deal with; she didn't need another. Especially a ghostly man. "I don't think it sounds crazy at all."

He gave her a questioning look. "Most people don't believe in the ability to talk to the dead.'"

"I'm not most people, I guess."

"Because you have that ability, too."

"I…" How could she possibly respond without lying to him? "I don't talk to ghosts. Let's just say I have strong intuition."

He gave her hand a squeeze. "Miss Selene, I spent my life as a cultural anthropologist, traveling the world. I've seen things that can't be explained, frightening things. Wondrous things. I also know how cruel people can be when I learned early on the meaning of *quadroon* and *mulatto*. But I also learned that what makes us different only makes us unique, and we should be proud of those differences."

Selene lowered her gaze to their joined hands. "It's difficult though, being different."

He tipped her chin up with one careworn finger. "You will find someone someday who will understand and accept you. A man, I believe. If you haven't already found one."

Had she? No, not Adrien. He would never understand her powers any better than she would ever understand the root of his pain.

Tisha stuck her head in the door and called, "Time for lunch, Mr. Gutherie."

Selene stood and offered her hand to Jeb again. "As soon as I have the plantation back in order, I would love to have you visit, maybe even stay a day or two. I'd be glad to pick you up and drive you."

He gave her a mock frown. "Don't take too long, otherwise I might be six feet under."

She laughed softly. "I have a feeling you'll be with us for a while."

His expression turned serious once more. "Miss Selene, I've buried two wives and two sons. I'm ready to go when the Lord calls me home. But seeing the Sunshine House again would give me a reason to stay a little longer, so I'll just tell Saint Peter he'll have to wait until that happens."

Filled with a fondness for this astonishing man, Selene leaned over and gave him a hug. "You be sure to do that."

She headed to the door but pulled up short when Jeb said, "One more thing, Miss Selene."

She turned and faced him again. "Anything."

"This lifetime passes quickly, until one day we turn around and we've seen a century come and go. That's why it's best not to ignore your destiny."

"I'll remember that," Selene said as she left him with a smile.

And she would, even though she had no idea where her destiny might lie.

"Where have you been?"

Selene set her bags on the kitchen counter, surprised to be greeted by Adrien, who both looked and sounded quite perturbed. He also looked like his usual sexy self dressed in worn jeans and tight white T-shirt. "I've been running some errands," she said as she began to unload the groceries.

"You should have told me you were leaving."

She slid two cartons of yogurt and a bottle of orange juice into the refrigerator, turned and closed the door with a push of her bottom. "I recall you telling me that I didn't need your permission to leave the house."

He took a quick check of his watch. "It's almost nine."

"I didn't realize I had a curfew."

He surveyed the two bags on the counter. "For someone who spent the day shopping, you didn't buy much."

"Actually, I didn't only go shopping today. I met with the man who owned this house before your grandfather bought it."

Adrien looked only mildly curious. "How did you find him?"

"Through a friend. He was very nice and accommodating."

"The friend or the previous owner?"

He sounded jealous, and Selene loved it. "Both. The owner's name is Jeb Gutherie. We had a very nice visit."

"Where did you meet with him?" His tone was laced with suspicion.

She could extend the game, or admit the truth and be done with it. "At the retirement home in Baton Rouge. He lives there."

If Adrien was at all relieved, he didn't show it. "You spent the better part of the day with him?"

She'd spent the better part of the day in a bookstore with a mocha cappuccino, reading a sex manual. She'd also made a purchase that she hoped might prove beneficial later tonight. "I spent less than an hour with him, but I've solved the mystery of our lovers. He told me—"

"Spare me the details."

She shrugged, said, "Okay," and opened the cabinet to put away a few staples. If he was too stubborn to hear the news, she'd save it for later.

"You didn't stop anywhere on your way back?" he asked.

His third degree was getting just a bit tired. "I grabbed some fast food on the way home. Oh, and I stopped at a biker bar and played pool with the locals. I even got a tattoo on my butt. It says Helpless Georgia Peach." She turned from the cabinet and sent him a sunny smile. "Would like to see it?"

His expression turned stony. "I'm glad you find this humorous, but I damn sure don't. Anything could have happened to you on the back roads at night."

She couldn't resist rolling her eyes. "Oh, please. I drove all the way from Georgia alone and that took nine hours, not thirty minutes." She propped one elbow on the counter and leaned into it. "Did you miss me?"

When he didn't respond, she walked right up to him, wrapped a hand around his neck and pulled his mouth to hers. At first he failed to respond, but with a little cajoling, he soon became an active participant in the kiss. She relished the hardness of his body, the play of his tongue and the feel of his palms sliding over her bottom.

But Selene only allowed it for a while before she pulled away and reclaimed her place at the counter. "Well, I guess that answers my question. You did miss me."

He stared at her for a few moments and Selene knew what he wanted to do. Saw what he wanted to do in a series of images, all involving hoisting her up onto the counter and having his way with her right there. But instead of acting on the fantasy, he turned and muttered, "I'm going to bed."

Selene knew better. Maybe he was retiring to his bedroom, but he wasn't going to sleep. And if all went as planned, she would make certain of that.

When she was assured Adrien had gone upstairs, she grabbed the plastic boutique bag and walked quietly to her room, turning down the lights behind her. She'd grown more comfortable with the darkness even though she still dreaded the sounds. Even more so now that she knew Grace's and Zeke's stories. She paused at the top landing and stared down the darkened corridor housing the nursery that had never been used, again overcome with a strong feeling of sadness.

Shaking off the melancholy, Selene headed down the hall, purposefully avoiding the demon's steely glare. She took a quick bath, retired to her room and withdrew the negligee from the sack—a simple short satin slip of a gown, appropriately the color of her mother's Black Magic roses. She could definitely use a little magic tonight, as well as some courage.

After dressing in the gown, she collapsed onto the bed and ran her hand over the silky fabric, bringing about a host of memories of the last time she'd done this very thing with another man in mind, but for all the wrong reasons. As it turned out, Richard hadn't been at all receptive. With Adrien, she might be setting herself up for the same rejection. But she had to try. She'd spent a good two hours that day studying the philosophy behind tantric sex, and in turn realizing what Adrien's "modified" method had been missing—the part that dealt with enlightenment and illumination, and the purity of love. In order to reach that plane, one had to be open emotionally as well as physically. Adrien had avoided emotions altogether. He was still avoiding them.

Selene honestly believed that if she could convince him to let go of his resistance, his control, then maybe his internal wounds might begin to heal. Maybe he could allow himself to feel again. Or perhaps he might close himself off even more.

She wanted to take that chance. Had to take that chance. First, she had to find him, and she hoped that didn't entail searching the entire house.

When she heard the sound of his door opening onto the balcony, she knew that wouldn't be the case. The time had arrived to make her move. To show him that her patience had run out. And to make his fantasy a reality.

* * *

While he sat rigid on the wicker sofa, Adrien knew what Selene wanted the moment she walked onto the veranda. Aided only by moonlight, he could see she wore red, the mark of seduction, and a determined expression. He could also see the paleness of her skin set against the night sky, the way her golden hair curled around her shoulders like a halo. An angel bent on seducing the devil himself.

Not once had he ever passed up the opportunity to make love to a willing woman. Not once had he ever denied himself for such a long period of time since he'd discovered the benefits of sex at a relatively young age. And he'd never known a woman quite like Selene. He admired her wit as well as her body. He appreciated her strength. He respected her determination…except at the moment.

Exactly as he'd feared, she'd come to strip him of his control, to melt his emotional armor, to test him. She'd been testing him since she'd walked through the door earlier. And he'd failed miserably. He hadn't been able to mask his jealousy over the thought of her with another man. What she did or who she kept company with shouldn't matter to him. But it did matter, and that could be deadly for both of them.

As she moved toward him with intrinsic grace, he gripped the sofa's arms as if he could anchor himself against his body's sudden ambush. Against the purpose in her brown eyes.

Don't do this to me, Selene….

"I want to do this, Adrien," she said as if he'd voiced his thoughts out loud. "I have to do this."

A burst of fire surged through his body when she leaned over and rubbed her palms down his chest to his abdomen then back up again. "You don't need this tonight," she whispered as she lifted the medallion from his neck and set it beside him, symbolically removing his self-control.

He didn't issue a protest when she slipped the button on his fly and slid his zipper down. Didn't utter a sound when she worked his jeans and briefs down his hips to his thighs. When she straightened to study him, he grew painfully hard right before her eyes.

In business, he was shrewd, unforgiving, never bending to anyone's will. He demanded complete control of his life, at least the aspects that he could control. He didn't welcome any loss of authority. But when Selene knelt before him and lowered her head, he realized what happened next was entirely out of his hands.

She explored him with her tongue from tip to shaft before immersing him completely in the heat of her mouth, causing him to hiss a breath between his clenched teeth. Right now he'd give up what was left of his soul to let her have her way, even though he recognized the risk in that. If he didn't stop her soon, he wouldn't be able to stop her at all.

Selene offered him a reprieve when she came to her feet before him. She took it back when she lifted the gown over her head and tossed it aside, leaving her completely nude.

After she climbed into his lap, her thighs straddling his thighs, she ran her tongue along his bottom lip while brushing her breasts across his chest. "You have two choices, Adrien. You can tell me to leave you alone, and I will, for good. Or you can stop denying what you and I both need and just go with it."

In that moment, what was left of Adrien's resistance splintered. He kissed her hard, kissed her deeply as he lifted her hips with one hand and guided himself inside her with the other, ending months of self-imposed celibacy with one hard upward thrust. It took all his strength not to climax immediately when she surrounded him with tight, wet heat. He braced his palms on her waist, following her movements while keeping his grasp light in order not to bruise her fair skin.

Determined to take her to the limit, he parted his thighs and in turn, parted hers wider, filling her to the hilt. When he broke the kiss and lifted his hips only slightly, he saw awareness pass over her face, witnessed her transformation from genteel lady to unrestrained woman. She kept her gaze connected to his as she rode him hard and fast, as she had in his first fantasy. Now he was at her mercy, and she was taking extreme advantage of that. While she was empowered, he was powerless.

Adrien wanted it to last longer, but his body began to say otherwise, and so did Selene's. He lowered his hands between her legs and stroked her for only a few moments before he felt the pulse of her orgasm that threatened to push him over the edge as well. He cursed his limitations. Cursed his inability to hang on for a while longer. But he didn't curse the climax that charged through him, bringing about a violent shudder that ran the length of his body.

Selene collapsed against him, the sounds of their ragged breathing disrupting the virtually silent night. He threaded his fingers through her hair and rubbed her back until he felt her relax against him. They stayed that way for a time until she lifted her head and touched his face with reverence, looked at him as if he were a man, not a fiend.

"Now that wasn't so difficult, was it?" she asked.

She had no idea how difficult it had been, at least when it came to giving up his control. "You caught me off guard."

"I assumed that was the only way I could get you to cooperate."

"You assumed right."

"And now that my mission is accomplished, I'll leave you to go back to whatever it was you were doing."

Taking Adrien totally by surprise, Selene climbed off his

lap, retrieved the gown and put it back on, then turned and walked back into her room, leaving him with his pants down around his ankles and confusion rolling around in his brain. He'd expected her to request he join her in bed. He'd even secretly hoped she would. Instead, she'd deserted him without requiring more than a fast round of raw sex. And for some reason, that angered him.

In those moments when he'd been joined to her body, he'd felt as if she could absolve him of his sins. But if she discovered what he had done, he could expect only a temporary pardon. Regardless, he wanted more of Selene, and less misery, until she walked away for good.

An hour had passed when Selene felt the bend of the mattress behind her and two solid arms came around her. She was as surprised by Adrien's sudden appearance as she had been by her lack of inhibition on the balcony earlier.

She rolled to face him, separated from his incredible body by only a thin cotton sheet, since she had climbed into bed without clothes. She suspected he didn't have on a stitch, either, and hoped to confirm that soon. "To what do I owe this pleasure?" she asked.

"I didn't realize you were awake."

"Let's just say I'm not used to having a man show up in my bed without any warning."

"Do you want me to leave?"

"I didn't say that." If she did, she wouldn't mean it.

"Good, because I'm not leaving. Not yet." He proved his point by working his way beneath the covers, pulling her closer yet keeping his lower body angled away from her. As she'd suspected, he wasn't wearing a thing, and he smelled so good that Selene nuzzled her nose against his neck. His damp hair brushed against her cheek and her hand automatically traveled there to sift through the soft waves.

Selene had rarely known such euphoria. She delighted in his warmth, his undeniable strength and even his continuing mystery.

He rubbed her back softly, soothingly. "I'll be leaving eventually."

She plied his neck with a series of soft kisses. "I understand. You'd rather spend the night in your own bed."

"I meant I'll be leaving the plantation. I'm going to sell it after it's restored."

That gave her good cause to drag her feet on the renovations, and a reason not to jump into this relationship heart first. It also gave her a sinking feeling in the pit of her stomach. "Where will you be going?"

He curled his hand over her bottom and kneaded it gently. "I'm not sure. Someplace warm if it's winter. Maybe an island."

A deserted island, no doubt. "Are you going to take Ella?"

"No, although I'm sure she'll argue the point. But she won't win."

She suspected not many people experienced the thrill of victory when Adrien was the opposing general.

He slid his thigh between her legs, bringing them into closer contact and making Selene all too aware he was aroused, in turn arousing her. "In the meantime, I want to be your lover until you leave," he said with conviction.

He palmed her breasts lightly, bringing about Selene's sigh. "What about Ella?"

"Three's a crowd."

She laughed even though she wanted to moan. "I meant how is she going to feel about us being together?"

He brushed his knuckles across her belly. "We'll be discreet. And she already has her suspicions."

Surely Selene hadn't been that obvious in her admiration. "Why is that?"

He formed his palm between her thighs. "Because she knows me too well. She knows that I've wanted you since you walked through my door, even though I wanted you gone in the beginning."

"What do you want now, Adrien?" That simple question proved difficult for Selene in light of Adrien's current ministrations, and her fear that she might not like the answer.

"I would think that's obvious," he said as he caressed her without mercy. "I want to be inside you again."

He rolled her away from him and fitted himself against her back before returning his hand between her legs. "No expectations," he said.

"No expectations," she murmured as he lifted her leg over his hip.

"But you can always expect that I'll make you feel…" He eased inside of her. "Very good."

Selene had no doubt that he would exceed those expectations. He already had, and he did again as he rocked against her. Unlike their lovemaking on the veranda, this joining resembled a sensual slow dance, not at all fiery and frenetic, at least not at first. But soon the passion took over on the heels of the sheer electric need that had existed between them since their meeting, setting a feverish tempo until they were both sated and sapped of strength.

After their respiration slowed and their bodies had calmed, Adrien tipped Selene's head back and kissed her. A deep, meaningful kiss that threatened to bring her unsolicited emotions to the surface.

She had to remember to stay grounded, stay guarded. For however long he remained in her life, she would accept his gift of pleasure, yet she would also accept the reality of the situation—he might be the consummate lover, but he was also impossible to hold, and as Ella had so wisely put it, much too easy to love.

First morning light seeping through the window served as Adrien's cue to leave. He wasn't one to hang around for morning-after conversation, but for some reason he couldn't tear himself away. Couldn't stop watching Selene as she slept beside him, one hand curled next to her face, the other resting at her side. Couldn't resist taking another methodical look at her body. Then he would leave.

Careful not to wake her, he clasped the sheet and lowered it to her thighs. He studied her rose-colored nipples before visually tracking the path down her belly to the soft gold shading between her thighs, and went stone hard over the sight. He knew how she tasted all over, how she felt surrounding him when she climaxed, and he wanted to know it all again. And again.

Selene had seeped into his veins like pretty poison, and he needed to get her out of his system. Experience had taught him exactly how to do that. Now he only had to convince her to take the bait, beginning tonight.

Eight

Selene sensed Adrien's presence moments before she looked up to see him standing on the second-floor landing, a striking figure set against the heavenly ceiling. With his dark hair framing his face in soft waves and his translucent blue eyes, he could have fallen away from the band of angels circling overhead.

As she climbed the stairs, her pulse picked up speed in response to his charismatic pull. She hadn't seen him since he'd come to her bed last night, yet he'd never been out of her head for more than a few minutes during the day. She'd replayed their conversation over and over—no expectations, no promises. Only a sexual alliance that would last until her work was done. That bothered her more than she cared to admit, but she couldn't resist him any more than she could will her heart to stop beating, though she could swear it had skipped several beats as she continued her upward climb.

Selene paused at the second stair before the landing, her hand tightly gripping the rail. "I was about to come looking for you. I thought you would like to know that the contractor's set to begin the restoration next Monday, beginning with exterior repairs—"

"What do you have planned for the next two days?"

Apparently he wasn't in the mood to discuss the renovation. Considering the heat in his eyes, he didn't look as if he wanted to talk at all. "Actually, I have nothing scheduled tomorrow or Wednesday. I do have an appointment on Thursday with the woman who's going to restore the furniture, and a crew's coming out to get started on the landscaping."

He leaned forward and grasped the railing, his hands only inches from hers. "Good. I have something I need you to do."

"What would that be?"

"I want you to spend the next forty-eight hours with me, beginning tonight. No phones. No appointments. No interruptions. I only require your trust and undivided attention."

"What will we be doing?" As if she really had to ask. She could already see the mental preview playing out in his mind.

"You know what we'll be doing. And we'll stay in my bedroom where it's cooler, in case you get too hot."

Getting too hot was a given, especially if he planned to hold her captive for hours. "Aren't you afraid we'll get tired of each other?"

"I promise that won't happen."

Selene knew he would make good on that promise. Still, she worried that to take him up on his suggestion could mean certain peril to her emotions. But because her time with Adrien would be limited, she felt the need to make as many memories as possible, as long as she kept a firm hold on her feelings.

In order to avoid any possible interruptions, she had one

last task to complete before she joined him. "I need to call my mother first."

He gave her a wry grin. "To ask her permission?"

"To check in." A call she'd been avoiding for some time now.

"Don't take any longer than necessary." He straightened and subtly brushed his hand over his groin, drawing Selene's attention to the prominent crest outlined against his slacks.

She swallowed hard. "It can wait."

"Are you sure? I wouldn't want to keep you from your family."

"I'm sure." And she was. After all, the phone worked both ways, and her mother hadn't bothered to call her. Right now she had better things to do, interesting places to be, specifically in Adrien's arms. In Adrien's world. At times in Adrien's mind.

Selene took his offered hand without hesitation, more than willing to follow wherever he might lead her. She only hoped that when their time together was over, she wasn't so lost she couldn't find her way back.

Without speaking, Adrien led her into his bedroom that he'd transformed into a seductive lair. Lit candles were scattered about the area, bathing the darkened room in a golden glow. No music played in the background, but the open windows allowed in the sounds of nature's symphony coming from the swamp below.

Adrien pulled Selene down onto a nest of pillows he'd arranged on the floor in the sitting area and removed only their shoes. She noticed a stick of incense burning on the table, emitting an exotic scent that reminded her of warm summer nights in a forest. "That smells really nice."

He reached out and pushed her hair away from her shoulder as he studied her face. "It's a special blend I discovered during my travels. It reportedly has a favorable effect on lovers."

"It's an aphrodisiac, you mean."

"I'd prefer to think of it as an enhancement to an already favorable situation."

She really didn't need any enhancement; she was already experiencing the effects of his smile, the blue fire in his eyes.

"I only have one rule," he said as he began to slip the buttons on her blouse. "No talk of the past. As far as I'm concerned, it doesn't exist as long as we're in this room. Other than that, there are no other rules."

Selene had no concern for the past, only the present when he slid the blouse off her shoulders and removed her bra. He took off his own shirt at his usual leisurely pace while she watched his dynamic chest come into view. Oddly enough, his medallion was missing, which led her to believe that during this respite, he was willing to relinquish his willpower.

Leaving their slacks still intact, he laid her back on the pillows, slid an arm beneath her and settled her against his shoulder. He drew random designs up and down her bare arm with his fingertips as he took her on a journey to the exotic places he'd visited. She watched his mouth as he spoke, admired the way the flickering candlelight played out over his perfect profile, lulled by the sound of his deep voice as he painted a picture with words and, unbeknownst to him, through his thoughts.

Midway through his musings on his travels in Mexico, Selene began to experience a strange tingling in her breasts that took a slow trek downward, followed by a stream of heat. In response, a small sound climbed up her throat and filtered out of her mouth before she could stop it.

Adrien stopped mid-sentence and turned his gaze to her. "You feel it, don't you?"

She highly doubted the incense was responsible for the sudden flash fire of need. It was simply Adrien—a man who was as powerful as any opiate. "I definitely feel something." Her voice sounded winded and raspy.

He tipped her face up and ran the tip of his tongue over her bottom lip. "I'm already hard just thinking about what I want to do to you. What I'm going to do to you."

Selene silently willed him to begin and she got her wish when Adrien sat up and worked her slacks and panties away. She noted a momentary chink in his armor when he stood and fumbled with his fly before removing his slacks and briefs. Now completely nude, he hovered above her and allowed her a long visual exploration, which she gladly took. Because of the limited light, parts of his body had been cast in shadows, but she could see enough to know he was definitely aroused.

He dropped to his knees beside her and leaned to kiss her thoroughly before straightening again. All Selene's senses were heightened—sight, taste, smell and touch. Definitely touch as Adrien sent his hands over her body in a heady excursion. "Tell me what feels good," he whispered as he divined her flesh with a fingertip. "Here?"

"Yes, there," she managed to say on a broken breath when he hit the mark.

He urged her to verbally express her desires as he used both his hands and mouth to bring her to a searing climax, the likes of which she had never known. When her turn came to explore him, he openly talked about what he liked in explicit terms, what drove him wild. And without hesitation, she met every one of his requests with the enthusiasm of a woman caught in the throes of self-discovery.

By the time Adrien eased into her body, Selene felt as if she had traveled to another dimension where nothing existed beyond overwhelming sensation. Where only they existed. As he lifted her hips toward him with his palms and thrust deeply inside her, she experienced another orgasm that seemed to go on for endless moments. Not long after, Adrien released a feral moan as his frame went rigid in her arms. He collapsed against her, his heart pounding against her breasts, his respiration harsh and uneven. Selene breezed her palms down his sculpted back, over his buttocks and up to the damp curls at his nape. She loved the smell of him, the feel of him, even the weight of him.

When he didn't move, she thought maybe he'd fallen asleep until he muttered, "I'm wasted," in her ear.

Selene wasn't wasted at all. In fact, she had already begun to feel the stirrings of more need. Framing his jaws in her palms, she lifted his head and forced him to look at her. "Please don't tell me we're through for the night."

His grin lit up his eyes—and Selene's heart. "I said I'm wasted, not dead. I predict I'll recover quickly."

Adrien's prediction proved to be correct as they again made love two more times during the night. Shortly before dawn, they fell asleep curled together on the pillows and Selene awoke to find him staring at her.

"Good morning," she said as she stretched her arms above her head. "What time is it?"

"Does it matter?"

She supposed it really didn't. After all, she had nothing better to do than stay in his arms. She could think of nothing better to do. "I'm just used to being up by now."

"I'm already up."

Her gaze immediately tracked downward to discover proof of that. "Well, you can always count on three things. Death, taxes and a man's morning erection."

Adrien laughed then, a deep throaty laugh that lifted Selene's spirits even more. "Why, sir, I didn't realize you had a sense of humor," she said.

He tugged her against him. "And I didn't realize the extent of your charms."

As far as Selene was concerned, he had a surplus of charm that matched his monetary worth. "Could I charm you into some more of what we had last night?"

"Do you really have to ask?"

As it turned out, she didn't.

In the following hours, time seemed to suspend as Adrien kept Selene captive in an erotic haze. At noon, he led her outside onto the veranda, backing her up against the alcove surrounding the doors where anyone could come upon them, their bodies soon slick from the heat of the blazing sun and their unrestrained lovemaking. Selene had never felt so liberated, nor had she realized that taking such a risk could be such a turn-on. But Adrien knew, just like he knew exactly how and when to bring her to a glorious climax while he was seated deep within her body.

Though they left the room only when necessary, they didn't devote every moment to lovemaking. Adrien insisted on attending to her every need, including bringing them food and drink. He seemed more open, more relaxed than before as they talked about many things, including their preference for Southern authors and their disdain for politics. When she asked about his parents, he only said they were both gone, and left it at that. His apparent distress, which he unsuccessfully tried to hide, prevented Selene from asking for details. In accordance with his insistence they forget the past, he didn't mention her ex-husband, and she didn't inquire about the woman who'd once been in his life. But when she told him the ill-fated lovers' story, stressing her sadness over Grace's death and Zeke wasting away due to grief, she knew he could relate.

Several times she'd considered telling him about her abilities, but she'd worried he might not understand. That he might even call an end to their interlude before she was ready. Eventually she would tell him, when she felt the time was right.

At sundown, he prodded her to try his eighty-year-old scotch and when she wrinkled her nose and coughed, he laughed. She loved hearing his laughter, loved that he seemed to be transforming right before her eyes though he still retained the mystery that had drawn her from the beginning. They dined in bed and showered together in Adrien's well-appointed bathroom. Even that had been an experience Selene would never forget, as Adrien made love to her in ways she'd never dreamed possible, always careful to concentrate on her pleasure, never once causing her pain. And on the second day, they did more of the same—more touches, more talk, more unbelievable lovemaking.

Selene had never had such control of her own pleasure and, at times, of Adrien. She'd learned how to taunt him just so she could hear him plead with her in his low, drugging voice. She delighted in her newfound power as well as her recently discovered freedom. She reveled in what Adrien had shown her—that she was a desirable woman who could bring a man to his knees with only a touch.

By the time they reached the end of their escape from reality, Selene had done things she'd never considered doing before, had talked about things she'd never considered discussing, and had totally fallen for Adrien. She felt as if in many ways they were not only connected by their minds but also by their souls. Yet she still didn't completely understand the source of his sorrow even though he'd seemed to let go of that during the past two days. But when she awoke in the middle of the night to find him staring out the window, she realized he'd only had a temporary reprieve from his torment. She did all she could think to do—ask him to make love to her one final time, which he did, with a surprising tenderness forever imprinted in her memories.

And before she drifted off once more in his arms, Selene accepted that he would forever occupy a special place in her heart, and intended or not, he had won her love.

On Thursday morning, Selene awoke to find Adrien gone, and she felt completely bereft, as if she'd lost a lifelong friend, a cherished lover. She gave herself a good mental scolding for doing exactly what she'd vowed to avoid—falling in love with him. But she didn't know how to quell the feelings that continued to bubble up to the surface. How to stop thinking about him for more than a few minutes during the day even though she hadn't seen him since the night before. Unfortunately, she had no choice but to return to the real world.

After meeting with the furniture restorer at half-past noon, Selene gathered up a few fabric samples to use as an excuse to see Adrien.

She arrived at his office to find the door partially ajar and stepped inside, where Adrien paced the area behind his desk, clutching a cordless phone tightly in his grasp. "I said just do it, dammit. You're being paid well for your services."

After he slammed the phone down on the charger, Selene considered backing out quietly until his gaze shot to hers and his anger seemed to diminish.

"I've obviously caught you at a bad time," she said as she hugged the samples to her breasts. "I'll come back later."

He ran a fast hand through his hair before bracing his palms on the back of his chair. "You don't have to leave. I could use a distraction right now."

She took a few steps forward and held up the pieces of fabric. "For the main parlor downstairs, do you like the red-and-gold pinstripe or the green brocade?"

He rubbed his chin, sat down in his chair and smiled. "Tell you what. Take off your clothes and wrap up in them, one at a time, and I'll tell you which one I prefer."

She feigned a frown. "You're insatiable."

"I could say the same about you."

He could, and he would be correct. Right now she wanted to climb into his lap as she had on the veranda when she'd set their lovemaking into full swing. Climb all over him, as a matter of fact. "Now back to business. Which one do you like?"

He sat and leaned back in his chair. "You choose. I'm sure you have a better eye for color than I do."

She definitely had an eye for gorgeous men, and her eye was on the one sitting before her, with his wavy rogue's hair and his irrefutable sensual aura. "All right, if I must. Or I can consult with Ella when she returns. Any idea when that might be?"

"On Saturday. I told her to stay longer, but she refused. She claims she's wearing out her welcome."

As much as Selene wanted to see Ella, she couldn't prevent the nip of disappointment that their alone time had come to an end. But hopefully not their lovemaking. "I'm looking forward to seeing her."

He pushed back his chair, stood and braced his palms on the desk. "I'm not. I planned to make love to you in every room in this house. Of course, we could manage that in the next two days."

And that would quite possibly be the death of Selene. "We'll see, but right now I have something I'd like for you to do."

He presented *that* look, the one that said he meant business. Sensual business. "Climb up on my desk and I'll take care of it."

And she knew exactly how he would take care of it

through the mental signals he sent out that her brain picked up like a high-frequency scanner. "This isn't about sex, Adrien. I want to take a walk around the place as soon as it cools off a bit." She definitely needed to cool off, too. "I want you to come with me."

"Any particular reason why?"

"Mr. Gutherie told me he used to come here during the summers and play in a tree house. I want to see if it's still there."

"It is," he said. "In a pecan grove."

"You've seen it?"

The sparkle in his eyes gave way to recognizable regret "Yeah. I've explored most of the acreage surrounding the house."

"That must have taken quite a while."

"I had nothing better to do at the time."

She wanted desperately to ask him why he was so sad, but instead of coming right out and posing the query, she decided to take an indirect route. "Before I forget, I need to know what you want me to do about the guest room across from yours. Ella told me you didn't want it disturbed, but if you're worried about valuables, I can help you move them to a safe place while the redecorating is in progress."

Now he looked annoyed. "I want the room to stay as it is."

"For how long?"

"Until I say otherwise. Is that understood?"

He had all but confirmed that the clue to his distress could be found in that room. But would she risk trying to find out? Maybe after Ella's return she would consider it. Right now, she simply needed to lighten the mood. "Why, yes sir, I understand you completely. I might be insatiable, but I am certainly not deaf. Or stupid."

Selene could tell he didn't want to let go of the anger,

but he lost the battle and smiled. "No, you're definitely not stupid."

She pointed behind her. "Now that I know my intelligence is not in question, I'll go and let you get back to business. I'll meet you downstairs on the front porch at around six, if that works for you."

He rounded the desk and approached her with his usual slow, stalking gait. "Have you ever made love up against a tree, Selene?"

"I've never even considered it." She was now.

He slid his arms around her waist and pulled her to him. "Don't underestimate the power of nature. Don't underestimate my power."

That power was palpable, particularly when he kissed her. She was veritable putty in his arms, available for him to shape however he saw fit. And right then she understood she was hurling at breakneck speed straight into trouble.

With Adrien at her side, Selene walked backward through the field, studying the plantation now washed in the glow of the setting sun, trying to visualize what it would look like once the black columns had been painted white. *"Maison de Soleil.* The House of Sunshine," she said as she turned to face forward and plucked a lone dandelion from the grass. "We definitely need to rename the house after it's restored."

When Adrien didn't immediately respond, she tapped him on his shoulder. "Don't you agree?"

He glanced at her as they continued walking. "With what?"

"That we should rename the plantation *Maison de Soleil,* what it was called before."

"Before what?"

Obviously his thoughts had left for parts unknown.

"Before Grace passed away. Maybe we should ask Zeke, the former owner, his opinion. Jeb Gutherie told me his grandmother used to talk to him after he died, although Jeb claims Zeke has gone on to the great unknown."

That earned her a sour look from Adrien. "I don't believe people can commune with the dead," he said. "I don't believe in ghosts or voodoo or the sight."

Of course he wouldn't, Selene thought. He was a businessman. Pragmatic to a fault. And probably not yet ready to accept her "gift." "Then you don't believe that some things can't be explained?"

"No, I don't." He sounded insulted that she'd even asked.

"What about destiny?"

"We create our own destinies. We're responsible for our actions and our choices."

Selene plucked the petals from the flower, silently chanting, *Tell him, or tell him not.* She reached the last petal and ended with *Tell him not.* Maybe later. Much later. Or never.

"It's over there," he said, pointing to a grove of large pecan trees bordering the open field.

Selene quickened her pace when she caught sight of the log platform braced by two heavy limbs. She couldn't believe the tree house had survived all these years. She also couldn't quite fathom why she had the urge to run to it and climb, but she did exactly that. She'd barely gotten one foot up onto one low-hanging branch when Adrien said, "Don't do it, Selene."

She chose to ignore him and hoisted herself up onto the larger limb. "I want to do it. I wasn't allowed to climb when I was a child."

"Get down now."

With one foot planted on the log platform, ready to take the final step, she regarded him over her shoulder. "Why? It looks sturdy enough."

He strode to the tree and gave her a harsh stare. "Looks can be deceptive. It's old and probably rotted. You could fall and break something."

She appreciated his concern on one level, but resented that he believed she was incapable of taking care of herself on another. "I'm just going to test it with my foot. I won't put all my weight on it yet."

Before she could make her next move, she felt a solid grip on her ankle. "I said get down. Now."

Although he sounded livid, Selene noted a hint of real fear in his tone. "If you're that worried, okay."

As she began to climb down, her foot slipped and so did her grasp on the limb. Before she tumbled out of the tree, Adrien was there, gathering her into his arms. He immediately set her on her feet and backed away from her. "I told you not to do it, dammit."

Selene braced her hands on her hips. "I wasn't that far from the ground, Adrien. If I had fallen, I probably would have injured only my pride."

"Or you could have broken your neck, and God knows you wouldn't want to deal with that."

He spun away from her and headed toward the house. Selene had a hard time keeping up with him and an even more difficult time understanding why he was so angry. She managed to clutch his arm but he shook off her grasp and kept walking.

"What is wrong with you?" she said through her ragged respiration.

He stopped dead and faced her. "There's not a damn thing wrong with me. But you're too stubborn."

Her mouth dropped open a few seconds before she momentarily clamped it closed. "And you're being hypocritical, he who has jumped from planes and dived off of cliffs."

"That was a long time ago. The risk isn't worth it. I learned that the hard way."

Again he tried to move on but this time she wouldn't let him. She sprinted until she was in front of him and put up both her hands to stop his progress. "Don't walk away from me, Adrien. Not until you explain what this is all about."

"Your safety."

She held out her arms and slowly turned around. "See? I'm still in one piece."

"I don't have the energy or desire to deal with your carelessness."

"I'm not asking you to deal with anything. I'm a big girl and quite capable of taking care of myself."

A few brief images filtered into Selene's mind—a smiling young woman, and that same woman in a free fall, her eyes filled with terror, before everything faded to black.

Adrien turned away again and managed a few steps until Selene said, "Does this have something to do with Chloe?" He faced her again with a menacing look that made her shrink back. Made her want to run for the cover of the trees.

"Has Ella been talking to you?" he said, his tone as irate as his expression.

Selene folded her arms across her middle. "No, she hasn't. But I know Chloe existed. I know she's someone you cared about. Maybe even someone you loved."

He fisted his hands at his sides. "You don't know a damn thing about me. And you're better off not knowing."

With that, he turned and headed back for the house and, this time, Selene let him go. She was no closer to having the answers she craved. No closer to understanding his relationship with Chloe. But she did understand the depth of his grief and that Chloe had indeed been an important part of his life. She also knew something had happened to her. Something horrible, and that loss was still eating away at Adrien.

Selene vowed to find out all the facts eventually, hopefully not before it was too late to save him from a future of utter despair.

Adrien had no idea how she'd found out about Chloe. He only knew that she was coming too close to the truth.

Overcome with rage, he cleared his desk with one sweep of his arm before he paced the room, restless with turmoil and confusion. He despised indecision and weakness, almost as much as he'd despised himself at the moment.

He'd mistakenly believed that by spending so much time with Selene, he would discover something about her he didn't like. Something that would make it easy for him to let her go. Instead, he'd fallen victim to his own machinations. She wasn't out of his system at all. He was consumed by her.

In her presence, he'd begun to forget his failings, and that was something he couldn't allow himself to do. Forgetting would be the true mark of a man who was devoid of conscience, and totally beyond salvation. He hadn't arrived at that place. At least not yet.

He also recognized that Selene didn't deserve the brunt of his anger. She deserved a man who was whole. A man without a history of irreparable mistakes. A man who could love her the way she should be loved.

Yet in those hours he'd spent with her, at times he'd believed he could be that man. She'd given him hope that maybe he could move beyond what had been to what might be. Until the memories had been resurrected that afternoon, reminding him of the impossible.

He knew of only one way to assure her imminent

rejection—by telling her the truth. An extreme measure, and a last resort.

In the meantime, he would spend one last evening pretending he was the man she believed him to be—before he returned to damnation.

Nine

After spending the night restless and alone, Selene decided to return to the near-barren nursery the following morning. She sat in the rocking chair and set it in motion with her heel, staring at the cradle while thinking about poor Grace, who'd never had the chance to hold her baby. Who'd been torn from her husband's life all too soon, sending him spiraling into a state of grief from which he'd never emerged. That kind of devastating loss was totally foreign to Selene. Of course, several of her relatives had succumbed to old age. Otherwise, she'd not suffered too much loss, with the exception of her marriage—a marriage that had been hopeless from the beginning. At least she hadn't made the fatal mistake of getting pregnant, although at times she'd wondered if a child could have alleviated some of the loneliness. Yet bringing a baby into a world with two parents who didn't really love each other would have been cruel.

Selene sighed and nudged the cradle that was as empty as she felt at the moment. Every instinct told her to leave Adrien alone, maybe even to leave this place. But something was keeping her here. An unknown force, or fate. Or perhaps it was simply her hope that Adrien might eventually love her, too.

"Wishful thinking, Selene?"

Selene shifted around to find him leaning against the doorjamb wearing his standard white shirt and black slacks, as if he'd recently walked out of a corporate meeting. She couldn't stop her spirits from soaring or her heart's quickening.

She came to her feet and opted for business talk to mask her continuing hurt over his behavior. "I was thinking maybe this would make a nice family room. It could be more modern than the rest of the house, and that might provide a good selling point when you put it on the market."

He continued to study her for a long moment before he said, "I'm sorry."

Selene hadn't expected that at all. "Apology accepted."

He rubbed a hand over his nape and studied the floor in very un-Adrien-like fashion. "I know it's a lot to ask, but I would like to make it up to you tonight."

Another surprise. "How do you propose to do that?"

"By having dinner with you. A real dinner that you don't have to prepare."

A real date? That was probably too much to ask, Selene decided. "Will we be dining out?"

He finally lifted his gaze to her. "No. I've arranged for the meal to be brought in."

Her disappointment filtered out on a long sigh. "It wouldn't hurt you to get out of the house now and then."

He slid his hands into his pockets. "I have my reasons for not wanting to leave tonight."

She suspected that might have to do with what he planned as an after-dinner treat. But she wasn't going to go there, not until she had some answers.

Selene strolled toward him but kept a safe distance. "What time?"

"Seven."

"Fine. I guess I'll see you then."

When she brushed past him, he caught her hand and tugged her into his arms. She expected a kiss, but what she got was an embrace. He simply held her for a long moment, his palms pressed against her back and his cheek resting against her cheek. When he kissed her forehead, Selene asked, "What was that for?"

"For being you." She noted a warmth in his eyes that she'd never seen before, as if his emotional fortress had dissolved, at least for the time being.

Ironically, in all the years she'd been with Richard, not once had he ever remotely made her feel as special as she did with Adrien. "Thank you," she said. "I like you, too." In truth, she loved him. All his mystery, his hidden humanity, the man she knew resided beneath the steely exterior. A man so wrought with pain that he couldn't get past it to save his life.

His expression turned somber. "Your respect means a lot to me, Selene. More than you know."

But she did know. Her intuition was screaming that he cared about her. That he could love her, too, in the future. But not unless he finally unveiled the foundation of his tragic past.

And when he let her go and walked away, she understood they were quickly approaching the proverbial point of no return. If she couldn't get him to come clean tonight, then she would have to decide whether to fight or accept defeat. Accept that she wasn't "the one," as Ella had predicted.

But as long as she was with him, she still had hope that maybe, just maybe, he was an important part of her destiny.

Wearing the black satin dress she'd purchased that day, her hair done up in a neat twist, Selene descended the stairs as fast as her strappy heels would let her. She'd waited until five minutes after the hour in order to be fashionably late, and to let Adrien know she wasn't completely under his command. As she reached the dining room, she pulled up short when she spotted a lanky gray-haired stranger wearing a black tuxedo standing outside the opening.

"Good evening, miss," he said. "I'm Mr. Renaldo, your waiter for the evening. Right this way."

Speechless, Selene took his offered arm and allowed him to escort her into the dining room. When she entered, she found Adrien standing by the table dressed in a black silk jacket and slacks and a crisp white shirt. She immediately noticed their place settings had been set side by side, not at opposite ends of the table. The waiter pulled back Selene's chair and, after she was seated, draped a pink cloth napkin in her lap.

When the man disappeared into the kitchen and Adrien was settled in beside her, Selene asked, "Where did he come from?"

"Atlanta. He accompanied the chef from Chez Gaston. I thought you might miss your hometown, and this was a way to bring it to you."

"I know the place well, and I can't believe they drove all the way here on a Friday night." She couldn't believe Adrien had been so thoughtful.

"I had them flown in by private jet."

Unbelievable. "That seems like quite a bit of expense.

I really had no problem heating up one of the dinners Ella made for us."

Adrien draped an arm over the back of her chair. "Do you have something against having a top-rate meal?"

No, but Selene did have somewhat of an aversion to money. She also surmised that the extent of Adrien's wealth went beyond her expectations. Nothing she hadn't known all of her life, another aspect she'd been trying to escape. Now here she sat, with a man who had enough funds to bring in his own preeminent chef and waiter. And enough emotional baggage to fill an airport. "I'm sorry. I didn't mean to sound ungrateful. I appreciate it very much."

His eyes took on that smoky hue she found so hard to resist. "You'll definitely appreciate everything I have planned tonight."

Adrien unabashedly studied her breasts unencumbered beneath the black silk and a sudden fantasy-flash called out from his mind and landed in hers.

He never arranged for a private dining room in an exclusive restaurant, then touched you beneath the table until you wanted it right then, right there....

Surely he wasn't considering... Oh, but he was, that much Selene knew. And just thinking about it sent a hot blush rushing to her cheeks. At this rate, she was going to have a difficult time maintaining her resolve to avoid any more intimacy until she had answers.

He circled his fingertips round and round her bare shoulder. "I like this dress," he said. "But I would have preferred something a little lower cut."

She touched the high collar that now felt like a noose around her neck. "I wanted to wear something special, but I didn't have anything appropriate so I had to go into town to buy it. Unfortunately, this was the best I could do on such short notice. But the lady at the boutique was very helpful and accommodating."

"I certainly plan to be accommodating."

Selene had no doubt about that. She also had little doubt that the meal would be unforgettable when Mr. Renaldo brought in the shrimp-and-scallop appetizer. As soon as he left, Adrien laid his hand on Selene's knee beneath the napkin. As each course was served, his palm inched higher, and her pulse rose in anticipation. He was definitely teasing her. And it was working very well.

By the time the entrée arrived, she wasn't certain she could choke down another bite even though her dinner companion had yet to do anything questionable other than stroke his thumb along the inside of her leg.

Adrien managed to consume all the food, including the strawberry crepes that Selene waved away. She did accept the offer of a second glass of wine though Adrien hadn't finished half of his first.

After Mr. Renaldo cleared the final plate and retreated into the kitchen, Adrien leaned over and whispered, "You know, he's totally oblivious. I could—"

She slapped her palm on his hand before he hit the intended target. "But he's not blind, and if you do what I think you're going to do, I promise he'll know."

Adrien took her hand and held it to his lips for a kiss. "I was only wondering if you're wearing anything underneath this dress."

"Yes, I am." A barely-there scrap of black silk.

Before the discussion could continue, the waiter re-entered the room with the man who introduced himself as Chef Stephan Aucoin, a portly gentleman who looked as if he routinely consumed most of the food he prepared.

Adrien pushed away from the table and came to his feet. "Gentlemen, as always, you did an excellent job."

The chef executed a little bow. "Our pleasure, Mr. Morrell." He turned his attention to Selene. "Ms. Winston, you barely ate. Did you not find the food to your liking?"

"She doesn't eat well when she's hot," Adrien said, followed by a wry grin aimed at her.

"It's the summer weather," Selene quickly added. If she could reach Adrien's foot, she'd stomp it.

"Then we will have to return when the weather's cooler," Renaldo said.

Unbeknownst to them, she would probably be gone before the weather turned cooler.

Adrien checked his watch and rounded the table. "Your car's waiting to take you back to the airport." He reached inside his jacket, withdrew an envelope and handed it to the chef. "I'll see you out."

After Adrien escorted the men out of the room, Selene slumped down in her chair and fanned her face, surprised that she'd gotten through the evening without fainting. She was high on adrenaline and definitely warm, but not because of the elements. She grew warmer still when Adrien strolled into the dining room, hands in his pockets and a sultry look on his face.

Selene stood and pushed her chair beneath the table, using it for support. "She doesn't eat when she's hot? I cannot believe you said that."

He had the nerve to grin. "You are hot, aren't you?"

She was, and damn him, he knew it. "I'm cooling off now."

He stalked toward her and before she could move out of his path, he had her securely in his arms. After lifting the back of her dress, he ran his palm over her bottom. "I want these off of you."

She wrested out of his arms and stepped back, earning Adrien's frown. "First, we need to talk."

"About what?"

"About our secrets. Yours and mine."

He narrowed his eyes. "Everyone should be entitled to their secrets, Selene. I don't need your revelations."

Folding her arms beneath her breasts, she strolled to the opposite side of the room, putting the table between them. "Well, I'm going to make one. And you're going to listen."

He pulled back a chair and dropped down into it. "Go ahead and confess if it makes you feel better. But don't expect me to do the same."

Oh, but she did, especially after she said what should have been said a while ago. She drew in a cleansing breath and remained standing, her hands braced on the back of a chair. "When I was a little girl, I learned I had this innate ability to tap into other people's thoughts. I also learned it wasn't always a good thing, knowing what other people thought about you. Knowing what you were going to get on your birthday and Christmas. I taught myself how to block it out."

She waited for his response, but when he just sat there, looking cynical, she continued. "After my ex-husband started staying out well into the night with the excuse he was working, I decided to utilize my *gift* for the first time in years. Imagine my surprise when I discovered while he was in bed with me, he was fantasizing about a mutual friend. I called him on it, he admitted to the affair. End of story and end of marriage."

He shifted slightly in the chair. "I told you, I don't believe in that kind of thing."

In other words, he didn't believe her, but he would. "The moment I stepped into this house, your thoughts began to come to me. I didn't invite them, but they were too strong to block."

He pushed back from the table and stood up. "This is ridiculous."

"Is it?" Selene tightened her grip on the chair. "When I came to you on the veranda the first time we made love, I knew you'd fantasized about it because I'd been privy to those fantasies."

He seemed to mull it over for a minute before the skepticism returned to his expression. "Is there a point to all this?"

"Yes, there is." She moved around the table and stood only a few feet from him. "I've picked up other images from you. Images about the woman named Chloe. In fact, you're the one who told me her name inadvertently."

He shoved one chair and knocked it over. "I don't have to listen to this."

"Yes, you do, because I know something happened to her. And whatever it is, it's eating away at you like acid."

Without saying a word, he stormed out of the room and into the vestibule, Selene close on his heels.

"Stop and listen to me, Adrien," she demanded before he managed the first stair.

He faced her again, his expression heralding a bitter anger. "Why should I?"

"Because I've given you my trust from the beginning. Because I trusted you enough to tell you something only one other living soul knows. And now I'm asking you to trust me enough to tell me about her."

"If you really have this ability to read minds, you already know the whole sordid story."

She took another step toward him. "I don't know everything because you've managed to keep those thoughts from me. And maybe I've made a subconscious effort not to know because I was afraid you've done something terrible."

"You would be right about that."

She moved to the bottom of the staircase within his reach, determined to prod him until she had all the answers. "Then you owe it to me to tell me the truth. I want to know about Chloe. What happened to her. What it was about her that made you love her so much that you completely bowed out of life when she was gone."

He collapsed onto the second stair and lowered his head into his hands. When he looked up, his eyes reflected a sorrow so deep, it took Selene's breath.

Adrien's mind became an open floodgate then, sending a barrage of images into Selene's mind in rapid-fire succession. A young, dark-haired, blue-eyed woman climbing, then reaching out for a hand, unable to hold on. Falling, her body twisting, slamming against the wall of rock before dangling lifeless from a tether. The same woman who'd come to Selene in her dreams.

When the visions began to fade, Selene dropped down beside Adrien on the stair. "She fell."

He studied her with weary eyes. "She wasn't an experienced climber. She shouldn't have gone with me, but she begged me to go. And I didn't refuse her. I never could."

"You must have loved her very much."

"As much as anyone could love a sister."

Selene's shock came out in a slight gasp. "Sister?"

He swiped a hand over his forehead. "Yeah. She was born when I was twelve to my mother and my bastard of a stepfather. Chloe was the only good thing that came out of that sham of a marriage." He released a caustic laugh. "Ironically, Giles had control of the inheritance, and he willed it all to me. He made me administrator of Chloe's trust. Needless to say, that didn't set too well with my mother or her sorry husband who had designs on her money. Neither did the fact that Chloe remained in touch with me after I left home at sixteen to live with Giles. And now they blame me for the accident, and as bad as I hate to admit it, that blame is justified."

Selene draped an arm around his shoulder. "It's not your fault. You said yourself it was an accident."

He leaned forward, bent elbows resting on his knees, and streaked both hands over his face. "I don't want to talk about this anymore."

Instinct told Selene several pieces of the puzzle were still missing. But since he looked as if he'd been put through the wringer, she decided she'd learned enough for now. "I'm sorry, Adrien. But I'm not sorry you finally told me. I just wanted to take some of this burden away from you."

His blue eyes held a cast of confusion. "Why, Selene?"

"Because I care about you. When we're together, I'm happier than I've been in years. When we're apart, I feel like a part of me is missing. And I know you told me no expectations, no promises, but I can't help the way I feel."

He turned toward her and framed her face in his palms. "I don't deserve your compassion. I don't deserve spending even another minute with you. But God help me, I can't stay away from you."

His kiss was demanding and desperate, his touch deliberate as he leaned her back and sent his hands down her body to lift her dress. When he slid her panties away, she didn't bother to protest because she knew it would be futile—she wanted this as much as he did. When he undid his fly and nudged her legs apart, she saw no point in telling him they might be more comfortable in bed, because comfort wasn't his immediate concern. He wasn't seeking the unconventional, either; he needed a connection. Needed the one thing that had provided solace from the pain he had endured, and she was more than willing to provide that comfort.

He levered his knee on the stair and thrust inside her,

sending a slow-moving flame flowing throughout Selene's body. When he buried his face in the bend of her neck, she looked up at the cherubs soaring above them in the blissful blue sky. A fitting scene in so many ways since Adrien's mastery was pure paradise. But his torment contrasted with the peaceful depiction.

She closed her eyes and let the sensations take over, allowed Adrien to take the lead as he guided her back to the place where no painful past existed, only pleasure. As always, her body responded to his touch and her mind reached out to share in his physical gratification, as well as his emotional turmoil.

After a time, his frame went rigid and, following a long shudder, he whispered, "Don't leave me, Selene."

She assumed he meant only tonight, though she didn't want to leave him now, or ever for that matter. She was un-mistakably connected to him, heart and soul. Destiny *had* played a part in their meeting, and now that she knew the truth, knew that he was simply a wounded man, not a murderer, Selene didn't intend to ignore it.

She couldn't move her arms or legs. Couldn't utter a word or a scream. Couldn't pull away the fingers tighten-ing around her throat. In a matter of minutes, she would die at the hand of some unknown assailant. When she saw the flash of a gold medallion, she realized he wasn't a stranger after all.

Selene bolted upright, gasping for air and shaking un-controllably. Her gaze zipped to the now-empty space once occupied by Adrien, her mind running rampant with the un-speakable possibilities. Had she given her heart to a mur-dering demon, not a fallen angel?

Adrien had said he was administrator of Chloe's trust, but would he stage an accident to claim her inheritance all because of greed? She refused to believe that her instincts about him had failed her completely, even as the disturbing images continued to play out in her mind while she dressed quickly in the clothes she'd so easily discarded the night before. But she didn't have time to make her escape before he came out of the bathroom wearing only a low-slung towel around his hips and a slight smile.

He leaned one shoulder against the wall and folded his arms across his bare chest. "Where are you going?"

Caught between walking into his arms and running away, Selene backed toward the door. "I thought I should get dressed before Ella comes home."

"She's already here."

That relieved Selene somewhat in case her concerns turned out to have merit—he'd murdered his own flesh and blood. "Good. I look forward to seeing how her trip went." And to demand answers. Beg for them if she had to.

When Adrien pushed off the wall, Selene backed up another step. "What's wrong, Selene?" he asked.

She didn't dare tell him about her visions. Didn't dare give her suspicions away. "Nothing's wrong. I'm just afraid Ella will catch me in your bedroom."

He released a low laugh. "As far as I'm concerned, she'll have to get used to it. I expect you to be in my bed from now on."

Last night, she would have given anything to hear him say that. But now, she didn't know what to think. "I'll see you later." Provided she wasn't forced to get out while she still could.

Without affording him another glance, Selene rushed into the hall bathroom and locked the door. She made quick work of her morning routine and when she hurried into her bedroom to dress, she noticed the message display flashing on her cell phone. One of her parents had tried to contact her only an hour ago, and although she was tempted to put off returning the call, she felt the need to make the connection with her family.

After collapsing onto the edge of the bed, she depressed the speed-dial number and her father immediately answered in his Southern-sophisticate tone.

"Hi, Dad. It's Selene. Sorry I missed your call."

"You're missing more than that, pumpkin. Your sister is in labor. She insisted I inform you immediately."

Hannah had been known for her bad timing, but perhaps in this instance, she'd displayed good timing. An excuse for Selene to leave. But would she have any peace at all if she didn't have the truth about Adrien before she returned home? No. "Have they said how long before the baby's born?"

"Last report from your mother, who by the way is still not speaking to you, the midwife said it could be several hours. Perhaps even tomorrow."

Not a surprise that her mother was still angry, something Selene would have to deal with later. "Then she's still determined to have the baby at home?"

"Yes, she is, although I have no idea why when hospitals and pain relievers are readily available in this day and time. Are you still in godforsaken Louisiana?"

Obviously Hannah had filled him in, which was okay since it saved Selene from explaining, although more questions were in the offing. "Yes, I'm still here." At least for now. "Tell Hannah good luck, and I'll be there as soon as I'm able."

As soon as she made the effort to find some answers. The decision to stay in Georgia for good, or return to Louisiana to be with Adrien, rested on what she discovered. The best place to begin was with the woman downstairs. And Selene had no time to waste.

* * *

"Welcome back, Ella."

Seated at a small desk in the kitchen, Ella glanced up from a stack of mail she'd been sorting. "Hello to you, too, Selene. I was beginning to think you'd left, considering it's almost noon and I hadn't seen you yet."

"Actually, I do have to leave for a couple of days. My sister's having her baby and I want to be there. But first, I need your help."

Ella stared at Selene over her half glasses. "I can hold down the fort while you're gone for a few days. Just let me know what I need to do."

Grabbing a nearby chair, Selene pulled it close to Ella. "This doesn't have anything to do with the restoration. It has to do with Adrien. I need to know what really happened to Chloe."

Ella turned back to the envelopes. "I've told you, I can't speak about that. I've given Adrien my word."

She touched Ella's arm to regain her attention. "Look, I know she suffered a fall while they were climbing and she died. Adrien told me that much. But I'm worried about what he's not telling me. I need to know if he's responsible for her death. If in fact it really was an accident."

"Why is this so important to you?"

"Because I care about Adrien. If he's done something horrible, I have to know."

Ella studied her a long moment. "You've fallen in love with him, haven't you?"

Denial seemed to be the best course, but Selene doubted she could pull it off. "I want to believe that it was only an accident. But my instincts are telling me there's more to it than that." Instincts she could no longer ignore.

"It *was* an accident, but that's only part of the story."

She sent Ella a pleading look. "Then tell me everything. Please."

Without commenting further, Ella pulled a key from a cubbyhole in the shelf above the desk, then slid it toward Selene. "In the room across from his. Second drawer in the nightstand. You'll find the answers there."

Selene went to her feet and laid a palm on Ella's shoulder. "Thank you," she said before she rushed out of the kitchen.

She hurried up the staircase, but the uncertainty over what she might discover in the drawer slowed her steps as she reached the dim hallway. When she noticed Adrien's door ajar, she assumed he had gone to his office. She *prayed* he had gone to his office.

While the bronze demon looked on with his treacherous eyes and frightening sneer, Selene fumbled with the key, dropping it twice before finally tripping the lock. She opened the door, expecting to find a room that housed treasured memories of Chloe. She found no keepsakes, no pictures, nothing that would indicate a young woman had resided there at all. Instead, she discovered a narrow hospital bed set lengthwise against one window, the nightstand Ella had mentioned beside it. And leaning against the wall at the end of that bed, a folded wheelchair.

Seeing the room only served to bring about more questions, not answers. She speculated that Chloe hadn't died in the accident and instead suffered some sort of paralysis. In order to confirm that fact, Selene walked to the nightstand and slid open the drawer to find several pieces of paper. Sketches, she realized when she lifted them from the bottom of the drawer, took at seat on the wooden floor and laid them on her crossed legs. Watercolor depictions of butterflies and trees, winged birds taking flight, including a little girl with dark curls running across what appeared to be the plantation's front lawn, with the house—painted all yellow—serving as a backdrop. But the saddest one of all featured a young woman, sitting profile in a wheelchair, her face covering her hands—the tragic portrayal of what Chloe had become. And below that, Selene came upon a note written in precise script.

Dear Adrien,
    I hate that I've become such a burden for you and Ella. But I hate leaving you both even more. Please don't make me do this. I'm not that strong.
    Forgive me,
    Chloe

More questions filtered into Selene's mind. Inconceivable questions. What had Adrien wanted his sister to do, and why was she asking his forgiveness? Had he tried to convince her that dying was the only way out, and she'd refused? Had he in turn taken her life to release her from her misery, or himself from the burden?

Needing more clues, Selene stood and opened the top drawer, the drawings and note still clutched in one hand. She found myriad medical supplies, including syringes and bottles, but the item in the corner drew all her attention. She lifted the photo from the drawer, a snapshot of Adrien and Chloe dressed in winter gear, snowcapped mountains surrounding them, their heads tipped together and energetic smiles on their faces. One thing Selene couldn't deny—this brother and sister loved each other very much. Yet something had gone terribly wrong....

"What in the hell are you doing in here, Selene?"

Ten

Selene nearly dropped everything when she turned to find Adrien standing in the open doorway, fury flashing in his blue eyes. She held up the pictures and note. "I was looking for these."

His gaze shot to the papers. "What did you expect to find?"

"Answers. I now know that Chloe lived through the accident, and that she ended up in a wheelchair. I still don't know what happened after that, and I need to know." She prepared to ask the question weighing heaviest on her mind, despite the possible fallout. "Did you have something to do with her death?"

If he was at all shocked that she'd asked, he didn't show it. "Yes."

Selene's worst fears had been realized. "What did you do to her?"

While he remained silent, another round of mental signals jumped into Selene's brain—Chloe in bed with her eyes closed, Adrien pulling her into his arms, his hands at her throat…checking for a pulse. And following that, the sound of Adrien's mournful moan so full of abject pain, it took her breath.

A heavy blanket of sadness settled over Selene. "Did she take her own life?"

He paced the room a few moments before pausing at the window and turning his back to Selene. "I've already endured a coroner's inquest, Selene. I don't need one from you."

"I'm only trying to put together what happened."

"My disregard caused her death. That's all you need to know."

"Adrien, you need to talk about it. You've carried it around for so long it's destroying you."

He remained silent for a while before he finally said, "Fine, I'll give you the details. But it's not the kind of thing you've faced in your safe world."

"I don't care. I need to know."

He turned toward Selene, all his emotions on display, from his red-rimmed eyes to his remorseful expression. "Chloe was quadriplegic, paralyzed from mid-chest down, with some use of her right hand. She could breathe on her own, at least for a time." He began to pace as he continued. "The day before she died, I insisted she needed to move closer to a hospital so she could have more intensive care because she wasn't getting better. In fact, she was getting worse. She didn't want to go, but I forced the issue."

"And after that?" she asked when he looked as if he might clam up again.

Again he turned his back on her, as if he couldn't quite face her with the rest of the facts. "Ella took care of her during the day, and every night I read to her until she fell asleep. I stayed up and watched her to make sure she was okay. But that night…" He lowered his head. "I was exhausted and I fell asleep. When I woke up, she wasn't breathing. I tried to perform CPR, but it was too late. I honestly believed she gave up."

Her heart heavy from the utter sorrow in his voice, Selene set the papers on the bed and moved behind him. "How long did you take care of her?"

"For two years." Although he had yet to face her, Selene took the mental journey with him as he continued. "In the evening, I took her for walks along the grounds so she could enjoy some fresh air. She liked to draw during those times and even though she struggled, she still managed to do what she loved most. But it wasn't enough. I didn't do enough to keep her fighting."

Selene disagreed. Her opinion of him had only elevated because of his sacrifice. And now she understood why he couldn't sleep, the extent of his pain that she felt as keenly as if it were her own. In many ways, it was. "Not many people would have made that commitment to someone, Adrien. You thought you were doing the right thing. You *were* doing the right thing."

He spun around, stormed to the bed and swept the papers off onto the floor. "If I'd stayed awake, I could have called the paramedics. She would still be alive."

Selene moved in front of him and laid her palm on his face. "Or it might have only delayed the inevitable. If her health was failing, no one could predict how long she would have lingered on."

He sighed. "She deserved more time."

"She deserved some peace. When are you going to stop blaming yourself?"

"I can't."

She slipped her arms around his waist. "Yes, you can. You have to. I know Chloe wouldn't want you to continue to live this way. No one expects you to forget her, but she's asked for your forgiveness. Can you forgive her?"

He closed his eyes briefly and when he opened them, Selene saw a hint of tears he seemed determined to hold at bay. "I already have forgiven her."

"Now you have to forgive yourself. She had no choice but to let you go, and now it's time for you to let her go, too."

"What I did to her is unforgivable. I failed her twice."

She laid her head against his chest, relieved when his arms came around her. "Chloe forgives you, Adrien. And I forgive you, too."

He framed her face with his palms and forced her gaze to his. "Come away with me, Selene. Away from this place. I only have to make one phone call and we can be anywhere in the world you want to go in a matter of hours."

It would be so easy for her to say yes. So easy to disregard her responsibility to her family to spend time with him. But she'd made a promise to Hannah. "I can't, Adrien. Not now."

He took a step back. "You're afraid of me. You're still not sure I'm telling you the truth."

"I know you're telling me the truth. I have to go home for a few days to be with Hannah while she has her baby. We can go away after that if you'd like."

The coldness in his eyes cut Selene's heart to the quick. "Go. Be with your family. They need you more than I do."

She wasn't so sure about that. "I won't be gone more than two days, Adrien. I promise."

"No promises," he said. "Stay in Georgia, Selene. You don't belong here. You sure as hell don't belong with me. I'll only bring you down."

A deep ache radiated from her heart as tears threatened to cloud her eyes. "You don't mean that."

He turned and walked back to the window. "Yes, I do."

She tried to tune into his thoughts but received nothing but blackness. No emotions. No latent regret. Nothing.

"You want me to walk away from everything we've shared?" she asked.

"We shared our bodies and time. That's all."

Selene's eyes clouded with tears but she refused to let them fall, even if something deep inside her did. "Maybe that's all it meant to you, but it meant more to me. Much more."

As the world Adrien had shown her crashed down around her, Selene headed for the door, her thoughts a jumble of confusion. Yet before she walked away for good, she decided to make a last stand. "You know, I've wondered why I didn't stay in Baton Rouge that first night when I arrived in Louisiana. I've wondered why I kept driving even thought it was late. Why I stopped in St. Edwards and didn't bother to leave that following day, or several days after that. Now I know why."

He turned and stared at her, his face a mask of stone. "To save me from myself?"

"No. To love you."

"Well, you've really done it this time, Mr. Morrell."

Adrien looked up from where he was seated on the cursed hospital bed to meet Ella's scorn. "You shouldn't have let her in here."

"You gave me no choice." Ella strode into the room and sat beside him. "She had to know the truth, that you aren't a monster. She loves you, Adrien, and you should accept that love. Accept that you love her, too."

He didn't want Selene to love him. And he didn't want to love her, but he did. "If you knew everything about her, you'd probably be glad she's gone."

"If you're talking about her mind-reading abilities, she told me before she left."

He bolted from the bed and walked to the window. "That doesn't make any sense."

"It makes perfect sense."

That drew Adrien around to face her. "You're an intelligent woman, Ella. You know as well as I do that reading minds sure as hell isn't logical."

Ella folded her hands in her lap. "I've also lived in this culture long enough to know it's possible. I've seen it. And I knew the minute she showed up on our doorstep that she was different. That she was here for a reason, otherwise I wouldn't have hired her because of her lack of experience."

Adrien gritted his teeth and spoke through them. "Damn you for buying into this crazy concept of fate."

Her expression remained emotionless, even when she said, "And damn you for dishonoring your sister by wallowing in self-pity."

"I don't want to hear this, Ella."

"Maybe not, but you're going to listen." She pushed off the bed and stood face-to-face with him. "We both made mistakes with Chloe, not realizing the extent of her decline and possibly doing too little too late. But we had good intentions. Selene did, too. She forced you to feel something other than guilt. She made you realize you're still a man and not some hollow shell. You might hate that, but you don't hate her. In fact, she is a part of you now. Now I want to know what you intend to do about it."

What the hell could he do? He'd already screwed everything up, destroyed any chance of being with her because of stupid pride. "Nothing. I told her to leave and she's not coming back."

"She'll be back if you ask her to come back."

God, he wanted that. More than he'd realized until that moment. "I have no idea how to get in touch with her."

"Good grief, Adrien. You can find anyone if you so choose." Ella looked thoughtful. "Or if she can read your thoughts as she's claimed she can, then I imagine she'll be able to know how you feel without you saying a word, even if you don't make a conscious effort. You can't stop thinking about her, even now. And you won't stop torturing yourself until you can finally tell her that you've made a mistake. A mistake you can't afford to make. Otherwise you will truly be damned to a life of loneliness. And Chloe would despise you for wasting your life."

Ella left Adrien alone then to ponder her words as well as feelings so deep that he felt as if he might suffocate. He did want Selene with him. He wanted all the things that he'd denied himself, including the love that Chloe had made him promise he would find after she was gone.

His thoughts of his remorse over his role in his sister's demise had been replaced by a biting regret over letting Selene go. If Selene had been telling the truth, that she could read his thoughts, then she would soon know that she had not left his mind for a moment. And she never would, even if he never saw her again.

"He's beautiful, Hannah." Selene looked up from the perfect little boy cradled in her arms to meet her sister's prideful expression. "What are you going to call him?"

"Trey, since he's Douglas the third."

"He looks like a Trey." To Selene, he looked like an angel. *An angel.* Her thoughts immediately turned to Adrien. Her own fallen angel. She tried to concentrate on the future, not the past, as she ran her fingertip down the baby's downy-soft cheek. "I don't know how you're going to handle having a little boy."

Hannah smiled. "I've always been able to handle boys, sis."

True, Selene thought, and she only wished she had been as skilled with men as Hannah had always been. Or at least the one man who continued to play upon her mind and heart like a favorite song.

When the baby stirred, Selene stood and laid him in the bassinet next to the bed. "You should get some rest while he's still sleeping. You look tired."

"You looked tired, too. Feel free to sleep in the guest room, unless you planned on staying with Mom and Dad."

"I hadn't really thought much about where I'll be staying." It suddenly hit Selene that she had no place to go. No real home to speak of. "I can stay here and help out with the baby as long as you need me."

Hannah frowned. "What about your job?"

"It's over." As was her relationship with Adrien, and that made her eyes begin to blur with unshed tears, just when she'd thought she'd had none left.

Hannah looked alarmed. "Oh no, sis. You didn't get fired, did you?"

Selene pinched the bridge of her nose briefly to try and thwart the threatening tears. "In a manner of speaking, yes."

"What are you going to do now?"

"I have no idea." All Selene could consider at the moment was a hot shower and a comfortable bed, though she doubted she would get much sleep. "I'll think about it tomorrow, just like a good Southern girl."

"You were always one to procrastinate, dear daughter."

At the sound of the genteel voice coming from behind her, Selene's frame went as rigid as the bedpost. She turned to discover Lynette Albright standing in the door clutching an overnight bag, looking every bit the prosperous society queen in her chic white suit, not a blond hair out of place in her perfect chignon, though it was well past the dinner hour.

Selene forced a slight smile around her discomfort. "Hello, Mother."

Lynette looked appropriately appalled. "Hello? That's all you have to say to me after you disappeared without a word?"

An argument with her matriarch was the last thing Selene needed tonight. "Look, Mother, I'm tired. Right now I only want to go to bed."

"Selene's staying in the guest room," Hannah said. "And since she'll be here, you can go home to Dad."

Lynette gave Hannah a scolding look. "I will do no such thing. You might need help during the night with the baby."

"I'm breast-feeding, Mother. I don't think you can help me with that since the whole concept of wet nurses went out with the dark ages."

Selene stifled a chuckle in spite of what awaited her—a long overdue sit-down with her mother. "Why don't you and I have a cup of chamomile tea before we go to bed, Mother? Hannah could use a little bonding time with the baby."

Still looking somewhat disgruntled, Lynette said, "Fine." She pointed at Hannah. "Don't hesitate to wake me if you need a break. I can still rock a baby even if I'm not lactating."

After Selene and Lynette doled out kisses to Hannah and little Trey, Selene followed her mother into Hannah's small kitchen. While her mother retrieved the cups, Selene put on the teakettle, a heavy silence hanging over the room. That silence continued until they were seated at the dinette, teacups in hand, though much had been left unsaid between them.

"Tell me about this job, Selene."

Not a topic Selene wanted to broach, but she might as well get it over with. "Actually, I was restoring an historical home. But I'm finished."

Lynette raised a thin eyebrow. "That was certainly fast. I assume there wasn't much to do then?"

So much more to do, and Selene hated that she wouldn't

be finishing the job. Hated even more that she would never see Adrien again. "I basically got the ball rolling and now someone else will take over." Maybe another woman. Someone else for Adrien to seduce. Someone else's heart for him to steal.

"What are you going to do now?" Lynette asked.

Selene shrugged. "I thought I'd put that degree to use that you and Dad paid for. Maybe go to work for an interior-design firm. Or maybe even start my own business specializing in historical restoration."

"Jan Myers has a nice shop downtown. I'm sure she'd love to have you. Would you like me to call her?"

"Jan is an interior decorator, Mother. What I do is a bit more extensive." When Lynette appeared hurt, Selene added, "But I appreciate the offer. And if it's okay, I could use a place to live for a while, until I find an apartment."

Her expression brightened. "Of course we'd love to have you. Your old room is still in order."

"Thank you. I won't stay too long." Selene released a humorless laugh. "It's sad, moving back home at my age."

"You know you're always welcome. You can stay as long as you'd like." Lynette stared into her cup for a long moment before turning her attention back to Selene. "I suppose I should apologize for giving you such grief over the divorce. But I had such high hopes for your marriage to Richard."

Selene took a quick sip of tea to wet her dry mouth. "It was more of a merger than a marriage, Mother. We didn't make each other happy."

"I know that now. All I've ever wanted for you and Hannah is your happiness." She sighed. "I wasn't happy about your sister's marriage to Doug, but it didn't take long to realize how much they love each other. And that, my dear, is much more precious than all the gold in Georgia."

Finally, her mother had come around to seeing that a

man's worth wasn't directly related to his bank account. "I know what you mean about that kind of love," Selene said as she focused on the floral painting across the room. "A love so strong you can't catch your breath whenever he comes into the room. And even when he's gone, you miss him so much you physically ache. You feel connected to him, as if he's a part of your soul."

Selene looked up to discover curiosity splashed across her mother's face. "I had no idea you felt that strongly about Richard, Selene."

"Not with Richard, Mother, and that was the problem. I loved someone else that way at one time." She still loved him, still longed for him. Still suffered because of that love, though she would never take a moment of it back.

Lynette laid her palm on Selene's arm. "You'll know it again, dear. Anything is possible."

Selene wanted to believe in the possibilities but right then she couldn't get past her recent loss. "I hope so." She stretched her arms above her head then dropped her hands into her lap. "It's definitely bedtime."

"Yes, it is. And I'm afraid you and I are going to have to share a bed."

Selene scooted back the chair and stood. "I can sleep on the sofa."

Lynette came to her feet. "That's not necessary. We can manage in the same bed. I remember many a night when you'd had a bad dream and crawled in between me and your father."

Selene smiled with remembrance of all the nights her mother had lulled her back to sleep with soft lullabies and soothing words. How terribly wrong that she had forgotten. "I'm a little bigger now."

"Yes, but your father won't be in bed with us, either, thank heavens. The man snores louder than a steam engine."

They shared in a laugh along with a few recollections of wonderful days gone by as they walked to the guest room. Selene realized that although her mother had always been quick with her opinions, she'd always been the same when it came to comfort. And before they settled in for the night, Selene thought about Adrien's estrangement from his mother, the forgiveness that might never come, and recognized her relief over bridging the gap with her mother.

Before they turned down the lights, she gave Lynette a long hug. "I love you, Mom."

The joy Selene witnessed in her mother's expression warmed her heart, which had felt so cold all day in spite of the summer heat. "I love you, too, Selene. And I'll love you even more if you don't steal the covers."

"I'll try to be good."

After Selene turned down the lights, her thoughts again turned to Adrien. And as she drifted off, he was once more the last thing on her mind. The last thing she saw.

Selene…

The sound of her name, said in a deep, desolate voice, sent Selene upright in bed as she frantically searched the room. For a moment, she was disoriented in time and place until awareness settled over her like the mists that blanketed the swamps at midnight. She wasn't back at the plantation; she was at Hannah's. Her mother, not Adrien, occupied the space beside her. Yet she could have sworn she had heard him, but apparently she'd been dreaming. Until she heard it again…

God, I need you….

Even hundreds of miles away, Adrien had managed to encroach into her mind. Not only could she hear his words, she could feel his anguish as intensely as if it were her own. It was.

She could ignore his pain, or she could return to Louisiana and force him to acknowledge what she knew to be true—they belonged together. She could prove to him that she didn't intend to leave him, as long as he welcomed her in his life. By doing so, she could meet imminent rejection, or she could come face-to-face with her future. A future with Adrien.

A strong sense of purpose drove Selene from the bed and, as quietly as possible, she dressed in a pair of jeans and a T-shirt. Apparently she hadn't been quiet enough because while tying her sneakers, she looked up from her perch on the edge of the bed to find her mother staring at her.

"It's four o'clock in the morning, Selene. Where are you going?"

"Back to Louisiana."

"What on earth for?"

"To take care of something that needs my attention." Namely, Adrien.

Lynette tossed back the covers and slipped on her robe. "It can't possibly wait for a few days?"

Selene stood and grabbed the overnight bag, shoving in what she'd unpacked, which hadn't been much. Maybe she'd known all along that she wouldn't be staying for any length of time. "No, it can't wait. It's important."

"More important than your sister? Your family?"

"*As* important." She ran a brush through her hair and then zipped the bag before facing her mother again. "Remember that speech you gave earlier about wanting us to be happy? And the one about never leaving unfinished business behind that you repeated several times while I was growing up?"

"Yes, but—"

"No buts. Now is not the time to take back your motherly platitudes. I have some unfinished business and it could directly relate to my happiness."

Lynette frowned in her usual fashion. "Does this have something to do with a man?"

Selene piled her hair atop her head and secured it with a plastic clip. "Yes, it does. A man I love so much that I'm willing to fight for him. For us."

"I can't talk you out of this?"

"No, you can't. It's something I have to do or I'll never have any peace." She slipped the bag's strap over one shoulder. "Please tell Hannah I stopped being so cautious and that I love her and I'll try to see her soon. She'll understand."

Lynette looked as if she didn't understand at all. "How long will you be gone?"

Selene gave her a quick hug and a kiss on the cheek. "That depends on him."

"Does this 'him' have a name?"

"Adrien Morrell."

"Is he a good man, Selene?"

"Yes, he is. But he doesn't realize it. At least not yet."

Lynette groaned. "Don't tell me. He doesn't have a penny to his name."

She smiled as she backed toward the bedroom door. "He has lots of pennies, Mother. But more important, he has my love, and as you've said, that's worth more than all the gold in Georgia."

By the time Selene reached the plantation at noon, she relied on the support of sheer adrenaline and the prospect of seeing Adrien again to keep her going. She left her keys in the ignition and her purse in the front seat in case he again sent her away. Now if she could just hang on to her courage.

As it had been that first day she'd arrived, Ella took her time answering the summons and, when she opened the door, she didn't appear at all shocked to see Selene. "I've been expecting you," Ella said, confirming Selene's speculation.

Selene strode past Ella and into the foyer. "Where is he?"

"In his office. Where else?"

"Good. I have to talk to him."

"Did your sister have her baby?"

"Yes. A boy. I'll tell you all about it later." She hooked a thumb over her shoulder. "I need to do this before I lose my nerve."

Ella waved her away. "Of course. I have to warn you, though. He's in a foul mood."

"That makes two of us."

Despite her exhaustion, Selene practically sprinted into the rotunda and up the stairs, calling, "Yes, I'm back," at Demon Giles over one shoulder as she headed toward Adrien's office.

She paused at the door, her hand gripping the knob, while she took a moment to consider what she would say. A moment to prepare for the possibilities. He could turn her away, causing her heart to cave in once more. Or he could finally admit that he loved her.

Without bothering to knock, Selene opened the door to find the room practically absent of light due to the closed curtains. But the area wasn't so dark that she couldn't see Adrien seated behind his desk.

She immediately crossed the room and tore open the curtains on one of the windows flanking his desk. "Before you say anything, I know you told me not to come back." She moved to the other curtain and yanked it open. "But I've realized a few things in my absence."

She rounded the desk, braced her hands on the wooden surface and leaned into them while he simply stared at her. "First, as you've said, I don't work for you. Second, I signed a contract, one that you prepared, I might add, and I plan to adhere to the terms. I'm not going anywhere until I return this house to what it once was."

After drawing a quick breath, she continued. "And furthermore, I refuse to let you keep playing the role of tragic hero. Chloe's death was horrible, but it wasn't your fault. She made choices, tough ones, just like I'm making the choice not to give up on you, even if you've given up on yourself."

When he failed to move, or to speak, she said, "Well, what do you think about this so far?"

He leaned back in his chair. "Don't let me stop you since you're obviously on a roll."

"Yes, I am. And I'm going to stay on a roll until I make you realize that nothing is beyond forgiveness when you love someone. And I do love you, even if you don't love yourself right now. We're good together and I'm going to prove it to you. And if you think I'm being the belle from hell now, just wait. I'm not going to let up until—"

God, I love you.

His silent declaration came to her as clearly as cut glass. "Say it out loud, dammit."

He shoved out of his chair and turned his back to her.
I can't do this, Selene. I can't do this to you.

That sent her around his desk where she grabbed his arm and yanked as hard as she could, turning him to face her. "Yes, you can do this. You only have to be honest and admit how you feel." She clutched the front of his shirt. "Please, Adrien. I have to hear you say it."

When he remained silent, she tipped her forehead against his chest, unwelcome tears rolling down her cheeks and dampening the front of his shirt. His arms came around her and he rested his lips against her ear. "I love you."

She lifted her face and met his gaze, finally seeing the emotion that she had craved so strongly. "I love you, too."

He cradled her head against him and held her tighter for a few more moments before he leaned back and studied her eyes. "Belle from hell?"

She laughed through residual tears. "Yes, and don't forget it."

He kissed her then, first her damp cheeks and finally her lips. After a time, he broke the kiss and rested his forehead against hers. "What are we going to do about this?"

She leaned back and smiled. "There's nothing to be done. We'll just go with it and see what happens."

"You're taking a huge leap of faith, Selene, believing in me."

"I believe in us, Adrien. And I'm not trying to save you because only you can do that. But I can be there every step of the way while you heal. And you will heal, I know it."

He looked at her with so much love in his eyes that Selene fought back another rush of tears. "For the first time in a long time, I think you're probably right."

She held him tightly. "That means we can take up where we left off, spending more quality time together, getting to know each other better, beginning right now."

"I have to leave this afternoon. I'm going to Los Angeles."

Selene experienced the bite of disappointment. "Is this a business trip?"

"In part, yes. My offices are in California. I've neglected several important projects, including a foundation I've set up in Chloe's name with her trust monies. It provides funding for spinal-cord-injury research."

"That's a wonderful tribute, Adrien. I'm sure she would be pleased."

"Yeah, she would. I have to spend a few hours in Florida first. I need to see my mother."

Selene was more than willing to sacrifice some time with him if he was willing to restore his relationship with his mother. "How long has it been since you've seen her?"

"Almost a year. She came to visit Chloe a few times to

try to convince her to go home with her, but I made sure I wasn't around. We didn't speak at the funeral."

"Then I think it's past time to mend fences."

He pressed another kiss on her lips. "And I want you to come with me."

Considering Selene's sudden euphoria, he could have told her he planned to hand her the moon and stars on a silver platter. Make that a gold platter. "What about the house? The contractor should begin work soon."

"Ella can take care of that until we return. Is your passport valid?"

Her confusion came out in a frown. "Yes, but last I heard, you don't need one for California, unless it's declared independence without my knowledge."

"I don't plan to spend more than a couple of days in L.A. After that, we can go somewhere exotic. I'm thinking Barbados."

Selene was thinking she must be hallucinating. "You're going to show me that beach you've talked about." The one she had seen through his thoughts.

He thumbed away one rogue tear from her cheek. "I'm going to make love to you on that beach."

"I'm looking forward to it, but I have two conditions. First, I never want to have to delve into your mind to know how you feel about me."

"I promise to tell you often. What's the second condition?"

"That we get rid of that darn demon in the hallway."

Adrien's laughter was pure music to Selene's ears. "What do you propose I do with him?"

"Well, if you'd kicked me out again, I would have made a very improper suggestion on where you could stick him. But since you've been most accommodating, I believe we'll just have to carry him up to the attic."

Adrien swept her up into his arms. "We'll do that later.

Right now I'm going to carry you to my bed and make love to you."

"Now that's new and different, making love in a bed." Selene checked her watch as they headed out the door. "What time does our flight leave?"

"Whenever I tell it to leave. We have a few hours to make up for the twenty-four we've been apart."

"That's twenty-four hours and twenty-two minutes, I believe. But who's counting?"

He sent her a devilish smile. "I am."

When they reached his bedroom, Adrien set Selene on her feet and gave her a thorough and highly suggestive kiss before he gave her the softest of smiles. "I'm going to show you the world as you've never seen it before."

As far as Selene was concerned, in many ways, he already had.

They made love with the bright sunlight streaming into the open windows, leaving nothing undisclosed, including Adrien's sadness as he finally grieved in Selene's arms, something that was long overdue.

During those precious moments, when she glimpsed the man she'd known had existed all along, Selene knew that she never wanted to leave Adrien's world again. And she never would.

Epilogue

Two years later

Maison de Soleil. The House of Sunshine.

The newly restored Louisiana plantation had proven to be Selene Winston Morrell's first step toward freedom—and a blessed life.

The facade had been painted white and yellow, not a speck of black to be found. Inside, the downstairs chambers had been restored to their original grandeur, the nursery upstairs now a family room, and the room across the hall that at one time had been a place of sadness had become Selene's sanctuary—the office where she now ran her design consulting business.

Although the successful restoration had been one of Selene's greatest achievements, her most treasured accomplishment could be found coming out the front door in Adrien's arms.

When father and daughter strolled toward the picnic table set out on the front lawn, Selene stopped gathering the last remnants of the birthday party to survey the scene. With her cap of dark curls and her eyes as blue as the summer sky above them, the little girl looked so much like her daddy that it made Selene's heart soar from pure joy. A precious child that had been born almost a year to the day from when Selene and Adrien had spontaneously exchanged marriage vows on a remote beach in Barbados.

After stuffing the paper tablecloth into the garbage can, Selene rounded the table, knelt down and held out her arms. "Come here, Chloe."

Adrien set the baby on her feet and she toddled across the lawn as fast her newfound steps allowed, her curls bouncing in time with her gait, a vibrant smile splashed across her round face. Their fiercely independent child who was so full of life, much like the young woman for whom she'd been named.

Selene swept her up into her arms and rested her face against the crown of her head. "You smell so good, sweetie. Did you have a nice bath?"

"Between keeping her in the tub and getting the icing out of her hair and ears, that bath was a challenge."

Selene looked up to meet Adrien's smile. "Your efforts earn you five stars in the good-daddy department."

Chloe yawned and laid her head against Selene's shoulder. "She's definitely tired," Selene said. "But at least she'll sleep for Ella on the trip to Shreveport."

Adrien frowned. "Are we sure we still want to do this?"

Selene had to admit she was already missing her daughter, but she still believed they could use the break. "We've talked about it nonstop since Ella made the offer. It's only for a week, and we have to let her out of our sight sooner or later."

Adrien rubbed a hand across his neck. "Yeah, you're right. Did your family leave already?"

"Just a few minutes ago. Did you speak with your mother?"

"She called earlier to wish Chloe a happy birthday, and to ask if she could take Chloe for a day or two this summer. I told her yes."

"I'm glad." Selene had hoped her mother-in-law might come to the party, but at least Adrien had begun to communicate with her again, and she wanted to get to know her granddaughter. "Well, everyone has left except—"

"Come give your uncle Jeb a kiss goodbye, honey."

The request had barely left the man's lips before Chloe was wriggling out of Selene's grasp to head toward Ella's SUV.

Adrien came to Selene's side and slid an arm around her waist as they watched their daughter climb into Jeb's wheelchair, something else she had recently learned.

"She loves him so much," Selene said, a hint of melancholy in her tone.

"Yeah. He's definitely been a good surrogate grandfather to her."

"You know, in a way it makes me sad that she might not remember him after he's gone. But then that might be a good thing because it's going to be so hard to let him go when the time comes."

"We'll just have to hang on to the good memories."

Something Adrien had learned over the past two years, much to Selene's relief. "You're absolutely right about that."

Adrien gave her a slight squeeze. "Besides, he's made it this long, he could last another five years or so."

Selene wanted to believe that, but she sensed that Jeb's time on earth might be coming to a close though he'd managed to stay around even after the restoration had been finished. And while she was pregnant. And after Chloe's birth. "I better go rescue him before your daughter chokes him to death with his own bow tie."

"Why is it she's always *my* daughter when she does something wrong?"

"Because that is the mother's law, according to me."

After sending Adrien a smile to counter his scowl, Selene walked over to the wheelchair and crouched beside it. "Chloe, don't chew on Uncle Jeb's tie."

Jeb rested a hand on the baby's head. "She's not hurting me, Miss Selene. In fact, she makes me feel like a younger man again. That's what new life does to a person."

Selene couldn't agree more. She'd quickly learned the healing power of a child, and of love. Although at times Adrien still withdrew, his moments of grief had lessened greatly since their marriage, and even more so since Chloe's birth.

Ella walked up with a large purple bag hanging from one shoulder. "Are we ready to get on the road now?"

"If you don't mind, Miss Ella, I'd like to have a private word with Miss Selene," Jeb said.

Ella lifted Chloe from his lap. "I'll just take the little one to say bye-bye to her daddy."

Chloe immediately curled her fingers into a wave and repeated, "Bye-bye."

Jeb waved back. "Live well, girl child. You are a gift to this world."

A lump formed in Selene's throat when she realized Jeb could be saying goodbye for good. While Adrien strolled around the yard with his daughter, and Ella loaded several things into the back of the SUV, Selene pushed Jeb's wheelchair across the lawn to the grove of pecan trees and stopped beneath the one that housed his childhood fort. After setting the brake, she knelt in front of him once more. "What is it, Jeb?"

He released a long sigh. "I spoke with Miss Chloe earlier today."

"I know. She's really starting to talk now."

"Not the baby. Mr. Adrien's sister."

Selene kept a calm demeanor despite her surprise. "Where did you see her?"

"In the place with all the angels while I was looking at her picture that hangs next to Miss Grace. She wanted me to give you a message."

Some might claim this was nothing more than the ramblings of an old man, but she knew better. "What did Chloe say?"

"She said thank you for bringing her brother back to life, for loving him and that she's going home now."

In so many ways, Adrien had returned her to life, too. A better life. Not always perfect, but pretty darned close. "I appreciate you passing that on."

He sighed. "I'm tired, Miss Selene. I'm ready to go home, too."

"I know. It's been a long day."

"I meant I'm ready to see my family in my glory home."

She laid her palm on his careworn cheek, her eyes misty. "I understand. But I'm going to miss you."

Jeb thumbed a tear away from Selene's cheek. "Now don't you cry for me, Miss Selene. I've had a good life, and you will, too. Take care of that baby girl and that man of yours. He relies on your love to keep him grounded."

"I rely on him, too."

"Of course you do, because it was his destiny to understand you. And yours to love him."

She stood and leaned to give him a long hug. "And I didn't ignore it."

As the warm breeze whispered around them and the locusts called to each other, Selene took her time wheeling

Jeb back to the awaiting vehicle. He'd become such an integral part of their lives that each parting had become more difficult for fear it might be the last time she enjoyed his presence.

But when she turned to him one last time, he gave her a wink and a smile. "Don't look so sad, Miss Selene. I don't know exactly *when* I'll be called home, so if I could have one more piece of Miss Ella's peach pie, I might be persuaded to make at least one more Sunday dinner. Or several."

Selene grinned. "I think that can be arranged in the near future."

While Adrien helped Jeb into the front seat and Ella stored the wheelchair in the rear of the SUV, Selene leaned through the open door to say goodbye to her daughter. She double-checked the car seat's strap then kissed Chloe's soft cheek. "You be good for Ella, sweetie. Mommy and Daddy will see you in a few days."

Chloe responded by popping her thumb in her mouth, her eyes looking as heavy as Selene's heart felt.

Ella slid into the front seat and shifted toward Selene. "She'll be fine, *shâ*. She'll have a good time playing with my new grand-niece."

"I know she'll be fine. But call if she's too fussy and you need us to pick her up. And be sure to call when you get there."

Ella presented her usual wily grin. "I'll call and let the phone ring once to let you know I've arrived, in case you are otherwise preoccupied."

Selene started to ask what she meant, but she already knew. And she did intend to be preoccupied with her husband for hours on end.

After giving both the baby and Jeb one last kiss and hug, Selene backed up and closed the door. She waved as she watched her daughter leave the plantation for the first time without her. But only the first of many times until she left for good to be her own person. At least that wouldn't happen any time soon.

Adrien circled his arms around Selene's waist and pulled her back against him. "I'm worried about her driving."

Selene looked back at him and frowned. "Ella's a good driver. Much better than you, in fact."

"I meant Chloe's driving."

She pulled his arms tighter against her and laughed. "Unless Ella's going to let her take the wheel as soon as they pull onto the interstate, I think we have about fifteen years or so to worry about that."

"It will be here before we know it."

So true, Selene thought. The past two years had practically flown by, yet she'd stored every memory in the haven of her heart.

After the vehicle disappeared from sight, she turned to find Adrien sporting a somber expression. "What's wrong, Adrien? And don't make me climb into that mind of yours to find out." Something she had promised not to do, and she hadn't, though he still tended to send out mental signals, especially when he wanted her, and that had been often.

"Nothing's wrong. I was thinking how much she would have loved you. How much you would have loved her."

Selene didn't have to ask who "her" was. "If she was anything like her brother, that's definitely true." She rose up on tiptoe and kissed his lips. "Now that we have a whole week of free time, how do you propose we spend it?"

"In bed."

She couldn't help but tease him a little. "Well, considering your daughter inherited your insomniac ways, we could probably use a few good nights' sleep."

He pulled her against him and kneaded her bottom with his palms. "That's not what I meant and you know it."

"I know no such thing because the only time we utilize the bed is to sleep."

He ran his tongue along the shell of her ear. "Okay, then let's go to the blue parlor."

She shivered. "We've been there. In fact, I believe we've been in every room at least once, if not twice since they were complete."

Adrien donned the look that had enchanted her from the moment she'd met him. "Have you ever made love against a tree, Mrs. Morrell?"

"Yes, Mr. Morrell. And I'd prefer the red room to bark burns."

"Then the red room it is." He grinned. "As long as you agree to something first."

"You know I'm always open to all the possibilities."

"Would you be open to having another baby?"

Since they hadn't really talked about another child, Selene was more than open to discuss it now. "I would not be opposed to having a son, especially if he looks like me since our daughter doesn't."

Adrien shook his head. "I prefer girls. They're much more interesting and complex than the male species."

"Adrien, you are anything but simple." He still retained that complexity, a riddle Selene might never solve, yet that mystery kept her on her toes, and their relationship as exciting as it had been since the day they'd met.

Following a down-and-dirty kiss and a few suggestive touches, Adrien said, "Why don't we take this inside and start on that baby?"

She squeezed his bottom. "Best idea you've had all day. You can play the tortured hero and I'll be the belle from hell."

"We can play it out however you want to, babe, as long we play."

As they headed into their house, arms around waists, Selene realized how very far they had come, from sullen sadness to easy laughter. From the shadows into the sunshine. As he'd promised, Adrien had taken her to special places, both outside and inside his private world. But most importantly, he had shown her his heart that had finally begun to heal, as well as the absolute power of love.

* * * * *

If you enjoyed this book, don't miss the next in the RICH & RECLUSIVE *mini-series.* Forced to the Altar *by Susan Crosby is available in May 2007.*

A SINGLE DEMAND

by

Margaret Allison

MARGARET ALLISON

was raised in the suburbs of Detroit, Michigan, and received a BA in political science from the University of Michigan. A former marketing executive, she has also worked as a model and actress. The author of several novels, *At Any Price* marked her return to the world of romance after taking some time off to care for her young children. Margaret currently divides her time between her computer, the washing machine and the grocery store. She loves to hear from readers. Please write to her c/o Silhouette Books, 233 Broadway, Suite 1001, New York, NY 10279, USA.

For Melissa Jeglinski, with gratitude

One

Cassie Edwards sank her feet into the sand and sipped her piña colada as she watched the man pouring drinks behind the bar. He reminded her of the prince from Cinderella—tall, almost regal looking, with dark-brown hair, and eyes framed by crinkly laugh lines. He had the physique of an athlete and was wearing a soft linen shirt tucked into a pair of faded jeans.

Although she had not spoken a word to him, she felt a connection, a magnetism that made it difficult to look away. She couldn't help but fantasize what it would be like to be with such a man. How it would feel to touch him. To kiss him. To belong to him.

What had gotten into her?

Cassie glanced around the restaurant. It was situated directly on the beach, an open-air saloon framed in little white lights, complete with a tiki bar and waiters and waitresses wearing Hawaiian shirts. It seemed to be a mecca for romance. Couples were everywhere, holding hands, kissing, cuddling together. It was enough to make even the die-hard cynic a little sentimental.

Cassie felt the sting of loneliness. The Bahamas, she thought, was not the place to mend a broken heart.

But she couldn't think about her ex-fiancé right now. Nor could she allow herself a harmless flirtation. She had not come here in search of love.

She had come to meet with Hunter Axon, one of the most ruthless corporate raiders in the world.

It was a strange assignment for a woman with no business expertise, a woman who was employed as a weaver in an old historical mill.

"Can I bring you another piña colada?"

Cassie glanced up. A tingle ran down her spine as she recognized the bartender she had been admiring. As she stared into his deep, brown eyes, she felt the rest of the world fade away. What was he doing at her table? He wasn't her waiter. Cassie shook her head. "No. No, thank you."

The man hesitated a moment. Then he nodded toward her camera. "Have you taken many pictures?"

He was flirting with her.

Unfortunately, Cassie didn't really know how to flirt. She had never had much of an opportunity. Cassie's and Oliver's families had chosen them for each other ever since they were born two days apart at the same hospital. Growing up, all of the boys back in Shanville, New York, knew she was Oliver Demion's girl. She was off-limits.

Cassie felt a rush of nerves. How did people do this? "No," she mumbled. *What?* "I mean yes."

The man smiled. "Have you been down to the reefs?"

She shook her head. "I haven't had time. I've just taken pictures of the beach. I prefer abstract photos, the kind that capture the essence not the reality. Do you know what I mean? The radiance but not necessarily the, um…" The what? Why was she talking like the nutty professor?

"You're a serious photographer."

She laughed. "No. At least, not anymore. I went to school to study the arts but I dropped out before I graduated." Because my grandma got sick and I had to return home to help her. So I went to work in the mill my fiancé owned and then he dumped me right before he sold the company that everyone in town worked for. Aren't you glad you asked?

Fortunately she kept those details to herself. "It's just a hobby now."

He paused for a moment, looking at her. She felt as if he was studying her, almost undressing her with his eyes. Dear God, he was handsome! She swallowed and shifted her eyes.

"Let me know if there's anything else."

"Right," she said meekly. Was she supposed to say something else? Invite him to sit down? But she couldn't. Or could she?

After all, she reminded herself for the umpteenth time that day, she was not engaged anymore.

But she still felt guilty. And it had nothing to do with her past relationship. It had to do with the reason she had come to this exotic locale in the first place.

She glanced back toward the bartender. How could she have fun when she knew the devastation her friends were about to face? How could she relax when she knew she would have to return to Shanville and disappoint everyone?

How had she ended up in this predicament?

Until a few months ago, she'd thought she'd known exactly who she was and where she was headed. She was engaged to be married. She had a job she loved, a community and town she adored. But life had thrown her a curve ball. In the blink of an eye, everything changed.

In retrospect Cassie should not have been surprised that Oliver broke off their engagement. After all, their relationship had been riddled with problems ever since he took control of the mill. She would've broken off their engagement years ago if she hadn't been afraid of upsetting her fragile grandmother. But it had been her grandmother's wish that she marry Oliver. Her grandmother had claimed that their engagement was the one thing that brightened her days.

It wasn't that she didn't love him. She had grown up with him.

They'd gone to school together and spent their summers working side by side at the mill. But when Oliver took over the helm of the mill, he changed. He became obsessed with money. It became obvious to Cassie that Oliver had big dreams—dreams that did not involve owning a small mill.

In hindsight the writing had been on the wall. Oliver may have talked a good game, but as her grandmother always said, actions speak louder than words. Oliver's actions ultimately proved that he did not want to marry a small-town girl who worked as a weaver in his family's textile mill. And he would never be happy living in Shanville. Oliver was destined to seek love and fortune elsewhere.

But as obvious as Oliver's feelings toward her might have been, Cassie never guessed how deeply he disdained Shanville. She had also never guessed that Shanville would one day be destroyed by one of its own.

But that was exactly what had happened. Oliver had mismanaged the mill so badly he had brought it to the brink of financial ruin. Then, just when she thought things couldn't get worse, he betrayed Shanville and the people who loved him. He announced he was selling the mill—the pillar of their community, the employer of generations of Shanville residents—to Hunter Axon.

Hunter Axon. A corporate raider who had made a fortune taking advantage of others' misfortunes. He was famous for taking over small businesses, firing the workers and closing the factories, moving production overseas.

The sale had caught everyone unaware, even Cassie. How had Oliver arranged this? How had he convinced Hunter Axon to buy a small textile mill that hadn't seen a profit in years?

It took some research, but she finally found her answer. Bodyguard.

Oliver had stumbled upon a patent the mill owned for Bodyguard, a soft, absorbent material. A material, he realized, that would be perfect for athletic wear. And instead of using the patent to turn the mill's fortunes around and make amends, Oliver had gotten greedy.

She had tried to convince Oliver to keep the mill and just sell the patent, but he refused. The mill was as good as sold; the deal done.

So Cassie had no choice but to try to meet with Hunter Axon himself. She was convinced that the mill's fortunes could be turned around if it was allowed to produce the patented fabric.

Cassie had cashed out her meager bank account and flown to the Bahamas to try to talk to him. But her mission hadn't been as simple as it sounded. Hunter's receptionist had refused her an audience with her boss. Desperate, Cassie had even gone to his house, but was once again refused entry. In the two days she'd been in the Bahamas, she had not so much as caught a glimpse of the elusive man.

Now, on the eve of her departure, she was forced to face the truth: she had failed. Demion Mills was doomed to become just another deserted warehouse, its beautiful old looms designated to museums or scrapped for parts.

Cassie picked up her bill. Twenty-four dollars. Twenty more than she should have spent. After all, she only had thirty left, and she needed cab fare for tomorrow morning. She knew she shouldn't have splurged on eight-dollar piña coladas, but she couldn't help herself. She glanced back toward the aquamarine water and set the bill back down. A warm breeze swayed the graceful palm trees that flanked the beach. Perhaps, she thought, she could afford to stay just a few more minutes.

She picked up her empty glass and popped a half-melted ice cube into her mouth. Sinking back down in her chair, she stared at the fiery red sun sinking into the Atlantic.

"Can I buy you a drink?" asked a husky voice.

Cassie almost jumped out of her chair. But it was not her hunky bartender. It was a blond-haired, portly gentleman sporting a sunburn that outlined the shape of sunglasses, making him look like a red raccoon.

"No, thank you," she said. She swallowed the cube. "I was just leaving."

"What's a beautiful girl like you doing all alone?"

"Excuse me?"

"It's a crime, that's what it is. But I have good news. You're not going to be alone any longer." He flashed a thumbs-up sign to some men sitting at the bar. They were snickering and laughing, giving him the thumbs-up back in encouragement.

"If you'll excuse me," she said, "I have to get going."

"Oh, come on," he said. "Let us buy you another drink."

"No, but thank you."

She opened up her wallet, and before she could stop him, he had reached over and pulled out her license. "Miss Edwards of 345 Hickamore Street. Shanville, New York."

"Give that back to me, please."

"You're a long way from home, Miss Edwards."

"I asked for that back." She stood up and glanced around. The music had picked up, and although there were quite a few tables around her, the patrons seemed too busy with each other to notice.

He raised the license above his head. He glanced at his friends at the bar. They snickered and laughed, encouraging him. "For a kiss," he said. Before Cassie could move away, he had grabbed her by the waist. "One kiss."

"Is there a problem?" said a voice from behind.

The man dropped his hands. Cassie turned around and found herself staring into the deep, brown eyes of her bartender.

"No problem," the blond man said.

The bartender's eyes narrowed as he crossed his muscular arms against his chest. He was an intimidating figure with an inherent air of authority.

"The lady here just dropped her license. That's all," the man said, flicking Cassie's license toward the table. His eyes darted nervously toward his friends. They were still at the bar but were staring down at their drinks, pretending not to notice the drama unfolding only feet away.

The bartender's eyes blazed. It was obvious he didn't like being lied to. He took another step toward the man and said in a lethal voice, "I want you out of here now. I prefer to avoid a scene. However," he said, unfolding his arms, "if it's necessary—"

Before he could finish, the man swung a punch. But the bartender was too fast. Like a trained fighter, he spun around and grabbed the man by the lapels, lifting him off the ground. "I'm not going to ask you nicely again."

"Okay," the man said, raising his hands in surrender. "I give."

The bartender set him back down. The man glanced toward the bar. His friends had disappeared. "Some vacation," he mumbled, stumbling away.

Cassie could feel the bartender's eyes on her once again. "Are you all right?" he asked gently.

"Fine," she said. Her camera was sitting on top of the table, its lens cap off. She glanced back at the bartender. Despite her scuffle, all she could think about was his deep, brown eyes. She didn't think she had ever seen eyes so intense.

"You're welcome to use the house phone if you'd like to call someone."

"Call someone?"

"Someone to pick you up. Drive you home."

"No," she said.

"All right, then," he said. "I'll call you a cab."

She remembered the lack of cash. "No, I'm staying close. I'll just walk."

Actually, it was not close at all. After her unsuccessful attempts at meeting with Axon, she had gone back to the motel, a sorry-looking building blocks from the beach. But she couldn't see spending her last night in the Bahamas cooped up in a small, dark room, so she had walked the beach, stopping to photograph anything and everything that caught her fancy: a woman braiding hair, an old man selling shell necklaces, a young child splashing in the waves.

How far away was that hotel, anyway? A half hour? An hour?

She was distracted by a loud holler from down the beach. In the distance she could see her perpetrator. He had rejoined his friends and they were jumping up and down and hollering, making lewd gestures at a group of women.

"I'll see you home," the bartender said. She turned back toward him. He was watching the men. "Where are you staying?"

She hesitated. She suddenly realized she could not tell him where she was staying. Nor did she want him to see her to her hotel. She didn't know him. And although only minutes earlier she had been dreaming about a seduction, the truth of the matter was she was still Cassie Edwards, the town Goody Two-shoes. The twenty-three-year-old virgin. The fiancée of Oliver Demion.

Make that ex-fiancée.

"Thank you for your help, but I'll be fine." No, she could not have him see her home. But there was one thing she desired of him.

He was staring at her, not saying a word.

She picked up her camera. "Would you mind if..." She hesitated.

"If what?"

"If I took your picture?"

He looked at her as if it was the first time anyone had ever asked for such a thing.

"I'll be quick," she said.

"Sure," he said. He stood still, not moving.

She looked through the lens and focused. He stared directly at the camera, looking at her with an intense, yet almost amused expression.

She snapped the photo and smiled. "Great. Thank you."

He shrugged. "No problem."

She wondered if he was just going to stand there until she left. She opened her purse and took out the money. She set it on the table. "Like I said, I'm a photography buff," she began. "Ever since I got my first camera I—"

But she was talking to the wind. He was gone.

She glanced around the bar. There was no sign of him. It was as if he had disappeared into thin air. She sighed. She had a chance and she blew it. What had she been thinking?

With one last glance toward the bar, she turned to leave. Suddenly she stopped. Her bartender was less than fifty feet away. He was leaning against a palm tree, his hands tucked in his pockets as he stared at the water.

She found herself suffering from yet another case of nerves.

Should she hurry by as if she hadn't noticed him? Or should she try and strike up a conversation?

He turned around. He smiled, almost as if he had been waiting for her. "Which way are you headed?" he asked.

There was something about his sweet, crooked smile that made her mind turn to mush and her heart beat faster. "That way," she said, nodding toward her left.

He said, "Me, too. Do you mind if I walk with you a bit?"

She laughed nervously. "Sure."

He stopped. "You do mind, or you don't?"

"I don't mind," she said quickly. He grinned. They began walking again.

She wasn't sure if his being there was a coincidence or not. She almost hoped it wasn't. She stole a peek at him out of the corner of her eye, and when she saw him looking at her, she blushed and glanced away. She realized they did not even know each others' names. But for some reason, it didn't seem to matter. She was content to escape her life and identity, if only for a while.

"Are you in the Bahamas for business or pleasure?" he asked.

"Business," she said.

"What do you do?"

She hesitated. "I'm a…" She paused. She did not want to talk about the mill. Not tonight. Not in this magical, beautiful place. Tonight she was Cinderella at the ball.

He said, "You don't have to tell me if you don't want to."

"I'm in town for a meeting."

"A meeting? Sounds mysterious."

"I assure you it's not." She smiled at him. "So," she said, quickly changing the subject, "I noticed you working the bar. How long have you lived here?"

"About ten years," he said.

"What a nice place to live."

"It can be." He stopped at a small marina and said, "I have to check on a boat. If you're not in a hurry, perhaps you'd like to come with me?"

Once again she found herself hesitating. Part of her would

have liked nothing better than to spend as much time with him as possible, but the other part was telling her she should leave while she still had her wits about her.

He said, "I should admit that I lied to you. I'm not going to let you walk home by yourself. It's not safe for a woman to walk this beach by herself after sunset."

She glanced down the beach. She could hear some male voices. Did they belong to the raccoon man and his friends?

It would be ridiculous to take a chance walking the beach by herself. But then again, wasn't it equally ridiculous to accept a stranger's invitation to his boat?

But was she ready to say goodbye? Besides, as he said, she didn't have much choice. She was not getting rid of him in either case. Not that she wanted to. Not by a long shot. "Thank you," she said.

She followed him down the dock. The boats seemed to increase in size as they walked. He stopped at the last and largest yacht. "There she is."

When he climbed aboard and held out his hand, she accepted his help. She jumped onboard and looked around. "Wow," was all she could say.

It was not only the size that was impressive. The boat looked brand-new. Everything seemed to sparkle with polish—the floors, the doors. It exuded wealth, from the rich mahogany of the hull to the beautiful cushioned deck chairs.

It was the type of boat that looked as if a tuxedoed butler might appear at any moment. The type of boat that was bought and sold with a crew. "Does somebody actually own this thing?"

He nodded and smiled. "Somebody actually does."

"Do you crew on this?"

He hesitated. "When needed."

"I bet that's a nice job."

He laughed. It was the first smile she had seen since they'd left the bar. "It beats sitting at a desk."

"Where is everybody?"

"There's only one crew member that actually lives onboard, and he's visiting his mother in Ohio this week."

"And the owner doesn't live onboard, I take it."

"No," he said. Once again he flashed his crooked smile.

"Mind if I take a look around?" she asked.

"I'll give you the guided tour."

She followed him through a pair of mahogany doors and into a galley. The cabins looked as if they were out of the pages of *Architectural Digest*, each grander than the previous one. At a bedroom door she stopped. She went over to the drapes and felt the material. "Jacquard silk lampas," she said, not realizing she was speaking out loud.

"What?"

"This material is woven by hand," she said. "It's very expensive."

"How do you know that?"

She blushed. How did she know that? Because she spent her days at a loom, making that exact material. "I've photographed it." She ran her hands over the sleek, heavy silk. "It has a wonderful texture."

"You really *are* a serious photographer."

She shook her head. "No. Not anymore."

"Not anymore?"

"When I was growing up, I thought I wanted to be a photographer. I took pictures of everyone and everything."

"Sounds interesting."

She nodded. "I was an arts major in college."

"But?"

"But life intervened. My grandmother got sick."

"And you never went back?"

"No. She needed me. And then when she didn't… Well, things had changed."

"That's too bad."

"No," she said. "I'm happy with my life and the path I've taken. It may not have been the path I thought I would choose, but I have no regrets." She looked at him and smiled. "I don't believe in them, anyway, do you?"

"Regrets?" He shook his head. "Not tonight, at least." He grinned.

Not tonight? She pondered the meaning as she followed him back out the galley and onto the deck. "That's it," he said, turning around to face her.

"No swimming pool?" she teased. "No grand ballroom?"

"I'm afraid not."

She shrugged her shoulders. "I guess it's okay."

His smile faded. For a second she thought she had offended him. He did know she was being sarcastic, right?

"Are you in a hurry?" he asked.

She shook her head.

He nodded toward the lounge chair. "Why don't you have a seat and I'll get us something to drink. What would you like?"

"Are you sure it's all right?"

Once again he smiled. "Yes. Do you like champagne?"

She nodded.

He came back carrying a bottle and two glasses. He opened it up and poured some into a flute. "Cheers," he said, handing it to her.

She took a sip as she leaned back in her chair and breathed in the warm, salty air. "This is nice," she said. "I almost wish I didn't have to go home tomorrow."

"Where's home?"

"New York," she said.

"Is that where your family lives?"

"Lived," she said. "My parents died when I was young. I was raised by my grandparents. My grandfather died about ten years ago and my grandmother…" She hesitated. "A few months ago."

"I'm sorry," he said. There was a tenderness in his eyes that made her feel like crying. "That must be hard for you."

"Yes," she said. She was suddenly tempted to tell him her whole sad story, but she stopped herself. She did not want to tell him about Oliver, nor did she want to tell him about the mill and the horrible Hunter Axon. She wanted to forget about all that, at least for tonight. She stopped talking and focused on drinking.

"You're not married."

She took another sip and said, "I almost was."

"Almost?" he repeated, refilling her glass.

Oh geesh, she just couldn't help herself. Why would she bring up her broken engagement? Didn't she have anything happy to say? Anything fun? "I was engaged but it didn't work out."

"So that's another reason why."

"Why what?"

"Why you looked so sad tonight."

"Tonight?"

"I was watching you."

He had been watching her. Was he…interested in her? "You were watching me?"

He nodded. "You looked like you were ready to cry."

No, he was not interested. He was a nice guy who was feeling sorry for her. Pity was not often a precursor to lust. She shook her head. "I might have been thinking about my grand-mother, but I wasn't thinking about *him*—at least, not like that."

"I'm sorry," he said.

"No more 'I'm sorrys,'" she begged. "Please. I'm beginning to feel like a pity case. Anyway, I'm over him. I am. I think everything happens for a reason."

"I agree," he said, nodding. "But it's still never easy saying goodbye to someone you cared about."

She sighed. "True. But sometimes exes can do things that make it a little easier."

"Like?"

"Like leaving you for another woman." Oh damn. There she went again. Couldn't she keep it buttoned up for two seconds?

No. It was not only the alcohol but the anonymity that was getting to her. The ability to talk to someone she would never see again. Someone who did not know her or Oliver, or their situation.

He was staring at her. "He left you for another woman?"

Her name was Willa Forchee. She was about ten years older than Oliver and worked as a vice president for Axon Enterprises. Cassie had met her several times and thought she seemed just as mean and vindictive as her boss was reported to be. In any case, Oliver admitted they had been involved for months. He claimed to be in love for the first time in his life.

Ouch.

But Cassie had not spent much time wallowing in the self-pity of a jilted lover. Every ounce of energy was used up in anger over the mill and herself for not stopping Oliver sooner.

"I'm sorr—" he began.

She put a finger to his lips to silence him. "No more 'I'm sorrys.' Please."

He took her finger away. But he did not let go. He began stroking it. Softly and gently. Even though it was a simple, tender act, it took her breath away. It was far more sensual than a kiss. And so intimate. What was happening? They didn't even know each other.

"What about you?" she asked as casually as she could manage. "Are you married? Have a girlfriend?"

He shook his head. "Neither. I work too much."

His gaze was as soft as a caress. He was still stroking her finger, as if stoking a gently burning fire. She swallowed and said, "You must meet tons of women at the bar. It seemed like the place was really hopping."

"I don't typically date women I meet at the bar."

"Typically?"

"There's an exception to every rule."

He had a mischievous twinkle in his eye. She, apparently, was the exception. It was enough to make her smile inwardly and out. He let go of her finger. "Are you hungry?" he asked. "You didn't eat anything at the bar."

Right. She had spent her dinner money on cocktails. And she didn't regret her decision. Not one bit. After all, she reasoned, a girl had to have priorities. "A little."

"Let's see what's in the kitchen."

She followed him into a large and sparkling galley kitchen. Every appliance was top of the line. "Nice dishwasher," she said.

"Thank you," he said, with mock sincerity. "That's the first time I've heard that."

"My dishwasher just died," she said. "So I'm particularly sensitive right now." Her dishwasher had joined a long list of dead appliances—her toaster oven, her cooktop and her washing machine. She looked around the kitchen. "The people who own this nice dishwasher, where are they?"

He looked at her and hesitated. "Standing in front of you."

"What?"

"I own this boat."

She started laughing. So he was funny, too. Smart and funny. A nice combination. "So you probably cook a lot in this kitchen."

"No," he said. "Usually my chef cooks for me."

She laughed again. When was the last time she had had this much fun? She couldn't remember. It had been a long time since she and Oliver had enjoyed each other's company. But it wasn't always that way. They had grown up the best of friends, enjoying the beautiful town they lived in. In the winter they went ice skating and in the summer they fished and swam in the creek.

Oliver had proposed while they were still in high school and she had accepted. But after Oliver started college, he changed. It was subtle at first. He was no longer satisfied to make a quiet dinner and stay in. Only an expensive restaurant would suffice. And that was not the only change. The boy who had grown up in jeans and a T-shirt began wearing designer clothes and getting manicures. His conversation always returned to money: who had received what job offer with what benefits, who was driving what new car.

Her grandmother had defended him. "He's growing up," she'd said. "Every man goes through it."

But it was more than that, Cassie realized now. They had been growing apart. And the distance had not been entirely due to Oliver.

She still cared about him, of course. She always would. But her love for him was that of a sister toward a brother. She had been more than happy to accept his distance, more than happy to date like a couple from the eighteen hundreds. Social calls that consisted of a glass of iced tea or two in the backyard.

At one point she questioned their youthful decision to marry. But Oliver had been adamant. He persuaded her they were destined to be together, that their decision to marry was still sound.

In retrospect, his were the words of someone who was desperately trying to convince himself. But at the time, she agreed to go ahead with their plans. After all, her grandmother was counting on it. Perhaps, Cassie thought, things between Oliver and her would improve after their marriage. But she was wrong. When Oliver had canceled their engagement, he had done her a favor, however brutal it had been.

"Hey," the bartender said. "Sad again?" And then he touched her.

It was an intimate touch, a hand to her cheek. A lover's touch.

She glanced at him, trying to read his eyes. Still looking at her, he let his fingers trail down her cheek. It had been a long time since a man had touched her like that, and the intimacy was enough to cause her emotions to flood to the surface. No, she thought. She could not cry. Not now.

"He was a fool," he said, obviously assuming she was lamenting the loss of her fiancé. "You deserve better."

"You don't even know me."

"I'm here with you right now," he said. "And that's all that matters." He removed his hand but continued to stare at her tenderly.

How could she be sad when her Prince Charming was standing before her? She only had one night before she turned back into a pumpkin. "So," she said brightly, "what does your chef usually cook in your kitchen?"

He shrugged and opened the fridge. Inside were ready-made bowls of pasta, some delicious-looking London broil and twice-baked potatoes. "Something I can heat up quite easily."

"You're getting into this ownership bit," she said. "Are you sure the owners won't mind if we eat their food?"

When he turned and glanced at her, she added, "I just don't want you to get into trouble."

He leaned forward. "I guarantee it."

"Guarantee you *will* get into trouble or you won't?"

He tucked a wisp of her hair behind her ear. His touch sent another tingle down her spine. "Are we talking about dinner?"

She swallowed.

He smiled and winked, then turned back toward the food and finished heating up the dishes.

When it was ready, he prepared the plates and lined them on his arms like a professional waiter.

"You've obviously had experience," she said, nodding to the way he was carrying the plates.

"Years," he said with a smile.

She grabbed the dinner plates and silverware and followed him to the table, which faced the sea. He lit the candles.

She sat, glancing back to shore. The docks were empty and the beach had emptied out, too. It was as if they were alone in the world. "Where is everyone?"

"It's a private marina."

She took a bite. The food was delicious. She suddenly realized how ravenous she was. She hadn't eaten anything since breakfast. Distracted by the dinner, she didn't even realize her host was barely eating, until she glanced up. He was leaning back in his chair, smiling at her. There was something regal about him, as if he really were a prince.

"I'm sorry," she said.

"For what?"

"My manners. I guess I was hungrier than I thought."

"You have perfect manners." He picked up the champagne and refilled her glass.

"Where are you from originally?" she thought to say.

"I was born in Maryland. But when I was ten my father lost his job and we moved to a little island not too far from here."

"It seems like paradise."

"It can be. But it wasn't quite paradise when I was growing up. It's hard to make a living as a fisherman—especially when you have no experience."

She nodded. "You're an only child?"

"Yes. My mother died when I was young. It was just my dad, my grandmother and me."

"Your grandmother?"

He nodded. "My dad thought I needed a mother figure, so he moved her here from France. She never learned to speak a word of English." He smiled as he remembered her. "I can still hear her now, yelling, *'Ne t'assois pas sur le canapé avec ton maillot de bain mouillé.'*"

"What does that mean?"

"Don't sit on the couch in your wet suit." He smiled at her. He took a sip of his champagne and said, "What about you? Any brothers or sisters?"

She shook her head. "No. I'm an only child, as well." But growing up she had never felt alone. Shanville was a small town filled with quaint Victorian houses, the occasional country store and a small Main Street that seemed to have most everything a person could desire. Nearly everyone who didn't work on Main Street worked for Demion Mills. Cassie still lived in the house where she had grown up, several streets away from Main Street and a short trip through the woods to the mill. She felt as if her co-workers and neighbors were her family. People who had known her since she was born. People who had supported her through the good times and bad. People who, like her, worked at the mill.

They tended the old looms with care and love, producing fabrics that sold for up to $1,000 a yard. They were proud of their work, proud to have covered not one, but three presidential chairs in Demion fabrics. But it wasn't only presidents who had benefited from their expertise. Their fabrics had draped the homes of the rich and famous, the kings and queens around the world. And even, Cassie thought, a millionaire's yacht in the Bahamas.

"Are you done?" he asked quietly.

She suddenly realized she had once again been staring morosely at her plate. He was probably anxious to get rid of her. Cheer up, she commanded herself once again. Stop thinking about the mill. "Yes," she said.

He held out his hand. "Follow me. It's time for dessert."

Two

Cassie accepted his hand, and he pulled her to her feet. But he did not let go. He led her off the boat and back down the dock.

"Where are we going?"

"I want to give you a truly tropical experience." When he reached the end of the dock he said, "Take off your shoes."

"What?"

"Trust me."

She wasn't sure why she needed to take off her shoes, but she kicked them off and followed him onto the beach. He walked over to a palm tree and shook it. "What are you doing?" she asked as a coconut fell to the beach.

He picked it up and said, "I know how much you like piña coladas." He knocked the coconut against the side of the tree, revealing the nut inside. Taking out his tool knife, he used the corkscrew to make a hole in the end and offered it to her. "Take a sip."

She put the brown, hairy shell to her lips and drank some of the sweet, clear liquid.

"Do you like it?"

She nodded and handed the coconut back to him.

"You can finish it if you like."

"No," she said. It was good, but it would taste even better with pineapple juice and rum.

He accepted the coconut and drank the rest of the liquid. Then he cracked it and used his knife to carve out a piece of the meat. "Dessert," he said, holding it to her lips as if he were feeding her candy.

She smiled and bit off a small piece. The whole experience was so sensual that she almost forgot to taste it.

"Well," he said, taking a step toward her. They were so close she could feel his breath on her forehead.

She glanced up at him. "It's wonderful. But why did I take off my shoes?"

He took her hand once again and led her along the water's edge. The warm, sandy water slid in between her toes.

"So you could feel that," he said, nodding toward her toes.

She laughed. She took the coconut out of his hands and held it up to the moonlight.

"What are you doing?" he asked.

"I think this would make a great picture. The coconut blocking out the moon. The light radiating behind it."

"Do you want me to get your camera?"

"No," she replied. For once she did not want to see life from behind the sanctity of her lens.

He set the coconut on the beach, then took her hand and said, "Come on."

"Where are we going?" she asked.

"Absolutely nowhere."

They moved together as one, their arms wrapped around each other. Every now and then they would pass another couple and smile. It was easy to believe, she thought, that they were like them. Husband and wife, honeymooners, lovers.

"My hotel is just up here," she said.

"But your shoes and your camera are back at the dock."

She smiled. "Right."

He stopped walking and she turned back toward him. "Ready to turn around?"

But he didn't answer her. He was staring at her intently, his eyes full of fire. He said, "My God, you're beautiful."

She felt the color rush to her cheeks as she swallowed hard.

He took a step toward her. He towered over her, still staring into her eyes. She couldn't look away. She stood there, hypnotized, completely under his spell.

"May I kiss you?" he asked softly.

She nodded and tilted her head toward him. He leaned forward and brushed his lips against hers. He pulled away and hesitated, as if waiting.

She responded instinctively, reaching her hand around his neck and steering him back toward her lips. He responded with a kiss that took her breath away. His tongue was inside her mouth, exploring the recesses. Deep and sensual, it was unlike any kiss she had ever received.

Only when she thought she might faint from lack of oxygen did he pull away. He stood there for a moment, resting his forehead against hers.

Finally, in a raspy voice, he said, "Let's head back."

He pulled her close to his side, resting his hand on her hip.

It was an intimate gesture, one that intimated ownership. She was his...for the moment. She reciprocated, looping a finger around his belt loop.

What was she doing? She barely knew this man. This...interlude was a fantasy, nothing more. Where could it possibly lead?

But she couldn't think about that right now. She wanted to just close her eyes and enjoy the feeling of a handsome man holding her close, the feeling of being desired.

Before she knew it, they were back at the dock. She sighed, sad that their time together was at an end.

She picked up her shoes. "I need to get my camera before I leave."

"Okay," he said. He almost sounded disappointed as well.

They walked down the dock without touching. He climbed

aboard and once again held out his hand. She accepted it and jumped on. But this time he didn't let go.

She knew it was time to go home. Their night together was over. But before she could speak, he had taken a finger and delicately trailed it around her face. "Don't go back," he breathed, as if desperate for her to stay. Without even questioning her response, she leaned forward and kissed him.

He responded slowly and softly, as if he had been waiting for her an eternity. As if they had kissed a million times before. His hand slid around her waist as he pulled her in closer.

She felt as if the world was spinning away. All that mattered was the energy they alone were creating.

She pulled back and took several deep breaths. Another kiss like that and she would be physically incapable of going anywhere. She needed to leave. Now. "I…I have an early flight. I really should be—"

But she didn't have a chance to finish. He kissed her again, harder this time. All her senses spun to life. She wanted him to touch her, to hold her all night. She wanted to feel his lips on hers for the rest of her life.

Finally he stopped and said, "At least finish your champagne."

She glanced toward the table. The champagne bottle sat in a bucket of half-melted ice. "It seems a shame to waste such good champagne," she said finally. She would have a drink, and that was all. She would go home with her virginity intact.

Smiling, he led her back toward the table. Once she was seated, he dragged his chair closer to her and sat down. He took the champagne out of the ice bucket and refilled their glasses.

They sat in silence, enjoying each other's company. Finally Cassie said, "If this was my boat, I don't think I'd ever leave."

"No?"

"No. I can't imagine a place more beautiful than this."

"Especially tonight," he said. He took her hand and held it. "I'm not often by myself on this boat but when I am, I love to sit out here at night and look at the stars."

She said, "I once tried to photograph the night sky."

"But?"

"I decided some things in life are just too perfect to capture."

He touched her cheek, directing her face back toward him. He kissed her and said, "Stay with me tonight."

She asked the first question that popped into her mind. "Where?" After all, this was not his boat. Was he even allowed to sleep here? She needed all the facts before she made her decision.

"Right here, on the boat. No one else will be here."

It was tempting, but...

"Nothing has to happen," he said, brushing a tendril of hair away from her face. "I'm just...I'm not ready to say goodbye," he said.

Neither was she. "Okay," she heard herself reply.

He picked up her hand and kissed it. "Thank you." Standing up, he offered her his hand.

As she stared at his hand, panic welled up in her throat. She knew that by accepting it, she was embarking on a journey unlike any other.

She glanced at him, hesitating. His eyes glowed with a savage inner fire.

As if hypnotized, she took his hand and he pulled her to her feet. As she followed the bartender toward what she assumed was the ultimate destination, a bedroom, she couldn't help but remember two previous scary moments. As a child, she had once watched a frightening movie her grandmother had forbidden her to see. That night she had lain in her bed, certain that every creak was a ghost with an ax. She had been so terrified she had awakened her grandmother and confessed her sin.

The other time was when Oliver asked her to marry him. She'd had a sudden sick feeling that had taken away her voice, as though a golf ball was being jammed in the back of her throat. Her heart had begun to beat fast and her stomach had tied in knots.

But, she reminded herself, both those times she had recovered. And she hadn't been harmed. Not physically, at least.

Not that she was worried about being harmed. She looked at him once again. He seemed so kind, so gentle.

And she had no doubt he was experienced. He had probably done this a million times before.

Done what? What was she worried about? Hadn't he said that nothing had to happen?

The problem, she realized, was that she *wanted* something to happen.

She swallowed.

No wonder she was terrified. It had nothing to do with him. She was worried about herself. Worried that she might be just a little too anxious to unload herself of the twenty-three-year-old sexual albatross hanging around her neck.

"Hey," he said softly, stopping outside a bedroom. "Are you all right?"

It was now or never. Her last chance to turn back. "Sure."

"Look," he said, brushing the hair away from her eyes. "If you'd prefer that we go back on deck…"

After all, shouldn't she be proud to be a twenty-three-year-old virgin? And in June, on her birthday, she'd be a twenty-four-year-old virgin. Next year she'd be a twenty-five-year-old virgin, then twenty-six, twenty-seven, twenty-eight…. Hallelujah! She might even be eligible for the *Guinness Book of World Records*.

"I want to be with you," she said.

He picked up her hand and kissed it. He led her into a bedroom that had a king-size bed with a velvet coverlet. "Are you sure this is okay?" he asked.

"Yes," she said.

"I just want to lie with you for a while. To feel you next to me."

She smiled, trying to hide her nervousness. They were still standing in the small, narrow hallway. He took a step toward her. She instinctively backed away, up against the wall.

Their eyes locked. For a moment she thought he might kiss her. Instead, he swept her up in his arms. He was strong, stronger than she had guessed. Her heart raced as she leaned back against his chest. She wrapped her arms around his neck, and he placed her gently on the bed. Without removing a stitch of clothing, he slid down next to her and wrapped his arms around her.

He gently massaged her arms as he kissed her. It was a tease, just enough to encourage her to turn toward him for more. He slowly raised her arms above her head. Pinning them down with one hand, he kissed her softly.

They kissed for what seemed like hours, his tongue slipping inside her mouth, probing and exploring ever so gently.

He seemed to be waiting for her silent okay before progressing to the next step. Only when she sighed with desire did he begin to explore her body. He ran his hands over her sundress, slipping his fingers underneath her spaghetti straps. In a practiced move, he pulled down the straps, exposing her bare breasts. His fingers ran over her nipples, followed closely by his tongue.

As he took her in his mouth she felt a warmth spread up from her legs. This was what she had read about. This was what making love was supposed to be.

He reached inside her panties and pulled them off in one smooth motion.

She was no longer thinking with reason. She had gone too far to stop. She needed him inside her.

She pulled at his shirt, clawing him like an animal. Within a second it was off. His pants and shorts followed suit. He was above her, all naked muscle, shining in the moonlight. Once again she was reminded of the powerful fighter she had seen at the bar. But she was not intimidated by his power. She felt safe and protected. Desired.

She took him in her hands and directed him toward her.

It was all the encouragement he needed. With a single thrust, he entered her.

Thick and heavy, he ripped through the last vestige of her virginity. As a searing pain tore through her, she dug her nails into his back and cried out.

He stopped. "I'm sorry," he said as he began to pull out. "I didn't know...."

"Don't stop," she whispered. "Please."

He hesitated, as if unsure what to do. She raised her hips and brought him deeper inside her. She saw him close his eyes, saw the anticipation tighten his face. He was no more capable of stopping now than she was. She moved her hips once again.

He opened his eyes and began to move, gently and slowly. He stared straight at her, his eyes searing into her soul. They were as connected as two people could possibly be.

The pain gave way to pleasure. Intense and primitive, it took control of her body. They moved together, both dependent upon the other. As she moved her body up against him, the momentum built within her, taking control of her mind and body. When release finally came, however, she was not prepared for the intensity. She held on to him for dear life as the dam of sensual pleasure burst, sending her body into spasms of relief. Only then did she feel his body shudder as a slight groan passed his lips.

He kissed her cheek and ran a finger around her lips. "Are you all right?"

She smiled. "Better than all right."

"You're a virgin."

"Not anymore."

He picked up her hand and kissed it, pulling out slowly. "Definitely not anymore." He swallowed. "Had I known...well, I never would have suggested you stay."

"So, I'm glad I didn't tell you."

He smiled, but it was not a happy smile. He looked sad, almost guilty.

"It's okay," she said. "I'm a big girl."

"You were waiting to make love on your wedding night, weren't you?"

She nodded.

He sighed and glanced away. "Did you think this would mend your broken heart?"

"My heart," she said, "is definitely not broken." At least not yet. But she had a feeling things might change tomorrow. He pulled her close and lay there, his arms wrapped around her.

* * *

Cassie awoke to the rocking of the boat. She glanced beside her. He was laying there, his roughly hewn body totally visible on top of the covers. She turned away, embarrassed.

But how could she be embarrassed to look at him when they had been so intimate? Not once, but twice?

She couldn't help but blush as she remembered what had transpired the night before. Making love to him had been everything she had dreamed of. As she looked at him sleeping, she could feel herself melt. His thick hair had fallen over one eye, his arms were spread around the pillow. She would like nothing better than to snuggle up to him and—

He sighed and turned over.

She froze.

She needed to get out of there, before he awoke. After all, what would she say? She could not bear to hear him promise to call and stay in touch. It would ruin everything. Right now it still seemed to be a dream.

And that was exactly the way she wanted it.

She tiptoed out of bed and slipped on her clothes and left without making a sound. She had less than an hour to get to the airport.

Three

Cassie stared at her cold cup of coffee. It was difficult to believe that only a day ago she had been in the Bahamas. Twelve hours earlier she had been making love to a man whose name she did not know.

And now, here she was sitting in a boardroom across from her ex-fiancé. To make matters worse, the cool, impeccably dressed blonde sitting next to him was his girlfriend, Willa, otherwise known as Hunter Axon's henchman.

But if Oliver was bothered by having his ex-fiancée in such close quarters with the woman he had left her for, he didn't show it. He thumbed through a manila envelope and set it back down. "Willa told me what you did."

She perked up. "What are you talking about?"

"Axon's receptionist told Willa about your little trip to the Bahamas."

So that was why he had wanted to see her. When she'd arrived at the mill late this morning, she had been told that Oliver wanted to talk to her the minute she arrived. "It's no secret," she said. "I wanted to see Hunter Axon."

He nodded. "I knew it! You think you're so sly. I know everything that goes on around here."

"Not everything," she said, thinking about her bartender once again. She hadn't told a single soul about her romantic night. It was her secret, one that she would carry to her grave.

"How can you do this to me?" Oliver asked. "You know how important this deal is."

Was he kidding? Was he really narcissistic enough to think she was on a personal vendetta? "This has nothing to do with you, Oliver," she said.

"What, then?"

"This has to do with preserving a way of life, a tradition that has been passed down from generation to generation."

"Oh, please, Cassie. You're talking like a history professor. This is a business. A weak one at that. It hasn't been profitable in years."

She raised an eyebrow as her eyes narrowed. "And whose fault is that?"

But he waved her off, oblivious. "Do you know how lucky I am that I could even sell it? That a company of Axon Enterprises' stature would even be interested?" He was turning red in the face, each word seemingly making him more frustrated.

How could she ever have thought of marrying him? He was not her friend. The man sitting in front of her had become a complete and total stranger. "Well," Cassie said, "you'll be happy to know that I didn't meet with him. I tried, but he wouldn't see me."

"We already know that," Willa said. She reached out a manicured hand and patted Oliver's arm. It was the kind of touch one would bestow on a loyal pet. "Let me speak to Cassie alone." She turned toward Cassie and flashed her a smile that threw daggers. "Privately."

Oliver glanced at Willa. His blue eyes grew large, and he smiled softly, as if melting at the mere sight of his beloved. So, Cassie thought, he really did love her. She knew for a fact that he had never looked at her that way. But she was not jealous. In fact, she had begun to despair of Oliver's humanity and was relieved to learn he was still capable of human emotion.

He nodded and reluctantly walked out, shutting the door behind him.

"Look, Cass," Willa said, in the most patronizing tone Cassie had ever heard.

"Cassie," she corrected her.

"Cassie. I know what's going on with you. I really do."

Cassie looked at her. "What's going on with me?"

"Revenge. Pure and simple."

"Revenge?" Cassie felt as if she'd been slapped. This woman was as bad as Oliver. Did they really believe that Cassie would be so self-centered? Hundreds of jobs and the town's future were dependent on this mill. "This has nothing to do with revenge."

"Well then, what?"

"This town can't afford to lose the mill."

Willa sighed dramatically, as if the conversation was exhausting her. "Cass…Cassie, I want to make a deal with you. I've spoken with Hunter and he's assured me that not everyone will be laid off. I'm in a position to guarantee you a job—but I have a condition."

"And that is?"

"Help us make this transition as smooth as possible."

"What transition?"

"The sale. Hunter Axon is coming here to firm up the deal. I want you to promise you won't…interfere."

Cassie was unmoved. She was not afraid of Willa. She was angry. She suddenly realized why she had been unable to see Hunter Axon. His assistants had been warned by Willa to keep her away from him. "Did you tell your people to prevent me from seeing Mr. Axon?"

"I work for him. It's my job to put out the fires."

"Put out the fires?"

"So to speak." Willa sighed. "Look, Cassie, I'm sorry about Oliver. I really am. But I suggest you take the deal I'm offering you. For if you think I'm tough—well, I guarantee you I'm a sweetheart compared to Mr. Axon."

Willa had offered severance pay of one week for each year of employment. On paper it was a decent amount. But did it make up for the loss of the mill? The mill was the largest employer in Shanville. It supported the town's economy. What kind of job would the people who had spent their lives working as artisans be suited for? And where would they find these jobs? "I'm willing to take my chances."

"You don't know with whom you're dealing. You think Mr. Axon will be inspired by your little sob story? You think he's going to give a damn about you or your little community? He cares about one thing—making money." She smiled. But it was not a kind smile. It was a smile that caused flowers to wilt and water to freeze. She said, "I've known him for years, even before I came to work for him. He is, quite simply, the best in the business. And he does not look kindly on those who stand in the way of his getting what he wants."

"I just want to talk to him."

"If you cause him trouble, bringing this case to the media and what have you, I guarantee he's going to squash you like a bug. Do you understand me?"

Cassie's hand instinctively went to the necklace she had worn since childhood, a gold heart her mother had received as an engagement present from her father. But it was not there to reassure her. Cassie had lost it in the Bahamas.

"I'm not afraid of him."

"Then you're even more of a fool than I suspected."

Cassie glanced away. As much as she hated to admit it, she had a feeling Willa was right. How could she be so foolish as to think she could actually make a difference?

"Let me be clear," Willa said, putting an icy hand on Cassie's. "If you continue to interfere, I'm going to pull the severance package we've offered."

"I don't care about your lousy severance."

"I'm sure you don't. But what about…" She picked up a file from her desk and squinted her eyes as she read, "Luanne Anderson? I believe her daughter has some problems, doesn't she? It would be a shame if she found herself out of work with no severance."

"Are you threatening to punish me by taking away Luanne's severance package?"

"Not just Luanne's." Willa glanced down at the file once again. "But Mabel's…Larry's… Well," she said, putting the list down, "let's just make it a clean sweep, shall we? I mean it's not really fair to give it to some and not others."

"You can't do that," Cassie breathed.

"I can't. But Hunter Axon can."

Cassie swallowed.

"He's done it before, in fact. Several times. He usually gives the workers a choice. They can either be poor losers and get everyone all stirred up, or they can be good sports and concede graciously. Take the money and run, so to speak."

Cassie glanced away.

"In this particular situation I'm going to save Hunter some trouble. If you attempt in any way to contact him when he arrives, I will personally cancel the severance package." Willa smiled once again. She leaned forward and said in a conspiratorial tone, "Oliver told me about some of your recent travails. I've arranged for a severance package that is more than fair. Why don't you take the money and go back to school. Get that arts degree you wanted."

Cassie could feel her cheeks burn. Oliver had clearly spoken about her to this woman. She could just imagine the conversation, just imagine Oliver telling Willa about the simple, small-town girlfriend he was about to dump.

Cassie was tempted to defend her job and her life. But what was the point? Willa would never believe her. To her, Demion Mills was just an old textile factory. As far as Willa was concerned, Cassie should be grateful to her for rescuing her from despair.

"Do we have an understanding?" Willa asked.

"Understanding? This is not about me or you or Oliver. This is about all the people who are losing their only means of support. All the people who have to move away from the only homes they've ever known."

"You're wasting my time," Willa said. "I've offered you a deal."

"Stand by quietly and watch you destroy our town—or try to save it and risk financial ruin for my friends?"

"That's a little dramatic, but basically, yes."

Cassie stood. "Are you finished?"

"Of course." Willa stood and held out her hand. "I admire your spunk, however misdirected it may be. I really hope that your past history with Oliver won't prevent us from being friends."

Cassie left without shaking her hand.

Hunter checked his watch. His plane was late, due to a violent and unexpected thunderstorm. No matter. He was in no rush to reach his destination.

In fact, for once he hated to leave the Bahamas. He hated to think that there was even the slightest chance he was leaving her behind.

"You'll never find her," said the investigator he'd hired. "It's like looking for a needle in a haystack. How can we find a woman with no name?"

But Hunter wouldn't admit it was hopeless. He couldn't. Ever since he had first laid eyes on her he thought of little else.

Hunter felt in his pocket for the only thing that had provided solace in the days since, a heart-shaped necklace.

He had found it on her pillow, its clasp broken. As he clutched it in his hands he felt the conviction surge once again. He would find her. But where? He had searched everywhere. Damn. Why hadn't he gotten her name?

To make matters worse, she didn't know his, either. What if she returned home and had a change of heart? How would she contact him?

He hadn't intended for this to happen. The bar happened to be one of the many properties he owned on the island. He'd stopped in, not for a romantic interlude, but to speak with his employees. But it had been so busy he'd pitched in, helping to tend bar. When he'd seen Cassie sitting by herself, he'd been intrigued. She possessed an almost ethereal beauty with her creamy white skin and deep green eyes. A cloud of long, curly, reddish-brown hair ran down her back. She had the figure of a ballerina, petite with long, slender legs.

But it was not just her beauty that had mesmerized him. She had seemed oblivious to the activity surrounding her. She had stared at the water as if lost in her own sad world.

He didn't usually find himself tongue-tied among women, but when he'd attempted to speak with her, he'd stumbled over his words like a child.

Afterward he realized she'd thought him a bartender, and although he did admit he owned the boat, it had been clear she did not believe him. He had let the mistaken identity slide. After all, he'd thought at the time, what difference did it make? For once it was nice to be with a woman who was not interested in his fortune or his name.

As the evening progressed it became obvious she was lonely, the victim of a broken heart. She needed solace and comfort. He was more than happy to provide it.

But he had misjudged her and the situation. She had not escaped to the Bahamas to lose herself in the arms of another man. She was not looking for a companion with whom to share a bed and some physical comfort.

She was a virgin.

Had he known, he never would have slept with her.

Or would he?

Knowing the pleasure he'd experienced, the incredible connection they had shared, he did not regret a moment. But did she?

Was that why she'd left without saying goodbye?

Had she chosen him out of loneliness? Despair?

It didn't matter. Much to his surprise, he awoke with an overwhelming desire to see her again. When he awoke to find her gone, he was filled with despair. He knew right then and there that he had to find her again.

It had been years since a woman had made such an impression.

He'd been with a lot of women since the demise of his engagement. But he'd kept them all at arm's length. "She permanently scarred you," one woman had said of his ex-fiancée. And until he met his mysterious, auburn-haired stranger, he'd thought she might be right. After all, he had been young and naive when he'd fallen in love with Lisa. She was a fellow college student and together they'd planned their future. When he received an internship at a prestigious New York equity firm, he had asked her to marry him. But shortly afterward he had come home early to find Lisa in bed with another man. To make matters worse, it was his boss at the firm. She married his boss, but not before telling Hunter why. Years later he could still hear her words. *I could never marry a poor man.*

Her rejection had only fueled his desire to become wealthy and powerful. And he had discovered what Lisa had no doubt realized by now, as well. Money did not guarantee happiness.

He glanced back out the window as the plane began its descent. He was surprising himself. He did not consider himself a sentimental type, but he was a man obsessed, consumed by a sweet, brief memory. It had been a long time since he'd enjoyed the simple pleasures in life like a stroll on the beach, a drink from a coconut.

The plane lurched as it touched the ground. He looked out the window. It was snowing in Shanville.

Four

"**A**re you still going to try to talk to Mr. Axon?"

Cassie glanced at her friend, whom she'd known her entire life. She hated to disappoint Frances. Sixty-five years old, Frances Wells—like most of the people in Shanville—lived paycheck to paycheck. If she lost her job at the mill, she would not be able to find employment elsewhere.

Unfortunately, Frances was not alone. The community was aging, and most of the workers were fifty or older. Cassie might be able to move on, but they would not. Still, she couldn't risk losing their severance packages. "I can't gamble with everyone's future. It's a long shot, anyway."

"But it's Oliver. He loves you."

"No," Cassie said quickly. "According to him, he never did. But even if I did have some pull with him, he no longer has any control. He's already given over the reins to Axon Enterprises."

"I don't know how Oliver can stand by and let this happen. If I had known what a devil he would become, I would've swatted his behind while I still had the chance."

"So would I, if I'd thought it would've made any difference."
Frances smiled. "Well, at least I'm happy for you."

"What do you mean?" Cassie asked.

"The severance is just what you need. You'll have the money to move away and return to school." The older woman smiled sadly and patted her hand. "You don't belong in a mill, Cassie. You never did. You belong behind that camera of yours, taking pictures. Working for *National Geographic* or someplace where you can make your dream come true."

"Oh, Frances," Cassie said. Once again, she felt as if she might cry. "I would be more than happy to never take another picture again if it meant you would all be able to keep your jobs." Cassie glanced around her. "And I'm not so sure that's my dream anymore."

"What are you talking about? Ever since you were a little girl you loved that camera."

Cassie shrugged. "All I know is that I can't stand the thought of losing this mill."

Frances glanced at the old stone building in front of them and shrugged. "I guess it was bound to happen sooner or later. We all knew that things haven't been right around here for years. It was foolish to think young Oliver could handle it, just because he had a fancy education."

"I think he could've saved it if he wanted to," Cassie said. "He chose not to." She shook her head. "I wish I'd seen what he was intending. Perhaps I could've talked some sense into him while there was still a chance."

"Nonsense," Frances said. "You know as well as me, Oliver always had a mind of his own." She put an arm around Cassie and squeezed. "At least I can sleep easier knowing that you're going to be okay."

"Okay?" Cassie asked.

"Your grandmother and I never thought Oliver was right for you."

"What?" The news astounded her. "I thought Grandma loved Oliver."

"She loved him like one loves a wayward child. She knew you

two had been friends your entire lives, but she had grave concerns about your future together. 'He makes Cassie happy,' she used to say. 'And that is all that matters.'"

Could this be true? Had there just been a colossal misunderstanding? Had both she and her grandmother tried to convince themselves Oliver was Mr. Right because they'd assumed it to be what the other wanted?

But what did it matter? Her grandmother was gone, and Oliver was engaged to someone else. And she, well, she had moved on, too. With a little help from her Bahamian bartender.

It was days since they were together, but Cassie couldn't stop thinking about him. It was as if he was seared into her consciousness. Everywhere she looked she was reminded of him. Everything she did made her long for him.

It wasn't supposed to be this way.

It was a one-night stand with a stranger. Intimacy without commitment. Lust without love. She didn't even know his name.

So why couldn't she forget about him?

She felt nothing but irritation when she saw her ex-fiancé, but when she looked at the picture she had taken of her bartender on the beach, she felt like crying. She couldn't help but hope that one day she would see him again.

But would he even remember her?

Probably not. His experience with women was obvious. She had little doubt that he had found someone else to share his bed.

She followed Frances into the cafeteria. Employees were packed inside like cattle. At the front of the room were three chairs. Oliver and Willa sat on either side of an empty chair as if waiting for the king. Oliver stood up and said, "Mr. Axon was delayed. But he called a while ago and said he should be here shortly." His face brightened as he nodded behind her. "There he is now."

Cassie turned. There, walking toward her, was none other than her bartender.

Hunter walked through the crowded auditorium, trying not to make eye contact. He had been in this situation many times before. He knew what the questions would be. These people would not be receiving the answers they wanted to hear.

He would be closing the mill within six months. All employees, however, would receive a generous severance package. According to Willa, who had done a thorough study of the area surrounding Shanville, it was more than enough to give them time to find another job.

He looked at Oliver. Oliver jumped to his feet and began applauding.

Applauding? It was overkill, but Oliver couldn't seem to help himself. Oliver reminded Hunter of the rich kid in prep school, the one who was always complimenting the teacher and making fun of the unpopular kids. "Stop please," Hunter said, annoyed. Oliver was kidding himself if he thought these people would welcome him. Willa had said that she had already informed everyone of his intentions.

Oliver's face fell, and he dropped back in his chair. "Sorry, Mr. Axon," Oliver said. "Did you have a nice flight?"

"No," Hunter said. He couldn't help himself. Oliver just annoyed him for some reason. Once again he reminded himself to be civil.

He turned back toward the crowd. "I apologize for the wait. My flight was delayed due to inclement weather. Now, I know you all have a lot of questions. I promise you I will do my best to answer every single one of them." He scanned the crowd. This would not be easy. Most of the workers were older than he had expected. Younger workers typically welcomed the severance package as it was intended, a means to a better way of life. But these people would have a difficult time finding employment elsewhere. "Why don't I begin by telling you a little about my company—"

He stopped. She was standing toward the back of the room, staring at him as if he were a ghost.

She was there.

Run.

Cassie turned and made her way through the crowd, back toward the exit. It was an instinctive reaction, an urge for self-preservation. She hurried as if her very life depended upon it.

Cassie flung open the door and escaped outside. She paused for a moment to catch her breath. She was winded, not from the rush, but from the shock.

She had slept with Hunter Axon.

The realization was enough to give her another surge of energy. She rushed toward the stairwell as her head continued to pound. She had lost her virginity to Public Enemy Number One. The man who was closing the mill and putting her friends out of work.

How could this have happened?

But it had. There was no denying it.

Why had he lied to her? Why had he pretended to be someone he wasn't?

Cassie threw open the stairwell door and began rushing down the steps. She needed to get back to her loom. She needed the comfort of something familiar. A quiet place where she could recover from brain overload.

"Wait!"

The sound of his voice made her stop. But not for long. In a flash she was back on track, moving as fast as she possibly could.

But it was not fast enough. "Wait," he said again, practically jumping down the steps. He grabbed her arm, stopping her. "I've looked everywhere for you."

Looking at him, at the tortured expression on his face, she almost believed him. Almost.

"Hunter Axon?" she said.

He smiled and extended his hand. "Nice to meet you. And you are…?"

As she stared into his brown eyes, her confusion faded. What difference did it make who he was? What mattered was that she had found him again. What mattered was that he had not forgotten her. That he had been looking for her. She took his hand and said, "Cassie Edwards."

"Cassie," he said gently, as if he had been reading the tenderness in her eyes. He held on to her hand firmly, as if he had no intention of letting go. "What are you doing here?"

"I work here," she said, abruptly dropping his hand. She had to forget about their past history. She had to ignore whatever feelings were choking her. This man was not the man she had thought. He was Hunter Axon. And he was destroying the life she had known.

The smile faded from his face. "I don't understand."

"I went to the Bahamas to meet with you."

"What?" he said, the muscles tightening in his jaw. It was obvious that his surprise was genuine. He had not been told of her visit, despite his assistant's assurance to the contrary. "Why?"

"I wanted to talk to you about your intention for the mill. I tried for two days to get in to see you. I went to your office as well as your home."

He hesitated. "So, when you saw me in the bar…?"

"I didn't know who you were. I never would've…" She swallowed.

"A coincidence," he said, taking a step back. It was as if she had thrown a bucket of cold water over his head. All earlier signs of intimacy were gone.

"Yes," she repeated quietly.

The door opened and the sound of high heels echoed through the stairwell. "Hunter? Hunter?" It was Willa.

Immediately Cassie was reminded of Willa's threat. *Let's just make it a clean sweep, shall we? I mean it's not really fair to give it to some and not others.* If Willa saw her talking to Hunter, would she retract the severance packages, as threatened?

It was not something Cassie wanted to find out. "I have to go," she said, turning and heading back down the stairs.

"Cassie!" Willa yelled, stopping her. Willa was peeking over the railing. "Wait!"

Hunter closed his eyes briefly and sighed, as if frustrated by Willa's intrusion.

"What's going on here?" Willa asked, making her way down the stairs.

Hunter replied, "We were just—"

"Mr. Axon was looking for the men's room," Cassie said. She

turned back toward Hunter and said, "And I'm afraid you passed it. It's upstairs, right outside the doors."

Hunter was looking at her strangely.

"Is this true?" Willa asked him.

He glanced at his associate. "How the hell would I know? I've never been in this building before."

Cassie suppressed a smile.

"I'm relieved that you're all right," Willa said to Hunter, flashing a fake smile. "I was concerned when you dashed out of the auditorium in midsentence."

"I was overwhelmed by a sudden urge to…" He glanced at Cassie. "Use the men's room."

"Like I said," Cassie repeated, "upstairs to the left. You can't miss it."

"Thank you." He turned to Willa. "Please give the workers my apologies and explain the situation. I'll be back momentarily."

"Certainly," Willa said.

Hunter ran up the stairs. Cassie heard the swing of the doors. She glanced at Willa and shrugged, then turned and began walking back down the steps.

"I thought you said you didn't meet Hunter when you were in the Bahamas."

Cassie felt her heart jump into her throat. Perhaps their charade was not as convincing as she thought. Cassie swallowed as she met Willa's eyes. "Are you accusing me of lying?"

Willa walked down the steps, approaching Cassie slowly. "It's just a bit confusing. He suddenly bolts out of a conference and I find you huddled together in a stairwell. Quite a coincidence."

"I didn't discuss the mill, if that's what you're worried about."

"Why would I be worried? After all, we have an agreement, right?"

Cassie glanced away.

"It would be dreadful to see so many nice people put out of work, with no money to see them through the long, hot summer."

"Yes," Cassie said. "It would."

Willa hesitated, as if thinking. "Cassie," she said, "I'm glad we had this little talk. I want you to know that I do trust you. And I'm sorry that we've gotten off to such a rough start. I'd like to make it up to you."

Make it up to her? Cassie felt a chill run down her spine. This woman was creepy. She almost radiated evil. "Oliver and I are hosting a little party for Hunter tonight at Oliver's estate."

Estate? Cassie couldn't help but smile. The Demion house sat on top of a hill overlooking all of Shanville. Although it was the closest thing the town had to a mansion, it was hardly an estate. It had been built by a wealthy family in the mid eighteen hundreds. It consisted of twenty-two spacious rooms and ten working fireplaces. Oliver had moved in several years ago, when his parents had officially gone to Florida and given him the reins of his family business. His house was large, Cassie would give him that. But an estate—in Shanville? Hardly.

"Why don't you come."

Cassie looked at her. What was she up to? Was she trying to encourage her to talk to Hunter, just so she could pull the plug on the severance packages?

But could she really do such a horrible thing? And would Hunter allow it…or even encourage it? Or had Willa been bluffing?

Cassie needed to decide whether her hunch about Hunter was right. Would he hear her out? Would he actually listen to what she had to say?

If she was wrong, her friends could lose their severance. But if she was right…maybe they had a chance after all.

"It should be quite the event," Willa continued. "I just got word today that the governor is coming."

The governor? Would he be able to help Demion Mills? It was worth finding out. Willa may have forbidden her from talking to Hunter Axon, but she could not forbid her from talking to the governor.

"Thank you," Cassie said. "I'd love to attend."

"Good," said Willa. "Oh, and, Cassie, it's a formal event so dress is..."

"Formal," said Cassie.

"Exactly," said Willa, flashing her the same, creepy Cheshire Cat grin once again.

Five

Cassie took a step and stopped. It was not too late to turn back.

She glanced up at the Demion "estate." The granite Victorian, never a cheery place, looked almost haunted in the moonlight. Through the windows Cassie could see bits and pieces of the elaborate party inside, a woman's bejeweled wrist and hand, part of a man's tuxedo.

Who were these people?

And why had they come to Shanville?

For an opportunity to meet the great and ruthless Hunter Axon?

It had taken Cassie much of the day to recover from the shock of discovering that the man who had inspired her dreams had also been the one to cause her nightmares.

A coincidence, he had said.

An unbelievable twist of fate. One that could have been avoided by asking the most obvious of questions: What is your name?

That was what she wished had happened, wasn't it? That she had learned of his identity? That the whole evening had been avoided, and that she had returned home with her virginity intact?

No.

As much as she hated to admit it, that was not the case. She did not regret their time together, even though she knew she should.

After all, she had slept with Hunter Axon. So why didn't she regret it?

Because it had been the most perfect night of her entire life.

She sighed deeply. How could this be? How could her tender, sweet lover, the man who had whisked her off her feet both literally and figuratively, be Hunter Axon? Hunter Axon should be a glib, burly man, as grotesque looking and acting as his actions would merit.

He should not look and act like a prince.

But apparently she was not the only one who was susceptible to his charm. Why else would the governor be coming to a party in his honor? One would think the mere sound of Hunter Axon's name would inspire trepidation. After all, his projects typically left a trail of devastation. Joblessness and homelessness were two of the more common side effects.

But as Cassie marched bravely to the door, the governor was not on her mind. All she could think about was Hunter and the fact that within minutes, she would be seeing him once again.

Before ringing the doorbell she paused and glanced down at her dress. Her grandmother had made the material herself, working after hours at the mill. Ruby had sewn the gown. Luanne had added the trimmings. Years ago Cassie had thought it to be the most beautiful dress she had ever seen, and she still felt that way.

Regardless of the dress, Cassie still felt awkward. But why should she? She had been to Oliver's house many times before.

But back then she had come as Oliver's friend. Not as the guest of his girlfriend. She took a deep breath and rang the bell.

Willa answered. "Hello, Cassie." She raised a perfectly shaped eyebrow and gave her a quick nod. "Please come in."

Cassie entered. She winced as she noticed what Willa was wearing. And Willa was not alone. Everyone was dressed in their work attire. The only people dressed for a ball were the tuxedoed waiters.

And Oliver. Although he was wearing casual pants and shirt, he had attempted to make his outfit more festive by tying an ascot around his neck. Cassie couldn't help but think he was taking this owner-of-an-estate thing a little too far. She felt like sending him back to his room to change. But then, her outfit was not much more appropriate.

His eyes opened wide as he saw her. He came marching over, a martini glass in his hand. "Cassie?" He looked at her, confused. "What are you doing here?" She saw him glance at her dress with an expression that was somewhere between curiosity and horror.

"Willa invited me," Cassie said weakly.

"Yes," Willa said. "I was in a jam. Cassie was kind enough to help me out."

"I don't follow," Oliver said, still holding his martini glass. "Why are you wearing your prom dress?"

Cassie stood still. She glanced at her dress, wishing she could close her eyes and transport herself back to her house. Normally she would be in her sweats getting ready to curl up with a good book.

But she did not have to worry about answering. Willa took care of that for her. "One of the servers fell ill. Cassie is going to be taking her place tonight."

Cassie blinked as the words sunk in. It was worse than she thought. Willa had not invited her there as a guest but as a servant. She had walked enthusiastically into a trap.

"Really?" Oliver said, confused. "I thought—"

"You thought what? She's obviously dressed to work." Willa winked at Cassie and said, "You were smart to wear your old clothes, dear. You'll be serving pasta."

Cassie glanced past Oliver, searching the room for Hunter. Was he there? What would he think when he saw her?

But what did she care? It did not matter what she was wearing; what mattered was what she had to say.

No, she thought, she would not allow Willa to interfere with her plans. The governor would be there tonight, and she needed to talk to him. She had a job to do.

"Cassie?" said Willa. "Are you all right? Oh, dear. I do hope there wasn't a miscommunication. You did realize I had asked you here to work."

"Of course," Cassie said quickly. She would not allow Willa, Oliver or Hunter, for that matter, to get the best of her. Though she worked as a weaver and struggled to pay her bills, she was every bit as good as the rest of them. She took off her coat and began to roll up her sleeves. She met Willa's gaze directly. "I'm ready."

"Hello," said a familiar voice behind her. Cassie felt a flutter in her belly. Although she was doing her best to forget him, her body still craved his touch.

"You can start by taking Mr. Axon's coat," Willa said to Cassie before turning her attention to Hunter. "Welcome to Oliver's humble home."

Cassie turned to face him. He was wearing a black designer suit, a bright-blue silk tie and a starched white shirt. It was an outfit that radiated money, power and prestige. His brown hair was slicked back, and his brown eyes were focused on her as if to say, What are you doing here? Willa helped him off with his coat and handed it to Cassie.

"Can I get you something to drink?" Willa asked him.

"Just water for now," he replied, still looking at Cassie.

She had to say something. But what? "Hello, Mr. Axon," she said. "It's nice to see you again."

"And you," he replied, staring at her intently.

No. It was not nice to see him again. It was terrible. Awful. Every time she looked at him she wanted to kiss him.

"You heard Mr. Axon," Willa said to Cassie. "He'll take a glass of water." She handed Cassie her empty glass. "And I'd like some more champagne."

What was going on?

Hunter watched Cassie walk away.

He glanced angrily at Willa. Why was she treating Cassie like a servant?

He was tempted to run after Cassie but he knew better. For

whatever reason, it was clear that Cassie did not want Willa to know about their previous relationship.

"What do you know about that woman?" he asked Willa.

"What woman?" she replied, as if she had no idea whom he was talking about.

"The one who's getting our drinks."

"Cassie? The one you were talking to in the stairwell this morning?"

So, he thought, Willa was suspicious. "Ah," Hunter said. "That's why she looked familiar."

Willa smiled. "I think she works the loom, but I'm not certain."

"The loom?"

"She's a factory worker. She's actually been a bit of a troublemaker, as well. She's threatened to start a rebellion of sorts if we don't acquiesce to her demands."

"Really?"

"I'm afraid so. She even went to the Bahamas to try to meet with you." Willa smiled. "But I took care of it for you. And I've informed her that she's to go through me in the future. You're much too busy to be bothered by details."

Details? Was Cassie a detail?

Hunter felt his blood boil. He did not want Cassie dealt with by Willa or anyone else for that matter. He would take care of her himself. But how could he tell Willa that without making her suspicious? After all, he was usually more than happy to have Willa take care of the personnel matters.

Willa smiled. "That's what you pay me for. To handle problems."

"You seem to have handled her well," he said. He was not liking this, not at all. Willa was an excellent employee, one who had given him years of dedicated service. In her difficult and prestigious position in his company, she was responsible for researching potential properties and companies and determining which ones Axon would attempt to purchase. Many of these were hostile, and Willa had become adept at dealing with difficult employees. Although her methods were sometimes coldhearted and cruel, she was successful. Most of the times he appreciated Willa's skills. But not in this situation. He couldn't help but wonder how Cassie, after threatening to start a rebellion, had fared with Willa's wrath.

Her smile faded. "What do you mean?"

"Well, she's here, isn't she? She must have come to terms with the situation."

"One can only hope," Willa said. Her grip on his arm tightened.

"I wouldn't worry, Willa," he said, searching the room for another glimpse of Cassie. "I can handle myself."

Willa said, "Of course you can." She squeezed his arm again before letting go. "Anyway, we have more important things to think about at the moment." She glanced around. "Like where the governor disappeared to."

Cassie tightened her apron. Her face burned with embarrassment as she thought about the way Willa had ordered her to get Hunter's drink. The woman had succeeded in making her feel uncomfortable, embarrassed her in front of everyone.

But she had not succeeded in distracting Cassie from her mission. If anything, she was more determined than ever to talk to the governor.

Still, she could not help but wonder what Hunter thought when he saw her standing there dressed as if attending a ball. Did he feel sorry for her? Or perhaps instead of pity, he felt something even worse—antipathy. After all, she was certain Willa had wasted little time explaining that she worked the loom in Demion Mills. She had no doubt that Hunter was even more snobby than her ex-fiancé. Hunter Axon, like Oliver, would never be happy with a factory worker.

But what did it matter? She had to forget about Hunter, forget about their night together. For that was all they were destined to have. A memory of a beautiful night.

She walked through the hall, carrying Hunter's and Willa's drinks on a tiny silver tray. Fortunately, Oliver's caterers had a wide selection of aprons. Cassie was able to find one long enough to almost cover her formal attire. But from the guests' reaction she had worried unnecessarily about what she wore. Her apron was a signal that she was part of the catering staff, a servant. In this crowd of snobbish people, that meant one thing: she was all but invisible.

Cassie walked back out to the hall, but Hunter and Willa were no longer there. She peeked in the dining room and stopped. The governor of New York was standing not three feet away, glancing at the lavish spread.

She set the tray down on an antique table and took off her apron. She was determined to act before Willa intervened.

As she made her way toward the governor, she went over the key details of her plea. She would emphasize the importance of the mill to the community, then segue into Hunter's plans to move production overseas. She would ask the governor for his help in preventing the purchase of Demion Mills by Axon Enterprises.

"Excuse me, Governor," she said. "Can I please have a word with you?"

"What?" he asked, turning around to face her. The woman standing next to him stiffened. Cassie suddenly noticed the earpiece in the woman's ear. Like Cassie, she was not a guest. The woman was his security detail.

Would the security woman ask her to leave? It didn't matter. Cassie had bigger problems. Out of the corner of her eye, she could see Willa and Hunter making their way toward her.

"I'm sorry to interrupt, Governor," she said. "But I need to talk to you. I work at Demion Mills. I think you should know that the people of Shanville are not happy about Axon Enterprises buying Demion Mills."

The governor looked startled for a moment, as if surprised by her intrusion. "Well, Miss…" He hesitated.

"Cassie Edwards."

"I'm sorry to hear that, Miss Edwards." His voice, however, was anything but. Bored maybe. Or tired. But not sorry.

He helped himself to a generous portion of roast beef.

"He's going to close the plant," she said.

He shook his head as he speared a tomato with a toothpick. "I was under the impression that he was saving it from bankruptcy."

"That's not true," Cassie said. "All we need is a change in management."

"I'm afraid that's not what I've understood—"

"Please," Cassie said, interrupting him. "Isn't there something you can do to stop this sale? Hunter Axon has the ability to ruin this community. Shanville can't survive the loss of the mill."

But she had already lost his attention. "Hunter," he said with a smile, looking over her shoulder.

She could feel Hunter beside her, standing so close their arms were touching. "This woman," the governor continued, "has some concerns about Demion Mills."

"Really," Hunter said. He glanced down at her. Cassie could see the fire burning behind his icy eyes. So, she thought, he was not happy with her for talking to the governor. Too bad.

"Well," he said, "I'd welcome an opportunity to address them."

To undress them? Her ears were playing tricks on her.

Willa stepped forward and tucked her arm into the governor's as she grabbed his plate. "Axon Enterprises has an excellent community outreach program," she said, steering the governor into the other room and away from Cassie. "Why don't I tell you about it over dinner?"

Cassie watched the governor walk away. That was it. She had lost her chance. To make matters worse, she was quite certain her actions would have unpleasant repercussions. She glanced toward Hunter, readying herself for a fight.

"What are you doing?" he asked quietly.

"I was curious as to whether or not the governor knew about your plans to close down the mill when—and if—you buy the mill."

"And did you satisfy…your curiosity?"

"No," she said.

He gazed at her, studying her carefully. The hardness in his eyes disappeared, replaced by kindness. "You didn't come here tonight to serve food, did you?" he asked, touching her arm.

The feel of his hand was enough to make her quiver. But she

could not allow herself to be distracted. She pulled her arm away. "I came here to talk to the governor. To stop you from buying Demion Mills."

The coldness in his eyes had returned. "Then I have bad news for you."

She stopped.

"I've already bought the mill, Cassie."

Cassie felt winded, as if the news had knocked the last bit of breath from her. "What?"

"I signed the papers this afternoon." He took a step toward her. "I'm your new boss."

"I'm sorry to hear that," she said weakly.

"Why?"

She backed away.

"How can I be happy when a business that has been in operation for generations is being shut down? When hundreds of friends will be losing their jobs?"

"This is not the time for this discussion," he said, eyeing the group of people that was quickly approaching.

When she saw Willa making her way over, she knew she was in for yet another confrontation. And she was in no hurry to cause the loss of her friends' severance. Especially when she wasn't getting anywhere. She looked Hunter straight in the eye and said, "I wish you had told me who you were."

At the mention of the Bahamas, he glanced away. "You left before I had a chance," he said.

"If you knew I was there, if your assistant told you a weaver from the mill had come all the way from Shanville, would you have met with me?"

He paused.

It was all the answer she needed. No. Hunter Axon would never have wasted his time with a mere factory worker. And she had little doubt that he would not have been willing to share his bed with one, either.

"Yes," he said finally.

She glanced away. What was the point? It was hopeless. Hunter

Axon had bought the mill. She was soon to be an out-of-work weaver, an unemployed factory worker, plain and simple. She was not in Hunter Axon's league personally or professionally.

How could she ever have thought that he would listen to her? He couldn't care less about preserving a time-honored tradition or saving the jobs and way of life for hundreds of families. He was interested in one thing: money.

"Hunter?" said Willa. "Is everything all right?"

Cassie did not care to hear Hunter's response. Before he had a chance to answer, she left.

As Cassie pulled into her driveway, she glanced up at the house. The porch light had burned out months ago, and she had not yet changed the bulb. She sighed, making a mental note to add it to the list.

She knew her grandmother would not approve of the way she was keeping house. Her grandmother would've been in the midst of spring cleaning, scrubbing the floors and airing out the carpets. Outside she would've been busy as well, bundling up all the sticks that had fallen during the long, hard winter and stacking them neatly next to the woodpile. She would've raked and tilled her gardens in preparation for her bulbs.

But Cassie had not done any of that. She had meant to, truly, but the last few weeks had been spent in meetings with her co-workers, plotting strategies.

At least, that was her excuse. Although a hard worker, Cassie did not have a natural knack for homemaking.

"You need to pay attention," her grandmother had once said in exasperation. And so Cassie tried. But it didn't seem to help much. When her grandmother would mention that the watering can Cassie left in the backyard was turning rusty, Cassie would grab her camera to photograph it. When her grandmother had mentioned that a mouse had gotten into the cupboards, Cassie stayed awake all night with her camera, ready to snap.

Finally her grandmother had given up. Cassie, it seemed, was forever doomed to make bread that did not rise, sour spaghetti sauce and hard-as-rock cookies. But despite her lack of home-making skills, she knew her grandmother was proud of her.

She had worked hours of overtime to buy Cassie her camera. She'd filled the house with Cassie's photos, hanging them on the wall as if they were great works of art. When Cassie received a scholarship to college, her grandmother had told her that Cassie had made her the happiest woman in the world.

She had been devastated when Cassie dropped out to return home to care for her. "I'm fine," she had protested. "Don't be ridiculous."

But Cassie knew otherwise. The women at the mill had told Cassie of her grandmother's fainting spells and terrible head-aches. They told her that they feared her time was limited.

And so, Cassie returned. This time, however, things were dif-ferent. Cassie was the caretaker. For nearly two years she took care of her grandmother and the house as well as she could. But she had enjoyed every minute. She had loved her grandmother more than anyone in the world, and her death had left her feeling sad and alone. It was a loss from which she doubted she would ever recover.

Cassie reached back inside the car and pulled out the carton of ice cream she had bought at the convenience store. She planned on handling her sorrows her own special way. The past week called for a pint of chocolate chip ice cream and a spoon.

Out of the corner of her eye she saw a shadow pass under the eaves of the house. She paused. Although Shanville was so safe that most people didn't bother locking their doors, there were exceptions.

Cassie moved back toward her car and put her hand on the handle. "Who is it?" she asked. "Who's there?"

A tall, dark figure stepped into the moonlight. "We need to talk."

Her heart skipped a beat at the sight of Hunter Axon. She felt paralyzed, unable to move.

He stepped closer. "That was the second time you walked out on me."

He was standing in front of her, so close they were almost touching.

She forced herself to shift her eyes, breaking the spell. "What are you doing here?" she asked, making her way toward the house.

He grabbed her back. "Don't walk away, Cassie. You went to a lot of trouble to talk to me. I'm here now. I suggest you take advantage," he said, his eyes hardening.

She paused, looking him over. Would it make any difference? Doubtful. Still, she owed it to her friends to try. But would it help them? Or would it hurt them?

"I would like to talk to you," she said. "But I can't."

"I don't understand. You felt so strongly you traveled all the way to the Bahamas to meet with me."

"That was before..." Her voice drifted off.

"Before our night together?"

"No," she said, meeting his gaze directly. "Before I found out that talking to you could cost everyone their severance pay."

She could see the surprise in his eyes. "What?" he said.

"Willa told me that if I even try and talk to you, she would cancel the severance packages. She said I would never convince you, and we, meaning everyone who works at the mill, would be left with nothing."

He held her gaze. "There are situations where we have been forced to cancel a severance package. But it's not something I enjoy."

Was that supposed to comfort her?

He said, "I give you my word that anything said between us tonight is off the record. I will not hold it against you or the workers of Demion Mills."

He was staring at her intently. His eyes, although cold, were honest.

"Please," he said. "I would like the chance to talk to you."

He had just handed her a pass to get out of jail free. "Okay," she heard herself say finally.

He followed her inside the house. She turned on the light in the hall and said, "I think you know what I'm going to say."

"Is there a place where we can sit down?" he asked.

She straightened. Sit down. Good idea. She nodded toward

the living room. "In there." She moved a pile of newspapers off the couch and made room for him to sit.

She hurried to the kitchen and put her ice cream in the freezer. When she returned, he was looking at a series of photos of a blossoming flower.

"Did you do these?" he asked.

She nodded. "A long time ago."

"And this?" he asked, moving over to the next. It was a picture of a sunflower.

"My grandmother wanted flower photos in this room."

"You're good."

"Thanks."

"Really good. You could be a professional."

"But I'm not," she said curtly. She was not about to give in to flattery. As much as she appreciated the compliment, she didn't trust it. From what she was learning, Hunter Axon was capable of great charm when necessary.

"Your grandmother was not happy about your decision to drop out of school, was she?"

She looked at him.

"I did some research on you today," he said.

Research? He had been curious about her?

"Discreetly, of course," he added.

Of course. Hunter might be a lot of things but she had the feeling he was very discreet when it came to his women. All of his women. Hundreds and hundreds of women...

What was she doing? What did it matter how many women Hunter Axon had slept with?

"Why don't you sit down," she suggested again, motioning toward the couch she had cleared off.

He sat on the edge of the couch and glanced around. "Nice room."

Was he making fun of her? The room was nothing fancy, but Cassie thought it cozy. The furniture was old but comfortable.

"My grandmother decorated it forty years ago and I don't think it's ever been changed."

He was looking at her. She had seen that look before, in the Bahamas. It was a tender look, one normally reserved for sweethearts and lovers. He said, "It must be hard for you, living here without her."

Intellectually, she wasn't sure if he was sincere or not, but emotionally, it didn't seem to matter. She could feel the ice around her heart begin to thaw. "It is," she said.

Get a grip, she warned herself. This was no friendly conversation. She had to stay objective. "But I'm glad that she's not here to witness what you're doing to the community she loved so much."

Hunter glanced away and sighed. "Cassie," he said quietly, "you've made it clear what you think about my intentions for the mill. But you haven't talked about what happened in the Bahamas."

Cassie straightened. Did he really want to talk about that? What was he worried about—that since she knew who he was, she might stalk him or something? Or maybe pretend she was pregnant with his child? "What's to talk about? It was a weird case of mistaken identity. A bizarre twist of fate."

He sighed. "I never meant for any of this to happen. Had I known who you were…" His voice trailed off. But he didn't need to finish. If he had come all the way out here to tell her that he would not have slept with her if he had known that she was not just a factory worker, but *his* factory worker, he had wasted his time.

"Obviously," she said coldly. "If we had known the other's true identity, this would not have happened."

"I didn't say that," he responded. "I said I never intended for this to happen. I didn't say that I had any regrets or that if I had known who you were and why you were in the Bahamas I would have done anything different."

She paused. Now, *that* she was not expecting.

He stepped forward, taking her hand in his. "I've looked everywhere for you. I've had people calling hotels, searching their records."

"Why?"

"Because I wanted to…" He hesitated, glancing down at her hand. "I needed to see you again."

"You…you wanted to see me again?"

"And I found you," he said. "In the last place I expected."

She could feel the world fade away. They were once again back in the Bahamas. He was not Hunter Axon but her prince.

Unfortunately, it was a fantasy. And like all fantasies, the sooner this one came to an end the better. She let go of his hand. "You should go."

He looked at her. Finally he said, "I had hoped that perhaps we might…"

"Might what?" She shook her head. "Even if you weren't buying this company you'd still be Hunter Axon. And I'd still be a factory worker. But because you are Hunter—"

"Why does that change anything?" he interrupted.

"It changes everything. Because of you I'll soon be an unemployed factory worker."

"With the severance, you don't have to be a factory worker anymore. You can go back to school. You can study photography."

"I don't want to go back to school," she said. She shook her head. How could she expect him to understand? "I grew up at the mill, watching my mother and grandmother work."

Her eyes grew distant as she traveled back through time. "I remember looking at the way their fingers seemed to fly over the looms. They worked together, tying the threads and hanging them over the loom. They turned those pieces of thread into masterpieces."

She shook her head as she continued. "There was a time when I wanted to leave. I took up photography and went off to school. But then…" Her voice faded. "I came back." She glanced at Hunter. "And I've never regretted my decision. I love being a part of history, carrying on the family tradition of weaving. I'm not ashamed of what I do. I'm proud of it."

"I'm not saying you shouldn't be proud of the work you do…the work you've done. I'm just saying that perhaps you could look at this a little differently. Perhaps this is not as bad as it may seem. It will give you a chance to reevaluate."

"I don't want to reevaluate. I want to stay here at the mill."

"But the mill can't afford to stay open. I've seen the financials. It has not turned a profit in years."

"It could've. If Oliver had done something with the patent to Bodyguard."

"Not necessarily. I'm not sure the mill could handle the production for that patent. And I know it couldn't handle the marketing. That patent is a gamble. And the mill has no money to put behind it."

Cassie turned away. He had a point. But she was not ready to concede defeat. There had to be some way of saving the mill.

"Cassie," he said quietly, "surely you knew the mill was having financial problems."

She turned back to face him. "The mill was mismanaged. Oliver Demion single-handedly ran a once-profitable institution into the ground. He paid himself an enormous salary and offended some of our biggest clients. He's also never done any marketing or advertising. I know that, under the right management, this mill could be profitable once again."

He shook his head. "I'm sorry, Cassie."

"So that's it," she said. "Your mind is made up. You're going to close Demion Mills?"

"It will be another several months before we will be able to transfer production to our plant overseas, at which point you will all receive a generous severance."

She shook her head and glanced away. "Please go."

He sighed, his vexation obvious. "All right," he said resolutely. "But before I go…" He moved toward her. For a moment she thought he was planning on giving her one last kiss. Instead he reached into his pocket and pulled out her necklace.

"You found it," she said, breathing a sigh of relief. "It was my mother's. I never take it off. The clasp broke a while ago and I jerry-rigged it but—" She stopped. A brand-new clasp sparkled in the light. "You fixed it."

She looked at him and said, "Thank you."

It was a moment of tenderness. She glanced away and fumbled with the necklace, attempting to put it around her neck once more. "Let me help you," he said. Before she could object, he was behind her. His fingers brushed against her neck, causing a tingle that ran down her spine and into her toes. She closed her eyes, her willpower fading. Maybe they still had a chance. Maybe she could still talk some sense into him.

"You can't close this mill," she said, turning to face him.

"What?"

"It's going to kill the town. I don't expect you to care about that, but the people... Almost all of them have worked at the mill their entire lives. It's all they know."

"Which is probably why they've stayed. I'm not cutting them loose without anything. With the mill staying open for a while and the severance package, they will have more than enough to give them time to find another—"

"Even if you're right, and they can find another job, what makes you think they want to?"

Hunter looked at her. She could see his gaze harden. Unfortunately, it only made him look more handsome.

"This is what I do, Cassie. And if it wasn't me, Oliver Demion would sell to someone else. Someone not so generous."

She could feel his gaze sweep over her. He stepped forward and touched her cheek.

She froze. She didn't want to speak any longer. She wanted to touch him. To kiss him.

It was enough to give him one more chance. She took a breath and said, "What about the people who can't find another job?"

"What do you mean?"

"People like Ruby Myers, who's worked for the mill for the last forty years. If the mill closes, how will she make a living?"

He was in front of her. He raised her chin toward him with his index finger. "She will have social security and a handsome severance."

Cassie took a step back, moving away from him. "That's not good enough. Frances Wells can't leave town, either. She's caring for a sick husband. Xavier Scott can't leave, neither can Miranda Peters or Richard Smith."

"Perhaps we can work out a different severance. Perhaps we can give them more money."

"That's very generous of you, but I'm not interested in negotiating a severance."

"What exactly were you suggesting, then?"

She straightened. "Sell us back the mill."

"Are you prepared to make me an offer?"

Cassie glanced away. She had spoken with many banks since she found out Oliver was trying to sell the mill. But none had been willing to finance a loan.

"Cassie," Hunter said, and once again the warmth was gone from his voice. From the cold way in which he regarded her, she thought for a moment she might have gone too far. That perhaps he would renege and cancel the severance package. "I'm not in the business of giving away properties. And I'm not about to finance an operation that has not turned a profit for years."

She nodded. It was hopeless. He would not change his mind. "Goodbye, Mr. Axon."

He sighed. "Just ask yourself this, Cassie. What will you and all your friends do if I sold you the mill and you were forced to declare bankruptcy? Just imagine. No severance package, no last pay period. Just gone."

"We won't have the opportunity to find out, will we?"

He gave her one last glance before turning away. As he walked toward the door, he stopped.

Suddenly Cassie realized what he was looking at. The photo she had taken of Hunter on the beach was sitting on top of the table. She had printed it out as soon as she returned home, a reminder of the mysterious and kind man to whom she had given her heart.

He glanced back at her and looked, for a moment, as if he might speak. Instead he turned back toward the door and left. Cassie ran to the door and leaned outside.

"Hunter," she said, her voice stopping him. "Thank you for returning my heart."

And with that she slammed the door.

Six

Cassie looked at the white posterboard. She picked up a red marker and wrote: Workers on Strike.

"Here you go, Mabel," she said, handing it to the grey-haired woman in front of her. "You can go join the others."

It was a cold, drizzly day, typical of early spring. The winds whipped in from the mountains, swirling around town and chilling even the sturdiest of souls. But no one noticed the biting rain or the invincible wind. They had more important things on their minds. Like the strike.

After Hunter had left, Cassie had called everyone and anyone she could think of. Her message was the same: Hunter Axon would not listen. Urgent action was needed.

But what?

Christine Humblegot, who worked as Oliver's secretary, said she had overheard Willa tell Oliver that because the plant in China would not be up and running for another three months, she was counting on the workers at Demion Mills to begin producing Bodyguard samples so that they could deliver on time.

In other words, Hunter needed them. At least temporarily.

It was their only bargaining chip.

A strike might make him more willing to negotiate. Of course, a man like Hunter would be able to find a way to work around the strike—but it would cause him some headaches.

"This is so exciting," Mabel said. "I've never done anything like this in all my sixty-three years." Mabel held the poster proudly above her head and stopped. "Do you think the police will arrest us?"

"I doubt it," Cassie said. "Herb has his hands full." Cassie nodded toward Herb Blansfield, Shanville's sheriff. He was standing by the entrance to the mill, waving a sign that said Keep Jobs In Shanville. Although it had been years since he last worked in the mill, his wife and daughter were employed as weavers.

Cassie smiled as she looked over the crowd. She had explained the risks to each and every one of them. But that seemed to only firm their resolve. Despite the risk, every single member of the mill had enthusiastically joined the strike. They were courageous and determined. No one was willing to see the mill disappear into the hands of a company who had only one intention: to destroy it.

So the whole community had turned out to show its resolve. Luanne was there with her six daughters, all mill employees. Christine was there with her grandparents.

If Hunter Axon thought they would just roll over and hand him the keys to their beloved mill, he was wrong.

Hunter left Cassie's with one agenda: he wanted to kiss her.

Not that a simple kiss would quench his thirst. His need for her had taken on a life of its own, growing stronger by the day. The thought of never seeing her again had brought him to the brink of despair.

To have found her was a miracle.

But their reunion had fallen quite short of his anticipation. Instead of falling into his arms, she had been ready to run him out of town on a rail.

Once again he found himself thinking about what had transpired the previous evening. Instead of making love they'd argued about Cassie's desire to save a broken-down mill.

How could she expect him to fund a business that had not shown a profit for years, a business that was on the verge of bankruptcy?

Yet Cassie's reaction was not unique. In his years of business he had encountered many workers who, like Cassie, made him desperate offers to save their businesses. He had been vilified as a devil, an unfeeling corporate raider who took advantage of other people's misfortune.

Some of them had given him pause. A few had made him wonder if he had done the right thing.

But of course he had. After all, he did not buy successful businesses. Their misfortune was brought on by the same reasons that were responsible for the demise of Demion Mills—a greedy heir who had no business expertise and workers who were paid more than the company could afford. Sometimes the product needed to be redefined; sometimes the whole concept of the business needed to be simplified.

He would figure out the solution and roll the company into Axon Enterprises where it would become part of a profitable, money-making organization.

It was the only way. And, most of the time at least, the workers eventually realized that they had no choice but to accept their fate.

Sooner or later Cassie would realize that, too. In the meantime he needed to win her back. He needed to make her forget about the mill.

But how? She had made it clear the night before where she stood. She was not interested in him unless he reconsidered his plans for the mill.

But that was not an option.

He needed to persuade her that his buying the mill was the best scenario in a long list of awful ones. And then they would pick up where they left off in the Bahamas. Once again he remembered how she felt next to him, her warm silky body resting beside him.

Flowers, he thought. He would start with flowers. A dozen roses each day and—

As he pulled into the parking lot he was suddenly distracted by the people waving signs in front of the mill. He stepped out of his car and discovered Willa and Oliver standing side by side, looking at the strikers.

"I can't believe it," he heard Oliver say.

"What's going on?" asked Hunter.

"They're striking," said Willa.

"What do we care?" Oliver said. "We're moving the operations to China, anyway." He smiled at Willa. But she did not smile back.

"We do care," she said. "We need to keep this mill operational until China is set up and ready to go."

"So," Oliver said, the smile fading from his lips, "what do we do?"

Hunter glanced at Willa. "Find out who the organizer is."

"And?"

"Bring them to me," he said in a voice that inspired fear in even the strongest of men. With that he brushed past Oliver and headed toward the mill.

If these people thought he could be taken down by a simple strike, they were mistaken. If they wanted a fight, they were going to get it. He was done being Mr. Nice Guy.

Cassie sipped her steaming hot chocolate. She had seen Hunter from a distance, and the unhappy look on his face was enough to bring a smile to her lips. He was learning that the artisans at the mill were a bit tougher and more well organized than he thought.

"Look who's coming," Ruby said, motioning behind Cassie. Cassie turned around. Willa was walking toward her, her lips taut in a half smirk, half smile. As she walked, the crowd became silent and parted, staring as she passed. She did not acknowledge them but kept her eyes focused on Cassie.

Cassie stood up straight and inhaled, as if bracing for a fight.

Willa stopped in front of her. "Cassie," she said, "can I talk to you for a minute?"

Cassie nodded. She handed the remainder of her hot chocolate to Ruby, who accepted it with a comforting nod. Then Cassie turned and followed Willa back into the empty building. They walked in silence to the cafeteria. Once inside the cavernous room, Willa turned to face her. She said, "I believe you owe me an apology."

"We had no choice but to strike," Cassie explained. "I tried to speak with you—"

"I'm not talking about the strike," Willa said in a tone so sweet it was bitter. "I was talking about last night."

Cassie suddenly remembered that she had left the party shortly after her confrontation with Hunter.

"Honestly, Cassie," Willa said, hands on her hips. "I have a mind to fire you right now. How dare you harass the governor."

Cassie did not look away. She was not afraid of Willa, nor was she intimidated by her threats.

Willa raised an eyebrow. "Don't make the mistake of thinking that your...relationship with Hunter will protect you."

Cassie swallowed. Had Hunter confided in Willa? "I don't have a relationship with Mr. Axon." And she wasn't lying. A one-night stand hardly qualified as a relationship.

"You're a fool," Willa said. "Whatever it is you're doing to him or with him, it's not going to make any difference in the long run. Do you understand me?"

"No," Cassie said. "I don't."

"Hunter Axon is a kiss-and-don't-call type of guy. He may be intrigued by you, but it'll fade as soon as you start interfering with business. If you're interested in landing more than a job, I'd suggest you stop interfering with Hunter's plans."

"You're wrong about my interest in Hunter. I want to save this mill. I'll do whatever I can to make that happen."

"Even if it means giving Hunter your virginity?"

"What?" Cassie said, startled. How could she know about that? How could Hunter have confided such an intimate detail?

"Don't think Oliver didn't tell me about how you've held on to it for all these long years."

Oliver. Oliver had told her she was a virgin. Hunter had kept his silence.

"Is that what you've offered Hunter?" Willa asked. "A night with a virgin?"

"I've had enough," Cassie said. She turned to leave.

But Willa stopped her with her words. "Do your friends know of your feelings for the man who's destroying their company?"

"I told you, Willa, you're wrong." Once again Cassie reminded herself that the man who had captured her heart was fictitious, a figment of her imagination. He bore no resemblance to the man known as Hunter Axon.

Willa looked her over carefully. "Perhaps," she said. "But I doubt it. I'm never wrong."

Cassie glanced away. She wanted to say something, but what?

"He'll never care about you," Willa said. "Other women have tried, just like you, to get his attention. They only succeeded in irritating him. Hunter does not like to be distracted from his mission."

Once again Cassie faced Willa. "And what is that?"

Willa smiled. "Making money, of course."

Hunter had made a decision. He would cancel one week of severance for every hour of the strike. A person who had worked there for eight years would erase his entire severance in one day.

It was a drastic measure, but necessary. He had little patience for games.

Willa entered without knocking and crossed her arms.

Hunter snapped his phone shut. "What are their demands?" he asked, rolling up his sleeves as if readying for a fight.

Willa smiled smugly. "I've found the organizer. I think she should tell you herself." With a dramatic sweep of her arm, Willa stepped aside.

Cassie.

She stood still, her arms crossed in front of her and her eyes defiant. A bandanna was tied around her head, holding back her beautiful reddish-brown hair. She was wearing a loose-fitting flannel shirt rolled up at the sleeves and an old pair of jeans.

As far as Hunter was concerned, he had never been presented with a more worthy foe. Nor had he ever seen anyone so beautiful.

"You?" he heard himself say.

Willa said, "She's the one behind this ridiculous strike. She was working the phones all night, organizing the workers. According to Oliver, they've never done anything like this before."

He continued to look at Cassie. "Why?"

Cassie stood up straight and said, "We're not going to let you take this mill away from us. Not without a fight."

"I didn't take this mill away from you," he said. "The Demions did."

"You are the owner," she said, narrowing her fiery green eyes. "Correct?"

As he stared at the woman in front of him, he could feel his resolve melt. How could he tell her that he was canceling her severance? How could he hurt her?

He had to admit he admired her spirit. But what could she possibly hope to gain by such a ruse? The mill would be closing in a few months. He could bring in other workers in the meantime. Or could he? This was not a typical factory. Loom weaving was a dying skill. Machines had taken over for people. And in the rare cases where human skills were needed, production had been moved, as he intended, to China. Where would he find skilled artisans who were familiar with the antiquated looms?

He stopped himself. Was he just trying to make a case for Cassie? Were his personal feelings affecting his business decisions?

Hell, yes. Anyone else would have already received an ultimatum and been shown the door.

"This is ridiculous," Willa said. "You are wasting Mr. Axon's time."

He held up a hand to silence her. "What are your demands?" he asked Cassie.

"Give up the plant in China. Keep the jobs here."

He shook his head. He might be amenable to a demand for more severance, but did she really think he would abandon his intention so easily? "That's impossible."

Willa said, "The cost benefit will not—"

"So sell us the mill," Cassie said, interrupting her.

"What?" Willa asked.

Hunter looked at her intently and said, "Have you found a bank to finance the sale?"

She swallowed and glanced away. "We will."

Willa laughed. It was a shrill, almost piercing sound. "Axon Enterprises is not a bank."

"This isn't right," Cassie said, staring at him with burning, reproachful eyes. "You have no interest in running a mill, nor do you have any appreciation for the work that we do."

"Whether I appreciate it or not is beside the point," Hunter said calmly. "I bought it. And I own it."

"All you want is the Bodyguard patent. So take it. But give us back the mill."

He was silent for a moment. "Sell you the mill, but keep the patent?"

"That's right. You can go produce the patent in China. And we'll stay right here, making beautiful fabrics."

He sighed. He felt for her. He did. And he wanted to help her. But even well-meaning workers would not be able to keep this mill afloat. It had been hemorrhaging money for years. "What will that do? You'll still have a mill on the verge of bankruptcy."

"We'll take that chance."

"Cassie," Oliver said, appearing in the doorway. He looked shocked to see her there. "What are you doing?"

"I'm talking to your new boss," she said simply.

He took her by the arm. "Why are you doing this to me?"

Hunter's blood boiled at the sight of another man touching Cassie. Get your hands off her, he ached to say. Instead he said in a voice that commanded attention, "Let her speak."

Cassie shrugged her arm away from Oliver's grasp.

"We're not going down without a fight," she said, looking directly at Hunter. "We will not go back to work until you agree to our demands."

He did not like being threatened. "I can bring in others to do your jobs," he said.

"It will take time. Time which, we understand, you don't have."

Under any other circumstance, he would have been furious. He did not negotiate with soon-to-be-obsolete factory workers. But the frustration he felt toward the situation only seemed to fuel his desire for Cassie.

She crossed her arms, defiant. "We're not going to stop at the strike, either. We'll call the news media, we'll write letters to politicians...."

"The news media?" Willa said. "What news media?"

"The Albany stations."

Willa scoffed. "As if they care about a local-yokel mill an hour away."

"I'm not going to give up until you listen to me," Cassie said to Hunter. "I may not succeed but I can make this very, very difficult for you."

Willa took a step toward Cassie. "How dare you threaten Mr. Axon like that." She turned back toward Hunter and said, "I apologize for this insolence. I suggest you let me deal with this little insurgence."

Still looking at Cassie, Hunter said to Willa, "Will you give me a minute alone with Cassie, please?"

Willa said, "I think this is setting a poor example. If you kowtow to these ridiculous demands, any of them, it will hinder our efforts in other communities."

"I'll deal with Cassie," Hunter repeated through clenched jaws.

"Oh," Willa said, as if he had been communicating in code. "Alone. Right, I got it." Willa shot Cassie a nasty smile. "Of course, Hunter," she said. "Come along, Oliver."

When Oliver and Willa had left, Hunter took a step toward Cassie and said, "Sit down."

"No, thanks," she said.

He took another step toward her. "I wasn't asking you. I was telling you."

"Thanks for the explanation, but I wasn't confused."

"Yes," he said, "I think you are. This is not personal, Cassie. Whether you like it or not, I'm your boss. And you are costing me money."

"So fire me," she said.

"If I thought that would solve anything, I would. But I'm not about to give up the one degree of control I have."

This time it was Cassie's turn to step toward him. She looked up at him with anger smoldering in her eyes. "I don't care who you are. I'm not afraid of you. You can't control me."

It was a dare, plain and simple. But as he stared into Cassie's cool green eyes, his anger once again gave way to passion. She was wrong. He may not be able to control her mind but he damn well could control her body. He had done it before and was desperate to do it again. He wanted to take her in his arms, to make her sigh with pleasure and burn with desire.

"I see," he said. He swallowed and forced himself to turn away. "What are you offering?"

"What?"

"You're the mediator," he said. He glanced back at her. "You want to buy this mill. Tell your people to give me an offer."

"You'll consider it?"

He paused. "I'll consider just about anything."

She took a step backward and glanced away. But she was not quick enough. Hunter had seen the surprise in her eyes. She had not expected him to negotiate. So why was she doing this?

"I have to discuss this with my co-workers," she said.

"I'll give you twenty-four hours. You can present your proposal to my board."

"Tomorrow?"

Hunter thought he could detect a hint of panic. "Correct."

"Your board is coming here?"

"No," he said. "You're going to them."

"Where?"

"The Bahamas."

She paled, revealing a hint of despair. Normally he would

enjoy watching an antagonizer squirm. But not this time. He wanted to comfort her. To tell her everything would be all right.

"Be at the airport at noon tomorrow," he said. "My plane will be waiting."

She cleared her throat and asked, "Are we going together?"

"No," he said. "I'm leaving momentarily. After all, there's no reason for me to stay. Unless…"

"Unless what?"

"Unless you want me to."

He let his eyes gaze over her, drinking in her beauty.

She swallowed and touched the top button of her shirt as if making sure it was still closed. "No."

"So be it." He walked over to the door and opened it. "Until tomorrow."

She stood up and walked past him, accidentally brushing up against his arm as she passed. After she had left he shut the door and smiled. At that moment he would've been willing to sell her the mill for another night of passion.

Seven

By the time Cassie landed in Nassau it was nearly six. The attendant directed her out of the plane and toward the waiting limousine.

As she walked across the tarmac, she found herself shaking her head. It seemed unbelievable that she, Cassie Edwards, would be flying in a private plane and driving around in a limousine. After all, she was the girl who had to stick a hairbrush in her choke to start her car, the girl whose car engine leaked oil so badly she was forced to carry a case of oil and a can opener so she could add more at each destination.

She wondered what it would be like to be as rich as Hunter Axon. She knew that some people assumed there was no such thing as having too much money, but she disagreed. To some unfortunate souls, money was like a drug, intoxicating and overwhelming. The more they had, the more they wanted.

Like Oliver. He had been the richest man in Shanville, living a life that most just dreamed of. But it was not enough. And his quest for more cost him his company, his town and the people who loved him. She was certain that Oliver would one day discover that wealth could not buy him what he wanted most: happiness.

She couldn't help but compare Oliver to Hunter Axon. Hunter was intense, serious and ambitious. Not to mention one of the richest men in the country. But was he happy? He did not have a wife or children. But he had his pick of women, which, in and of itself, would probably be enough to make most men happy.

Cassie nervously licked her lips. She had to stop thinking of Hunter in such personal terms. He was her employer, her boss. End of subject. It did not matter if he was happy or unhappy.

She stepped inside the limousine and introduced herself to the driver. She then opened up her proposal and went over her notes one last time. After a grueling seven-hour meeting, the employees of Demion Mills had agreed on an offer. They would not try to buy back the patent. They couldn't afford it. But they would give Hunter more than a fair price for the mill. The deal, however, was dependent on his cooperation. They would make payments to him, forcing him to act as a bank.

She knew that the offer was not strong enough. But they had little choice. No bank would give them a loan. Their homes were their only collateral, and if the mill failed, their homes and land would be worthless.

So why would Axon Enterprises agree to such a scheme?

Once again she questioned their decision to go forward. Had Hunter been right? Would they have been better off just quietly accepting the severance?

Perhaps. But Cassie couldn't shake the feeling that they still had a chance of saving their company. For, despite what she had heard about Hunter Axon's ruthlessness, she had seen other qualities in him as well. She was almost certain that beneath the veneer of invulnerability was the man she had seen the first night they met: sensitive, protective and caring.

But were her personal feelings affecting her perception?

As much as she hated to admit it, she still felt a connection to him. She was certain she always would. After all, he was the first man with whom she had made love. And nothing would ever change that.

The driver slowed down. Cassie suddenly realized they were not at an office, but a home. As they approached, the iron gates at the end of the driveway swung open.

They drove down the long, curving drive. The house, invisible from the road, loomed ahead. It was exactly what she had imagined—a rambling Spanish-style mansion that, with its manicured grounds, resembled a country club.

She half expected to see the flurry of activity that was typical of great estates: gardeners, maids and butlers rushing around. But there was none of that. In fact, it seemed serenely quiet and deserted. Cassie stepped out of the limousine as the front door opened. Instead of a uniformed butler, a plain-faced, middle-aged woman in jeans and a T-shirt stood at the doorway and smiled. "Come on in," she said. "Mr. Axon is out back."

Cassie paused inside the cavernous entrance. Huge oil paintings, two stories high, filled the foyer. A large sweeping staircase straight from Tara wrapped its way toward the sky.

Cassie followed the woman through the French doors at the far end of the hall and out to the patio.

It was a view out of a magazine. Lush green acres rolling down to a white sandy beach and the green water of the Atlantic. Off to the right, stone lions guarded an infinity swimming pool.

Hunter was sitting at a table on the veranda, his back toward her. He glanced up as Cassie approached.

"Hello, Mr. Axon," she said.

The term "Mr. Axon" brought a slight smile to his face. He stood up and held out his hand. He didn't look as if he was dressed for a business meeting. The brown hair that had been slicked back in Shanville was curly and natural. He was wearing an outfit similar to the one he had worn their first night together, a soft linen shirt tucked into linen pants. "Miss Edwards."

She took his hand. Once again he held it as though he wasn't about to let go. And part of her wished he wouldn't. She gave herself a mental slap. Focus. She pulled away. "Where is everyone?"

"You mean the board?"

She nodded.

"We have to go to them." Still looking at her, he asked, "Are you ready?"

She nodded. "I hope so."

"Good." He nodded toward the setting sun. "I had hoped to do it today, but because of the delay in your arrival, I bumped it to tomorrow morning."

Which left...the night. And she had not made hotel reservations. As if reading her mind, he said, "I took the liberty of making reservations for you at a hotel around the corner. I think you'll find it has all the amenities you need."

And she had no doubt it cost a fortune, as well. She had investigated all the hotels on her last visit. Nothing was as inexpensive as the Barter Hotel.

"Thank you," she said, "But I prefer the hotel I stayed in the last time."

"Ah," he said. "The Barter Hotel by any chance?"

She nodded. How did he know that?

"It's closed temporarily."

"But I was just there."

"They're renovating."

"Oh," she said, disappointed.

"Of course, you're welcome to stay here. I have several guest rooms."

She shook her head. "No. No, thank you."

He nodded. She could see a twinkle in his eyes. Was he teasing her?

"In that case," he said, glancing at his watch, "I'll see you to the car."

"I'm leaving?"

When he paused, she glanced away. What was wrong with her? She had sounded disappointed, as if she had wanted to stay with him. For good reason. As much as she hated to admit it, she *was* disappointed.

"I'm afraid I have dinner plans this evening."

His news took her breath away. Dinner plans? With whom?

She tried to ignore the jealousy ripping through her heart. What did she expect? She was not dating him. She had merely slept with him. But if he had dinner plans, why would he invite her to spend the night?

Was he willing to go out to dinner with another woman and return home to sleep with her?

"Unfortunately it's an engagement I cannot cancel," he said, turning away as if dismissing her.

"I wouldn't expect you to," she said coldly. Hmph! What did she care if he had a date? He was free to see whomever he liked.

Right? Right!

The thin veneer of anger could not hide the deep well of despair.

But she was not allowed to feel despair. Nor was she allowed to feel territorial. She barely knew Hunter.

She swallowed her emotions as he led her through the house and back to the limo, where the driver stood outside her door, waiting. Hunter said, "I hope you enjoy your stay at the hotel. Everything is taken care of, so feel free to order anything you like from the room service menu."

"That's not necessary," she said. "I have my own money."

"My company has a suite of rooms at the hotel, permanently reserved for visitors," he said. "We have never charged a guest."

"Oh," she said. "Well then, thank you."

"I'll see you tomorrow morning," he said, slamming her door.

Hours later Hunter was once again staring out over the water. He shook his head as he remembered the expression on his comptroller's face at dinner when he had informed him that he was thinking about selling the mill to its employees. "Are you crazy?" the man had asked.

Hunter had not seen the offer, but he knew it would not be titillating enough to convince his staff. After all, the risk was so significant no bank would finance the loan. There was no way the workers could afford to offer him enough to make it worth his while.

"So why?" the comptroller had asked. "Why would you even consider this?"

Hunter had not answered his question. After all, what could he say? That he was smitten with one of the women who wanted to buy it? It seemed ridiculous. He barely knew Cassie.

But the mere thought of her was enough to bring a smile to his lips. He remembered the way she had walked into his office, her arms crossed, her beautiful face turned up in defiance. She had been wearing her work attire as if to remind him of who she was: Cassie Edwards, factory worker. What she didn't realize was that he didn't care whether she was a photographer or a factory worker. He was not impressed by fancy titles and clothes. Even external beauty rarely moved him. His attraction to Cassie was based on something else, something he couldn't define. A quality or qualities that, when put together, made her the most intriguing woman he had ever met.

But was that reason enough to give her what she wanted?

No. Intellectually he knew that selling the workers back the mill would be a mistake. But he had to consider it. He couldn't bear the thought of disappointing Cassie, a woman he barely knew. But was she worth the risk?

He needed another opinion. So tomorrow he would take Cassie to his board. And if his board approved, well then, so be it. Regardless of his future with Cassie, he would give her what she wanted.

Eight

Cassie brushed the bread crumbs off her skirt as she stared out the limousine window. She usually skipped breakfast, but today she had made an exception. She was presenting her offer to Hunter's board and she certainly didn't want her stomach growling in the middle of the presentation.

But her stomach was tied in such knots that she found it almost impossible to eat the large breakfast that had appeared at her door that morning, "Compliments of Mr. Axon." She had choked down a piece of toast and swallowed a few sips of coffee before heading out the door.

She tapped her fingers nervously on her legs. She had hardly slept the night before and she was certain she looked as tired as she felt. She had stayed up, tossing and turning, her mind going a million miles a minute.

She had every reason to be nervous. After all, she had never given a business presentation before. She did not know what to expect.

As much as she wished that that alone was responsible for her insomnia, the truth of the matter lay elsewhere. She didn't want to admit it, but she couldn't stop thinking about Hunter. How could he have invited her to spend the night at his house when he had a dinner date with someone else?

Was he trying to make her jealous? She doubted it. If he felt anything for her at all, it was lust, plain and simple.

But what did she care? So their one-night stand had turned into just that. That was what she had intended, right?

But she had not expected to see him again. She had expected to return home with a beautiful memory of a kind and gentle man. And now that she knew who he was...well, the beautiful memory had turned into an embarrassment. Instead of feeling grateful for the time they shared, she felt guilty. It was as if she had done something wrong. Something illicit. And she had. Instead of protecting her friends from Hunter Axon, she had slept with him.

And for some terrible reason, she wanted to do it again.

Ugh. What was wrong with her? How could she even think such a thing?

The limousine stopped at a red light. Cassie glanced out the window. They were approaching Hunter's estate. She swallowed and stared at the beautiful palm trees lining both sides of the street. Suddenly something caught her eye. It was a brightly colored bird, unlike any she had ever seen before.

She instinctively reached for her camera, but for the first time she could remember, her camera was not there. She had purposely not brought it. She was pretending to be a corporate executive, and an executive would not walk into a meeting with a camera slung around her neck.

Cassie's stomach growled. She patted it and sighed. It was hopeless.

As they approached the entrance to Hunter's estate, the iron gates swung open once again and the limousine drove down the long, narrow driveway. The driver stopped in front of Hunter's house and hurried out to open her door.

Cassie stepped out of the limousine and, after thanking her

driver, clutched her folder against her chest and strode up the steps. Just as she was raising her hand to knock, the door opened.

The woman who had answered the door the day before appeared in front of her. She greeted Cassie pleasantly and once again led her through the house and out the back. Hunter was outside, talking on the phone.

He was not dressed as she might have expected. He was wearing the most casual outfit he had worn so far: khaki Bermuda shorts and a short-sleeved linen shirt.

What was going on? "Is the meeting canceled?" she asked.

"No," he said. Perhaps it did not matter what he wore. After all, he was the boss. And maybe the dress code for professionals in the Bahamas was different from in the States.

If that was the case, then once again she was dressed inappropriately. She was wearing a vintage suit she had found at a flea market—a simple cotton skirt and a sleeveless silk blouse topped by a tight-fitting cotton blazer.

As the heat crept up her cheeks, Hunter smiled sweetly, putting her fears to rest. "You look nice."

She couldn't help but appreciate the gesture. "Thanks," she said.

"All right," he said. "Let's go." With that, he turned and began to walk toward the water.

"Isn't the car that way?" she asked, motioning behind her.

"Yes," he said, continuing to walk.

She hurried to catch up with him. "I don't understand."

"We're traveling by boat," he said, nodding toward the cigarette boat in front of them.

"A boat?" Now she really was confused. "I just assumed we were going to your office."

"We're meeting at an island offshore," he said, jumping aboard. Like his yacht, the boat looked brand-new. Hunter said, "You might want to take those shoes off. And, uh, the stockings as well."

She just looked at him. The stockings?

As if reading her mind, he shrugged and said, "You're welcome to keep them on if you like but this deck is slick. I know you wouldn't want to end up in the water before your presentation."

She glanced down. How in the world would she get her panty hose off? Was it possible to do it and somehow keep her dignity? No. She'd just have to take her chances.

"It's all right," she said. She held on to the rail and hopped on. The minute her feet hit the deck of the boat she felt them give way. In that split second she knew that Hunter had been right. It was no time for a swim.

But before she hit the water, he grabbed her. He swung her around as if she were no heavier than a feather. He held her close. Looking in her eyes he said, "You might want to reconsider your decision."

"My decision?" she murmured. What decision was he referring to? Her decision to spend the night alone in a hotel room when she could've been snuggled up next to him?

He leaned forward, and for a split second she thought he was going to kiss her. Instead he righted her and, glancing at her panty hose, said, "You can take them off below if you prefer."

She nodded. He slowly removed his hands. As he turned the key in the ignition, she went below, where she took off her panty hose, rolled them up and stuck them in her purse.

She took off her jacket and walked back up, barefoot and sleeveless. She sat down next to him.

He was idling the boat in the water. "Ready?"

She nodded.

"Hold on," he said. He revved the engine, and with a start, they took off across the water.

"Isn't this a little unorthodox?'" she asked over the din of the engine.

"What do you mean?"

"Taking a boat to a board meeting."

He shrugged his shoulders. "I don't like doing things by the book."

The boat seemed to glide across the water. They were headed straight into the Atlantic. Up to the left, Cassie could see a school of dolphins. "Look," she said, excited. She pointed them out to Hunter.

He slowed the boat down. When she glanced at him, she saw that he was looking not at the dolphins but at her. "Was the hotel suitable?" he asked.

She nodded and turned back toward the dolphins. "Great," she said. "Thanks for breakfast."

She glanced sideways at him. Once again she found herself wondering about his evening. Whom had he spent it with? "What about you?" she asked.

"What do you mean?"

"I remember you said you had dinner plans."

He nodded. "Oh, yes." He glanced back at her. "It was a long night."

A long night. She got it. He wanted her to know that he'd slept with her. Whoever she was.

How dare he? How could he be so narcissistic as to assume that she would even care—

The boat hit a wave straight on. Water splashed against her silk blouse, making it cling to her skin. Her bra was clearly visible. Not exactly the kind of outfit you wanted to wear on a boat, beside a man with whom you had just slept, a man who was now sleeping with someone else. But that was the least of her worries.

"Sorry," Hunter said. "It's choppier than I thought." She saw his eyes glance toward her chest. He nodded toward the back. "There's a towel back there."

She grabbed the towel and wrapped it around her. When she sat back down, he pointed toward the island they were approaching. "That's where we're going."

"But…it looks almost deserted."

"It is. Almost."

He drove up to an old dock. He turned off the boat and began securing it to the dock.

"Where are we meeting your board?"

"Right there," he said, pointing to an old rambling shack on the beach.

"There?" she asked, more surprised than horrified. "In that hut?"

He grinned.

"What is this, Hunter?" she asked. "What's going on?" This had to be some sort of joke. Where was the fancy marina? Where were the hotels? Where were the conference rooms? "You promised me—"

"I promised you an opportunity to meet my board. My board consists of one person—the only person whose advice I trust. My father. This is where he lives." He held out his hand. "That man there," he said, nodding behind him, "is the man who will decide your future."

She glanced toward the shore. The man approaching them was wearing a bright Hawaiian shirt with blue-jean shorts. His gray, bushy hair was partially covered by a baseball cap. He waved and smiled.

"Don't let his sweet-old-man demeanor fool you," Hunter said. "He's every bit as mean and tough as I am."

"Your father?"

"That's right."

"Why didn't you tell me?"

"Does it matter?" he asked. "If you had asked me who was on my board I would've been happy to tell you." He nodded toward her purse and her folder. "Now, why don't you hand those down to me so you can meet him."

Cassie glanced at her belongings. It seemed ridiculous to bring a purse on the beach. She pulled out her shoes and handed her folder to Hunter.

"Morning," Hunter's father said. He held out his hand to Cassie, helping her off the boat. "You must be Cassie. Hunter's told me all about you."

Cassie glanced at Hunter. "Really?"

"Yep," his father said. "You're every bit as pretty as he claimed."

She saw Hunter wince. "Let's keep it professional, Dad. Remember, this isn't a social visit."

Hunter had described her as pretty? She couldn't help but feel pleased.

"Whatever you say," his father replied with a big grin.

Cassie smiled in return. As she glanced at the older man's friendly smile, she could feel her apprehension fade. He seemed to radiate sincerity. "It's nice to meet you, Mr. Axon."

"Phil. Call me Phil."

"Hey, Phil," said Hunter. He nodded toward the cottage. "Are we meeting at the house?"

"Inside?" he asked. "On such a beautiful day?"

It was beautiful. Cassie glanced at the sky. Eighty degrees and sunny, with not a drop of humidity.

"I was hoping," Phil continued, "that we might be able to discuss things over a pole."

"Excuse me?" Cassie asked.

"I don't think Cassie is interested in fishing, Dad."

"Actually," Cassie said, "I would love to." She still wasn't sure if Hunter had been telling her the truth when he said the future of the mill rested in the hands of his board—his father. But if her fate really did rest in the hands of this seemingly kind and simple man, then so be it. Perhaps she still had a chance of saving the mill after all.

Phil smiled and held out his arm. Cassie looped her hand through it and together they walked toward an embankment at the top of which were four chairs.

It didn't take Cassie long to start talking about Shanville and Demion Mills. She told Hunter's father the story of how the mill began and described how it had become the anchor of the town. She told him about the looms and explained how they hand wove the material. She talked about the people who worked there and explained why their futures were dependent on the mill.

Hunter's father listened patiently. When she was finished, Phil asked her the same question Hunter had asked. "What makes you think you can save it?"

She looked at Hunter. "I'm not sure I can. But I know I have to try."

He shrugged. "Fair enough." He glanced at Hunter. "How much of a hit will you take?"

"He's keeping the patent," Cassie said defensively, before Hunter could answer. "We're just asking him to finance the buy-back."

Hunter raised his eyebrows. "The mill has not made a profit in five years."

Phil maintained eye contact with his son. "So this is not a business decision, is it?"

Cassie swallowed. Perhaps she had been wrong about Phil Axon's understanding nature. She said, "We'll pay him back regardless. Even if we have to sell our homes to do it."

Hunter said to his father, "You and I can talk about this later."

"There's nothing to talk about."

"What?" both Hunter and Cassie asked simultaneously.

Phil glanced at his son. "I think she's a woman of her word. If she says she'll pay you back, then she'll pay you back."

"With interest," Cassie said.

Hunter glanced away, obviously surprised by his father's proclamation. Before he had a chance to respond, however, his phone rang. He flipped it open and turned away as he spoke in a low voice.

Cassie looked at Phil and smiled. "Thank you," she said.

"You're more than welcome. But I think you should know it's ultimately Hunter's decision."

"Then," she said wistfully, "I doubt we stand a chance."

"I disagree."

She gave him a puzzled look.

"I understand why you might say that. I know his reputation. The corporate robber baron. And I'm not saying it's not deserved. But I know a different side."

She glanced away.

"You know," his father said, "life hasn't been easy for Hunter. Not easy at all. After his mother died, I went through a hard time. Things just got worse when I lost my job. I came here to figure things out. My mother—Hunter's grandmother—was worried about us living out here alone. She didn't have much faith in my ability to bring up a child. And I suppose she was right. I could barely take care of myself.

"We never had much money," he continued. "I did my best,

but I was dependent on the sea. Sometimes the fish were plentiful, sometimes they weren't. We never had any extra money for books, clothes, medicine, the stuff most kids take for granted."

Hunter's father was a nice man who obviously loved his son. But how could he excuse Hunter's behavior? Lots of children grew up poor. They didn't turn into money-hungry tycoons.

"One year Hunter's grandma got sick. She'd never been in good shape. Well, we put her in the boat and got her over to the mainland. But we waited and waited for them to check her into the hospital. In the meantime, we kept watching all these other people just walk right in and get service. See, it didn't matter if she was dying. We were poor. They took the ones with money or insurance first. By the time we finally got in, it was too late. She died. They tried to save her, but they couldn't. Hunter was convinced if we'd had money, things would've turned out differently."

"I'm sorry," she said.

"His goals were commendable. He was driven not by greed but by compassion."

She didn't answer. She did not want to be the one to tell him that honorable intentions did not necessarily make an honorable man. But still, she couldn't help but be touched by Hunter's history. If her grandmother had suffered the same fate, who knew what impression that might have made on her?

"How did he end up at Yale?"

"After his grandma died, Hunter applied to a boarding school. He got in, and when he graduated he applied to the best of schools, determined to work his way through college." He smiled. "He's done it all by himself, every step of the way."

She understood why he would be proud. It was an impressive feat—a boy of simple means turning himself into one of the richest men in the country.

Phil shrugged. "I know I'm rambling."

"Not at all," she said with a smile.

He looked back at the water. "I must say, when Hunter told me he was bringing a lady out here I just assumed it was a date. He doesn't often bring his associates."

She glanced at Hunter. He was still talking on the phone, his back to them, oblivious to the conversation occurring behind him. She felt a pang of jealousy. Did he bring dates often? How many women had he brought to meet his father?

As if reading her mind, Phil said, "Although I don't know why I'd think it was anything but a business associate, I can't remember the last time he brought a girlfriend out here."

She breathed a sigh of relief. But what did she care? She was not dating him. Phil said, "He's a good man, my Hunter."

She glanced down. A good man? He was a powerful man, a man who had made millions. But he was not exactly known for his philanthropic nature. Then again, from what Phil had just told her, she could understand why he might think such a thing. "I've always felt the one thing my son needed was a good woman."

"I don't think your son has any trouble finding women."

"Just not the right one." He shook his head. "He thought he found her once."

"What do you mean?" Cassie asked, stabbed by a momentary pang of jealousy.

"He was going to marry her. Darn near broke his heart, she did. I tried to warn him. Saw it coming a mile away." He shrugged. "But he's always had a mind of his own."

"Well," Hunter said, appearing behind him, "what did I miss?" Cassie glanced up at him. Hunter had suffered a broken heart? She found it difficult to imagine. She had just assumed him to be the heartbreaker, not the other way around.

"Oh, we're just getting to know each other. Right, Cassie?" Phil asked with a wink.

She nodded.

"Cassie," Phil said, "it seems a shame to go back to the mainland so soon. Would you like to see the island?"

She glanced at Hunter, who looked at his watch. She picked up on his cue and said, "I'm not sure we have time."

"Come on now, Hunter," Phil said. "She's come a long way. And it's lunchtime."

"All right," Hunter reluctantly agreed.

Phil smiled. "You should take her to the fishmonger." He shrugged. "The island only has one decent restaurant and it's not much."

"Aren't you coming?" Cassie asked hesitantly. The only reason she had been amenable to staying was that she thought *he* was inviting her.

"Me?" he asked, as if the thought had never occurred to him. "I've got too much work to do. But you two go on."

"Too much work?" Hunter asked, surprised.

"You got it," Phil said. "Now go on."

Hunter rolled his eyes.

Cassie stood up. "I'm not exactly dressed for an island tour."

"Leave your shoes here. Besides that, you're fine."

"My shoes?" Cassie repeated.

Hunter shrugged. "People rarely wear shoes on the island."

"I'll hold on to them for you," Phil said. "Don't you worry."

As they walked away, Hunter whispered, "Don't let my dad pressure you. You don't have to do this if you don't want to. I can take you back."

She glanced around. The sweet smell of jasmine filled the air. She could feel her resolve weaken. After all, how often did she travel to an island paradise? "No," she said. "I would like to stay. If, of course, it's okay with you."

"My schedule is clear for the day."

She nodded. Once again she found herself wondering why Hunter had brought her there. "I like your dad," she said. "He seems like a nice man."

"He is."

She stopped walking. "Does his opinion really make a difference?"

"Not typically," he said, without looking away.

Any optimism she might have felt disappeared with his words. She swallowed hard, trying not to reveal her frustration. "So, why am I here?"

"Because," he said, "this is not a typical situation."

"So you're honestly considering my proposal?" she said, as hope once again filled her heart.

"You wouldn't be here if I wasn't." His expression stilled and grew serious. He looked as if he was waiting for her to speak. But what did he want her to say?

He glanced away and nodded toward a small motorbike next to the house. "This is our transportation."

"That?" she said, looking at the bike. There was barely room for one person, not to mention two.

He jumped on. "Climb on," he said, turning the key to the ignition.

Cassie hesitated. Hunter met her eyes, as if daring her. He said, "You wanted to see the island. This is how people travel here."

She hiked up her skirt and sat behind him. Her bare legs rested against his.

"Hold on," he said.

As the bike jolted forward, she instinctively grabbed on to Hunter's waist. Through his shirt she could feel his taut muscles. Once again she saw his naked body, towering above her as he penetrated deep inside her. At the memory she stiffened slightly and leaned back.

They were traveling down a narrow dirt road carved out of a jungle. She could see glimpses of island life—brightly colored birds, the deep blue Atlantic. Finally they came out into a clearing. It was as if she had stepped back in time. Vendors of exotic fruit and fish crowded the streets. Although there was a small marina, it was wooden and rickety.

"This is the island that time has forgotten," Hunter said, stopping the bike in front of a small building.

"I'm surprised that some big resort hasn't gobbled this up yet."

"No," he said. "It's not going to happen, either."

"I wouldn't be too sure." She glanced at him. But she could tell by the expression on his face that he was not making an educated guess. He knew for a fact this island was safe from development. "You own this island, don't you?"

He held back a grin. "Let's eat."

So he owned an island, too. "I'm surprised you haven't sold it off to a developer. I bet you could make some money."

He stopped. "Believe it or not, I'm not all about money."

"Prove it."

"If I was all about money, you wouldn't be here right now." He was towering above her. His voice was low and his eyes were cold.

He held her gaze for a moment before turning and opening the door. The bright sunlight disappeared. They were in a small, dark room with a long bar behind which a man was grilling fish.

Hunter nodded toward a stool. "Have a seat."

"Hunter!" the man said, beaming when he saw him. "This is a surprise."

"I was in the neighborhood," Hunter said.

"I talked to your father," the man said. "He tells me you're very busy these days." The man looked at Cassie and smiled again. "I can see why."

Hunter raised an eyebrow. "I'm afraid you're wrong." He glanced at Cassie. "She thinks I'm an arrogant bastard."

The man looked at Cassie and frowned.

Embarrassed, she said, "I never said—"

"I didn't say you did. I said you thought it." She could see the mischievous twinkle in his eye. "Freddy, I'd like you to meet Cassie Edwards, a business associate."

"Nice to meet you, Miss Edwards," Freddy said with a smile. He grasped her hand warmly. "But you're wrong about this man here. He's the most decent man I've ever met."

"I think you give me a little too much credit, Freddy. But thank you."

Freddy chuckled. "I'll give you two the specials. It will fix you right up."

She glanced at Hunter. He was obviously still tickled by his own joke. "I enjoyed talking to your father. He's not what I would've expected," she said, as Freddy chopped a head off a fish. She looked away.

"How so?"

Who would think the father of a corporate giant would be so down to earth and nice? "He seems so…perceptive."

"He can be," Hunter said.

As they ate their meal, Hunter glanced at the woman beside him. He had enjoyed introducing her to his family and friends and the island he still referred to as home. Hunter turned back toward Freddy. He had known him his whole life. The two had grown up together, attended the local school, graduated in the same class. Although Hunter had never told another soul, it was he who had bought Freddy this restaurant. He had offered to set him up anyplace in the world he desired but Freddy had not wanted to move. He confessed his dream had always been to have a little restaurant right there on the beach. And so, that was exactly what Hunter had given him. But it was his friend who had made the restaurant a success.

"What about dessert?" Freddy asked when they were finished.

Cassie shook her head. "No thanks. That was delicious, though."

Freddy smiled and flashed Hunter the thumbs-up. Hunter could see Cassie turn red with embarrassment. "I like her!" Freddy said.

"Don't get too excited there," Hunter said. "Like I said, she's a business associate."

Freddy winked. "Well, maybe your business associate would like to see Blind Man's Peak."

"I don't think so," Hunter said, looking at her. "She needs to get back to the mainland."

"What's Blind Man's Peak?" she asked.

"We used to go there as kids. It's on top of an old volcano. It's got a view of all the islands around here."

"Sounds interesting."

What did that mean? Did she want to go? "It's a little bit of a hike. The path is too steep for the bike."

She put her napkin on her plate. "I can handle it."

"You can't go in bare feet."

"So let's go get my shoes."

"You can't wear high heels, Cassie. You could break something."

"Shoes? Does someone need shoes?" asked Freddy.

"Freddy…" began Hunter.

"What size?"

She smiled at Freddy. "Nine."

"Big feet," he said. "I'll be right back."

"Don't tell me he's gone out to find a pair of shoes for me."

"I'm afraid so."

"They sell shoes?"

He nodded. "Freddy has a big family. Most of them work in the vendor stands you saw out front. You could purchase a whole new wardrobe, if you like."

Freddy burst back in the front door. He ran over to the grill and flipped some more fish. Then he turned back toward Cassie and said, "Try these."

He handed her a pair of flip-flops on which someone had painstakingly glued shells. She said, "They're much too beautiful to wear."

"That's what they're for," Freddy argued.

She slipped them on. "They're wonderful. Thank you."

"Anything for a friend of Hunter's."

Hunter smiled appreciatively. "Thanks, Freddy."

Freddy winked and handed Hunter a pair of plain flip-flops. "I didn't want you to feel bad."

"I owe you one, my friend," Hunter said with a grin.

Hunter turned back toward Cassie. "Whenever you're ready…"

"I'm ready." She stood up. "Thank you for this delicious lunch," she said to Freddy. "And," she said, pointing to her feet, "for the shoes."

Hunter led Cassie out. They were almost to the door when Freddy once again flashed him a thumbs-up. Hunter was not surprised by his friend's opinion of Cassie. Nor was he surprised by his father's. It only cemented what he had suspected.

Cassie was not like Lisa.

He had taken Lisa to the island only once. Despite her kind words and pleasant smile, she had been all too anxious to escape back to the mainland and the comforts of an expensive hotel.

He got on the bike. Cassie jumped on behind him. She slid back as far as possible, but she could not stop her breasts from pushing up against him. She held her hands stiff, barely touching his waist.

He drove off the road, heading toward a familiar path. After a while they came out at another clearing. Hunter parked his bike. "We have to walk from here."

It had been years since Hunter had walked along this narrow dirt path. He had once made the trip at least once a day, but after he left the island, his trips were limited to an annual visit at best.

"Are you okay?" he asked Cassie, glancing at her flip-flops.

"Fine," she said.

He smiled to himself. He was impressed. Most women would never have agreed to such an adventure. Especially when dressed in a fancy skirt and blouse. But Cassie did not seem to care what she was wearing. She seemed completely at ease, as if taking a walk to the edge of a volcano was a typical outing.

"It's right up here," Hunter said.

Cassie passed him, climbing up the peak. The crater had long since filled in, leaving just a grassy, narrow knoll. "It's beautiful," she said, looking at the blue-green Atlantic and the islands dotting the sea.

He nodded as he stood beside her. "I used to come here a lot."

"Did you grow up on this island?"

He nodded. "I grew up in that 'hut,' as I believe you described it."

Cassie swallowed as the color drained out of her face. "I'm sorry," she said. "I didn't mean to insult you. I thought it was a cute house. I should've said bungalow."

The look on her face made Hunter regret he had even mentioned it. Cassie was not a snob. It was his own clumsy way of proving that he wasn't, either. "I know," he said.

She nodded, seemingly relieved.

"You think it looks small now," he said. "You should've seen it when my grandmother was alive." He rolled his eyes and laughed. Out of the corner of his eye he could see her smile.

"Your grandmother lived there, too?"

"Yes. She took the bedroom and my father the couch, and I had a mattress on the floor."

"You're kidding?"

He shook his head. "No. We didn't have much money. But my grandmother kept it together. You'd be surprised how far she could stretch one fish."

"My grandmother was the same way," she said. "She could stretch one pot roast a week." She smiled.

"What about you?"

"Me?" She shook her head. "I can't cook. I never felt the urge to try."

"You'd rather be out taking pictures."

She grinned. "I guess." They walked in silence for a while. Hunter couldn't help but think about her interest in photography. If Cassie did not have the mill, would she pursue a career behind the camera?

"What happened to your mother?" she asked.

"She died soon after I was born. My dad couldn't cope, so my grandmother came out from France to help. She raised me."

"Right," she said, flashing him a bright smile. "I remember now."

"What?"

"Say something in French."

He hesitated. *"Tu es la femme la plus belle que j'ai jamais vu,"* he said quietly. You are the most beautiful woman I have ever seen.

"What does that mean?"

"It means…" He paused and glanced up at the sky. "I hope it doesn't rain."

She nodded as if she didn't quite believe him. He shrugged and glanced away.

"Do you still have relatives in France?"

"Distant. My grandmother wanted to be buried back there, so I met some of them at her funeral."

"That must have been interesting."

"It was deafening."

"What?"

"We're a very loud family."

She laughed, and he felt his spirits soar.

She glanced back toward the water. "This is so beautiful. It feels like we're on the top of the world."

"That's why I loved it here. I could spend the day working and get home exhausted. But when I came up here I forgot everything. I felt as if I could take over the world."

She paused a minute. "Why are you telling me all this?" she asked quietly, a slight hesitation in her voice.

Why was he? He was getting personal. He couldn't seem to help himself. He wanted to open up to her, to prove to her he was not the bastard she thought he was. But there was only one way to do that.

"Hunter?" she said, still waiting for an answer.

"Cassie, I have to tell you, selling the mill to you does not make sense."

He could see her stiffen.

"But I'm going to accept your offer."

Her eyes opened wide in astonishment. "You are?"

He nodded. "I am."

"So the mill will stay open?"

"That's right."

"Why?"

Why? Wasn't it obvious? Because he couldn't stand the thought of disappointing her.

Instead he said, "I didn't realize that there was going to be such an insurgence from the locals. That's not the way I do business."

She stood still, almost as if she was afraid to breathe. "And you'll still produce the Bodyguard cloth in China?"

Why had she brought up the patent? Was she insinuating that she wanted the patent, too? A mill that size could never handle the production of a mass-market product.

"That was the deal." He could feel his defenses rise. He was angry. Didn't she understand that this was a financial risk that he would never have assumed in any other circumstance? He was not a bank that reached out to nonprofit clients. He bought companies. He didn't save them. "There will be some conditions of the sale, however," he said, taking a step back. "After all, I need to know that my investment will be returned."

"Of course," she said. Her arms were crossed in front of her chest. She was looking everywhere but at him. What had happened? Shouldn't she be happy? After all, he just gave her back the mill.

In any case, it was clear the cliff had lost its magic.

"Come on," he said. "Let's go."

Cassie barely said a word when they returned to his father's bungalow and retrieved her shoes, jacket and folder. She was polite and kind, but distant. Neither mentioned to his father that Hunter had agreed to sell the mill.

She was equally silent on the boat ride back. As they neared the dock, she finally said, "I'd like to return home as soon as possible."

Hunter glanced at her. "Okay."

"I have to get back and tell everyone the good news."

And Hunter had to deal with Willa. He knew she would not be pleased. She was already talking to museums about which items would be donated, looking forward to the large tax credit. And she had already taken several companies through who were interested in purchasing the space. She would immediately recognize that his selling the mill back to the workers was based on emotion rather than reason.

But he didn't care what Willa might think. At the moment all he could think about was Cassie.

He had half hoped that their rendezvous might suddenly turn romantic. But it hadn't. Even before he brought up the mill, Cassie had maintained her distance. It was as if she was purposely keeping him at arm's length. What had happened to the spontaneous woman he had met on the beach?

"I'll arrange your flight back," he said.

"Thank you," she said. "Will you be returning with me?"

"No." It was obvious that Cassie was only interested in a business relationship. Unfortunately, he was not willing or able to accept a platonic relationship. He could not be near her without wanting to touch her, without being tempted to kiss her.

Therefore, it was best if he stayed away from her. He would not return to Shanville. The lawyers would handle it from there.

"Tomorrow, then?" she asked.

He shook his head. "There's no reason to wait till tomorrow." He glanced at her. She was staring at him. "Is there?" he asked. Give me a reason, he pleaded silently. Please.

She shook her head. "I guess not."

His heart sank. He pulled up to the dock and stopped the boat. He stepped out and turned to offer her his hand. When she was safely on the dock, he let go.

He said, "I'll drive you to your hotel so you can gather your things. I'll let my office know that you'll be ready to leave in an hour."

"Wait," she said, stopping him.

He turned back toward her.

"I...I wanted to thank you."

"Sure," he said. "It's business, right?"

"No, it's not just business. You have been so kind. More than kind. I will always be grateful."

Her soft silk blouse fluttered in the wind. Her long auburn hair, tousled by the wind and water, was a mass of wild and sexy curls.

"Hunter," she said. Her emerald green eyes sparkled. "I think my first impression of you was correct."

"What was that?"

"That you were a kind and gentle man."

He smiled sadly. Unfortunately, that didn't seem to be enough. He turned and began walking toward the house.

"I don't want it to end like this," she said.

He stopped.

"I want to stay here tonight," she continued. "With you."

Nine

She said it. The words that had been floating in her head just came spilling out. And it was too late to take them back.

Not that she wanted to. In fact, she had meant every word.

She had been surprised by the turn of events. She had expected a stiff, informal board meeting, not a visit to his childhood home to meet his family and friends. She had been given a rare glimpse at the person behind the facade. Instead of a corporate jerk, she had found a man who still had a close relationship with his father and childhood friends, a man who had saved the island on which he had grown up.

He had a heart.

And up there on that cliff it had seemed as if he might have wanted to share it with her. In front of her eyes, he had metamorphosed back into the man she had originally met on the beach, the one who had split a coconut with his hands. The one with whom she had shared the most intimate of experiences.

But when he told her he was giving her back the mill, she could think of only one thing: returning to Shanville.

Why?

Because she had been frightened.

She was more terrified of Hunter, the man, than she had ever been of Hunter Axon, ruthless business tycoon.

It had taken a while to digest the information, taken a while to pump up her confidence. But ultimately she remembered that she had never run away from a challenge in her life. She was not about to start now.

And so she had offered to stay.

More than stay.

She had offered herself.

And from his reaction she could tell it was an offer he was not prepared to accept.

Hunter stood there, looking at her as if deciding what to do with her.

Perhaps, she thought, as her heart dropped, he had changed his mind. Perhaps she had misread the cues, the subtle signs of his interest. Perhaps she was wrong. Perhaps he didn't want her anymore.

The deal was done, the offer accepted. He was ready for her to go home.

He nodded, still looking at her. "Good," he said. Then he turned and began walking back toward the house.

Good? What did that mean?

As she hurried to catch up, Hunter swung open his phone. She could hear him arrange to have her things brought over from the hotel. That was that. He was about as excited as if she had offered him a bowl of soup.

"If it's not convenient for you, I can stay at the hotel," she said, still hurrying to keep up with him.

He stopped so short she almost ran into him.

"I don't like games," he said.

They were standing nose to nose, eye to eye. "Neither do I," she said.

"Then why are you playing them? If you want to stay here tonight, you're more than welcome. If not, I'll see to your return to Shanville."

Why was he being so cold and indifferent? Didn't he want her to stay? "If you don't want me here, I'll—" She stopped talking. His gaze had softened and he was looking at her tenderly.

He touched her cheek. His fingers trailed downward, outlining her chin. He gently lifted her head toward him and kissed her. It was deep and sensual, filled with a passion that belied his outward calm. Her senses reeled and her knees grew weak. Finally he said, "I've wanted to do that ever since I saw you in that auditorium."

He took her hand, walking more slowly now. "Unfortunately, I have some business to attend to. But it shouldn't take me long."

"That's fine," she said. "Is there a place where I can freshen up?"

He touched her hair. "You look beautiful," he said, practically caressing her with his eyes.

"Thanks," she said. "But I would love a shower."

He nodded. "We can arrange that." They entered through the back. He led her through his grand rooms and up the sweeping staircase. As she walked up the stairs, she admired the paintings hanging on the wall. Most were by contemporary artists she had studied in school. "Is this a Kandinsky?" she asked, stopping in front of a painting with brightly colored cubes.

He nodded. "Do you like modern art?"

"Sometimes," she replied honestly.

He smiled.

"But I can't imagine having art like this in my house. I'd be so worried."

"Worried?"

"What if there's a hurricane…what if there's a leak…?" She shrugged.

"It is a responsibility," he said. "I'll eventually donate most of these to a museum. In the meantime, I have a vault downstairs where I can put the paintings in case of a hurricane or leak."

He stood there, looking at her as he continued to hold her hand. He started to walk again, but more slowly. He took her into a room that looked like an expensive hotel suite. A king-size bed faced French doors that overlooked the pool and the Atlantic beyond. Off to the side were two comfortable-looking lounge chairs.

Like the rest of the house, it looked brand-new. "Please make yourself at home. In the bathroom there are toiletries, robes, towels…anything you might need. I'll see that you receive your things as soon as they arrive." He held her hand to his lips and kissed it. It was a chivalrous, gallant act that had the desired effect. It left her wanting more.

He turned and left, closing the door behind him. She closed her eyes, fighting off a sudden case of nerves. Was she sure about this?

Could she handle another night with Hunter? After all, she still hadn't quite recovered from the last one.

But she had little choice. In the argument between mind and body, her body was pulling rank.

One night. One more night.

And then she would be on a plane back to Shanville. She would be so busy she would forget all about her elusive lover. Right?

She walked into the bathroom. Like the rest of the house, it was grand, elegant and looked brand-new. White marble was everywhere, the countertop, the floor, the shower. Everything appeared to have been designed with women in mind—right down to the little basket of lilac-scented toiletries and the woman's robe.

She suddenly realized that this was not just any old guest room. This was exactly what it looked like: a suite reserved for his female guests.

But why would he give them a separate room? Why not have them use his private quarters?

She wondered how many women had used this room to "freshen up." Had the woman he'd gone out with the previous night used it, as well?

She glanced around the brightly colored walls. So what if she had? Cassie reminded herself that she could not think about the future or the past. She was there now, and that was all that mattered.

She scrubbed off the salt and sand, relaxing in the steamy heat of the shower. Afterward she wrapped herself in the fluffy robe and brushed her hair.

She stepped out of the bathroom. On the table between the

lounge chairs was an open bottle of champagne and a crystal glass. Someone had delivered it to her room while she had been in the shower.

She helped herself to a glass of champagne and walked out on the balcony.

She wondered whether she should dress in the same clothes she had worn to the island. After all, who knew when her clothes might arrive?

Then again, she thought, admiring the view, who cared? She was perfectly content to take a while to admire her beautiful surroundings and rehash the day's events.

But she didn't have long to wait. Within moments there was a knock on her door. When she opened it, Hunter himself was standing in front of her, carrying her suitcase.

She said, "I'm surprised you brought that up yourself."

"Why?"

"I thought you'd have one of your..." Servants? Helpers? "One of the people who work for you."

"The only person who works here is Gehta," he said, walking past her and setting the suitcase on the bed. He had showered as well, and his wet hair was slicked back. He had changed out of the clothes he had worn that day and was wearing a linen shirt and pants.

"And she's gone for the day," he continued. "I'd never ask her to carry it up those steps, anyway."

So they were alone. He was the one who had brought in the champagne.

"Are you enjoying the champagne?" he asked softly. She saw him swallow as his eyes slowly grazed down her body.

She nodded. "Yes, thank you."

He took another step toward her, staring into her eyes. He touched her cheek.

It was just a touch, but it was enough to cause her body to react. Maybe the champagne, the shower, the beautiful and warm evening were all to blame.

Still looking into her eyes, he undid the tie to her robe. He paused, as if waiting for her to stop him. But she didn't. All of her concerns faded away. All she could think about was how much she wanted him to touch her, to hold her. How much she wanted to feel him inside her.

He put his hands on her shoulders and gently pushed off her robe. It fell to the ground, leaving her naked and exposed.

He had not taken his eyes off hers. Usually she was modest and reserved, but there was something about Hunter that made her throw caution to the wind. She felt bold and passionate. Adventurous. She straightened her back, not afraid to display her body.

"You're so beautiful," he said again, gently touching her shoulders. His breathing became ragged and harsh, as if an electrical current ran through the air. She half expected him to pounce on her, to toss her down on the bed and take her hard and rough. He moved slowly, teasing her with time. One hand slid down her back and cupped her rear end. The other worked its way down her front, massaging her breasts before sliding down toward her belly. She breathed in his warm, musky scent as a current ran through her.

As he moved behind her, he placed a hand over her breast, gently encouraging her to relax against him. They were in front of the open window. "Look at the sun," he said as his right hand continued to explore. She forced herself to look outside. She felt the warm breeze against her bare body, felt the crispness of his linen shirt pressed against her back and his warm breath against her neck.

He caressed her gently, his fingers working their way down her belly. She inhaled sharply as he touched the delicate skin inside her thighs, making his way toward her most sensitive spot. Her thoughts fragmented as his fingers ran up the delicate arch and back down through the soft folds, giving her the most intimate of massages.

She raised her arms and wrapped them around the back of his head as she reveled in the pleasure that came from being rubbed and touched so sensuously.

Finally, she had no choice but to surrender. He held her tight as her body released, causing her to shudder in his arms. When she finished he turned her toward him and touched her hair. "Cassie," he said softly.

But she did not want him to speak. Not yet.

She began unbuttoning his shirt. She wanted to do for him what he had done for her. After his shirt she concentrated on his pants. She reached for him, taking him in her hands before bringing him to her lips.

She heard him moan slightly and felt his fingers run through her hair as if encouraging her to continue.

When she paused, he took the opportunity to lift her off her feet and carry her to the bed. As he stared into her eyes, she felt as if he were looking into her soul.

Their lovemaking was passionate, almost desperate. He held her hands as he moved deeper and deeper.

As the pleasure once again began to build, she arched her hips, bringing him deeper. She closed her eyes only when she felt her body begin to release. Hunter let go at the same time, joining her in a deep climax.

Afterward he pulled her to him, holding her close.

They lay there, their naked bodies wrapped around each other, quietly watching the sun sink into the sea.

When just a fringe of orange appeared above the water, he touched her hair. "You're warm."

"A little."

"Do you want to go for a swim?"

"I didn't bring a suit." It hadn't occurred to her. After all, technically she was here on business, not pleasure. But Demion Mills seemed worlds away.

"You don't need a suit," he said. "There's no one around."

He stood up and handed her a towel. It was a dare. And she accepted. But the brazenness she had experienced only moments earlier was gone. She felt vulnerable from their emotionally charged intimacy. She was too modest to walk around the house naked, people or no people. She wrapped the towel around her. "All right." He laughed, following suit and tying a towel around his waist.

He led her back down the grand staircase and through the open French doors. She paused before walking outside.

"No one will know," he said, kissing her shoulder. "We're alone."

He led her to the pool. Once again she felt as though she were at an exotic resort. The only light came from the moon, the blue-and-gold spotlights framing the palm trees and the lit, black-bottomed pool. Flashing her a mischievous grin, he dropped his towel and dove in. She watched him glide underwater, his form that of an experienced swimmer.

She dropped her towel as well and stood there for a moment, enjoying the tropical breeze. He reached the end of the pool and glanced back toward her, motioning for her to join him.

She held her nose and jumped. But she didn't hit bottom. In the flash of a second he was there. He caught her in the water and swung her up in his arms. "Do you do this often?" she asked as he lifted her above the water.

"Do what?"

"Skinny-dipping."

"Actually, I don't think I've ever even been in this pool."

"What? How long have you lived here?"

"Years. But I'm fairly certain I've never used the pool."

"Why not?"

He shrugged. "I don't know. I guess I'm always working."

"I know you have time to date," she said. "Even the women of Shanville know that."

"Really?" he said. "Well, I'm flattered the women of Shanville care so much about my personal life."

"So none of your women ever wanted to go swimming?"

"My women?"

"You know what I mean."

"None of them was invited."

She didn't know whether to believe him or not, but it didn't matter. She was there with him right then, and he made her feel as if she was the only one.

"Thank you," she said.

"For what?"

"For making me feel special."

"You are special." He kissed her again. And then he tossed her into the water.

They splashed around the pool like children. After a while, he pulled himself out and grabbed a towel. "I'm going to order dinner," he said. "I'll be back."

She floated on her back, staring up at the stars. She felt as if she was having a dream, a beautiful hazy dream. When he came back outside he was wearing swim trunks and carrying a robe.

"Is the pizza already here?" she asked.

He grinned and shook his head. "I would be surprised if it arrived at all. I didn't order pizza. But if that's what you'd like…"

"No," she said, resting her arms on the side of the pool. "Whatever you ordered is fine. I like everything. Chinese…"

"How about lobster?"

"What's that dish called again?" she asked. "That one with the lobster sauce."

"No, no. I meant cooked lobsters."

"Lobster? For carryout?"

"The Four Seasons is delivering."

"The Four Seasons?" When she had been in the Bahamas before, she had wandered into the hotel, impressed by the spectacular view and surroundings. But she had nearly passed out when she saw the menu. A simple cocktail had been fifteen dollars.

She nodded toward his swim trunks and said, "Is that why you're so dressed up?"

"Exactly." He knelt close to her and said, "I'm glad you're here."

She smiled back up at him. "I am, too."

She kicked back from the edge of the pool and floated toward the middle. When she glanced back toward him, she realized that he hadn't moved. He was still kneeling at the edge of the pool, staring at her. He smiled. She swam back toward him. "What's so funny?" she asked.

"Not funny," he said. "I'm enjoying watching a beautiful mermaid swim naked in my pool."

She grinned. "If the people of Shanville could see me now, they'd never believe it."

"I'm having a hard enough time believing it myself," he said. He leaned over and kissed her.

They were interrupted by the doorbell. She gasped in horror and started to pull herself out of the pool. She had no desire to have anyone but Hunter see her naked. "Don't worry," he said. "Take your time. I'll have them set it up on the veranda."

As Hunter disappeared inside the house, Cassie wrapped the robe around her. She ran her fingers through her hair and sat down on the edge of a cushioned lounge chair. A few minutes later Hunter appeared at the door. He held out his hand to her and said, "It's ready."

The veranda was on the highest part of the property, with a sweeping view of the Atlantic. In the distance she could see the tour boats docked in the harbor, twinkling with lights.

He pulled out her chair and she sat down. He handed her a glass of champagne.

"To you," he said, sitting down and raising his glass. She took a sip.

The lobster had been cracked open, but still Cassie was unsure of how to eat it.

Hunter must have noticed because he leaned forward and stabbed a piece from the tail. He dipped it in butter and held it to her lips. She took a bite. "This is wonderful," she said, tasting the delicious, tender white meat.

They ate in silence, content to be together. It was comfortable and relaxed, as if they had been a couple for years. She felt herself wishing that they could prolong the night forever. That she would never have to leave Hunter's side.

But it was ridiculous. After all, she barely knew him. And chances were slim that their evening together would ever be repeated. A relationship was out of the question. After all, according to Hunter's father, only one woman had ever captured his heart. Cassie couldn't help but feel another twinge of jealousy as she thought of her. What had she been like? What kind of special qualities had she possessed? Before she could stop herself she said, "Your father mentioned a woman in your past."

"Sounds mysterious," he said. "What woman?"

"Your…" She hesitated. She knew she was getting into sensitive territory, and she knew it was none of her business. But she couldn't help herself. She wanted to know more about this mysterious woman. "Your fiancée," she said. She continued to chew as if she had asked him nothing more significant than the time.

"My fiancée?"

She nodded and swallowed. "Your father said you were engaged."

He shook his head. "No. I may have thought for a time that I wanted to marry her, but it was never official."

"Why not?"

He put down his fork.

She said, "You don't have to tell me if you don't want to."

"It was a long time ago," he said. "I met her when I was in college, struggling to pay the bills. We both had similar backgrounds, wanted similar things."

"You fell in love." There. She said it.

He looked at her. "I thought so."

"So what happened?"

He sighed.

"Let me guess. You became rich and famous. You changed. And she couldn't handle it."

"No. As a matter of fact, she's married to an extremely wealthy man. A man who was at one time my boss."

She glanced at him. His fiancée had married his boss?

"She broke up with me so that she could be with him," he said.

It was her turn to put down her fork.

He continued. "She told me that she could never marry a poor man."

Hunter's old girlfriend had broken his heart? "So that explains it."

"What?"

"Your drive and ambition."

"I'm not following," he said.

"Revenge."

He shook his head. "I've always been driven. And she had little effect on my ambition. But unfortunately, she did affect my relationships."

"How so?"

He shrugged. "I learned that it's impossible to really know someone."

She had to ask one more question. "What does that mean?"

"It means that for me, relationships have been at best a distraction."

He could not have inflicted more pain if he had slapped her. She was a distraction. But what did she think? Did she honestly think she would leave the Bahamas with a husband in tow? What made her think she would be any different from the rest of the women he'd slept with?

"What's wrong?" he asked.

"Nothing," she said, focusing on her empty plate. "I should thank you for your honesty. I mean, most men would lead a woman on, telling her all sorts of things she wanted to hear."

"You misunderstood." He shook his head. "I was speaking in the past tense. I thought you were looking for an explanation as to why I've never married."

She glanced up.

He stood, walked over to her and held out his hand. She accepted it, standing to face him. He said, "You're much more than a simple distraction." He cupped her face. "What about you? What happened to your marriage plans?"

She pulled away. "I don't really want to discuss that."

"Why not?"

She did not want to talk about Oliver. Not now or ever. "Because I prefer to discuss you."

"But how can I get to know you if you don't tell me more about yourself?"

She looked away. He was saying and doing all the right things. It was enough to make her believe in the future, believe that there might be a chance of a future. But how could there be?

"What's wrong?" he said. "I lost you again."

"No." She smiled sadly. "I'm just enjoying our time together."

"I am, too," he said, touching her cheek. "I am, too."

Ten

Cassie opened her eyes. Sunlight flooded the room. She was in Hunter's bedroom, a huge room with massive doors that opened to a deck.

She lay in bed as her mind replayed the wonderful scenes from the previous evening.

After dinner she and Hunter had gone back to the pool, where they had sat and held hands for what seemed like hours. Neither wanted the evening to end. Finally she had fallen asleep resting her head against Hunter's shoulder.

She awoke to him carrying her up the stairs and gently setting her down on his bed. Though half-asleep, she was still happy to realize that Hunter had brought her into his very own bedroom, his private sanctuary. He had crawled in beside her and wrapped his arms around her. They had fallen asleep with their bodies melded together.

She stretched lazily, glancing around the room for a sign of Hunter. She could hear him talking in the other room. With a burst of energy, she pulled the sheet off the bed and wrapped it around her. She followed the sound of his voice to a room down the hall. Unlike the bright, tropical tones of the other rooms, this room was done in deep, rich colors. The walls were lined with books.

Hunter stood with his back toward her. He was naked with the exception of his drawstring pajama bottoms. "Dammit!" she heard him say. She could see his back muscles flex with tension.

"I understand, Willa. But that doesn't change my mind. Had I known there was going to be a groundswell of activity, we never would've gone in there, anyway."

He turned around and smiled when he saw Cassie. His voice and appearance seemed to soften at the sight of her. "I have to go," he said into the receiver. He snapped the phone shut without saying goodbye.

He went over to Cassie and kissed her smack on the lips. "How did you sleep?"

"Great," she said. She glanced toward his phone and said, "I overheard you talking to Willa."

"I'm sorry," he said. "Not a very pleasant way to wake up."

"Is there a problem?"

"No," he said. "No problem."

He nodded toward the tray beside her. "Breakfast?" There were croissants, bagels, cream cheese and butter.

"Wow," she said. "The royal treatment."

He grasped her shoulders and said, "I was thinking…"

"What?"

"I have to attend a fund-raiser this afternoon."

Of course, she thought, her heart stopping. He wanted her to leave. Their night of passion was over. He was once again Hunter Axon, womanizer extraordinaire.

This was what she had expected, right? She should be grateful for their evening together and leave with as much dignity as possible. "That's okay," she said. "I should get going anyway…."

"No," he said with a smile. "I'd like you to come with me."

He wanted her to stay? With him?

She found herself suddenly hesitating.

The heart that had been so wounded only seconds before suddenly filled with fear. She was already more attached than she would like. Could she handle another day…and night with him? Or would that be enough to cause her to fall hopelessly in love? "I should get back," she said quickly. "Everyone is going to be wondering what happened."

"Call them and tell them it's taking longer than you thought."

What difference could one more day make? After all, hadn't she already passed the point of no return? No matter how hard she tried, she would never forget Hunter. The damage had already been done. "Okay," she said.

He smiled. "Thank you."

"You're welcome." She kissed him and said, "Do I need a special outfit, because all I have is what you saw yesterday."

She suddenly realized that he was looking at her like a hungry lion watching its prey. "I like what you're wearing today much better," he said, moving toward her.

She pulled the sheet up around her neck as she smiled and backed up, moving toward his bedroom. "I think it's too…summery."

"Hmm," he said. He ran his hands down her sides. "I see what you mean."

"What kind of fund-raiser is this?" She was almost in the bedroom.

"A typical one. Politicians looking for rich people. Rich people looking for politicians."

"Is it supposed to benefit anyone beside rich people and politicians?"

"Children in need."

"Where is it?" Her foot hit the bed.

"It's at the racetrack," he said, gently pushing her back on the bed.

"What racetrack?"

He began unpeeling the sheet from her body. "The horse racetrack."

"The outfit I had on yesterday is dirty."

He slid his hand inside the sheet, caressing her breasts. The feeling was intoxicating. "I'll buy you a new one."

Focus. "I don't want a new one. Is there a dry cleaners on the island?" He kissed her neck.

"I think so."

"You think so?"

"I don't usually deal with laundry."

"Of course," she said sarcastically. She playfully pushed him away.

"You don't have to get hostile," he said, with a twinkle in his eye. Within a second she was flat on her back.

"Like I said," he repeated, completely removing the sheet. He took his time, his eyes seemingly drinking in every detail of her naked form. "I think the suit you have on looks just fine."

He kissed her and let go of her arms, allowing her to wrap them around his neck and hold him close.

She said, "I just can't believe that..."

"That what?"

"That I'm with you. You're so different from my expectation."

"Different good?" he asked, kissing her. "Or different bad?"

They were interrupted by his cell phone. He pushed himself up and glanced at the number. "It's my office."

"Go ahead," she said.

He sighed and swung open his phone. "Yes?"

He glanced at her. "No," he said finally. He turned away. "She spoke out of turn. Don't start yet." He closed the phone and turned back toward her. But something in his demeanor had changed.

"Is everything all right?"

"Fine," he said simply.

But she had the feeling she was not being told the whole truth. "There's not a problem, is there? A problem with Demion Mills?"

"You tell me," he said. He held a hand to her cheek. "Are you sure about this?"

She nodded.

He said, "This buy-out is going to tie you to New York...to the mill for a long, long time."

She felt her blood run cold. She knew instinctively something was wrong. Why was he trying to talk her out of her decision? "What are you getting at, Hunter?" she asked, wrapping the sheet back around her.

"I can help you, Cassie. I can help you live the life you dreamed. You could go back to school. You could pursue a career in photography."

"But I don't want a career in photography."

He was quiet for a moment. "You're saying that you're happy to spend the rest of your life just working in a factory—"

"Just?" She sat up straight. She felt as if she had been slapped.

"I'm sorry," he said quickly. "I didn't mean it that way."

"I'm proud of what I do. And I'm happy. Is it what I dreamed about as a child? No. But dreams change. So do people." She shook her head. "This may be difficult for someone like you to understand, but I'm content to be who I am. Cassie Edwards, weaver. I don't need money to make me happy."

He glanced away. "I understand that. Unfortunately, in business, money and profitability are the bottom line. It's going to take a lot more than positive thinking to turn this mill around. This would be a difficult project for the most experienced of marketing people."

"We had a deal," she said softly.

"We still do." He crossed his arms and said, "I just want you to be aware of what's in store for you. I don't want to see you get hurt."

"I'm not going to get hurt."

He walked back toward the bed and took a seat beside her. "Look. I feel like we have a future here. I'm not sure what's happening to us but I think it might be something. I'd like for us to give it a chance."

"So would I."

"Well, that's going to be difficult when I'm the one who's going to have to go in there and foreclose on your home if need be. I'm afraid this stay of execution I've given you is only temporary."

"Don't ask me to choose between you and the mill."

"I would never do that," he said. He shook his head. "Why do you think I'm willing to do this, Cassie? I care about you more than…well, more than I've cared for anyone in a long, long time. I want to help you." He stood up and walked toward the balcony. At the French doors he stared silently at the Atlantic.

The anger that was building inside Cassie suddenly dissipated. He was talking to her like a…like a friend. She walked up to him and slipped her arm around his waist.

When he turned toward her, she could see the pain in his eyes.

"I have to do this, Hunter. I will never be happy if I let my friends down."

"But you may still," he said. "The Demions couldn't make this mill work with or without the patent."

"We're not going to make the same mistakes."

"You have no experience running a company. Neither does anyone else."

"I'll learn. We'll all learn." So he thought she would fail. It was one thing to question her decision, but to insult her intelligence was another.

After all, he was wrong. Wasn't he?

Or was he?

Perhaps she was just being foolish. Perhaps the Demions had been right to sell the mill. Perhaps, even with the patent, the mill was doomed. Machines could do it faster and more accurately. So why would people be willing to pay the higher price for hand-woven garments?

But how could she stand by and do nothing?

She couldn't. For one thing was certain: the mill was worth saving.

She turned away. "I guess I'll go get ready."

He grabbed her arm and swung her around to face him. He looked sad, almost tortured. "I want you to be happy."

She had no doubt he meant it. And that single statement touched her more than all the sweet nothings she had ever heard.

She reached up and kissed him. He pulled her toward him, crushing her lips with his. Suddenly he stopped. He cradled her head in his hands, staring into her eyes. Then, as if overtaken by passion, he kissed her once again.

They came together with the desperation of a drowning man in search of air. They made love as if the connection between them was vital to their very being. It had moved beyond desire. It was now a need.

Afterward he murmured, "What have you done to me?"

She laughed and pulled herself up. "I was about to ask you the same question."

"What do you mean?"

"I've gone from virgin to...I don't know."

He kissed her.

She glanced at the clock. "What time are we supposed to leave?"

He shrugged. "An hour or so."

An hour or so? "But my clothes!"

He glanced at the heap on the floor. He opened up the bottom of his nightstand and pulled out a phonebook. He opened it up and seconds later said, "There's a one-hour dry cleaner near here." He shut the phonebook and said, "I'll take them."

"Thank you," she said, relieved. He threw on jeans and a T-shirt. He looked years younger than his age, more like a muscular surfer than a businessman.

"I'll be back," he said, holding up her clothes.

He was gone less than an hour. When he returned, she had showered and was finishing drying her hair. "Thanks again," she said, turning off the dryer and giving him a kiss. "How much time?"

He looked at his watch. "Well, considering the limousine is already here...five minutes?"

She let out a yelp, grabbed her clothes and slammed the door.

A few minutes later he was showered and changed and she was wearing the identical outfit she had worn the day before. "You look beautiful," he said.

"Thank you." She kissed him on the cheek. "But you saw this outfit yesterday."

"That doesn't change anything," he said, keeping his hands around her waist. He kissed her neck and smiled.

Then he grabbed her hand and led her out of the house.

She said, "I've never been to the horse races before."

He opened the limousine door and stopped. "I hope you're not disappointed."

She knew for a fact she would not be. How could she be disappointed as long as she was with him?

He slid in beside her and wrapped his arm around her shoulders. She snuggled against him. She was overcome by emotion. For the first time in her life she felt as if she belonged to someone. She felt loved.

He did not tell the limousine driver where he was going. Apparently the driver already knew. She turned toward Hunter and smiled. "Do you ever drive yourself?"

He laughed. "Anyplace but here."

"Why not here?"

Suddenly the limousine driver spoke. "Because I need a job." The man turned around and flashed Cassie a smile from ear to ear.

Hunter shrugged. "There you have it," he said mischievously.

Cassie laughed.

He glanced at her purse. "Got your camera?"

She smiled and patted her purse. "Naturally."

The limousine pulled into the airport. "What are we doing here?" she asked.

"We're flying to the track."

He obviously liked surprising her with transportation. A boat to a board meeting, a motorbike to lunch, a plane to the racetrack… What was next?

But if Hunter thought she was impressed by such extravagance he was wrong. She would've been just as happy traveling by foot.

He led her into a private hangar. They were greeted by an employee and led out to the tarmac where a helicopter was waiting. Hunter opened the door and assisted her inside.

"When are you going to tell me where we're going?" she asked.

"I already told you. The—"

"Racetrack. Right. I guess I should've been more specific. Where is the racetrack located?"

"It's in Florida," he said. "Outside of Miami."

The helicopter lifted off the ground, and as the vehicle surged past the Nassau skyline, she held his hand. Twenty minutes later she was looking at the coastline of Miami.

She let go of Hunter's hand and pulled out her camera. She snapped her photos as the helicopter flew past towering glass buildings. At times they were so close she could see the occupants inside.

"That's where we're going," Hunter said, pointing out the window.

She held her breath as the helicopter landed on top of a narrow building. The door suddenly opened and she was being helped out.

Hunter grabbed her hand and together they walked down the flight of stairs leading into the hotel.

"Welcome, Mr. Axon," said a man in a uniform.

They followed the man out of the hotel and into another waiting limousine. The driver nodded as they entered, but once again he did not ask them where they were going. He already knew.

They drove for another half hour to the outskirts of Miami. He pulled into a large parking lot and drove up to the entrance of the building.

Hunter took her hand. "Show time."

She followed him through the gate and over to the betting booths. She could hear the din of the crowd cheering outside in the grandstand.

Hunter picked up a betting card and glanced over it. He headed toward a booth and placed his bets. All were for one hundred dollars.

When she looked at the card, one name stood out. "Hunter," she said. She pulled out her checkbook. "I want one hundred on Hunter."

"What?" he said, fumbling for the card. He grabbed the card and shook his head. "There's a horse named Hunter?"

"Yes," said Cassie, smiling. "What are the chances of that? I think it's a sign from the heavens. That's our winning horse."

"He's a long shot," said Hunter.

"Really?" she asked.

An impeccably dressed older gentleman standing nearby joined them. "That's what they say." He shook his head. "But I'm not so sure. The more distance for this horse, the better. He's definitely a horse that gets rolling late."

"So you think he can win?" Cassie asked the man.

He shrugged his linen-encased shoulders. "As much as any other horse. You just need luck and an animal that can handle the distance."

She turned to Hunter, who looked unconvinced. "What's wrong, Hunter?" she teased. "Don't think your namesake can handle the distance?"

He shrugged. "We'll see." He reached for his wallet and told the woman in the booth, "The lady would like one hundred on Hunter."

"No way," Cassie said. "This is my bet. Don't think you're going to crash it." She nudged him out of the way. "To whom do I make the check out?"

"Don't be ridiculous," Hunter said, putting his hand over her checkbook. "I'm paying for this."

"I have a hunch," she said.

She made out the check. But before she could hand it to the woman, he stopped her. "If you put your check away," he said, "I'll wager one thousand dollars."

She smiled. "Now that's a risky bet."

"I have a hunch," he said with a grin. "Besides, didn't you just remind me this was for a good cause?"

She reluctantly put her check back in her purse, and he put down his credit card. The woman in the booth handed him a ticket, which he gave to Cassie.

They walked out to the track to see a group of horses finishing a race. "Are you hungry?" he asked Cassie. "There's a clubhouse above us." He nodded toward the glass windows overlooking the track.

She shook her head. "No," she said. He smiled and led her toward the seats near the track.

Hunter scanned the crowd and said, "I think we're sitting down there."

All of a sudden they were interrupted by a busty brunette. "Hunter? Oh, my God!"

Hunter turned. Cassie could feel him stiffen.

"I heard you were going to be here today." The woman looked at Cassie and said, "Hi."

Hunter introduced her. "Cassie Edwards, this is a friend of mine."

"Val Forbes," the woman said, giving Cassie a quick, mechanical nod. Before Cassie had a chance to respond, Val said to Hunter, "I tried to call you but your office said you were out of town."

"Yes," Hunter said. "I've been traveling."

"You look good," the woman said, her breasts heaving. "Really good." Cassie raised an eyebrow as she let go of Hunter's hand. This was no ordinary old friend. It was obvious that they had just run into one of Hunter's warm-blooded women—one whose name he hadn't recalled. Cassie could feel the warmth seep up her back. She looked the woman over carefully. Had Hunter shared his bed with her? Would he share his bed with her again?

The thought was enough to make her ill. Or at least in need of some sweets.

"Why don't you two catch up?" Cassie said. "I'll meet you at the seats."

If he wanted to talk to this beautiful woman, then let him. After all, Cassie had no claims on him. She had made a promise to herself: no commitments. Despite their intimacy, she had to force herself to keep their relationship in perspective.

She marched up to the snack booth and said, "I'd like a chocolate ice cream cone, please." She hesitated. Drastic times called for drastic measures. "Make that a double."

The man gave her the ice cream cone and Cassie began to devour it like a woman deprived.

The voice from behind her almost made her jump. "I thought you said you weren't hungry."

Cassie wiped off her chin and said, "I thought you said she was a friend."

"She is."

"Hmm. We should all have friends like that," she said, taking another lick of her ice cream.

"What's that supposed to mean?"

Her head began to pound. Cassie touched her forehead, willing the pain away.

"Are you all right?" he asked.

"Brain freeze," she said.

"Brain freeze?"

"Too much, too fast. Ice cream, that is." She held it out to him. "I'm done."

"Thanks," he said sarcastically as he accepted the half-melted cone and dumped it in the trash. "Bend over," he said.

"What?"

"I used to get brain freezes all the time when I was a kid. Bend over. I don't know how, but it works."

He massaged the back of her neck. She didn't know if it was the massage or the bend, but he was right. Her headache disappeared.

She flipped her head back up. "Much better."

He smiled. "Come on," he said, taking her hand. "Let's go sit down."

She followed him toward their seats. She wanted to ask him more questions about Val but she knew she couldn't. After all, it was none of her business. "So how do you know that woman?" she heard herself ask.

He glanced at her and said, "You're not jealous, are you?"

"Jealous?" The mere thought was laughable. She and Hunter hardly had a commitment. Besides, she knew the score.

So why was her heart burning? "Why should I be jealous?" she said as coolly as she could manage.

"No reason at all."

"I couldn't care less," she added for good measure.

"I'm glad to hear that," he said, leading her toward the two empty front-row seats. "Because it looks like we're sitting next to her."

Cassie glanced where he was pointing. There was the busty

brunette, sitting next to an even more beautiful blonde. The women had not noticed them yet. They were huddled together, as if deep in conversation. "Talk about luck!" Cassie said as enthusiastically as she could manage.

As soon as all the introductions were made once again, Cassie slid in next to the brunette. She couldn't help but notice that Hunter had let go of her hand. Was it because he didn't want to appear affectionate in front of Val?

Once they were seated, Val and the blonde continued their tête-à-tête. Cassie tried not to listen, but she was helpless to do otherwise. In only five minutes she learned more about Val than she cared to know: she just received $300 highlights, the dress she was wearing cost $800, her shoes were by Manolo Blahnik, her dinner the previous evening cost $200. The most traumatic news, the one that received an onslaught of sympathy from the blonde, was that despite having just received a $100 manicure, the nail polish on her left pinkie was already chipped.

Finally Val turned to Cassie and said, "You look familiar. Have I met you before?"

Cassie rolled her eyes. "Just minutes ago…"

"No, no," the woman laughed. "Before today."

Cassie shook her head. "I doubt it."

"At the MS benefit?"

"No."

"Was it the Governor's ball in Washington?"

"No."

"Hmm," she said. "I know I'll remember sooner or later…." She tapped her pink, slightly chipped nail on Cassie's leg. "Wait. You work for that state senator…what's his name…?"

"I work in a factory," Cassie said. Normally she did not describe the mill as a factory, but what the heck. It made a better story.

The woman laughed. "Aptly put. The state senate is a madhouse."

"No," Cassie said. "I don't work in the state senate. I'm a factory worker."

"What?" said Val, leaning forward as if she didn't hear correctly.

"I work in a factory in upstate New York."

The news had the intended effect. The women glanced at each other, stunned. Cassie could almost read what they were thinking. *Hunter Axon is dating a factory worker?*

For a moment she wondered what Hunter would feel about her revelation. Would he be embarrassed by her proclamation? That she was, as he himself had described it, just a factory worker?

But her doubts were put to rest when she felt Hunter's arm slide around her shoulders, giving her a proud squeeze.

"I don't follow," piped the blonde, leaning in. "So how did you two meet?"

"Hunter bought the factory where I work."

"Technically, honey," interrupted Hunter, "we didn't know that when we met."

Val said, "How interesting. I've never actually met a…well, someone who works in a factory before."

"Me, neither," said the blonde. "Is it as boring as it looks in the movies?"

Cassie's blood began to boil. Could these women be any more pretentious?

But she didn't have time to continue their discussion, because at that very moment, a new batch of horses took to the track.

"That's your horse," said Hunter, nodding toward the long, lean chestnut-colored one.

A shot sounded and the horses broke from the gate. Hunter the horse ripped out of the gate and rounded the first turn. "I think you have a chance," she whispered.

Hunter the horse shook off the rest of the pack one by one as he barreled into the backstretch. Cassie forgot all about the women sitting next to her. She stood up in her seat and began to holler at the top of her lungs as Hunter took the lead, flying under the wire.

Her horse had won.

Cassie screamed and threw her arms around Hunter.

He picked her up and swung her around.

"You won?" Val asked.

Cassie nodded.

"Too bad it's for charity," the blonde said. "You would've made a lot of money."

Cassie's elation turned to disdain. She turned around, facing the blonde. Was she joking? Must everything be defined by money?

"Let's go," Hunter said, pulling her out of the row before she had a chance to speak her mind. As they walked up the steps, Hunter took her arm. "Were you having fun back there, Norma Rae?"

Cassie smiled. "I don't know what you mean," she said as innocently as she could.

"I thought you forgave me for my idiotic comment earlier today."

"Which idiotic comment might that be?"

"Touché," he said with a grin. But just as quickly as it had appeared, it faded. "I was referring to the comment I made about you being a factory worker."

"I believe you said *just* a factory worker."

He pulled her to a stop. "Please forgive me," he said. His eyes looked dark and pained with guilt.

"I already have," she said, touching his cheek. But had she really? Of one thing she was sure: she had not forgotten.

As if reading her mind, he said, "I don't care what you do for a living, Cassie."

"Your friends certainly do."

"Those women aren't my friends," he said. "I'm not like them. You've met my father. You've seen where I grew up."

"I've also seen where you live."

He hesitated and said, "The plane, the boats, the big house…I could walk away from everything tomorrow. Those things don't define me."

"How do you define yourself?"

"As a fisherman. And not a very good one, either."

She had no doubt that Hunter was speaking in earnest. But could he really walk away from all of his expensive toys? From his jet-setting life? From the adoring women? She doubted it.

One thing seemed certain: her opinion mattered. He wanted her to like him. And for some reason, that realization thrilled her more than she cared to admit. "You're a lousy fisherman?"

He grinned. It was an irresistibly sexy smile that sent her pulse racing. "Worse than lousy. That's why I applied to boarding school. I knew the only chance I had to survive was to get off that island."

They turned in their winning ticket. Cassie got back a receipt that read "Thank you for your donation of one hundred thousand dollars."

One hundred thousand dollars, all to charity.

It was enough to make her want to kiss him. Without hesitating, she threw her arms around his neck and did exactly what she desired. At the moment their lips touched, a crack of thunder sounded through the stadium, followed by an announcement stating that all races were postponed.

Hunter took Cassie's hand and led her outside as the first fat raindrops began to fall. He kissed her again, harder this time. She was mildly aware of the hubbub around them. The racetrack was closing. People were closing out their bets and leaving.

He slid his hand around her waist. The wind picked up and the palm trees swayed.

The rain fell more steadily, drenching the crowd outside the track. But they did not move. They stayed there, wrapped in each other's arms, aware only of each other.

Eleven

Hunter awoke early the next morning. He lay in bed, quietly watching Cassie sleep. Most mornings he began his day with a start, jumping out of bed and hurrying off to work. But not today. When he'd woken up and felt Cassie in his arms, it was as if time had stopped. It was a feeling unlike any he had ever experienced. For the first time in his life he did not wish he were somewhere else.

Or with someone else.

But then again he had known Cassie was special from the moment they met. With each passing day, he only grew more impressed.

Like the way she had handled herself the previous day. He knew how intimidating it could be to be thrown into a crowd of snobby, wealthy socialites. But Cassie had more than held her own.

In fact, she had put those offensive women in their place. But they weren't the only ones. She had done the same with him.

Just a factory worker...

He knew how it had sounded. He didn't blame Cassie for being angry. After all, he had criticized her livelihood.

But as much as he hated to admit it, a part of him assumed she could do better. That an intelligent, gifted woman such as she could not be happy working for minimum wage and making fabric.

There was no way around it. Cassie was right. He was behaving like an elitist.

And she was right to be offended. After all, what was wrong with working in a factory? Or, in this case, an old mill? Maybe it was not as lucrative as a corporate job, but then again, it didn't have the headaches, either. Cassie made a decent living at an honorable profession.

More important, Cassie worked with people she loved and trusted. And at the end of the day, she went home with the knowledge that she had helped to create something beautiful.

How many people could say that about their jobs?

Certainly not him.

Axon Enterprises was a profit-making machine, a corporate behemoth that cared little for humanity. Money was the bottom line, the definition of success. And ethics were nonexistent.

He would be the first to admit that the path he had chosen was a difficult one. With the exception of his father and a handful of others he had known from childhood, he trusted no one. He had learned firsthand that money did not buy happiness. He had a house he barely lived in, a boat he never used. He had grown accustomed to a life devoid of meaning.

But he had never been aware of it as much as he was right then and there.

He had wanted to prove to Cassie that he was not the cold, ruthless man she imagined. But perhaps she was right. After all, what kind of man was willing to make a living off other people's failures? What kind of man could displace workers who had worked at a factory for generations?

He shook off the covers and swung his feet to the floor.

He sat on the edge of the bed and put his head in his hands. What was he doing? Why was he suddenly so anxious to prove the morality of what he did?

Cassie.

He sat up straight and looked at her once again. She had not moved. Her beauty was intense, almost ethereal. She had the face of an angel, thick, black lashes, dusty-rose cheeks and a smooth, ivory complexion.

What was she doing to him?

Being with Cassie had forced him to deal with all the issues he had denied for too long.

Her power over him was as strong as it was undeniable. Cassie inspired him to be a better man.

But how could that be? He barely knew her.

But it didn't seem to matter. He had to help her.

He knew that in spite of her protestations, she did not fully realize how difficult it would be to increase the mill's revenues. Demion Mills produced only two to twenty yards of fabric a day. Computerized looms made twenty to one hundred yards a day.

And the machines in the mill were old; most original. The newer machines did the work of six iron-and-wood looms. He knew the Demions had borrowed heavily against the mill just to make payroll. Most of the mills like Demion had shut down, moving operations to the Far East, or replacing people with computers.

But what if Demion Mills was the sole producer of Bodyguard?

He had not agreed to sell them the patent, but was the mill worth anything without it?

And could the patent alone save the mill?

Probably not. Oliver Demion had realized this. When he found that the material his family had been producing for use in lawn chairs was suitable as an absorbent undergarment for athletes, he had done the most intelligent thing he could think of: sell it along with the mill. Oliver knew the patent was worth a small fortune, and the mill, even if it was capable of producing it, had no money to commit to marketing efforts.

But the mill needed that patent. Without it Cassie and her friends could never hope to stay in business. Within a year the mill would be hemorrhaging money. In two years it would be closed.

But the introduction of Bodyguard would require a substantial sum of money. An amount Demion Mills did not have.

So what should he do? What could he do?

"What are you thinking about?" Cassie asked, blinking her eyes sleepily. Her beautiful auburn hair was splayed over the white pillowcase.

"You," he said.

She reached out her hand and touched his cheek, smiled. She nodded toward his watch. "What time is it?"

"Nearly nine."

She sat up straight. "I should get back to Shanville."

He nodded. "I'm going with you."

"To Shanville?"

"Yes. I want to talk to some of the artisans and get a feel for your production capabilities."

"Oh. Okay. Why?"

"Because..." He stumbled. He did not want to tell her he was considering giving her back the patent until he was sure the mill could handle the production. "There are some things I need to take care of to get ready for the transfer."

She removed her hand. "You're not having second thoughts again, are you?" she asked.

Second thoughts? Was it possible that she still did not trust him? He pushed himself up on one arm. "No. I'm selling you the mill. But it's still complicated." He leaned over her. "I don't want you to fail."

"You don't need to worry," she said. "We're using our homes as leverage, remember?"

"So I should be content with the knowledge that I will be foreclosing on everyone's homes? That I would essentially own a town?"

She hesitated. He saw a flicker of apprehension cross her face. "You would rather have your money," she said, as if stating a fact. He saw the disappointment in her eyes.

She was wrong. It was not about money. At least, not this time. But he did not tell her that. He needed to prove that he could behave honorably. He needed her to trust him.

He kissed her shoulder. "Get dressed," he said quietly. "We have work to do."

Cassie stood on the factory floor. She looked around her. It had been a three-hour flight back to Shanville, yet she felt as if she were worlds away. The sleek glamour of Hunter's Bahamian world was nowhere to be seen. Instead it was as if she had been transported back through time. Heavy, Victorian-era machinery was packed into the large room. She closed her eyes and listened to the familiar thwack of silk threads being beaten back by wood battens, a sound so musical her grandmother had written a poem about it as a child.

All around her were friends, women she had known her entire life. They worked the clattering looms, nimble fingers flying over the taut ropes, cast-iron flywheels.

Cassie had told her co-workers that their offer had been accepted. But instead of joy and jubilation, it was a quiet peace. Everyone knew that they may have won the battle, but that did not mean they were going to win the war.

"Cassie." She felt a warm pat on her arm. Luanne said, "You did good. And we're all grateful." Luanne handed Cassie a small card to tuck into the loom. Cardboard cards, each punched with holes to determine the ornate patterns in the weave, were kept on long strings looped over the looms. A complex pattern might require as many as 20,000 cards. The system was developed in the eighteenth century and still used.

"Luanne's right," Ruby said. "You saved our mill all by yourself. Your grandma would be proud."

Luanne shook her head. "And she'd be happy that you're through with Oliver after what he did to us all."

"We have the mill back again. The past is the past," Cassie said.

"But we don't have the patent," Luanne said.

"No," Cassie admitted. And they never would. Hunter might

finance a loan for the mill, but the patent was too valuable. He would never agree to sell it for what they could offer.

Luanne sighed and shrugged her shoulders. "I guess Oliver did what he had to do. Can't blame a man for wanting to make money."

"Why not?" said Priscilla. She, too, had worked in the mill all her adult life. "Why can't you blame him?"

Cassie understood their anger. But she no longer felt anything toward Oliver one way or the other. Her mind had been taken over by Hunter. All she could think about was Hunter—what he had said, what he had done. How he had touched her. How they had kissed.

She felt as if he possessed not only her body but her soul as well.

And that troubled her.

In a way, she wished she'd never seen the man behind the image. That she'd never heard about the poor boy who had learned early on that money was a ticket to survival. That she had never heard about his grandmother's death and the brutal loss of the woman he loved.

But learning how he had come to be a corporate raider was not the same as accepting it. Money was his crutch, his way of self-protection. But his motives could not be glorified. Nor could they be excused.

She knew it was useless to think that perhaps she had a chance to convince him otherwise.

Or could she?

After all, it was obvious that he wanted to help her. Didn't he? And that was commendable.

The truth of the matter was she wanted to give him a chance. The man she had spent time with was capable of extreme caring and kindness. She was sure of it.

Wasn't she?

Could the man who had held her in his arms and stared into her eyes while making love to her take her house out from under her?

Yet hadn't he threatened to do just that? *So I should be content with the knowledge that I will be foreclosing on everyone's homes?*

The problem was, she realized, that she was already confusing business with pleasure. And she doubted Hunter would make the same mistake.

After all, he had seemed so cold and distant on the flight back. He had barely spoken with her, choosing instead to work on his computer. She had felt self-conscious and awkward. With nothing to do, she had busied herself by fiddling with her camera and taking the occasional picture.

"I don't understand why he's still here," Priscilla continued.

"Who?"

"Hunter Axon."

Cassie blushed at the mention of her lover's name. She still had not told anyone of their affair. "He wanted to talk to some of us about production," she said.

"But," Priscilla continued, "why should it matter, if he's selling us the mill?"

"Because he's financing it," Luanne said.

"He doesn't want to sell us back the mill only to see it fail," Cassie said. "If we don't succeed, he's not going to get any money."

"Is that it? Or does he have a more personal investment in our success?"

Cassie could not answer her old friend. How could she explain that she had fallen in love with the man they considered an enemy?

Priscilla put a hand on hers, stopping the loom.

Cassie looked at her, her eyes full of torment.

Priscilla smiled kindly and said, "Is he worried that you'll end up getting hurt?"

"He's a decent man…he is. I know you've all seen a side to him that's…well, less than flattering but…"

"We all know that, Cassie. He's giving us back our mill."

Luanne grinned and said, "I couldn't be happier for you. After Oliver, I was hoping that you might meet someone else soon. And who could you possibly meet around here?" She rolled her eyes in emphasis.

Cassie glanced around the room. The women were all nodding their heads supportively. Cassie smiled in appreciation and said, somewhat meekly, "I didn't mean for this to happen." Cassie slid in another card. "I doubt this...whatever it is between Hunter and me, will turn into anything." She sighed. "I'm sorry. I hope I haven't complicated things. I never should've gotten involved with him in the first place."

"He's back here, isn't he?" Luanne said. "He obviously cares."

Cassie hesitated. More than anything, she wanted to believe that Hunter cared about her.

"If I were you, I'd give him a chance. He's an important, busy man. And he's trying to help us. That's something."

Luanne was right. He had come back.

There was hope. There was definitely hope.

"You're not serious." Willa fixed her gaze on Hunter as she tapped her long, manicured nails on the wooden table in her makeshift office.

Hunter had just finished telling Willa of his plans. "I am."

"Do you have any idea how many hours I've spent on this project? How much time I've spent securing this deal?"

"You will be compensated, Willa. As usual."

"This is not a typical deal for me."

"I understand that."

"Oliver was counting on us moving production to the Far East."

"Oliver will receive the compensation he was promised."

"Don't be foolish, Hunter. You could lose millions."

Hunter appreciated Willa's concern, but she was not telling him anything he did not already know. He had little choice. He could not leave Cassie in Shanville with a mill that was headed for bankruptcy. "You're forgetting that with the deal I have in mind, I would still retain a percentage of the fees gained from the patent."

"That patent is worthless unless they know how to market it."

"So we will help them."

"Why not just do it ourselves? Why share the rights?" She shook her head.

"There's more at stake than money. These people…well, they've invested their entire lives in this mill."

"So what?" She shrugged. "That's never stopped you before."

What could he say? Willa was right. He'd never really cared before. But he did now. The people of Shanville were no longer anonymous small-town workers. How could he tell himself that taking over the mill was in their best interests, when he knew otherwise? He continued, "Instead of the Far East you will return to the Bahamas."

"Hunter, please. This is all that factory worker's doing."

He did not need to ask to whom she was referring. He felt a sting of tension in the back of his neck. How dare Willa refer to Cassie with that snobbish tone? "She's not a factory worker," he said. "She's a weaver who's trying to save her mill."

"This has nothing to do with saving a mill. This is about re-venge. Plain and simple."

"Revenge?"

Willa was silent for a moment. "You don't know?"

"Know what?"

"Cassie and Oliver were engaged."

Hunter hesitated. It wasn't possible. Cassie and…Oliver? The man from whom he bought the mill? The man who followed Willa around like a devoted puppy? "Oliver Demion?" he heard himself say.

"Apparently she had been in love with him since she was a child. But he never really loved her. He got engaged because he felt obligated. They had been together since they were kids."

Hunter was silent. Why hadn't Cassie told him that Oliver had been her fiancé?

"But once he met me, he knew he had to break things off with Cassie. She was devastated." Willa shook her head and sighed. "Poor Oliver. He felt so guilty." She shrugged. "In any case, he felt guilty until Cassie swore revenge."

Hunter couldn't believe what he was hearing. It couldn't be true. Cassie was interested in revenge?

"Oliver predicted she would set her sights on you. But I give her credit. I never thought you'd actually fall for it. And I certainly never thought she'd be able to persuade you to sell the company."

That was it. Hunter had heard enough.

"I don't have time for idle gossip, Willa, and neither do you."

With that he left the room. He walked down the hall toward his office. Had he misjudged Cassie? Had she been playing him all along just to get what she wanted?

Had he missed the cues? Was he just a pawn?

After all, it had happened before. He'd thought he'd known Lisa. Apparently he hadn't known her at all. Everyone had seen her for who she really was but him. He had been blinded by love.

He'd sworn it would never happen again. After all, he had been a boy when he was with Lisa. He had been with many women since. He thought he could tell the good from the bad. He thought he could recognize the diamond from the rhinestones.

But perhaps he had given himself too much credit. Perhaps Willa was right. Perhaps Cassie was only using him to win back an old love.

Did it matter?

Hell, yes.

He could feel himself close up, feel his heart freeze once again. He had given too much too soon. And he had no choice but to pay the price.

But what could he do?

He cared about her too much to walk away and leave her with an old mill destined for failure.

No.

He would do the honorable thing. He would give Cassie the mill and the patent.

But then he was through. His relationship with Cassie would be defined solely through business.

If it was revenge she was after, she would have to obtain it alone.

Twelve

Cassie stared at the phone. It was nearly nine o'clock at night, well past the dinner hour. Hunter hadn't called. And it was becoming more and more obvious that he had no intention of calling.

So what did that mean? Was he just busy? Or, she thought, her heart sinking, had he reached a decision regarding the mill that he knew she would not like?

What decision might that be, however? He had told her he would sell her the mill. She believed him. He would not renege.

So what was it, then? Why hadn't he called her?

She had heard he was leaving the next day and was spending the night at a hotel in town. She'd assumed he had booked the hotel room for the sake of appearances. It had never occurred to her he actually planned on sleeping there. Alone.

She swallowed. Perhaps his reason for not calling was a more personal one.

Cassie stood up and walked toward the window. A cold and bitter wind rattled the panes, seeping through the cracks. Despite her wool cardigan, Cassie shivered. She crossed her arms in an attempt to ward off the chill.

It was hard to believe that only the night before she had slept naked, enjoying the warm breeze from the open French doors. It was equally hard to believe that the man with whom she had shared a bed, the man who had made some passionate and tender love, was no longer interested in her.

But it was a scenario she had to consider.

In rapid progression, she imagined the worst. Perhaps he thought their differences too numerous. Perhaps he had grown tired of her. Perhaps he never really cared. Perhaps...their relationship was over.

If it was over, she should not be surprised. After all, they had become intimate very early in their relationship. She had known it was risky. She had known she was setting herself up for rejection, known that their relationship would end eventually. Hadn't she?

Maybe. But a part of her had hoped for a miracle. A part of her had actually believed that Hunter cared. That their lovemaking was every bit as special to him as it was to her.

Was she wrong?

It seemed difficult to believe that he suddenly had a change of heart. Yet from the moment they left the Bahamas she had sensed a difference. It was subtle, but still noticeable. A slight stiffening. A pulling away.

But would he leave town without so much as a goodbye?

Cassie turned away from the window. What was wrong with her? Why was she analyzing everything like the soon-to-be-jilted lover? Perhaps the reason he hadn't called was something less dramatic. Perhaps he was just distracted by work.

Or perhaps not. Perhaps he had no intention of calling her now or ever again.

She glanced once again at the phone. She checked her watch. She knew where he was staying. And if he had tired of her or was ready to break up with her, she wanted to hear it in person.

* * *

Hunter took off his watch and set it on the night table. He undid his cuff links and began unbuttoning his shirt. His mind, as it had been all day, was focused on Cassie.

He had spent the afternoon and evening holed up in an empty office, busying himself with work in an attempt to distract himself from the pain in his heart. But it had been in vain.

Damn!

How could he have been so naive?

He didn't want to believe that their relationship was based on revenge, yet the facts proved otherwise. Why else had she not told him the truth about who her fiancé was? Why was she so willing to give up her dream of a career in photography just to save the mill? Why did she lose her virginity to a stranger?

She had been motivated by love.

A love not for him, but for someone else.

He was interrupted from his reverie by a knock on the door. He was in no mood for distractions nor company. "Come in," he barked.

Cassie opened the door.

The mere sight of her was enough to take his breath away. But he could not give in to his body. He needed to control his feelings. He needed to focus. To concentrate. He turned away and continued unbuttoning his shirt. "What are you doing here?"

He could hear her shut the door.

"What's going on?" she asked quietly.

"What do you mean?"

"The way you just greeted me. Something is wrong, isn't it?"

"I'm tired, Cassie. It's not every day I give a company back."

"Is that it?" she asked, shutting the door. "Are you having second thoughts?"

"Would it matter?" he asked.

She glanced down.

"No," he said. "I didn't think so."

"So this is about money?"

"Why don't you tell me," Hunter said, facing her.

"What are you talking about?"

"As I mentioned to you before, everything usually boils down to money," he said, taking a step toward her.

She lifted her head, defiant. "Maybe with you."

"But not with you?" he said. He stood in front of her. He could see the outline of her firm breasts underneath her snug jacket. Her jeans seemed to wrap around her slender hips.

"No," she said. "I don't think money is all that important in the scheme of things."

He could feel himself weaken. Damn, she was beautiful. "Tell me," he said, "if money doesn't motivate you, what does?"

"What do you mean?"

He took a step toward her. "Why are you so desperate to keep the mill?"

"I told you. This mill is in our blood. It's who we are. Some of the people who work here have worked here their whole lives. They can't just pick up and move on."

"But you could. Right?"

"We've been over this," she said impatiently. "This is not about me."

"So there's no...personal reason for wanting the mill back."

"Of course. I love the mill, I love making fabric."

"And Oliver? Do you love him, as well?"

She swallowed.

He could see a change come over Cassie at the reference to Oliver. A flash of grief tore through him. So it was true. "Why didn't you tell me?"

She said, "I wasn't trying to keep Oliver's identity a secret. I would've told you about him if I thought it important. But he didn't have anything to do with us or what I wanted."

"You and Oliver were childhood sweethearts?"

"Yes." She shrugged. "Everyone just assumed that we would get married, including me."

He felt as if his heart was twisted in two. He hated this feeling of insecurity. Of uncertainty. "The breakup must have been painful for you," he said stiffly.

"Not for the reasons you might think. It was more difficult to find out that the person I thought I had loved no longer existed. I missed who he used to be, the friendship we once shared. But even still, I knew that he had done us both a favor. There was no passion in our relationship."

No passion? Was it true? Was her virginity due to a lack of physical chemistry?

He wanted to believe her. He wanted to think that the reason she gave him such a precious gift was because of their connection—the spark between them. Not because she was trying to erase another man's touch.

Cassie had not expected to be greeted by a barrage of questions regarding Oliver.

What was happening? Why was he so upset about her not telling him the name of her fiancé?

Hunter turned away from her and continued to unbutton his shirt.

She said, "Hunter…I'm sorry. Is that what's bothering you? The fact that I was engaged to Oliver?"

He turned back toward her. His eyes were dark and dangerous. "Of course not. Why would I care about your past romantic history?"

If he meant to injure her, he had succeeded. Why would he care? Because she wanted him to care. She wanted him to love her.

"My concerns are business related," he said coldly. "I don't want Axon Enterprises to get involved in a simple domestic dispute."

A domestic dispute? "Do you think I'm trying to buy the mill back just to spite Oliver?"

"Are you?"

She paused for a moment, speechless. How could he even think her capable of such a spiteful act? Did he really think that she would have risked losing her friends' severance just so she could exact revenge?

Yes.

She could tell from the way he was acting that he not only thought that, he was convinced. He had made up his mind. And nothing she said would make any difference. To argue otherwise would only make her appear defensive.

Her heart sank.

Why hadn't she told him about Oliver sooner? Didn't she realize that he would find out sooner or later the name of her ex-fiancé?

"Hunter," she said, making a move toward him.

He stepped away from her. It was a slight change, a shift in weight. But the message was clear. He did not want her near him.

What could she do to change his mind? What could she say? Nothing. The damage was done.

She glanced away and reached for the doorknob. "I made a mistake coming here. I'm sorry I bothered you."

Before she could leave, he grabbed her arm and pulled her to him. He stared into her eyes as if searching for something. "You didn't answer my question. Are you buying the mill out of spite?"

"No." She looked into his eyes. They were dark and angry, devoid of feeling.

She had spent the past few days loving him. But it was over. The realization was like an arrow through her heart.

"Why did you come here tonight?" he asked.

"I came here to see you," she said. "I couldn't stand the thought of you still being in town and not being with me."

Hunter let go of her and turned away. But not fast enough. She had seen something in his eyes. A softening. A glimmer of hope.

Suddenly it hit her like a bolt from the blue. He was jealous of Oliver.

Was it possible?

How could he be jealous of a man she never truly desired? Although she hadn't mentioned Oliver by name, she had spoken about the lack of passion in their relationship. Wasn't her virginity proof? She said, "I was never in love with Oliver. Never. I cared about him as a sister cares about a brother."

He turned back to face her. "Yet you were willing to marry him."

She sighed. "We got engaged while still in high school. He was different then. When we were growing up he was my best friend. I never thought he would end up being so deceitful. So motivated by money." She sighed. "In retrospect, I should've broken it off a long time ago, but—" she shrugged "—I don't think I would actually have gone through with it."

She stepped toward him again. "I'm sorry I didn't tell you about him," she said. "But the time with you was so special to me…so magical." She hesitated. "I didn't want to tarnish it by talking about Oliver."

He was looking at her as if deciding what to do with her. She glanced away and asked, "Do you want me to leave?"

She held her breath as she waited for the response.

He shook his head. "No," he said. She turned back toward him. His eyes lightened before her, becoming tender and kind once again.

She touched his bare chest as she breathed in the deep, musky scent of his aftershave. She would prove to him how she felt. How much she cared.

He did not touch her. Instead he turned his head ever so slightly and said hoarsely, "What are you doing to me?"

She was not ready to give up. She leaned forward and kissed him. It was like throwing a match on an oil spill. Flames ignited as he pulled her to him, kissing her mouth, her eyes, her cheeks. She reached inside his shirt, running her fingers down his bare torso.

He inhaled sharply as she made her way to the edge of his pants, tucking her fingers inside.

He pulled her hands away, and she looked at him. Why was he stopping her?

He met her gaze and said, "I want to see you."

"What?" she asked.

"I want to see you. All of you."

"You want me to take my clothes off?" She glanced toward the bathroom and said, "Okay. I'll be right back."

"No," he said, shaking his head as he pulled her back toward him. "Here." He was speaking matter-of-factly, as if giving instructions to an employee. "I want to watch you."

He wanted to…watch?

She felt a flutter of nerves. Like a striptease?

The thought was enough to bring a blush to her cheeks.

But why should she be embarrassed? After all, he had seen her naked before.

He was watching her carefully. Was this some sort of test? Whatever it was, she was up for it. Without answering him, she kicked off her shoes and socks. She stood before him and met his gaze directly, silently accepting his dare. Slowly she unzipped her pants, taking her time wiggling out of them.

His eyes darkened and his breath grew ragged as she pulled her turtleneck over her head and dropped it to the floor. Left with nothing but her bra and panties, she paused. She stood before him, teasing him with time. She unhooked her bra and tossed it on the bed. She stuck her thumbs into her panties and slowly pulled them off.

She knew he half expected her to get naked and jump under the covers, but she was emboldened by the heightened sense of passion. She could see the effect she was having on him. After a day of waiting for him to contact her, she was back in control.

And she was not ready to hand over the reins. She stood there, staring at him as his breath grew ragged. "What next?" she asked.

He held out his hand. When she took it, he yanked her on the bed, on top of him. Suddenly he was inside her, moving deeper and deeper.

They made love staring into each other's eyes, not even looking away when tension became unbearable and release necessary.

When he pulled her close to him afterward and tucked her inside the covers, she wrapped her arms around him. "I wish we could stay like this always," she said.

But Hunter did not answer. Instead, feigning sleep, he removed his arm and turned away from her.

Hours later Cassie was still awake.

Why hadn't he answered her? Why had he turned away?

She knew the answer without asking. It was as simple as it was undeniable: Hunter did not share her sentiment.

How could she have thought that Hunter was jealous of Oliver? The truth of the matter was that Hunter had been distant from the moment they set foot on the plane to return to Shanville, before he found out about Oliver. Oliver had just been a convenient excuse for him to escape.

She guessed that the real reason for Hunter's emotional distance was that their relationship had progressed too far too fast. And her coming to his hotel room had not helped matters.

But if he wasn't interested in her, how could he have made love to her?

Because he was a man. Sex and love were completely different things.

She felt like a fool. Why couldn't she just play it cool? Why did she have to act so…so desperate?

The truth of the matter was their relationship had been doomed from the night they met, the night they first made love. Her grandmother had warned her that making love changes things between a man and a woman. It was, she had said, the most intimate of connections, a connection that for some women, could never be undone.

Cassie had commended herself on refraining from premarital sex, but as she had admitted to Hunter, the wait had not been difficult. She had not been possessed by the instinctual, overwhelming desire she felt for Hunter.

And now that she had experienced such passion, her life was forever changed. For the rest of her life she would feel a bond with Hunter. And what kind of bond, if any, would he feel for her?

None. She would become another notch on his belt. Just another nameless woman with whom he had shared his bed.

She gingerly pushed the covers away and slipped out of bed. Moving in the dark, she found her clothes and put them back on. She stopped and paused, looking at him. It was time to say goodbye.

But as she turned away, he caught her in an iron grip. "Where are you going?"

"Home," she said, startled.

"Why?" he asked.

"I just…well, I should be getting back," she said. *Play it cool.* "I have to get up early tomorrow and I don't have my clothes here."

He let go of her arm and pushed himself up in bed. If she had been expecting a protest, she would've been disappointed. "Okay," he said.

All right, then. They were in agreement. She just needed to pick up her purse and walk out. Before she started crying.

"Wait," he said. He threw back the covers and turned on the light. "I'll see you home."

As he jumped out of bed, she watched his sinewy body tug on his boxers.

"No," she said quickly. "Go back to sleep. It's late."

"Did you drive here?" he asked, ignoring her protest.

"Really," she said, grabbing her coat. "I'll just be on my way. I'll talk to you tomorrow." She realized with horror that she sounded as if she was expecting him to call. "Or, um, whenever."

She opened the door but he was too quick. He shut it with his foot as he put on his coat. "Did you drive?" he repeated.

She gave up. He was too stubborn to be talked out of this. Even though it made no sense, no sense at all.

"This is ridiculous," she said. "What are you going to do? Follow me in your car?"

"My rental's already been returned. I'll drop you off and drive your car back. I'll see that it gets back to you."

Meaning he was not planning on spending the remainder of the night with her. In fact, he was willing to go to a lot of trouble to ensure that he did not have to sleep with her again.

He had his hand on the door when she touched his arm, stopping him. "Why are you doing this?"

"I'm not about to let you go home by yourself in the middle of the night."

"It's Shanville. It's perfectly safe."

He opened the door. "Let's go."

Thirteen

This was not the first time he had seen a date home after making love. He preferred it to spending the whole night together. He found the act of physically sleeping with someone even more intimate than intercourse.

But usually he didn't end up in this predicament. He rarely invited a woman into his own bed. He liked being able to leave when he wanted to.

It was just one of the ways he had managed to keep things simple. He had avoided heartbreaks by avoiding the pitfalls that encouraged a relationship.

But it was never much of a problem. Typically he was attracted to the very women who would welcome a casual liaison. Women who had little desire for a more permanent relationship. If, for some reason, things changed, he was quick to recognize the signs. Usually when a woman wanted him to meet her family he had one foot out the door already. For he had a simple rule—any mention of family meant he had taken the relationship one step too far. He did not want to meet the mother who "would absolutely love him" or the grandfather who "would never believe his granddaughter was dating a millionaire." Family only complicated things.

He always tried to be honest. He never promised a connection, a special relationship. Until now. And look what he had done. He had almost made a mistake. Or had he?

Cassie had claimed that she no longer felt anything for Oliver. That her need for the mill, her need for him, was not based on revenge.

But he was having a difficult time believing her. Not that he didn't want to. After all, he had hoped things might be different with Cassie. He wanted them to get to know each other. His usual rules regarding relationships and commitment had not applied.

He had made an exception and it had almost cost him.

As they walked outside, they were hit with a blast of cold air. The wind had died down and the night was eerily silent. Their footsteps echoed through the deserted parking lot as they made their way toward an old green Ford LTD.

"This is it," Cassie said, nodding toward the car. "The official grandparent mobile. Complete with a box of tissues in the back window."

"I'll drive," he said.

Cassie tossed him the keys. He caught them in his gloved hand and unlocked the door. Once they were settled, Hunter turned the ignition and...nothing.

She said, "Sometimes you have to turn it a couple of times. I think it might need a checkup."

Finally the engine roared to life. As usual, the car began to rattle and shake.

"I'm not an expert on cars," Hunter said, "but I think this one definitely needs some engine work."

She said, "The nearest car repair is a half hour away. And it's expensive."

"I'll take care of it for you."

"No," she said, mortified. Why had she said the part about it being expensive? And why, when it was obvious he wanted nothing more to do with her, would he volunteer to fix her car? "I don't want you to take care of it for me."

"Why not?"

"Because," she said. "I can take care of it myself."

They drove for a while. A heavy, awkward silence filled the car. Cassie was overwhelmed by a feeling of loss. How had this happened? How could they be so intimate yet so distant?

He pulled into the driveway and stopped. Once again it was time for goodbye. "Thank you," she said.

It was her eyes. They looked almost luminous in the moon-light. Open and trusting...and hurt. He could not go back to the hotel. Not without her.

He turned off the car and offered her the keys. "Aren't you leaving?" she asked.

"That's up to you."

"Hunter, I don't want you to stay because you feel pressured or something."

"Pressured?"

"I know you're trying to be honorable, but I didn't intend for this to be an all-nighter."

Had he misread her? Had his narcissistic mind been so busy focusing on his own reticence that he hadn't noticed that perhaps she wanted nothing more from him? Perhaps Willa had been wrong. Perhaps Cassie was not looking for revenge. Perhaps she was looking for some fun, a connection with another man. Per-haps loneliness had been her only motivation. "You were look-ing for sex?"

He could see her recoil at his harsh words. Right away, he cursed himself for insulting her. What was wrong with him? "I'm sorry. I just meant—"

"Is that what you're looking for?" she interrupted. "Sex?"

Something about the way she said it melted his heart. "No," he said. He pushed a tendril of hair away from her face. "No," he repeated, even more adamantly.

She glanced away.

He knew then why Cassie had insisted on going home. She had wanted to leave the warm comfort of his hotel room simply because she felt it was what he wanted.

He had heard her, of course, when she'd said she wished they could remain in each other's arms. But as much as he longed for the very same thing, he had been unable to respond. The news about Oliver had thrown him. He wanted to believe that Cassie was not using him, but he couldn't ignore the facts. Still, he didn't like to think that he'd somehow made Cassie uncomfortable. *"Je suis desolé,"* he murmured.

"What does that mean?"

He suddenly realized he had spoken to her in French. As a child he would lapse into French in moments of duress, usually when speaking to his grandmother. "It means I'm sorry."

She hesitated, allowing his words to sink in. Finally she said, "What did you say to me that day on the cliff?"

He said, *"Tu es la femme la plus belle que j'ai jamais vu.* You are the most beautiful woman I have ever seen."

"I had a feeling it didn't have to do with the weather." She smiled. "Thank you." She blushed slightly and glanced out the window. He had made her nervous. She tapped her hands against her knees and said, "Did you know the founder of the mill was French? William Demion?"

Hunter shook his head.

"He emigrated from France in the early nineteen hundreds. He headed toward Shanville because he'd heard that there was plenty of work mining slate. But when he arrived, he saw a truck-load of looms headed for the dump and offered the driver ten dollars for the lot."

"I take it he never mined slate."

She shook her head. "The driver of the truck turned out to be the weaver. He hired him, and Demion Mills was born."

He glanced away. He did not want to discuss Demion Mills. Nor did he want to discuss her ex-fiancé's ancestor.

"Do you feel like going for a walk?" she asked.

"A walk? It's almost midnight."

"There's something I want to show you."

"Sure," he said. After all, he was leaving for France the next day. And as much as he wanted to see Cassie again, would he?

When they stepped outside, she held out her hand. "Come on," she said.

He followed her through the cold, moonlit night. Scattered remnants of the winter's hard snow crunched under their feet as they headed toward the woods. The full moon lit the path. "It's strange, isn't it?" she said. "I mean, just two nights ago we were swimming in the buff. And here we are tromping through the snow."

As they walked out of the clearing, she paused. They were standing at the top of a hill. "This is my view at the top of the world."

The town of Shanville was lit below them. They could see the railroad tracks and the factory. He could even see his hotel.

She continued, "I started coming here right after my parents passed away. I figured it was the highest spot around, so it made me closer to heaven."

He pulled her close. "What happened to them?"

"They were in a car accident when I was five. My grandparents raised me."

"Did your parents both work at Demion Mills?"

"Yep. They met in college. When they graduated, my mother wanted to move back to Shanville. The mill was the only place they could find work."

He touched her cheek, as if brushing away an invisible tear. "What college did they go to?"

"Michigan State." She turned toward him. "I went to the same school myself...until my grandmother got sick."

"That's where you studied photography?"

"Yes."

He swallowed. As much as he hated to admit it, he wanted to ask about Oliver. "It must have been difficult being so far away from Oliver."

"No," she said without hesitation. She met his eyes and said, "I guess that should have been a clue that things were not right, but I just assumed it was because we were so secure in our relationship."

She hesitated and said, "I can't really explain why Oliver and I stayed together so long. All I can think was that, since I'd known him my whole life, our relationship was all I knew." She sighed. "But now that I've met you, I'm not so sure that I ever loved Oliver. Maybe it was just friendship. I know one thing for certain. I don't love who he has become. I never thought he could do this."

"Do this?"

"Destroy the mill. Then sell what was left to someone who… well…" She hesitated.

"Planned to close it down."

"It's in his blood, just like the rest of us. He grew up here."

"I wouldn't demonize him for his choice, Cassie. From what I can see, turning the mill's fortunes around at this point is not easy." What was he doing? Defending her ex-fiancé?

"It was his responsibility," she said, without hesitation.

Hunter could tell by the tone of her voice that Cassie felt betrayed and angry at Oliver's decision to sell the mill. But was there more to it than that? Would she still be angry if they were together? If Oliver had not left her for another woman?

She took his hand and held it. They stood there for a while, neither speaking as they stared back over the town. Finally she tugged on his hand and said, "Come on."

But she did not lead him back to the house. Instead they went down the ravine, walking in the opposite direction.

He knew where Cassie was taking him next. "Are we going to the mill?"

She nodded. "I want to show you something."

"Do you have a key on you?" he asked.

She shook her head. "We don't need a key."

They made their way through the ravine and back up the other side. He followed her down a moonlit path that led to the street. The mill was directly across from them.

Cassie said, "Wait here."

"I'm not going to let you walk around in the dark by yourself," he said.

"Why not? I've done this a million times. Besides, I don't want to give away my secret."

"What secret?" he asked.

She laughed as she led him around the side of the mill to the old cellar entrance. She yanked on the rusty lock.

"Breaking and entering?" he asked.

She smiled as the lock popped open. "Call the police."

He helped her open the door and followed her down the musty old steps. "Do many people know about your secret entrance?"

"Just me." She turned on a light. They were in an old, brick-lined basement. They were surrounded by stacks and stacks of old newspapers.

"These belonged to the original owner," she said, pointing to the papers. "He kept all the papers that had anything to do with the mill. Just piled them up in the basement. No one's ever moved them."

He followed her up a flight of rickety stairs that led to the main floor. She flicked on the lights. In front of her was the unofficial photo gallery, a series of framed pictures detailing the mill's history and its proudest achievements.

Hunter had walked past these pictures many times, but he had never really looked at them.

"That was the official presidential chair used in the Carter administration," Cassie said. He moved closer for a better look at the picture to which Cassie pointed. Two women stood behind a beautiful chair, smiling proudly.

She continued, "The young woman standing directly behind the chair is my mother. My grandmother is standing to her right. They made that material. Tuscan Vine Demion silk lampas. One thousand dollars a yard."

The women, like Cassie, had auburn hair and sharp green eyes. They looked more like sisters than mother and daughter. "I see a strong family resemblance."

She smiled softly. "My grandmother was very proud that day. She had just been promoted to master weaver."

"Is that difficult to achieve?"

"She studied for ten years, working as an apprentice for minimum wage. She was the first woman to ever achieve such an honor. Until then it had been only men."

Cassie moved to the next photo. "And this material," she said, "was used in the coronation gown of Queen Elizabeth." Like a docent in a museum, she walked him down the wall of pictures, patiently explaining each and every one.

When she was finished, she looked at him and smiled.

"Impressive," he said.

"Now close your eyes."

"What?"

"Close them." She took his hand. He heard a door opening and knew immediately that she had taken him into the heart of the factory. "Smell," she said.

He did as she asked, inhaling a distinct, sweet smell. "I noticed it on my first day here," he said. "What is it?"

"The smell of history. Old machinery and fresh silk."

He opened his eyes. She led him over to an old loom. "See those," she said, pointing to the threads gathered on the loom. "By the end of tomorrow those threads will be part of an intricately patterned piece of fabric."

He nodded toward a machine in the corner. It looked like something one might see in a museum. "What is that?"

"It's a device for twisting cords for tassels. It was invented by Leonardo da Vinci. It hasn't been changed much since."

She took his hand and ran it over the fabric on the loom. "Does this feel familiar?"

Despite the intricate pattern and the number of threads that had been used, the weave was so tight it felt like a single piece of sleek silk. "Should it?" he asked.

"This is the same material that's hanging in your bedroom in your boat. The material you don't even recognize took two people one whole week to make."

"I'll be sure to appreciate it when I get back."

She sighed. "Can you?"

"What do you mean by that?"

She shrugged, not wanting to answer. But she didn't have to.

He knew what she had been implying—perhaps he wasn't capable of recognizing beauty.

But she was wrong, he thought, as he admired her delicate, rosebud lips. He could not only recognize magnificence, he could appreciate it. "Just because I didn't recognize my drapes doesn't mean I don't appreciate them."

"It's not a matter of appreciation. It's a matter of noticing. I think if you had noticed you would have appreciated them. But you were too busy making the money needed to buy such luxuries." She shook her head. "I think a lot of people are like that. Life is something they endure. They're so busy surviving that they don't really live. So busy making money that it somehow loses its value." She looked around her. "That's why I'm so fond of this place. It reminds me of a simpler time. A time when making a living with your hands was nothing to be ashamed of."

"It's still not."

"Everything is equated with money. If it doesn't make money, it's not appreciated."

"That's true in a sense," he admitted. "But, Cassie, you can't stop progress. And you can't turn back the clock."

She hesitated and then nodded sadly. "Unfortunately."

Hunter knew right then and there that Willa was wrong. It was not revenge that motivated Cassie, but love.

It was nearly two in the morning by the time they returned to Cassie's house. Despite the late hour, neither was ready to end the evening. They built a roaring fire and settled next to each other on the couch with steaming mugs of hot chocolate.

Cassie leaned her head against Hunter's shoulder. Once again she was tempted to speak her thoughts out loud and tell him that she wished the night would never end.

But she had learned her lesson before. She would stay quiet, no matter how difficult that might be.

"This is nice," he said, brushing her cheek. "I almost wish I didn't have to leave tomorrow."

"Are you returning to the Bahamas?" she asked as coolly as she could manage.

He shook his head. "Paris."

"Oh," she said, obviously disappointed. "How long will you be gone?"

He hesitated. After a pause he said, "Look, Cassie…"

She knew what was coming next. And she was to blame. There had been desperation in her voice. And now she would get the speech. I never meant to lead you on. I never meant to imply that things were more serious than they seemed. We barely know each other….

And she had no doubt he meant it. But she had seen tenderness in his eyes and felt passion in his arms. She didn't want to think that the feelings he had brought to life inside her would be silenced once more.

But there was no choice. She had no more power over the fate of their relationship than she had over the fate of her beloved mill.

She held a finger to his lips. She couldn't bear to hear it. "Hunter, I didn't mean it to sound the way it did. Let's just enjoy tonight, okay?"

But the mood was ruined. She straightened slightly, pulling away. Hunter cupped her chin and directed her back toward him. "Cassie," he said. "I need to talk to you about the mill."

So she had been right about the speech. But she was wrong about the subject matter.

Had he changed his mind about selling her the mill? Is that why he seemed so distracted? Was he feeling guilty?

"I've decided to give you the patent."

She sat so still, she held her breath. "The patent for Bodyguard?" she said finally.

"That's right."

"But we can only afford our original offer—"

"I don't care about the money."

"You don't?"

He shook his head. "But I do care about you. And I can't sit back and watch you walk into a situation that I know is destined for failure. Which is why I'm going to provide the financial backing for the release of Bodyguard. I've assigned a marketing team to help you with the rollout."

It was better than she could have hoped. She hugged him. "Thank you."

But he did not respond. He pulled back and flashed her a sad smile. "You're still going to need a lot of luck, Cassie."

And suddenly all she could think about was him. She did not want to say goodbye. Not then. Not ever.

He said, "I do, however, have one demand."

There was a catch? "What?"

"Come with me to Paris."

"Paris?" She had dreamed of visiting Paris since she was a child.

"I have some work in a neighboring town, but it won't take me long."

"I don't know what to say."

"Say you'll come." He paused. "It's just a week. One week and you'll be back."

It was not Paris that enticed her so much, but the idea of spending an entire week with Hunter.

"Well?" he asked.

She looked into his kind and gentle eyes. They were not the eyes of a corporate baron. They were the eyes of a man who was willing to listen when others wouldn't. A man who was willing to give her a chance. They were the eyes of the man she loved.

There was no guarantee their relationship would last. Nor was there any guarantee she would not return from Paris with a broken heart. But it didn't seem to matter. "What time do we leave?"

Fourteen

Cassie's skilled fingers flew over the loom. She glanced around her. The floor where people normally worked in quiet or hushed tones was a flurry of activity. It had been a long time since Cassie had seen everyone so happy. It was as if the dark cloud had lifted.

So why wasn't she jumping for joy? After all, she had every reason to be ecstatic. The mill was saved, the patent returned. She had woken up in the arms of the man with whom she was desperately in love. They were leaving that night for Paris.

Luanne leaned forward and said, "When are you returning?"

"In a week."

"Take your time," said Ruby.

"You deserve it," said Luanne.

Cassie attempted to smile. What was wrong with her?

Why did she feel so vulnerable? As if the floor was about to give way underneath her?

Because Hunter had not said the words *I love you?*

Why would he? After all, they had only known each other for a short time.

Unfortunately it was not that simple. She suspected her affection would never be returned.

For, despite his humble origins, Hunter was a man who prized material wealth above all else. He was a product of the society he helped support, the fast-paced corporate world where emotional connections took a second place to business contacts.

Cassie was suddenly aware that the din in the room had silenced.

Suddenly she heard a voice that sent chills down her spine. "Cassie?"

She turned. Willa was standing behind her.

"Can I talk to you for a moment?"

"She's busy," Luanne said.

"It's all right," Cassie said. She smiled affectionately at her friends. She knew they were being protective, but she could handle herself.

She followed Willa into the empty hall.

Willa shut the door behind them and turned to face Cassie. "I'm going to be leaving soon. I wanted to congratulate you before I left."

Cassie couldn't help but think this was some sort of trick. What was Willa up to? "Thank you," she said.

"I hope there are no hard feelings."

"None."

"Excellent," Willa said. She nodded toward the picture behind Cassie. It was a black-and-white close-up of threads gathered in a ponytail on a Jacquard loom. "You took that photo, didn't you?"

Cassie glanced behind her. She had taken the picture while still in high school. Her grandmother had shown it to the manager of the mill, who had insisted on framing it and hanging it on the wall. "Yes," she said.

"You're really quite good. It's a shame you never had a chance to pursue your photography."

"I'm happy working here," Cassie said.

"So you say. Still, it's a shame your talent will never go anywhere. I mean, with your new responsibilities and all. You're hardly going to have time to brush your teeth, much less explore the arts."

"Is there a point to this, Willa? I need to get going."

"That's right," Willa said. "You have a plane to catch, don't you?"

Cassie glared at her.

"I wanted to congratulate you on that, as well. Scoring a trip with Hunter Axon. My, my. Very impressive. An affair with a man like him…well, that's quite a notch in your belt."

"Goodbye, Willa," Cassie said, her hand on the door.

"Of course, that's all it will ever be," Willa said. "An affair."

Had Cassie not been having the same thoughts, she might have been able to keep walking. But because Willa seemed to be reading her mind, because she was saying exactly what, deep down, Cassie had been thinking, she hesitated.

Willa took a step toward her and said, "Do you know why he's going to France?"

"He has business."

"He's buying a wine-making factory. It's in a small village outside of Paris. Families from the town have worked there for generations. We're getting it for quite a steal. See, they don't want to sell, but they have no choice. They're in debt. So Hunter's going to shut it down and produce the label in California."

Cassie was silent.

"All those families that have depended on this factory for hundreds of years are going to be displaced."

Cassie looked away. "Why are you telling me this?"

"I'm pointing out the obvious. I've known Hunter for years."

Cassie had heard all she could bear. She opened the door.

"It will never work," Willa said. "And you know that. You're just postponing the inevitable. And quite frankly, you have too much work to do to be so distracted. From one woman to another, the last thing you need is another heartbreak."

"I said goodbye."

"Oh, before I go… If you do get lonely, you might want to

call Oliver. I've broken it off with him, and the poor dear isn't handling it very well."

"Too bad," Cassie said. "You seemed so well suited for each other." She slipped inside, shutting the door behind her.

As she made her way back to the loom, she was aware that work had stopped and every eye was on her.

"Honey?" Luanne said. "Are you all right?"

No, she wasn't. In one split second her world had spun out of control, her hope for the future dashed.

Hunter was going to France to shut down another plant. To wreak havoc on more lives.

And for what? Money? Didn't he have enough of that?

But what did she think? That he had changed? That her short time with him had made him see the error of his ways?

"Why don't you sit down," Mabel said, touching her arm.

But Cassie barely heard her. How could Hunter do that? It was hard to understand how someone who could be so kind and caring one moment could be so unfeeling the next.

And as much as she cared about Hunter, could she really be with someone who could inflict so much pain on others?

But her question was, in all probability, moot.

Actions Speak Louder Than Words. And Hunter's actions were sending her a message. Nothing had changed. He was still the same man who had threatened their community. The man who worshipped money.

The man who would never love her.

And Willa, as much as she hated to admit it, was right. Cassie was too busy to let herself be distracted by a fling. Even if it came with a mill, a trip to Paris and a marketing plan.

Hunter finished reading the contract. It detailed the transfer of Demion Mills to the workers, emphasizing that his team would help with the marketing of Bodyguard.

It was the first time he had given back a property. Yet he had no regrets. It felt good to be helping the community. To have people thanking him instead of cursing his name.

In fact, he was, for the first time in years, happy.

Was it possible?

It was such a strange feeling for him that he wasn't quite sure how to respond.

Of course, his happiness was due to more than just the mill. The reason for his newfound bliss could be summed up in one word: Cassie.

From the moment he met her he realized this was no ordinary affair. He was entirely bewitched. It was difficult to believe that a woman who could be so enticing, give him the most sexual pleasure he had ever experienced, could also be so innocent.

But his attraction was based on more than just sex. She was the most honest, dedicated and loyal person he had ever met. Seemingly unimpressed by monetary wealth, she valued those things that Hunter had almost forgotten existed, the little everyday occurrences that made life special. Whether to admire a sunset or to feel soft fabric, she encouraged him to slow down, to stop and notice things that he had taken for granted.

His decision to invite Cassie to Paris had been spontaneous yet inevitable. Usually he did not enjoy having women with him on business trips. They were distractions at a time when he preferred to be focused. But Cassie was different. With Cassie, it was the business that was the distraction. He would've preferred to spend all of his time with her. He did not want to be apart from her. Not now or ever.

Hunter was distracted by a knock on the door. He glanced up and smiled as he saw Cassie.

"I was just about to come and see you," he said. "I spoke to the travel agent. She's booked us in an old inn in Loiret. The vineyard I'm buying isn't far away. You'll have a couple of days to sightsee but I'll be back in time for dinner." He stood up and walked over toward her, put his hands around her waist. "After which, I'm going to take you to Paris. I'm going to show you whatever you want to see."

She stepped backward, away from him. She bit her lower lip,

and her eyes, usually bright and full of life, looked glazed with despair.

Alarmed, he asked, "What's wrong?"

She met his gaze directly. "I can't go to Paris."

"Why not?"

"I have responsibilities here, responsibilities that can't wait."

"Cassie," he said patiently. "It's two weeks before the mill is officially transferred. And my marketing team isn't arriving until next week. You'll be back in plenty of time."

She glanced away. "My reason for not going has nothing to do with the mill."

An icy fear cloaked his heart. "What, then?"

"Why didn't you tell me you were going to Paris to take over a company?"

He felt a stab of guilt. But why should he feel guilty? He was not ashamed of what he did. Was he? "I didn't think it would make a difference."

She shook her head. "It's not right. Buying companies and putting people out of work."

"It's not that simple," he said. "I've built three brand-new factories in China employing hundreds of workers, people who were desperate to earn money."

"That's commendable, but it's not as if you're running a non-profit organization. What happens to all those people whose jobs you've taken away?"

"Not everyone lives in Shanville, Cassie. In some situations workers are more than happy to be offered a severance package." He argued mechanically, presenting her with the same defenses he used to ease his guilty conscience. "These are companies close to bankruptcy."

"You're putting people out of work. You're closing up mom-and-pop businesses that have been in families for years. You're making money off other people's misfortunes."

His eyes hardened as he was overcome by a raw and primitive grief. "Is that what you think of me? That I'm some sort of…monster?"

She stood up. "No. That's not the person I see. But..." Her voice faded.

"These businesses," he said, taking a step toward her, "these mom-and-pops that I take over, are destined for failure. I save whatever is left and turn them into profit-making ventures."

"For whom? Not for the families who have given them their life." She shook her head. "I'm sorry, Hunter. But I think it's commendable only if you prize money above all else."

So this was it? She was breaking off their relationship because she did not like his job?

He had the feeling it went deeper than that. And as much as it pained him, he needed to know.

He said, "Don't use my job as an excuse to stay away from me. If you have a problem with me or something I've done, I would hope you try and talk to me about it before you reach a decision."

"Talking about it won't change anything. You are who you are."

You are who you are.

It was personal.

"I see," he managed. "And your mind is made up?"

She nodded and turned to leave.

"Cassie," said Hunter, stopping her. But what could he say? How could he stop her from walking out the door when she was right? He did not deserve her. He never had.

He held up the papers on his desk. "Your contract."

She walked back toward him. As he handed her the contract, their hands touched. Hunter was once again overcome by the desire to say something, anything to change her mind. But what?

Instead she spoke. "I'm very grateful for everything you've done for me."

He let go of her hand. "Good luck, Cassie," he said.

That was it. It was over. It would have happened sooner or later, wouldn't it? So, better to get it out of the way. Better not to wait. She was right, he told himself.

When she glanced up at him, he could see her eyes were filled with tears. She reached around her neck and unclasped the necklace.

"I want you to have this," she said, offering it to him.

"No," he said. "I can't accept that."

"It's not worth anything but it means a lot to me." She put the necklace on the desk. She shook her head and turned away. "I will never forget you," she said softly.

Fifteen

Cassie stood behind her loom as the last of the workers left.

She was alone.

It was getting late and she knew that she should leave, as well. But she was not looking forward to returning home, back to the same place where, just that morning, she and Hunter had made love. She knew the minute she walked in the door she would be overcome by all the emotion she had struggled to hold at bay.

She closed her eyes. Once again she asked herself the question that had haunted her all day: Had she done the right thing?

Or had she just made the biggest mistake of her life?

She knew without a doubt she had passed up the chance of a lifetime. Hunter was unlike any man she had ever met before, any man she would ever meet again.

When she closed her eyes, she could still feel his touch. He had made her feel special. Desired.

She walked to the window and looked up at the stars. Hunter was miles away by now, his plane heading toward France. Did he regret the end of their relationship? Or was he looking forward to a new beginning?

She would never know. She doubted she would ever speak to Hunter again.

Hunter had been sitting in the airport for nearly two hours. Normally he would have been agitated, eager to get to his next destination.

But not tonight. In fact, he welcomed the delay. He was in no rush to leave Shanville.

To leave Cassie.

It had been hours since he last saw her, but it already felt like a lifetime. He had racked his brain trying to think of a solution. According to Cassie, however, the only solution would be for him to give up his company, to devote himself toward a more humanitarian profession.

He pulled out her necklace once again. *It's not worth much…*

How could she say that? It had been her mother's necklace. Cassie wore it every day. He knew how much it meant to her.

He had not felt right accepting such a gift.

He knew he would eventually return it to Cassie. But not yet. He could not bear to part with the only reminder he had of her.

"I just spoke to Jack," Willa said. "We should be leaving momentarily." She sat down next to Hunter and said, "I can't say I'm sorry to be leaving. The sooner I forget about Oliver the better."

"I'm sorry it didn't work out between you two."

She shrugged her shoulders. "I'm not. I guess you could say he lost his appeal."

"Coincidentally at the same time he lost his job."

She smiled. "Oh, well. Win some, lose some."

"You know," he said, "you haven't asked where Cassie is."

"Oh, Cassie. That's right. She was supposed to join you, wasn't she?"

Hunter looked at her, his eyes narrowing. He had suspected that Willa might have had something to do with Cassie's sudden change of heart. Her reaction just confirmed his suspicions.

"Oh, dear," Willa said. She sighed sympathetically. "Are you two having some problems?"

"You might say so," he said calmly.

"Well," she said, shrugging, "it's probably better this way. Cassie belongs here with her own kind."

His face paled with anger. "Own kind?"

Oblivious to his reaction, she smiled again. "You know what I mean. Her own class of people."

"I see," Hunter said, his voice heavy with contempt.

Willa checked her watch. "It's time for me to leave," she said, brushing off her skirt, "perhaps we should go."

"What did you say to her?" His voice was quiet, his tone cold and lashing.

"What?"

"What did you say to Cassie?"

Willa crossed her arms in front of her. "Nothing I wouldn't say to you—respectfully, of course."

"Like?"

"What does it matter?" She shook her head. "I think it was honorable of you to give her the mill, I really do. However, that said, what are you going to have to do to continue to please her? Every time she raises an objection about some poor people being displaced, what will you do? I mean, let's face it, you're not exactly a philanthropist."

No. No, he wasn't. But that didn't mean he couldn't be.

Suddenly he thought about the expressions on the workers' faces when he informed them he would be shutting down their plant. That the only job they had ever known would be gone forever. Sure there were instances when they welcomed the change, but more times than not there were tears, devastation, even hopelessness. He had done his best to ignore it, to push it out of his mind. He had told himself over and over again that he was actually doing them a favor, but who was he kidding?

He thought about his own father. He had grown up hearing stories about how his father had lost his job. Had his father been grateful to the man who had bought the company where he had worked? Hardly. He had lost the only life he had ever known.

How had this happened? Hunter looked down at his hands. When did he turn into one of the very people he'd grown up hating?

"We are who we are, Hunter. And I happen to think you're pretty terrific." Willa put her arm in his. "Shall we go?"

He was repulsed by Willa's touch. He suddenly saw her for who she was: a mean, vindictive, small-minded woman. He shook off her arm and asked her, "What do you think their chances are?"

"Their?"

"Cassie and the rest of the people trying to turn the mill around."

"The marketing team will help, that's for certain. But quite frankly, I think it's still a waste of your money. After all, they're going to have to price themselves out of the market. The wages they pay their workers are so high they'll never be able to make a product that people can actually afford. I don't care how good it is." She shook her head. "They were fools, each and every one of them. And they're about to pay the price."

Once again Hunter felt inside his pocket, desperately clutching the necklace that Cassie gave him.

Suddenly he had an idea. What if he were to provide financial backing until Demion Mills began turning a profit? What if, he thought, his pulse racing, he offered that service to other companies, as well?

Suddenly he felt as if the clouds had cleared. He saw his future as it could be. Instead of buying out the companies struggling for survival, he could use his expertise to turn their fortunes around.

But it would require a huge commitment. It would require walking away from the company he had built from scratch.

Only one thing was clear.

Nothing seemed to matter anymore but Cassie.

He stood. He took his briefcase and started toward the door.

"Hunter," Willa said. "Where are you going? The tarmac is that way."

He walked back toward Willa and stopped. "Do you think the severance package that we offered the Demion Mill workers was fair?"

"Yes, of course. I drew it up myself."

"Good. That's exactly what you'll receive. I'll direct the office to cut you a check. In the meantime, the plane will be happy to take you wherever you might want to go."

Willa stepped away, stunned. "You're firing me?"

"Just like you told the workers at Demion Mills: 'Don't view this as a negative. View it as a chance to start over.'" He nodded. "Goodbye, Willa."

Sixteen

Cassie closed her eyes and took her fingers off the loom, taking a momentary break. It was nearly midnight. Despite her fatigue, she had been unable to bring herself to leave the mill.

"Cassie?"

She opened her eyes. Hunter was standing in the doorway.

Cassie just stared, too astonished to speak.

"Can I talk to you?" he asked.

He looked exhausted. He was still wearing his suit, but his tie was loose, his rumpled shirt open at the neck. His hair was tousled, and he had circles under his eyes. "What are you doing here?" she asked. "I thought you went to France."

"I'm not going."

"What...why?"

He walked toward her. "You were right this afternoon. I am what I am. And my job is such that it doesn't allow for a lot of philanthropy."

"I'm sorry I said that."

"No," he said. "I didn't come here for apologies." He swallowed. "At least, not from you. I wanted to explain to you that my company is not what I had originally intended. I've always liked a challenge. I was attracted to the idea that I could go into businesses that were struggling and fix them. At least, that's what I told myself I was doing. I liked the idea of turning a business around—textiles, steel, wine, it didn't matter. I tried to ignore the fact that people were losing their jobs, that whole economies were ruined. I told myself that the businesses were struggling and if I didn't take them over, those people would lose their jobs anyway."

"That's probably true."

"But that doesn't make what I do right. And it doesn't excuse what I did, either."

She stared at him, her heart pounding. "What are you saying?"

"I'm saying I think it's time for a career change."

"A career change?"

"Instead of specializing in takeovers, I'm thinking that perhaps I should reconsider. Turn my energy toward helping those struggling companies survive."

Was she hearing him correctly? "Just like you're helping Demion Mills?"

"That's right."

He stopped at the loom. He ran his fingers over the threads she had just woven.

"That's what you came back to tell me?" she asked quietly.

He took another step toward her. He was standing so close their lips were practically touching. "That's not all," he said. His eyes blazed and glowed as he took her hands in his. "I've fallen in love with you."

He had fallen in love.

He loved her.

Cassie closed her eyes as the shock of his words hit her full force.

"If you give me a chance, I'm willing to try and be a better man."

She was certain she was dreaming. She had fallen asleep at her loom and would wake up alone in a cold, dark, empty room.

"Give me an opportunity to prove that I'm worthy of your love."

She opened her eyes and stared at him, unable to speak. He let go of her hands and pulled her necklace out of his pocket.

His fingers brushed her nape as he fastened it around her neck. "Do I have a chance?" he whispered in her ear.

She twisted around to face him. She once again remembered what her grandmother said. *Actions Speak Louder Than Words.* And with that, she kissed him.

Epilogue

It was the opening of the Shanville Gallery, a nonprofit center that featured the work of local artists. And from the crowd that had gathered in the small, renovated building in the center of town, it was a success.

Thanks to her husband's connections, the gathering included local and not-so-local stars. The governor of New York was there along with various politicians and personalities. All had turned out to show their support for Shanville, which was becoming known as a mecca for the arts.

But like Shanville itself, there was no pretension here. All the invitees were dressed casually, supping on a buffet that included dishes the local diner was famous for: meat loaf and macaroni and cheese.

Cassie spotted her husband across the room. They had been married for three years, but the sight of him still caused her heart to skip a beat. He stood in the doorway, a grin spreading across his lips as their eyes met.

Their wedding had been a fairy-tale ending to a not-so-traditional courtship—an affair that she felt certain would have restored her grandmother's pride and her belief in the power of sex.

Afterward, Hunter moved into Cassie's home, and together he and his new bride launched a foundation specifically designed to help family businesses in need.

In the three years that had passed since their wedding, Hunter had become a vital part of Shanville and Demion Mills. He seemed to have no problem leaving his corporate image and expensive toys behind, easily adapting to the down-to-earth lifestyle of small-town living.

It was a change, he claimed, that he had been anticipating a long time. All he needed was the right woman to make it all come true.

They walked toward each other, drawn together like magnets. He took her in his arms and kissed her on the lips. "I'm so proud of you," he said.

"Why?"

"You worked hard for this opening."

"We," she said. "We worked hard."

For the past few months Cassie and Hunter had met at the gallery after work, doing much of the refurbishing themselves. Hunter had long ago proven himself surprisingly adept with a hammer and nails. Some of Cassie's friends had been amazed that a man worth millions was willing to perform physical labor. But not Cassie. Hunter enjoyed working with his hands. He had become an excellent craftsman, capable of replicating the intricate wood carvings that were found on so many old homes.

"Cassie?"

Cassie turned. Her old friend Luanne was there behind her. "You have some visitors." She pointed to the door.

Willa and Oliver stood side by side.

"What are they doing here?" Ruby whispered, hurrying over.

But Cassie was not surprised to see them. After all, they had been invited.

Soon after she and Hunter married, Hunter had encouraged her to renew her friendship with Oliver. He had been her oldest and dearest friend, Hunter had argued. It was a relationship worth preserving. She took her husband's advice and she and Oliver re-defined their relationship as two old friends. Oliver soon confided that he had never recovered from the demise of his relationship with Willa. Cassie counseled him to reconcile, and one morning Oliver announced that not only had he and Willa reconciled, they had married.

Unfortunately for Oliver, however, it soon became clear that being the mistress of the "Demion estate" did not seem to satisfy Willa. Opinionated and haughty, Willa was every bit as abrasive as she had been at the mill. Still, Willa had become such a colorful personality in Shanville that it was hard to imagine the town without her. But most of the town residents were still cool to her, never having forgiven her for her previous offenses.

They seemed to delight in knocking Willa off her throne. And this, apparently, was another one of those times.

Cassie shook her head. Both Willa and Oliver were dressed in formal attire, as if attending a ball. Willa looked resplendent in a draping red dress. Oliver was wearing a white tuxedo.

Cassie saw Willa's eyes open wide in horror as she looked at the casually dressed guests. She gave Oliver a nasty look and swatted him across the stomach.

Cassie heard Luanne snicker. She looked at her friend suspiciously. "Luanne, is there a reason they might have thought this event was formal?"

Luanne shrugged and averted her gaze. "Maybe."

Cassie rolled her eyes. Hunter tried to hide his smile by pretending to cough.

She and Hunter went over to welcome their guests. Afterward, as they watched Willa and Oliver head toward the buffet, Hunter said, "You really are amazing. Only you could've made them feel so comfortable. That was very gracious of you."

She smiled and said, "I have every reason to be gracious. After all, as of today, all my wishes have come true."

He glanced at her. "Revenge on Willa?"

"No," she said, laughing.

"Let me guess," he said. "Saving Demion Mills was wish number one...."

"No," she said. "You were number one. Demion Mills was number two."

"And the art gallery was number three?"

"I wanted the gallery, but it wasn't a wish."

"Willa and Oliver come dressed to serve?"

She laughed and said, "Nope."

"You've been promoted to master weaver?"

"Not yet," she said.

Suddenly his eyes opened wide as she touched her stomach. He smiled.

Wish number three. They were soon to be family.

With a holler, Hunter picked her up and spun her around.

"But," she said, "I do have a single demand."

"Anything," he said. "As you know I've never been able to resist you."

"Just love me."

"That's a request I'll never deny," he said, settling the deal with a kiss.

* * * * *

SILHOUETTE®

Desire™

Dynasties:
THE ELLIOTTS

Mixing business with pleasure

January 2007
BILLIONAIRE PROPOSITION *Leanne Banks*
TAKING CARE OF BUSINESS *Brenda Jackson*

March 2007
CAUSE FOR SCANDAL *Anna DePalo*
THE FORBIDDEN TWIN *Susan Crosby*

May 2007
MR AND MISTRESS *Heidi Betts*
HEIRESS BEWARE *Charlene Sands*

July 2007
UNDER DEEPEST COVER *Kara Lennox*
MARRIAGE TERMS *Barbara Dunlop*

September 2007
THE INTERN AFFAIR *Roxanne St Claire*
FORBIDDEN MERGER *Emilie Rose*

November 2007
THE EXPECTANT EXECUTIVE *Kathie DeNosky*
BEYOND THE BOARDROOM *Maureen Child*

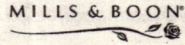

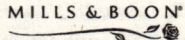

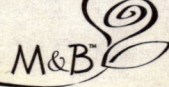

2 FREE

BOOKS AND A SURPRISE GIFT!

We would like to take this opportunity to thank you for reading this Mills & Boon® book by offering you the chance to take TWO more specially selected titles from the Desire™ series absolutely FREE! We're also making this offer to introduce you to the benefits of the Mills & Boon® Reader Service™—

- ★ FREE home delivery
- ★ FREE gifts and competitions
- ★ FREE monthly Newsletter
- ★ Exclusive Reader Service offers
- ★ Books available before they're in the shops

Accepting these FREE books and gift places you under no obligation to buy, you may cancel at any time, even after receiving your free shipment. Simply complete your details below and return the entire page to the address below. You don't even need a stamp!

YES! Please send me 2 free Desire volumes and a surprise gift. I understand that unless you hear from me, I will receive 3 superb new titles every month for just £4.99 each, postage and packing free. I am under no obligation to purchase any books and may cancel my subscription at any time. The free books and gift will be mine to keep in any case.

D7ZED

Ms/Mrs/Miss/Mr .... Initials ....

Surname .... BLOCK CAPITALS PLEASE

Address ....

....

....Postcode...

Send this whole page to:
UK: FREEPOST CN81, Croydon, CR9 3WZ